## Readers Love ANDREW GREY

*Fire and Sand*
"If you're looking for a lovely way to kill a cold, winter afternoon, this story will warm you up."
—Love Bytes Reviews

*Through the Flames*
"What a beautiful story of hate turning to love and putting the past where it belongs.... Sex, lies, suspense and forgiveness made this a must-read book."
—Paranormal Romance Guild

*In the Weeds*
"This story really has it all. If you like a great second chance, small town romance, cute kids, a touch of mystery and lots of feels, this is for you."
—TTC Books and More

*Lost and Found*
"Andrew Grey knows how to tug on the heart strings and make you feel the emotions the characters are feeling."
—Sparkling Book Reviews

*Borrowed Heart*
"...a delightful mix of heavy-hitting personal issues and fluffy happily ever after story telling."
—Joyfully Jay Reviews

# By Andrew Grey

Published by DREAMSPINNER PRESS
www.dreamspinnerpress.com

# By ANDREW GREY (cont'd)

Published by DREAMSPINNER PRESS
www.dreamspinnerpress.com

# By ANDREW GREY (cont'd)

Published by DREAMSPINNER PRESS
www.dreamspinnerpress.com

# BY FIRE
## ANTHOLOGY

REDEMPTION BY FIRE
STRENGTHENED BY FIRE
BURNISHED BY FIRE
HEAT UNDER FIRE

ANDREW GREY

DREAMSPINNER
PRESS

Published by
DREAMSPINNER PRESS

8219 Woodville Hwy #1245
Woodville, FL 32362 USA
www.dreamspinnerpress.com

This is a work of fiction. Names, characters, places, and incidents either are the product of author imagination or are used fictitiously, and any resemblance to actual persons, living or dead, business establishments, events, or locales is entirely coincidental.

By Fire Anthology
© 2023 Andrew Grey

Cover Art
© 2023 L.C. Chase
http://www.lcchase.com
Cover content is for illustrative purposes only and any person depicted on the cover is a model.

Trade Paperback ISBN: 978-1-64108-701-8
Trade Paperback published December 2023
v. 1.0

Redemption by Fire previously published by Dreamspinner Press, May 2012
Cover Art by Anne Cain, annecain.art@gmail.com
Strengthened by Fire previously published by Dreamspinner Press, August 2012
Cover Art by Anne Cain, annecain.art@gmail.com
Burnished by Fire previously published by Dreamspinner Press, October 2012
Cover Art by Paul Richmond, http://www.paulrichmondstudio.com
Heat Under Fire previously published by Dreamspinner Press, March 2013
Cover Art by Brooke Albrecht, http://brookealbrechtstudio.com

Printed in the United States of America

This paper meets the requirements of
ANSI/NISO Z39.48-1992 (Permanence of Paper).

# Table of Contents

# REDEMPTION BY FIRE

# Chapter 1

DIRK REACHED the room with the baby screaming so loudly he could hear it over the roar outside the door. After pushing open the door, Dirk rushed into the room and slammed the door closed behind him, ignoring the cries. Throwing a fire blanket over the child, he scooped it up and turned to head back through the burning Carlisle, Pennsylvania, row house. He would have loved to be able to go out the kid's window, but he was on the second floor, and no one could reach this portion of the house from the outside. The buildings were too close together. Why anyone would put a baby in a room with only one window that looked out over a brick wall was beyond him, but Dirk didn't have time to think about it. He yanked open the door. The flames that had just begun to lick up the hallway on his way up were nearly at the door, and the heat was incredible even inside his fire gear. He had to go down the stairs and out the front door; it was his only choice.

The sound of the fire told Dirk he probably had just enough time to get out, so he moved, the sound of his own breathing echoing in his head. The kid's screams died away, and Dirk hoped it was from exhaustion, but he didn't have time to find out. Everything in his brain screamed for him to get out of this death trap of a house and get out now. Sweat soaked Dirk's clothes and ran down his face as he reached the top of the steps. The walls all the way down were burning steadily, and the roar had increased exponentially. He could barely hear himself think as he picked his way down the stairs, his brain already telling him where he had to go at the bottom. He felt one of the steps give way under him. He managed not to fall and somehow reached the main floor. Dirk took one step and heard a crash as somewhere part of the house collapsed, and the sound of the fire went from revving jet engine to full-on sonic boom in a second.

All around him, he could see nothing but flame and black rolling smoke. He knew he only had one chance. Remembering the living room from his way in, Dirk dashed across it, dodging incinerated furniture, and he almost made it before part of the floor collapsed under him. He could see water spraying through the open front door. He could also hear the hiss of water as it trickled down through the roof, but this fire was so hot there wasn't much that would help in the next few seconds. More collapses sounded behind him, wood splitting, beams cracking, the house shifting and groaning, and the fire ramped up to blast furnace. The entire building was coming down around him. He knew it, and he had mere seconds. Taking another step, he was almost at the door when the floor moved under him. He leaped forward and almost made it, but then began to fall forward. He twisted so he wouldn't crush the baby and thrust the kid toward the doorway. It disappeared from his hands, and the last thing he knew, he was falling into a fiery abyss.

DIRK FIGURED he was dead. He spent days wandering through mist and smoke, trying to find God, but all he ever found were more and more swirls of gray and black. Maybe he was in hell. It wouldn't really surprise him because that's what he figured he deserved, anyway, at least if his father was right. Finally everything went dark, and Dirk figured this was it. Opening his eyes, he blinked through what felt like gravel and saw a tile ceiling. It took a few seconds for him to realize he was in a bed. Then the pain hit. His chest felt like the fucking fire was still burning in his lungs, his arm hurt like hell, and his legs throbbed. He tried to move a foot, and while it hurt, it at least moved, and so did the other one. Dirk did the same thing with a finger and breathed a sigh of relief that he was whole.

It wasn't until he tried to breathe in again that the real pain hit him, and Dirk closed his eyes to keep from crying as his lungs protested.

"You're awake," a perky female voice said.

"Fuck… yes… water." He needed some way to put out the fire inside him. Every breath felt like death. Dirk was aware of her moving through the room, and then something cold slid along his lips. Dirk started and gasped, which sent lightning through his chest, and he nearly bit the nurse. She squeaked and raced from the room. The ice melted, and the cold felt good in his mouth and on his throat, and Dirk relaxed, closing his eyes once again.

He must have slept, at least he thought he did, but it was hard to tell because when he opened his eyes again, he was still alone in the room and nothing seemed to have changed except there was a fresh cup of ice by his bed. It still hurt to move, but Dirk found a call button near his hand and pressed it. The same nurse from earlier came in and glowered at him. "Water," Dirk gasped.

"As long as you don't bite me again," she said and carefully placed some ice chips in his mouth. He did feel slightly better, but his arm and lungs still hurt like hell. "The doctor should be in soon," she explained as she took his temperature and blood pressure before turning to a portable computer.

"Chest hurts," he said carefully.

"You scalded parts of your lungs," she explained and kept typing. Dirk had already figured that out. She continued talking as she worked, and Dirk tuned out her blather, the pain taking most of his concentration. Once she left, he closed his eyes again.

AFTER A day, he began to feel better. He could breathe more easily even though he was still on oxygen. Once, when he'd woken, he'd found a card from his father, and one from his captain at the station, but other than that, he saw no signs of any visitors. He figured they were waiting until he got better.

He was wrong. The only person he saw other than the nurses and doctors was his father, and his visits were never pleasant.

"So after this, are you going to give up this fireman thing and get a real job? You have a degree. I could get you a job on my team at the brokerage," his father told him in his usual "I know best" voice. "I'll start the paperwork for when you get out of here."

"I don't—" Dirk began, but he started to cough, and it got worse and worse. A nurse hurried in and gave him something to calm the spasms, and he collapsed back into the bed, his injured arm aching and his chest hurting like hell. "Can't we just sit and talk?" Dirk asked, and his father looked at him like he'd asked for the moon.

"I have to be back in the office in half an hour," his father told him, and Dirk nodded.

Then his father left the room, and Dirk hadn't had a visitor since. That had been two days ago, three days since he'd awakened, and almost a week since the fire.

As the days went by, he fumed at everyone who walked into his room. He heard the nurses talking about him once in the hallway, but

he really didn't care. He spent most of his days watching television—
he couldn't get out of bed except to go to the bathroom, and it hurt to
fucking breathe. This was definitely no picnic! After swearing away
yet another nurse, he found himself with Brunhilda, the sadistic nurse
from hell, and that did nothing for his mood or his sense of misery. The
woman seemed to live to poke him with needles, and a sponge bath from
her could make prisoners spill their guts in two minutes flat. "You should
work for the CIA," he told her as she scraped yet more skin off him, but
she just grunted and paid no attention to him at all.

After that torture ended, Dirk lay watching television, feeling sorry
for himself. His lungs still hurt, but only when he took a deep breath.
The doctor had told him that they were hopeful he'd return to normal and
that his lungs were aching because they were healing. "Just give it time,"
he'd said before leaving.

Out of the corner of his eye, Dirk saw movement in his doorway
and steeled himself for another visit from Brunhilda. Instead, he saw what
looked like a brick wall casting a shadow carrying flowers in a plastic
fire helmet. "You Dirk Krause?" the man asked and slowly stepped into
the room, like he was nervous, setting the planter on the tray.

"Yeah, that's me," Dirk answered. "Who the hell are you?" The
kid might have been huge, but he had a definite baby face, and he looked
young as shit.

"Lee Stockton. I'm the new man on third shift, and the guys asked
me to bring you the flowers," the kid said pleasantly, and Dirk watched
him shuffle from foot to foot trying to figure out what to say next. "The
other guys have been really busy."

"I'll bet." Dirk shifted on the bed, looking at the huge kid. "You
draw the short straw or something?" Dirk had no time or use for a pity
plant in a cheap bit of plastic that the guys probably had the kid pick up
on his way over. "'Cause you're the first damned guy from the company
to visit. So you've done your job, and you can go now." Dirk turned
away and waited to hear the kid walk out of the room.

"You really are the biggest asshole on the planet," the kid said, his
voice deeper, and when Dirk turned to look at him, the kid's eyes blazed.
"I didn't believe them when they told me what a dickhead you could
be. But, boy, they weren't kidding. Two minutes, and you were already
acting like an ass. That must be some kind of record. No wonder none
of the other guys wanted to come up here." The kid moved to the side of

the bed, and Dirk got a good look at him. The kid's shirt barely held in his muscles, and when he moved his arm, it looked like the damned shirt was going to rip anytime.

"Well, fuck 'em all," Dirk said. He wanted to yell, but when he took the breath, his lungs reminded him of their condition by shooting pain down his chest. If they didn't want to see him, he didn't want to see those assholes, either. The kid didn't say anything. He just stared at Dirk like he was from another planet, and then his gaze heated, and Dirk squirmed a little, actually checking to make sure he was covered up. "What's wrong with you? You some sort of fag?" His arm was throbbing, and his lungs ached with this talking, and he wasn't in the mood for any crap. He expected the kid's look to shift to something approaching pity, and he was having none of that.

It had been his experience that whenever anyone was asked that question, they backed away fast, but the kid took a step closer to the bed with an unreadable look on his face. "You seem to have me mistaken with some sort of fucking doormat. I came down here 'cause no one else would visit your sorry ass, and this is the thanks I get. What are you doing calling people names and shit?" Lee took another step closer and stared straight into his eyes, which made Dirk squirm, especially since the kid was freakin' huge. "Anyone ever tell you not to poke the bear?" Lee said with a growl. "Because you're damned close." Lee continued stepping closer until he practically loomed over him. "Why are you such an asshole, anyway? You know what I think?" Lee leaned over the bed, uncomfortably close for Dirk. "I think you're one fucking huge closet case. I've met plenty of guys like you before. You're fucking miserable, and you make everyone around you pay for it. Well, I saw the way you looked at me, like I was dinner and you wanted to eat me whole. And don't think for a second you're ever going to get that chance, because I may fuck ass, but I don't fuck closet-case assholes like you."

"What the fuck, man?" Dirk managed to say as he pushed Lee away with his good hand.

"Hey, I see right through you. There's no hiding. I know a closet case a mile away, and I knew you were gay after being in the room for two seconds. You took one look at me, and I saw the way your eyes bulged and your mouth watered."

"Little full of yourself, aren't you?" Dirk pushed harder on Lee's chest, and damn if he didn't run up against a mountain of pure American muscle. "Now get the hell away from me. You don't know shit about shit." Dirk was more than a little uncomfortable, and Lee's words were hitting way too close to home.

"I don't, huh. You got yourself half a hard-on just thinking about me, and those sheets are thin enough that you really can't hide nothing. So you can cut the bullshit and stop being such an asshole. Now, I brought you your fucking flowers and did what I said I was going to do. You'll probably be in here for a while yet and at home for even longer, so I suggest you use that time to think about why you're here all alone and nobody wants to visit your sorry ass." Lee stepped back and looked toward the door. When he looked back, there was something in Lee's eyes that Dirk couldn't read at all. "See you around, closet case."

"I am not!" Dirk countered, and he really paid for that one as his lungs protested.

Lee turned back to him, and Dirk thought he was going to leave, but he waited for Dirk's coughing to subside, and then he moved close to the bed again. Dirk thought Lee was going to berate him again, but instead he leaned over the bed and planted a kiss on Dirk's lips. This was no soft girly kiss, but one hard and strong, with Lee taking possession of Dirk's mouth as though they'd been kissing forever. Fuck his lungs, the pain in his arms, and everything else. Dirk felt himself go instantly and painfully hard right then and there as his entire body reacted to Lee's touch. Lee moved his tongue to duel with Dirk's, and Dirk lost as Lee took what he wanted in almost every way. Damn, he felt good, and Dirk's body knew what it wanted and overrode his mind. Suddenly and without warning, Lee pulled back and stepped away from the bed. "Bullshit," Lee said and strode out of the room without looking back at all.

# Chapter 2

DIRK WAS finally on his way home. It took two more days before he could convince the doctor to let him leave, and by the looks on the faces of the hospital staff, they were just as happy to see him leave as he was to get the hell out of there. He needed a ride home, and when he'd called his captain, because his own father was too fucking busy, his captain said he would send someone to help him, and of course, and of course, sure as shit, there was Lee, waiting in the lobby. Dirk said nothing and hoped if he was silent, Lee would be, too, and he could get home fast and without too much fuss.

"I see the last few days haven't upgraded your disposition," Lee commented once Dirk was in the car and they were heading toward downtown. "Where do you live, anyway?"

"South side, near Walmart," answered Dirk before giving more detailed directions, and Lee nodded, continuing along the road toward town. "Thank you for doing this," Dirk said, and he saw the surprised look on Lee's face. "Contrary to what you think, I'm not a total asshole." But sitting in the car with Lee made him damned uncomfortable, particularly since all he'd thought about for the past two days was the way Lee had lit him on fire with his possessive kiss. He could not feel that way, and yet he couldn't stop thinking about it no matter what he did, and sitting in the car with Lee so close to him, the small space filled with the man's scent, he could almost taste him again, and that was not good at all.

"But you're close," Lee said. "After I got back from the hospital, the guys spent the rest of the day telling me stories about you. It seems you're quite the firefighter and when you're not fighting fires, you're impossible to get along with. Somehow I find that easy to believe." Lee shot him a wry grin, and Dirk's cock jumped in his pants.

"Hey," Dirk said, "I'm not always like that." He really wasn't. "I've had plenty of good times with the guys," Dirk countered, and Lee simply smirked at him and shook his head.

"Like I said, I see right through you. You're so afraid the guys will find out you like dick that you'll do anything to keep them away. Well, I know and I don't give a shit," Lee said as he stopped at a red light.

"So how long was it before you told them?" Dirk asked. He'd been stewing about that one for the past two days. How could he face the guys, or anyone else for that matter, if they knew?

Lee growled deep in his throat, and a zing shot up Dirk's spine for an instant. "I'd never out someone like that. You want to stay in the closet, that's your business." The light turned, and Lee hit the gas, propelling them through the intersection. A few minutes later, Lee glided his car to a stop in front of Dirk's house. Dirk opened the door and got out, carefully making his way up the walk. "You need these," Lee said and tossed him his keys. "I also have the rest of your stuff from your work locker."

Dirk had completely forgotten about everything other than getting home. "Thanks," Dirk mumbled and slowly climbed the stairs before unlocking the door and going inside with Lee behind him. Dirk made it to the living room and sat in one of the chairs, already out of breath. Fuck, he felt tired and weak. He heard the floorboards of the old house creak as Lee moved through the rooms, and then Lee returned with a glass of water that he placed on the table. To Dirk's surprise, Lee sat down on one of the chairs. "You don't have to stay," Dirk said, but Lee scoffed softly.

"You walked from the car to your couch and you're winded. I figure the stairs must look like Mount Everest about now. So I figured I'd make sure you were settled before I took off." Lee stood up again. "You got any food in this place?"

Dirk's contrary nature kicked in, and he was about to tell Lee to just go when he started to cough and cough. Reaching for the water, he tried to drink something but only succeeded in spraying water everywhere. Finally, he felt the spasms subside, and then he noticed that his back was being rubbed and his entire upper body steadied by Lee's huge hands. He jerked away and glared at Lee, who looked slightly hurt, and Dirk sighed softly to himself before reaching for the glass of water. Without saying anything, Lee left the room, and Dirk heard things moving and banging in the kitchen. He was too tired to fight, and it had been a long time since anyone took care of him, so he closed his eyes and reclined back on the sofa. "Knock yourself out," Dirk said softly to no one in particular.

Dirk rested and kept his eyes closed, ignoring any sounds that came from the rest of the house. As long as Lee didn't burn the place down, which wasn't likely, Dirk could deal with him. He lost track of time and simply concentrated on breathing. A jingling noise made him open his eyes, and he looked up as Lee carried in a tray and set it on the coffee table. After hospital food, a grilled cheese sandwich and tomato soup had never smelled so good in his life, and Dirk's stomach rumbled loudly. "I guess part of you approves," Lee said softly.

Dirk sat up slowly and reached for one half the sandwich, biting into it and chewing carefully. The last thing he wanted was to do anything to make him start coughing again. "Why are you still here?" Dirk swallowed and took a sip of the water. "You don't know me, and you've certainly done your duty for the brotherhood of firemen, and all that."

"You need some help," Lee said evenly as he picked up his own sandwich.

"What is it you want?" Dirk asked, holding his sandwich in midair. "No one does something for nothing." Sure, there was such a thing as watching each other's backs, but in his experience, everything had a cost.

"Cynical much?" Lee quipped. "God, no wonder you act like you do." Lee shook his head and said no more, which drove Dirk crazy because Lee hadn't answered his question. Since it didn't look like he was going to get an answer—or left alone for that matter—he sat back and tried to ignore the man, which was not easy. The kid was big, but he was also damned fine-looking. For as big as he was, Lee didn't look or act like some lumbering hulk. Instead he walked and even sat with a touch of grace. Dirk wasn't in the mood for talking, it took too much breath, so instead he looked, and there was plenty to look at. Lee's shirt barely covered his chest. Tree-trunk legs filled out a pair of jeans so tight Dirk thought he might be able to see the individual muscles through the fabric. As he raised his eyes, he willed himself not to look, but he did anyway, and it was readily apparent that Lee was big all over.

"I see you looking," Lee said, lifting his bowl of soup, spreading his legs further apart. Dirk turned his eyes away and looked down at his bowl of soup as he heard Lee chuckling deep in his ample chest. "You know there's nothing wrong with looking or even touching as long as both people are honest with themselves."

Dirk kept his eyes on his food and away from Lee, or at least he tried, but it didn't work. "Fuck." Dirk nearly dropped his spoon when Lee slouched slightly in the chair, putting everything on display. He knew Lee was doing this on purpose, and he got a very distinct impression that Lee was having a good time at his expense. "You just joined the department?" Dirk figured he'd try making small talk until he could finish eating and go upstairs… alone.

"A few weeks ago. I was originally supposed to be at Goodwill, but they assigned me to Union just before you got hurt. The place is a little old, but the people are really nice. Greg Martin's been showing me the ropes." Lee continued eating, and Dirk did the same, thankful that the conversation had gotten onto comfortable ground.

"Martin's a good man and a superior firefighter. He'll train you right, that's for sure." Dirk continued eating slowly, the soup sliding easily down his sore throat.

"The other guys seem all right too," Lee commented. "Everyone's been pretty welcoming to the newbie." Lee continued eating, and as they ate, Dirk found he kept sneaking peeks at him every now and then. A few times, he thought he saw a hint of a tattoo beneath Lee's shirt, but he couldn't be sure. The kid did have a bit of a baby face, but he also had amazing blue eyes, full lips, and blond hair clipped short. The kid was handsome, and his look pushed Dirk's buttons; well, it would if he let it, which he wouldn't. Lee settled back in the chair once again, and Dirk knew Lee was playing with him.

"They're a great group of guys that you can always count on to have your back." Dirk sincerely meant that. "Most of the guys there have saved me at one time or another, just like I've saved many of them. It's what we do." Dirk was proud to be a firefighter, and he was proud of his company. The best in Carlisle, as far as he was concerned. "You can count on them no matter what."

Lee looked skeptical. "But not to understand that you're gay." And here they were again.

"Are you some sort of broken record?" Dirk asked testily. Swallowing his last bite, he slowly got up off the sofa and carried his dishes into the kitchen. He'd had more than enough of this subject, and he wasn't interested in discussing his personal life with someone he barely knew. He wasn't comfortable talking about this with people he'd known for years. After taking care of his dishes, he walked to the stairs and slowly began to climb. The kid was right, those stairs felt like Mount Everest, and he got halfway up before grabbing the rail and starting to cough. He heard footsteps behind him, and before he knew what was happening, he'd been scooped off his feet. As Lee carried him up the stairs, Dirk continued coughing. Dirk finally got himself under control as Lee gently set him on his bed.

"How did you do that?" Dirk asked once the coughing had stopped. "I weigh two hundred pounds." And he felt weak as a kitten right now.

"In case you hadn't noticed, I'm big and strong."

Dirk settled on the bed and concentrated on taking careful breaths. "I noticed, but that's still a lot of weight." Dirk narrowed his eyes. "You aren't taking steroids, are you?"

Lee laughed. "Nope. Don't need that stuff. I've been lifting since I was a teenager, and I was always big." Lee shrugged and seemed to be waiting for something.

"What?"

"Get yourself undressed and into bed."

"I don't need you to tuck me in," Dirk protested. "Besides, I'll rest a little while before taking a shower. I feel all grungy."

Lee turned to leave. "I'll clean up downstairs and then take off." Dirk watched him go, and damn if his eyes didn't wander to Lee's ass, and he'd be double damned if Lee didn't turn around and catch him. Dirk said nothing, getting comfortable on the bed as he heard Lee go down the stairs. Dirk closed his eyes for a few seconds and then opened them again, swearing under his breath. Dirk had always fantasized about guys, he knew that, but now when he closed his eyes, he saw Lee… naked or at least how his filthy, perverted imagination conjured up Lee naked. To make matters worse, he got hard just thinking about him. He had no idea what he was going to do, but this had to stop. Dirk hated that he was this way. What he'd wanted ever since he was a teenager was to be like everyone else, and he'd ignored what his mind kept telling him for as long as he could. He'd always kept that part of himself a secret and under control, but with Lee, that control was getting harder to come by.

Breathing better, Dirk slowly stood up and padded to the bathroom, locking the door before turning on the water and getting undressed. He stepped beneath the hot spray and let it wash over him. He still had to be careful of his arm, but it hadn't been broken, and each day it was less and less painful. Washing himself single-handed was awkward, but he managed. What turned out to be a problem was his dick. It stood up, demanding attention the entire time. He thought about trying to whack off, but he'd end up breathing heavily, and he'd pay for that big time, so he ignored it as well as he could, turning the water colder toward the end. That seemed to do the trick, at least for the time being. After turning off the water, Dirk got out and carefully dried himself before wrapping a towel around his waist and opening the bathroom door. He nearly walked right into Lee, and the bigger man placed his hand on his shoulder, filling Dirk's nose with his scent, and fuck if his dick didn't take notice.

"What are you doing?" Dirk snapped and began to cough. At least that covered the bulge in his towel.

"I was just making sure you didn't fall or need anything." He looked so innocent that Dirk knew he was telling the truth.

"I'm fine. Thank you for everything," Dirk said before padding into his bedroom. "I appreciate your help." He really was grateful.

"Okay. I'll see you." Lee descended the stairs, and Dirk listened as the floors creaked and the front door opened and then closed. Going into his bedroom, he climbed into bed, found a semicomfortable position that allowed him to breathe relatively easily, and stared at the walls. Dirk was dog-tired, but his mind was running in a million different directions, all centered around one particular subject—Lee. Part of him was fascinated and turned-on as hell, while another part of him seriously wondered what Lee wanted. Because no one ever did anything for nothing.

# Chapter 3

DIRK WAS seriously beginning to rethink that sentiment about people doing something for nothing. It had been three weeks since he'd gotten out of the hospital, and Lee had stopped by almost every day either before or after work. Sometimes he didn't stay long, but he always made a point of asking how Dirk was feeling and if he was breathing better. The doctor had told Dirk he could return to work in a week, but he would be on restricted duty, which sucked, and he wouldn't be allowed to go out to any fires. Part of Dirk looked forward to Lee's visits. He was becoming more than company, and a few times they'd actually talked a little about something other than fighting fires. It seemed they both had a passion for motorcycles, and Lee had ridden his over a few times, and once he was feeling better, Dirk had taken Lee out to the garage to see his.

That was the good part. The hard part, in every sense of the word, was that after five minutes with Lee, Dirk was always aching in his pants and had to adjust himself until Lee left and Dirk could jerk off thinking about Lee's lips on him, hands, or, sweet mother of God, Lee's ass. Once Lee stopped by on his way to the gym in a tank top and shorts. Dirk jerked off to that image in his head for days. He knew he had to get over this, and there was no way he could act on it. At least he knew he *shouldn't* act on it, but his resolve weakened each time he saw Lee. Not that he was assuming Lee was interested.

Dirk heard footsteps on the porch and got up off the sofa, where he had been reading. He'd already watched enough television to last him a lifetime. Opening the door, Dirk stepped back as Lee walked inside. The sight stole Dirk's breath, and it had nothing to do with his injury. "Coming from the gym?" Dirk asked and swallowed. It was warm outside, and Lee was wearing a string tank that displayed his pecs and nipples perfectly and a small pair of running shorts that left very little to Dirk's imagination.

"Yeah, the water is off at the gym and at my place because of a main break. It's being repaired now, but I wasn't sure how long it would be. Do you mind if I use your shower?"

Dirk shook his head, and Lee headed upstairs, those shorts tightening around Lee's firm butt with every step. Dirk went back into the living room, picked up his book, and tried to read. After reading the same sentence eight times, he heard the water start and gave up on reading, knowing Lee was upstairs naked in his bathroom. Turning on the television, he found a show about earthquakes and began watching. Eventually he heard the water shut off and then heard Lee on the stairs. Turning down the volume, he twisted slightly to ask Lee if he wanted a beer, and his mouth dropped open. Lee was wearing an indecently tight pair of shorts and nothing else. "What are you doing?" Dirk asked gruffly.

"I'm not playing fair, is what I'm doing. You've been peeking looks at me and, I bet, jacking yourself off every night to what you think I look like. Don't think I haven't seen you, and don't you think for a minute that I mind one bit, because I don't. You see, I've been looking at you too." Lee stepped closer, standing between Dirk and the television, legs spread, bulge right at Dirk's eye level. "Like I told you, I see even what you don't want me to see, and I've spent three weeks doing everything I could to drive you crazy." Lee moved closer, his voice dropping and becoming richer, dripping with sex. "Do you think I wore those leather pants in the middle of summer just because I was riding my bike? Fuck no," Lee growled, and Dirk's cock jumped and throbbed. "I wore them so you could get a great view of my ass. You always ask what I want whenever I help you with something. Well, I want you to be honest with yourself and with me, even if you want to lie to the rest of the world." Lee motioned toward the windows. "You want me bad, and I want you. I didn't just come from the gym, and there's no water main break. I wanted you to see me in that string tank just like I want you to see me in these shorts."

"What if I tell you to leave?" Dirk asked pathetically, but it was all he could manage with a throat as dry as the desert.

"Then say so, and I'll leave," Lee murmured, so close to him Dirk could almost feel his breath. "I don't want anything you aren't willing to give. But you won't ask me to leave. I can see by your eyes you want this so bad you can't see straight." Lee leaned forward and touched his legs, his huge hands surprisingly gentle. "I know what it feels like to be in the closet and to want something so bad you can't stand it. But everyone's told you what you want is wrong, so you bury it and hold what you want inside."

Dirk nodded once because he almost had to. It felt like Lee could see into his soul and knew exactly what he wanted. The thought made him shiver, and when Lee's hand moved a little further up his leg, Dirk shivered once again.

"You don't have to do that. You can make yourself happy and stop hiding, at least for a while." Lee moved even closer, and Dirk felt his lips part in anticipation of another kiss. He still hadn't been able to get the one in the hospital out of his mind.

Dirk's heart pounded, and his breath shortened. Lee shifted his body ever closer, filling Dirk's line of sight with golden skin, and for the first time, Dirk allowed himself a touch, his fingers tracing the dark tattooed swirls that adorned Lee's left shoulder and part of his chest. "It's okay to be honest with yourself," Lee whispered, and Dirk felt himself nod. He knew what Lee said was right, but years of denial didn't fall away in an instant. He held back, and Lee moved still closer; then Dirk parted his lips and ran his tongue along them to get ready for what he was sure would be another amazing kiss.

It was. Dirk closed his eyes at the very instant Lee latched his mouth onto his. Just like the last time, Lee took immediate control, nibbling with hard, firm lips and probing Dirk's mouth with his tongue. Dirk felt Lee move closer, pressing him back against the cushions as the kiss continued to build. He felt Lee's fingers at the hem of his shirt, and Lee backed away just long enough to tug the fabric up and off him. Then he was being kissed again, Lee's massive chest pressed to his. Dirk's cock throbbed in the confines of his pants, and as Lee guided him down onto the sofa, his weight pressing onto him. Dirk could feel Lee's rock-hard cock pressing against his hip. This was what he wanted and had been denying himself—the feel, the warmth, the closeness of being held by another person, one that he wanted to be held by. In the past, all his encounters had been silent and anonymous, taking care of business in a video booth or some guy he neither knew nor cared about sucking him off in the bathroom of a club an hour away. And he always hated himself afterward. But this, God, this was completely different. Lee was kissing him, and he felt huge hands firmly stroking his skin, rough fingers occasionally plucking at one of his nipples, making him ache for more.

Dirk felt Lee move his hips, and the sensation of what felt like a long thick cock sliding beside his had him thrusting and bucking beneath Lee. "We got all the time you want," Lee said, his breath flowing warmly over Dirk's lips. Lee backed away and slowly got up from the sofa, his shorts massively tented, and Lee made no move to hide it. "See what you do to me?" Dirk nodded, his cock jumping and his ass throbbing at the sight. Lee extended his hand, and Dirk took it and got up off the sofa, heading for the stairs. As he did, he looked out the front window and saw his father's BMW pulling up in front of the house. Immediately, he pulled his hand away and raced back to the sofa, tugging on his shirt.

"Get dressed! Now!" he snapped between clenched teeth as he tried to control his breathing to keep from coughing. Turning around, he saw the passion that had burned in Lee's eyes die away, replaced with disappointment. Then Lee reached into his gym bag and pulled out a pair of workout pants and a T-shirt, slipping them on before gathering his things.

"I'll see you around," Lee said as he pulled open the door. Dirk heard Lee greet his father outside and then the sound of a motorcycle engine followed by the rumbling scream as Lee took off. Dirk sat on the sofa and turned on the television, keeping the volume low so it would look like they'd been watching television.

"Who was that?" Dirk's father asked gruffly as he walked into the house without knocking.

"One of the guys from the station," Dirk answered from the sofa. "He's been stopping in to make sure I'm doing okay." He tried to keep his tone neutral.

"Hmmmff," his father grunted as though he'd tasted something that wasn't quite right.

Dirk's stomach jumped, and he reminded himself that his dad was always like that. "I got the go-ahead to go back to work next week," he said, changing the subject. "I still get short of breath sometimes, but it's getting better all the time."

"Well, you won't have to worry about that too much longer. The brokerage is interested in having you join our team." His dad actually looked excited.

"What? Dad." When in hell had that happened? He loved his job and couldn't wait to return to work. The last thing he wanted was to be under his father's thumb for his living after giving up a job he was born to do. Dirk breathed too deeply and began to cough, his father ignoring it. "Tough it out" had always been his dad's motto, that and ignore anything he didn't want to see.

"I told you I was going to put out some feelers and start the paperwork when you were in the hospital," his father said firmly as he sat in one of the chairs. "Your job is way too dangerous, and you can make a hell of a lot more money working for me. I know you'll have to give your notice, so you can do that tomorrow and start with us in a few weeks."

"You got me to agree to this when I was under the influence of medication, and you haven't seen fit to talk it over or even see me in weeks."

"I called you!" his father snapped. "Don't talk back to me."

"Disagreeing with you is not talking back to you. I like being a firefighter, and I'm good at it." He felt just like he always did with his father, like he was still twelve and had just gotten caught playing doctor with Jimmy from up the street. "I don't want to be anyone's financial representative. I like being outside, and I like helping people."

"But you were almost killed," his father countered, and it was the first hint of parental concern he'd heard in his father's voice in years. "What sort of life can you possibly have? There's nowhere you can go. Don't you want more?" His father's usual tone was back in spades. "Just come down to the office next week and look it over. Don't dismiss this opportunity out of hand."

Dirk was more than a little uncomfortable. His father rarely took no for an answer. That was what made him an excellent broker and financial advisor, he got clients because he was persistent, but he carried that persistence into the rest of his life, and he rarely knew when to back off, especially with Dirk. The result was a mutual avoidance of each other. Well, mainly Dirk avoiding his father when he could. "I have to go back to work next week."

"Then come down late this week and see how things work," his father said, using his firm, "I'll not accept an argument" parental tone.

"No," Dirk responded with surprising firmness. "I'll keep the offer in mind, but I have things I need to do this week, and I'm still supposed to take it easy to make sure my lungs heal. I promise I'll think about it, but that's all." He'd never spoken like this to his father before, and Dirk was beginning to realize he probably should have long before now. Maybe there would be some mutual respect. "I need to lie down, and I know you have calls to return and clients to visit." Dirk knew where his father's priorities lay. Ever since his mother's death, when Dirk was in high school, his father's workaholic nature had taken over everything. His job and making money became paramount to Richard Krause, and that was what mattered, and to Dirk that was all that seemed to matter to him.

"I have already given assurances to my partners that you were interested in this position, and now you won't even come in. I stuck my neck out for you."

Dirk felt bile rise in his stomach. "You did what you wanted and nothing more. I have things I need to do, and you should have asked before this, or at the very least discussed this with me when I wasn't loopy on a bunch of pain medication." Dirk stood up and walked toward the stairs.

"Where are you going?" his father snapped.

"I told you I need to rest. I trust you know where the door is." Dirk didn't turn around as he climbed the stairs, and he was pretty pleased with himself when he heard the front door close without any more argument from his father. Not that he'd heard the last of this subject. His father would just regroup and attack some other way. If the man had stayed in the Marines, he could have made Commandant by now. At the top of the stairs, Dirk walked to his bedroom and sat on the edge of the bed for a few minutes before lying down. He knew he wouldn't sleep because his father had him all keyed up and because he couldn't stop thinking about Lee, hoping that he would come back. But he'd seen the hurt look on Lee's face.

Dirk reached for his phone, thumbing through the contacts, but there was no one he could call. Dirk didn't have many friends outside of the station, and his stay in the hospital had taught him that most of the men at work were just that, the guys he worked with. Lee had stopped by every day since he'd gotten out of the hospital. He'd even helped with things that Dirk couldn't do, and he'd done it all without complaining, not even when Dirk had needed help carrying a week's worth of dirty laundry to the basement before his arm was healed enough for him to do it. Setting his phone aside, Dirk closed his eyes, wrestling with his own thoughts. Eventually he dozed off, but with nothing resolved.

# Chapter 4

LEE HADN'T stopped by, and Dirk missed the company and his friendship. At that realization, Dirk blinked a few times. Not many guys would have helped someone out just because they needed some help, without being asked or anything. Over the past three days, every time he thought about Lee, he remembered his searing kisses and the way his skin felt against his or the way Lee's massively huge hands had touched him with an amazing combination of firmness and gentleness. The memory made him ache and throb every single time he thought about it. They hadn't even done anything other than kiss and touch a little, but that had been more meaningful than all the blowjobs and all the anonymous touching combined. He knew it was better if Lee stayed away. These feeling would fade away in time, and he could go back to his life the way it had been. But was that what he wanted?

Dirk was a good firefighter, he knew that, but none of the guys liked him. That was for sure, because they'd sent Lee to the hospital. He always knew the guys had his back in a fire, he never doubted that for a second, but other than that, he hadn't made any friends, and now he could see where he'd probably alienated the guys. He was an asshole, the way Lee had said. Over the past three days, he'd done a lot of thinking, and he'd realized there was a lot of his father in him. Sitting in his living room, Dirk turned off the television and booted up his computer and, after a few false starts, he managed to find out where Lee lived and decided to drive over and see if he was home.

He stopped on the way to pick up a six-pack of nice beer and parked on Hanover, the main street of town. He rang the bell to an apartment above an antique store. He wasn't sure anyone was home and was about to leave when he heard heavy footsteps approach. Lee opened the door, scowling at him for a few seconds before stepping back so he could enter. "What are you doing here?"

What was he doing here? What did he actually expect? Dirk swallowed, and Lee began climbing the stairs. "You may as well come up." Dirk followed and did his best not to look at Lee's ass, but he couldn't help it.

At the top of the stairs, Lee opened the door, and Dirk followed him into the tiny apartment. The place made Lee look even larger than he usually did, especially when he nearly had to duck to move from room to room. "Nice place," Dirk said, setting the beer on the small table in the kitchen area.

"What do you want, Dirk? You're on the mend and will be returning to work in a few days. You don't need me anymore."

"Well...."

"What? You need your laundry done or your lawn mowed? That's all I was to you, anyway. Some guy who did your shit for you. Well, that was fine, I helped you out, but not anymore. You made your feelings crystal clear the last time I was at your house." Lee moved toward the door and watched him. "You don't even get it do you? I saw the way you looked at me when your dad showed up. You couldn't even treat me like a human being. Did you ever think to introduce me to your father as a friend? No! You just looked at me like I was shit on your boots! Well, I'm not. I'm a person the same as everyone else. Not that I should have expected anything different, because you treat everyone like shit."

"I do not."

"Yes, you do. You're an asshole through and through. Why I thought otherwise is beyond me." Lee stalked over to where Dirk stood staring at him.

Suddenly it became important for Dirk to understand. "Why did you stick around in the first place?"

"The baby. I was the one you passed the baby to, and I figured a guy who would risk his life to save a baby couldn't be all bad. But I was wrong. You are an asshole extraordinaire. Now if you don't mind, I'd prefer if you left before I need to disinfect the place." Lee opened the door, and Dirk stepped toward the opening, feeling lower than he ever thought possible. This kid had actually maybe liked him, and Dirk had squashed that with a single look.

"You closet cases are all alike! You worry about nothing but yourself and protecting your precious little secret," Lee mocked in a childlike voice, and Dirk's temper began to rise. "You'll hurt anyone to protect your denial of who you are." Lee stomped toward him, his steps echoing through the room. Lee reached out, grabbing his shirt. "You think being gay makes you less of a man? Well, you're wrong. Being true to yourself makes you a man! Hiding yourself just turns you into an asshole!" Lee released his shirt with a small shove, and Dirk felt his temper begin to boil.

"You don't know what it's like for me, not one little bit." Dirk shoved back and stepped right into Lee's space. "You think you know everything, but you don't know shit about me or my life."

"I don't, huh," Lee said and reached for him. Dirk braced to get hit but instead Lee pulled him forward, slamming their lips together. In an instant, Dirk's anger evaporated, replaced by a crest of lust-driven passion. It slammed into him hard, and Dirk forgot to keep fighting as Lee pummeled his mouth. Just like the previous times, Lee took immediate charge, but this time Dirk fought back, nipping at Lee's lower lip, but Lee nipped back before using his huge hands to steady Dirk's head, taking complete control. "I know what you want. Believe me, I've seen it in your eyes and written all over your body." Lee kissed him again, another bruising kiss that seemed to dare him to tell Lee he was wrong, and while Dirk desperately wanted Lee to be wrong, he probably wasn't. Dirk was as hard as stone, throbbing in his pants, his legs shaking. He did want this desperately.

Lee tugged at the hem of Dirk's shirt, roughly pulling it over his head; then Lee did the same with his own, dropping it on the floor before slamming their bodies together. Lee tightened his gigantic arms around him. Dirk had never thought being held this way would turn him on, but Lee was so strong and big that Dirk felt surprisingly safe, like nothing could touch him. Dirk expected Lee to go back to kissing, and he did, but what he didn't expect was to be lifted off his feet like a child and carried through the room. He'd forgotten just how much strength Lee had at his disposal. Lee set him on the sofa, and Dirk stared up as Lee slid one of his tree-trunk legs between Dirk's.

"Are you sure about this?" Lee asked. "Because I want this too." Lee's eyes bored into Dirk's, and he squirmed slightly under Lee's intensely heated gaze. Dirk nodded, and then Lee kissed him again, and Dirk arched into the rough touch, holding onto Lee's shoulders for support. He needed to remain steady as Lee tugged at the waist of his jeans, the buttons opening one by one. There was no preamble or beating around the bush, Lee just shoved his pants past his hips. Standing up, Lee shoved his shorts down his legs, giving Dirk a look at his long, thick cock.

Dirk stared open-mouthed as Lee let him look his fill. "I imagined you naked plenty, but never like this," Dirk admitted, and Lee grinned. Dirk worked the pants off his legs, and Lee continued staring before shaking his head. Reaching for Dirk's good arm, Lee bent forward and shifted Dirk onto his shoulders in a fireman's carry. "What are you doing?" After all, he'd just been manhandled onto the sofa and now he was upside down with his ass in the air and a hand on it, his dick throbbing to beat the band.

"Taking you to bed," Lee explained, and very soon Dirk was bouncing on the mattress; then Lee was on top of him like they'd been on Dirk's sofa, but this was so much better. "Have you been with a lot of guys?" Lee asked him, and Dirk shrugged. Lee seemed to understand— his eyes went soft, and he stroked Dirk's forehead. He looked so sweet, and yet behind those eyes swirled a strength that turned Dirk on no end. Lee opened a drawer in his nightstand, setting the supplies on top. Then he prowled onto the bed. How a man as big as Lee pulled it off was beyond Dirk, but he did.

The intense kiss Lee gave him nearly stopped Dirk's brain, and when it ended, he gasped for breath, grateful he didn't cough. Instead, he ran his hand over Lee's chest, smooth skin covering muscle that held so much power, down his stomach with lines that felt like rift valleys, and finally, what he truly wanted, Dirk gripped Lee's thick, heavy cock. Fuck, he felt good, and Dirk swallowed a little, afraid of what he wanted. Lee seemed to sense it, shifting, bringing his cock closer to Dirk's mouth. "Is this what you want?" Lee asked with a gruff edge to his voice, and Dirk nodded, eyes bulging as he parted his lips, taking the thick head into his mouth. One taste of Lee was like ambrosia, he had to have more. Sucking, Lee's cock slid over his tongue, and Dirk stopped, closing his eyes as he bobbed his head slightly. "That's it, add a little suction," Lee encouraged, and Dirk took what he could. There was no way he was going to be able to take all of Lee, but, damn, he wanted as much as he could.

Lee pulled slowly away, and Dirk wondered if he'd done something wrong. Instead Lee turned around, straddling Dirk's head, lowering his cock into Dirk's mouth. Fuck. Lee tasted good, and while he sucked,

Dirk ran his hands over Lee's baby-smooth ass. Lee made soft moaning sounds and slowly flexed his hips, fucking Dirk's mouth at a leisurely pace. "Damn, you taste good," Dirk mumbled around a mouth full of Lee, and he heard a soft groan in reply, and then his own cock was engulfed, and Lee sucked him to the root in one swift movement. The things Lee did to his cock Dirk couldn't even begin to describe in words. Dirk felt Lee's hands work beneath his butt, and then Lee was lifting his hips.

"Wanted to taste you for a long time," Lee told Dirk before taking him deep once again. Dirk wasn't sure how much of this he was going to be able to take. Sucking Lee, getting sucked, the feel of Lee's skin, his masculine heady scent, his rich taste with just a hint of smoke from deep in his skin, all of it combined to a damned near sensory overload, and Dirk felt his climax rising already. He didn't want to come so soon, but the way Lee worked him, he couldn't stop it. Lee's cock slipped from his mouth as Dirk arched his back and came with a shout. He felt Lee stroking him hard, milking his release from him.

Dirk collapsed back onto the bed and felt Lee shift on the mattress. Opening his eyes, he saw Lee crouched over him, smiling widely. "Sorry I was so fast."

Lee smirked. "That was just to take the edge off," Lee explained with an evil grin on his face before kissing him hard and deep.

"Oh," Dirk said hopefully.

"Yeah, I'm going to get you ready and then fuck you until you can't form words."

Dirk wasn't sure about getting fucked. But before he could say anything Lee crouched between his legs, lifting them off the bed. His ass in the air, Dirk tensed, thinking Lee was going to fuck him right then. Fuck, was he wrong. Lee buried his face between Dirk's cheeks, his tongue probing Dirk's ass. Dirk gasped so hard and fast he nearly coughed.

"Jesus fucking Christ!" Dirk cried, and Lee actually chuckled before nibbling on his skin. Dirk's legs fell open further, and he pressed himself into the sensation, making sounds he never knew he could make.

"Like that?" Lee asked.

"Fuck, yes! God, please don't stop," Dirk begged. He was already hard again, and whatever Lee was doing to him made his head throb in complete and utter bliss. He'd never felt this way in his life. Before, sex was just an anonymous way to get off, but Lee made his entire being feel excited and alive, something only the adrenaline rush of fighting fires had ever done before.

A slick, full finger breached him slowly and then retreated, Lee continuing to rim him into the middle of next week. Then Lee's thick finger entered him again, and Dirk groaned as another one joined the first. "Feel full," Dirk whimpered.

"Do you want me to stop?"

"God, no. Please, God, never stop," Dirk moaned as Lee twisted his fingers. Fuck, that felt amazing. Lee added a third finger, really stretching him.

"Breathe evenly," Lee instructed in a caring, almost loving tone. "I'm going to make you feel so damned good." Dirk moaned his agreement as Lee's fingers scissored inside him. "Gonna make you feel loved." Lee slipped his fingers away, and Dirk lowered his legs to the bed. Dirk forced his mind not to concentrate on the "L" word Lee had just uttered. "Roll over, it'll be easier," Lee said. Dirk complied breathlessly, and he heard a package rip. A minute later, Lee lifted his hips, placing a pillow under him. "I promise I'll stop if you tell me to," Lee whispered into his ear, before sucking on it, and Dirk felt Lee's cock at his hole.

Dirk wasn't sure about this, but Lee didn't move, he held himself still and kept kissing him, and caressing his skin. "What are you waiting for?" Dirk asked, getting a little nervous.

"Just relax," Lee said against his lips. "Sometimes this requires patience and a little time to make it really good." Lee nibbled on his ear. "Your little hole is throbbing for me right now. It wants me and it's waiting. You can feel it, can't you? You're so ready for me to be inside, you can't stop vibrating. Your throat is dry, and you can't even take a deep breath without whimpering. You want me to fuck you, don't you? Your skin says you do," Lee added as Dirk arched his back, and Lee slipped his hands around to Dirk's chest, making tiny circles with his fingers over Dirk's nipples. "Your eyes said it too."

Everything Lee said was true. Dirk could not stop the adrenaline that coursed through his veins. His body ached for Lee right now, and it was all he could do to stop himself from pressing back, forcing Lee to enter his body. "I want you," Dirk gasped.

"What do you want? Tell me what it is you want," Lee whispered, licking the base of Dirk's neck. "Tell me everything you want."

"Everything?" Dirk asked, and he felt Lee move forward just a little, the pressure on his hole intense, but not quite enough. His cock throbbed and pulsed as his muscles went wild with anticipation.

"Yes, everything. What is it you really want?"

"I don't know," Dirk admitted, his voice breaking.

"Just say it!" Lee told him, his voice low, but forceful. "What does Dirk really want?"

"To be loved? I don't know." Dirk rocked his head on the pillow. "You to fuck me! I just need!"

Lee pressed forward, the pressure on Dirk's opening unbearable, and then Dirk felt his body give, and Lee pressed inside him. The stretch and burn were intense, and Dirk wasn't sure he could take it. Lee was stretching him almost beyond imagination. Then Dirk felt the cockhead slip inside, and Lee stilled again. Dirk cried out as his muscles spasmed and throbbed, going wild as Dirk's head seemed ready to explode.

"Breathe. I'm inside you and we're one."

The sounds of the traffic outside the apartment softened and slipped away as Lee sank deeper and deeper into him. It truly felt as though they were joined. More and more of Lee pressed into him until Dirk felt Lee's hips against his butt. Then Lee stilled, and Dirk buried his face in the pillow, chewing on the fabric as wave after wave of sensation rocked his body.

Then Lee moved, slowly pulling out, and Dirk whimpered when Lee completely pulled away, leaving him incredibly empty and surprisingly alone. "Please" was all Dirk could manage, and Lee tightened the hold around his chest, thrusting forward and filling him in a single, agonizingly slow stroke. Dirk was shaking by the time Lee was totally inside him again.

"I have you," Lee said into his ear, his huge chest plastered to Dirk's back. He could feel Lee's skin from his back to his butt and all the way down his legs. Dirk was nearly completely covered by Lee's body, and it felt incredible, like no one or nothing could get to him. "You're safe, and you can come apart all you want." Lee pulled out and thrust deep into him, the force vibrating through Dirk's entire body.

"Lee!" Dirk cried as he was filled, Lee's cock rubbing over a spot inside him that had Dirk seeing stars.

"I know. That's what you've been missing by not being true to yourself." Lee kept moving, thrusting slow and deep. "That's your body telling you what it wants."

Dirk nodded just as Lee pulled out of him, and Lee's weight shifted off his back. Then Dirk was rolled over, his knees lifted and pressed to his chest. Lee entered him again in a single stroke, his gaze boring into Dirk's. The intense expression on Lee's face made Dirk quiver even more than the intensely full feeling he experienced whenever Lee drove inside him.

"I can feel you," Dirk murmured almost under his breath when Lee drove deep and stopped, his cock jumping deep inside Dirk's body.

"I can feel you too. Every time your heart beats, you throb around me," Lee said, leaning forward to capture Dirk's lips in a soul-melting kiss. "You feel amazing, you know that? Every time you clench around me, it's all I can do not to let go, but I don't want to hurt you."

"This is holding back?" Dirk asked between shallow panting breaths.

"Oh yes." Lee began to move again, thrusting deep and hard, driving into Dirk's body. With each thrust, Lee picked up speed and intensity. The bed rocked, and Dirk's entire body reverberated with the energy from Lee's body.

Dirk had been holding his arms at his side, but now, he grabbed onto Lee's shoulders to steady himself as he felt Lee's intense power driving into him. Dirk held on as Lee pushed him to new heights. Lee was indeed keeping his promise, because shortly Dirk found he couldn't speak or form a coherent thought. His mouth hung open, and he tried to control his breathing as intense waves of sensation took over his entire body, overriding thought and everything that didn't center on Lee and the amazing things he was making him feel. As his passion built, Dirk dug his fingers into Lee's muscles, holding on as his climax built and built. At first Dirk thought they would never reach the top, but then the wave broke. Lee threw his head back, crying out his release in a deep growl that almost shook the walls, and Dirk followed right behind him, letting go of the last on his internal control and riding the wave of his desire until he couldn't hold it any longer.

Dirk opened his eyes and saw Lee still leaning over him. "Hey, you were out of it for a few seconds," Lee told him, and Dirk nodded slowly. Lee pulled out of his body, both of them groaning. "I'll be right back,"

Lee told him, and Dirk watched Lee's naked butt bounce as he hurried to the bathroom. He returned a few seconds later with a cloth and towel. Lee cleaned Dirk up and tossed the towel and cloth back toward the bathroom before climbing onto the bed, spooning against Dirk's back.

"Wow. I never," Dirk started to say, and Lee drew him closer, settling one of his big hands on Dirk's stomach.

"I know," Lee told him, and Dirk felt him lightly kiss his shoulder. "But that's how it should be all the time, and it can be with someone you care about, someone you might actually like and likes you before you have sex." Lee hugged him tighter, and Dirk knew he was right. Closing his eyes, Dirk almost instantly fell asleep, warm and comfortable in Lee's ample arms.

How long he slept, Dirk wasn't sure, but he woke sometime later, the light in the room having dimmed considerably. One thing he did notice almost immediately was his own painfully hard cock, and Lee's pressing against his butt. Rolling partway over, he felt Lee stir, and they kissed long and slow. There didn't seem to be the rush from earlier, but there was definitely the intensity. Lee feasted on his lips, lazily tracing his tongue around the outline of Dirk's mouth. Dirk felt Lee reach to the table and roll on a condom. Then he parted Dirk's legs and slowly slid inside.

Dirk's eyes drifted closed, the sensation familiar and wonderful. Lee filled him easily and moved his hand, which had been on Dirk's stomach while he slept, to slide it between Dirk's legs, where Lee wrapped his fingers around Dirk's cock.

"That's it," Lee crooned. "You feel so good." Slowly he began to move deep into Dirk's body, stroking his hand to the timing of his thrusts, passing his thumb over the head. Dirk began thrusting into Lee's hand, fucking it the way Lee was fucking him. The feelings were nearly overpowering, and he groaned softly. "Take it easy," Lee said, slowing down. "I want to make this really good for you."

"It already is," Dirk panted.

"I know. But we have lots of time. Just enjoy being together. There's something intimately special about being like this. It's not just about the sex, but about being close." Lee continued his leisurely thrusts, and Dirk could feel the desire building ever so slowly, and it was unbelievably amazing. Somehow, Lee knew just what he wanted and gave him just enough to keep him on the edge without tumbling over. Time seemed to have a life of its own as Lee leisurely fucked him into total oblivion. He never moved fast, but he drove Dirk wild with his hand and cock. Whenever Dirk got too close, he would back off and then speed up again. Dirk's eyes closed, and he let Lee take control of everything, giving himself and his pleasure over to him. As soon as he did that, the desire immediately ramped up simply because he trusted Lee.

"Not gonna last much longer," Dirk whispered, his hands clenching the bedding.

"Don't want you to," Lee whispered into his ear as he tightened his grip on Dirk's cock. "I want to come." Lee stroked harder, and Dirk clamped his eyes closed as he came, pressing Lee deeply into his body. As he did, he felt Lee pulse and jump inside him, and knew he was coming as well.

They both settled, Dirk trying to breathe and Lee holding him, their bodies still connected. Eventually Dirk felt Lee go soft and then slide out of his body. After a quick wipe-up, Lee held him a while longer. "I have to go into the station in a few hours," Lee told him, and Dirk was heartened because he sounded sad. "I would rather stay here with you." After lying quietly together for quite a while, Lee got out of bed. Dirk knew he had to leave, but it didn't make him feel any better. "I'll stop by your place after my shift if that's okay." Lee smiled at him.

"That would be really nice," Dirk told him, and Lee hugged him close.

"I'll see you sometime tomorrow morning."

Dirk agreed and got dressed and sat on the edge of the bed. Lee cleaned up and then began to change into his uniform.

"That looks amazing on you," Dirk said as Lee buttoned his shirt. "Did you always want to be a fireman?"

"Ever since I was a kid."

"Me too. My dad doesn't understand and wants me to work for him." Dirk hated the very thought of sitting behind a desk all day.

"He doesn't know about you, does he?" Lee asked, sitting next to him, and Dirk shook his head violently.

"He works at a Christian brokerage. I don't know what he really believes in other than money. But he'll do anything to protect it, and having a gay son would not help his reputation."

"What are you afraid of?" Lee asked softly, taking his hand.

"That if I tell him, he'll never have anything to do with me again." Dirk looked into Lee's eyes. "You don't know what that's like." Dirk felt miserable just thinking about how his father would react. He knew he would have nothing at all to do with him after that, and his father was the only family he had.

# Chapter 5

THE REST of the week before Dirk returned to work passed in a blur of mind-bending sex, dinners, watching television, and more sex. He and Lee spent all the time that Lee wasn't at work together. What surprised Dirk most was that while he loved the sex, it was being with Lee and having him to talk with about nothing at all that he really enjoyed. Normal things, like watching the Phillies on television, took on special meaning when he and Lee lay shirtless on the sofa, watching the game with his head resting on Lee's shoulder. Of course, they never seemed to make it completely through the game without becoming distracted, but that certainly didn't bother either of them.

Now he had to return to reality. Dirk was showered, dressed, and even had his medication in his pocket, ready to leave for work. He was looking forward to it, but he wasn't quite sure how he was going to feel. His hospital experience had been eye-opening in so many ways. Part of him was still hurt and angry that none of the guys had come to visit, but he also realized that he had a lot to make up for with the guys he worked with. He wasn't quite sure how he was going to go about it, but he knew he had to. Spending the past week or so with Lee had shown him just how solitary and lonely his life had become, and he wanted to make a change. Locking up the house, Dirk took a deep breath, testing his lungs, and breathed a small sigh of relief that his cough was largely gone.

The drive to the station took a few minutes, but he made a stop before parking in the lot and walking into the station house. He climbed the stairs toward the living area and braced himself for whatever faced him. "Morning, Charlie," Dirk said with a smile as the older firefighter passed him on the stairs.

"Dirk," Charlie said in reply and continued down the stairs. "Welcome back," he called without much real cheer.

"Thanks," Dirk continued, pretending not to notice. "How's your daughter doing? Getting bigger, I bet?" Charlie's wife had had a baby about six months earlier, and Dirk had pretty much ignored the event.

Charlie stopped and turned. "She's doing well. Crawling already and trying, unsuccessfully, to pull herself up." A ghost of a smile crossed Charlie's face before he turned and continued down the stairs. Dirk climbed the rest of the way and entered the room, where the television was already on and some of the guys were making breakfast while others talked. The conversation stilled as Dirk walked inside, and he could almost feel the tension in the room ramp up. A few of the men refused to meet his eyes.

"Morning," Dirk said to the group as he set the bag he'd been carrying on the counter. "I brought cinnamon rolls." Jones Bakery made the world's best, and they were a perennial treat around the station. Dirk opened the bag and pulled out the container, setting it in the middle of the table before walking toward the captain's office. The door was open, but he knocked anyway.

"Morning, Cap," Dirk called with a smile, and Captain Morris smiled at him and nodded, continuing his telephone conversation. They would talk later, he was sure, and Dirk returned to the station house area. "Do you need help?" Dirk asked Roger Smith, the station chef. The man was one of those old-time firefighters who'd seen it all, and he could cook like nobody's business.

Roger looked at him like he had three heads. Dirk never volunteered for kitchen duty. His father always said that was woman's work, and after his mother died, they rarely ate at home unless they could heat it up in the microwave. Lee, on the other hand, loved to cook, and Dirk had discovered that working in the kitchen could be fun. "I need to scramble the eggs," Roger answered. Dirk figured he could crack eggs, so he took the bowl Roger passed to him. The first two eggs did indeed crack on the edge of the bowl, but more egg ended up on the counter than in the bowl. By the third egg, he'd figured it out, and after cracking the rest of the two dozen eggs, Roger took the bowl and handed him a cloth to clean up the mess. "No wonder you order out when it's your turn to cook," Roger commented with a small smile.

"Sorry," Dirk said.

"It's cool," Roger answered. He began whipping the eggs and placing them in the frying pans, and Dirk turned, a sea of eyes instantly turning away from him to the television. Dirk sighed and walked back toward the stairs. He descended to the garage level and decided to check out the trucks.

They looked the same, and a few of the guys were laying out hoses to dry. Dirk picked up one end and helped Charlie hang them to dry. They didn't talk much, which was fine since Dirk was simply happy to have something to do. He hadn't realized how bad things had gotten. Before he'd been hurt, things had just seemed normal. He knew things weren't running as smoothly at the station as they should, but he hadn't realized that maybe he had been the problem when he'd pushed the other guys to do more or get more done.

"Thanks for the help," Charlie told him when they were done and then headed inside for breakfast while Dirk wandered around the engines.

"Come get one of the rolls before they're gone," Frank Jenkins told him from the doorway, his mouth half full. "It must seem strange to be back," Frank commented as they climbed the stairs.

"Sort of, I guess. Mostly it was long and rather lonely," Dirk said, and Frank stopped, turning around. He looked like he wanted to say something, but then shook his head and continued up the stairs.

Dirk went up to breakfast, sitting at the table in his usual spot, but everything felt off to him. He'd been looking forward to coming back to work, but he felt strange and out of place. Conversation swirled around the table the way it always did, but Dirk didn't feel like a part of it. He'd always thought these guys were his friends and his pushing and prodding was to make the unit better, but now he could see that he'd simply been critical and sometimes mean. No wonder they didn't like him.

"Thanks again for the help, Dirk," Charlie said from across the table.

"Anytime," Dirk answered. As the food was passed, Dirk took a little, but he wasn't really hungry. He wondered if he should say something, but decided to keep quiet. Actions spoke louder than words, and Dirk was always a do-it kind of guy, so he decided to be patient and hopefully the guys would see he was trying.

"You're on restricted duty?" Frank asked, and Dirk nodded.

"No fires until the doctor signs off on it, so I'll help as much as I can around here and try not to get in anyone's way. Hopefully it won't be too long, although that last fire did a number on my lungs even with the breathing gear."

"That was one of the most intense fires I've seen in a while, and the fact you got that baby out alive was a miracle," Charlie commented and returned to his food. After taking a bite, Charlie dropped his fork with a clang. "This is ridiculous." He turned to Dirk with a strange look on his face. "We owe you an apology. After you were hurt, we shouldn't have sent the newbie to the hospital. We all should have visited you in the hospital. We're brothers and we should stand by each other and have each other's backs, and that doesn't just mean in a fire." Heads nodded, and the other faces around the table had the same ashamed expression.

"I know I've been a pain in the ass—" Dirk started to say.

"You can be a real mean asshole sometimes," the captain said as he sat down. "But that's no excuse for anyone's bad behavior, including mine. We are a team, and we need to act like it." Captain Morris looked straight at Dirk. "That means that we do indeed watch each other's backs and help one another out. It also means that we don't belittle each other, make fun, or play the 'I work harder than you' game. Everyone in this company has strengths and weaknesses, and we all need to get along. We didn't get to be the oldest fire company in Carlisle for nothing. Now finish eating, because we have work to do." The captain left the room, and everyone began eating fast before heading out. Dirk stayed behind and helped with the cleanup before heading downstairs. Some of the men were washing the trucks, and Dirk joined in, doing some of the detail work.

One of the young volunteers manning the hose got him square in the ass with the water, and when Dirk glowered at him, he backed away. Dirk's first instinct was to yell and tell him to be more careful. It was an accident, so Dirk smiled at the kid and went back to work.

"Did you really almost die rescuing that baby, like the guys said?" the kid asked him as he moved closer to hose off the back side of the engine.

"I guess so," Dirk answered, looking at... Vinny. It took him a second to remember his name. "To tell you the truth, I don't really remember too much of it. By the end, I was pretty out of it, and I guess I acted on instinct. I'm no hero, if that's what you're asking. I was just doing my job." Dirk gave the kid a smile and went back to the detail work.

The siren sounded and everyone scrambled. The hoses were put away, and the guys jumped into their gear. Men called to one another, heavy boot steps pounded. Dirk's heart began to race until he remembered he wasn't going. Doors opened and closed, powerful engines started. Getting the buckets out of the way, it was only a matter of seconds before the engines were pulling out, sirens going. Dirk watched them leave, wishing more than anything that he could go, as well. Instead he watched as the engine turned the corner and the siren eventually faded into the distance. Dirk cleaned up the washing supplies, rinsing out everything before putting it away.

Dirk kept busy while they were gone. He listened to the radio and put on a fresh pot of coffee. The call turned out to be a false alarm, and soon the guys were on their way back. Once they arrived, Dirk helped with engine check, and the team restarted the job of washing the engines. After lunch, Dirk knocked on the captain's door, and he motioned him inside. Dirk closed the door.

"Before you went into the hospital, I was about to write you up as an impediment to the team. The guys hated you, and you got along with no one." The captain motioned Dirk toward a chair. "You're a hell of a firefighter, but you treat the men you work with like dirt. I debated letting you come back and decided I'll give you a final chance, and if what I've already seen is any indication, I made the right decision, and I'm going to give you a chance to prove it."

"Thanks, Captain, I won't let you down."

"See that you don't." Dirk stood up and was about to open the door, but the captain continued. "You always seemed to have a huge chip on your shoulder. It seems to be gone; make sure it stays that way." The captain gave him a firm look, and Dirk left the office. He deserved that, he could see that now. Dirk simply hoped he could actually change.

THE REST of the day and week were long, especially since Dirk was trying to watch everything he did and said. It was exhausting, but the guys were opening up to him more, and he was learning about things he never paid much attention to before. He and Lee worked opposite shifts, so he didn't see him at all, and by the time his days were over, Dirk ate and fell into bed. He hadn't known how much his injury had taken out of him until he tried to do his normal job. On Friday when he went into the station, Dirk was pleasantly surprised when Lee walked in at the same time.

"Looks like we're sharing a shift," Lee observed brightly, and Dirk returned Lee's smile.

As they climbed the stairs, Lee's scent reached him, and Dirk tingled slightly, remembering what they'd done together the last time Dirk had smelled his masculine spice. Dirk's cock went hard in an instant, and he had to take a minute to adjust himself.

"How did it go this week?"

"Tiring but pretty good," Dirk answered, hanging back because he had to have a few minutes to clear his thoughts and make his errant cock go back to sleep. God, this shift was going to be murder.

"Not too tiring, I hope," Lee said with a raised eyebrow, and Dirk groaned under his breath but kept a smile on his face. He was truly happy to see Lee. He hadn't seen him all week, and he really missed him. But at the same time, he'd been wondering how they would work together, and Dirk already had his answer. It was going to be hard, in more ways than one.

Breakfast was nearly ready when he arrived, so he took a place at the table, and sure enough, Lee sat right next to him. Dirk immediately tensed, because damn if his body didn't react again. The food was placed on the table and passed around. To keep his mind off all the erotic things having Lee so close to him evoked, Dirk concentrated on the conversation and, because Lee was next to him, he tried to keep the silly grin off his face. Once breakfast was over, Dirk helped with the dishes and then got to work. They had a number of calls, and Dirk did what he hated and stayed behind.

"How much longer are you on restricted duty?" Lee asked once they returned, and Dirk had to force himself not to react to Lee smelling slightly of smoke.

"I go to the doctor next week, and hopefully he'll sign my release. The breathing is good, and my arm is almost up to full strength again." The man drove him crazy, and at least at work, he wished he could keep under control. To make matters worse, Lee had caught up with him in the living quarters, near half a dozen beds. He was stripping off his clothes to get ready for a shower, and even though they were alone, anyone could walk in. When Lee dropped his pants and grabbed a towel, wrapping it around his waist, Dirk found himself staring at all that golden skin and the tattoo that he'd traced with his tongue the last time they were together. His gaze raked over Lee's chest down to where his skin disappeared into the white, impressively tented towel. Dirk squeezed his eyes closed as his cock throbbed and his balls tightened almost painfully. When he heard the door open behind him, Dirk made a hasty retreat, quietly gasping for air.

Dirk spent the rest of the day trying his best to avoid Lee. He hated that he was acting that way because he could see that he was hurting Lee, but he couldn't think straight when he was around him. He didn't want to work or do anything other than drag him to someplace quiet, drop his pants, and beg Lee to fuck him silly.

"Dirk, is something wrong?" Charlie asked as Dirk stared out into space, pictures of Lee running through his mind. "If I didn't know better, I'd swear you had it bad for someone."

"Why couldn't I?" Dirk challenged a little more forcefully than he'd intended.

"Not saying you couldn't," Charlie said evenly as he brought over two mugs of coffee, setting one in front of Dirk. "You've been working a lot, and that isn't a recipe for a relationship, is all I meant. You want to talk about it?" Charlie sat in the chair across from him. "I can see how hard you're trying, we all can. You had a life-altering experience, and I'm afraid we didn't help you much."

"You did more than you know," Dirk muttered as he lifted his mug, thinking of Lee. "But there isn't much to talk about. While I was gone, I had a lot of time to think, and I hope I figured out what was important."

"Those things take time, and you don't need to worry about it too much. I used to be a lot like you before I got all this gray hair. Full of piss and vinegar, they used to say. I had my close encounter with the fates in a fire off South Street that almost killed me and three other firefighters. One made it out, but was never able to work again. It was bad. After that, I settled down and learned what was important. Three months later, I met my wife." Charlie sipped from his mug. "I firmly believe you don't meet that person meant for you until you're ready for them."

Dirk stared across the table into the knowing eyes of the experienced man. Charlie had been around for a lot of years, and for the first time Dirk wondered if that was what was happening to him, with Lee.

"Whatever was stuck in your craw and got dislodged during that fire, take it as a sign. I did." Charlie sat quietly, and they sipped their coffee. Dirk settled into his own thoughts. Once he was finished with his coffee, Dirk cleaned both his and Charlie's mugs before returning to work.

At the end of his shift, Dirk was dog-tired and horny as hell. He'd spent the better part of the day trying to avoid the object of his horniness and failing miserable. It had turned into a hellishly hot day, and the guys had pulled the engines out to wash them. Dirk saw Lee working with them and stayed away, but apparently someone got a little wild with the hose and some of the neighborhood kids had gotten into the act. When Dirk wandered out, he was greeted by a very wet Lee, clothes clinging to his body, every contour and muscular ridge visible. Lee had grinned at him like a huge kid, and Dirk had raced inside so he wouldn't pop wood for the world to see.

"Who pissed in your cornflakes?" Lee asked him outside the station that evening at the end of their shift.

"What? No one, why?" Dirk didn't get it.

"You avoided me all day and then wouldn't even look at me. What did I do?" Lee sounded confused and hurt.

"You didn't do anything other than wind me up tighter than a drum," Dirk whispered as he walked to his car. "Do you want to come over?"

"I'm not sure I should," Lee said as he hitched his bag over his shoulder and then sighed. Dirk watched as Lee walked away from him toward his apartment. He wanted to call him back and apologize for whatever he'd done, but his pride, or stupidity, stopped him, and he watched Lee turn the corner before getting into his car and driving home.

HIS HOUSE felt as empty as ever when he walked in. Dirk was too tired to do anything other than eat, so when his doorbell sounded, he almost pretended not to be home, but loped down the stairs anyway. He wasn't expecting Lee to be standing on his front porch. Dirk opened the door in invitation as the fatigue vanished in an instant, replaced by happiness and deep desire. "Can I get you a beer?" Lee shrugged as he stood in the living room. "You look like a man with something to say."

"Am I just a fuck to you?" Lee asked with hurt and fear in his eyes. It was so palpable that Dirk swore he could smell it, like acid in the air. "Because if that's all I am, just tell me now, and I can deal with it. I mean, we spent a great week together, but if that was just about getting your rocks off on a regular basis, I need to know."

Quite frankly, Dirk didn't know what it was, and he shrugged. "I gotta be honest, I look forward to seeing you all the time. So, yeah, you're more than someone to get off with. You're my friend, I hope." Dirk knew he was doing this all wrong, but he wasn't sure about a goddamned thing right now. "I don't know anything about relationship stuff at all. I can't tell you what I feel except that when you're not with me, I wish you were. Does that count for something?" Dirk moved closer, and at least Lee didn't move away. "I won't blow smoke up your ass and tell you something that isn't true. I can tell you that I want you in my life more than I've wanted anyone before, but I don't know what that means."

"So I'm more than a fuck," Lee clarified, his eyebrows furrowing.

"You were never just a fuck. I felt that the first time we were together," Dirk said honestly. "I didn't mean to hurt you today, but every time I saw you, I stopped thinking. When I saw you all wet, I wanted to drag you somewhere, open your pants, and suck you off in your uniform. I had visions of how you'd look when you came, your cock down my throat and your uniform plastered to your skin. We have to be professional at work, and I was finding that hard to do, so I tried to stay away."

"You know it's okay to be civil to me. You can treat me like the other guys, at least," Lee said softly.

"But that's the problem. I don't want the other guys to fuck me, and I certainly don't see any of them the way I see you. If I'd been around you all day, everyone would know how I feel because they'd be able to see it."

Lee placed his arms around Dirk's neck. "Would that be so bad?"

"Me going around with a lump in my pants all day?" Dirk quipped.

"No, I mean the guys knowing how you felt," Lee said, and Dirk knew that they were back to the same subject, but now Dirk wasn't so sure of his answer.

"Just give me a little time. Please." Dirk's mouth was so close to Lee's he could feel their heat, and he took Lee's kiss as agreement, not knowing if he should. "Can we go upstairs?" Lee nodded, and Dirk led Lee up the stairs. He started toward his bedroom, but Lee seemed to have other ideas and tugged him toward the bathroom.

"Get naked," Lee said as he turned on the water and toed off his shoes before pulling off his shirt and pants. By the time he was done, Dirk's dick stood straight and tall, bobbing as he watched Lee strip off his pants. Dirk cupped Lee's heavy balls in his hand, stroking Lee's impressive shaft with the other. Lee let him feel and stroke his smooth steel before stepping under the shower spray. Dirk followed, and Lee immediately plastered him against the tile. "No coming until I tell you," Lee growled, and Dirk nodded with a slight whimper that turned into a groan as Lee thumbed his already pebbled nipples.

"Don't move," Lee whispered, and Dirk's breathing turned shallow with excitement. The warm water coursed over him, and Dirk's backside pressed to the cool tile. The difference was shocking and arousing at the same time. Dirk wasn't sure what Lee had planned, but from the heated look in his eyes, Dirk knew it would be good.

Lee reached for the soap, rubbing it between his hands before lathering Dirk's skin. Lee's hands felt warmly amazing, and Dirk rested his head back against the tile, sliding his eyes closed as he soaked up Lee's tactile attention. Lee swirled his hands over his shoulders and then down his chest, moving slick fingers to pay extra attention to his nipples. Dirk expected Lee to move lower, but he stroked his hands up to Dirk's neck, stroking around his ears, making him shiver with anticipation.

"God," Dirk moaned softly, refusing to open his eyes.

"You like this, don't you?" Lee asked sultrily, and Dirk's cock jumped just from Lee's voice, the evidence of just how much he liked it clearly visible. "Keep your eyes closed," Lee whispered as he slipped his hands away. Then Dirk's belly was soaped, with Lee's fingers teasing the skin around his cock. Dirk's knees shook with excitement, but Lee skimmed his hands on past, stroking up and down his legs, carefully avoiding what Dirk so badly wanted touched.

"Please, Lee….," Dirk begged, and he felt Lee stand back up, pressing his body close, the soap slicking both of them, bellies sliding past each other, Dirk's cock trapped between their bodies, sliding along Lee's.

"I know what you want, and you'll get it, but not quite yet. Neither of us will come until I'm buried in your tight, sweet body. Then and only then am I going to ride us both to heaven. This is about intimacy and care, not getting off, so relax and enjoy." Lee moved away, and Dirk felt surprisingly alone, and his instinct was to open his eyes to reconnect in some way with Lee.

Lee touched Dirk's hips, and he jumped slightly. Lee guided him to turn around, and Dirk stood with his hands against the tile as Lee washed his back. When Lee got to Dirk's butt, he automatically spread his legs, and Lee slid soap-slicked fingers along his cleft before lightly kneading his cheeks. "I love this," Lee whispered into his ear. "You're so responsive to my touch."

Dirk groaned, his head falling back slightly. He'd never thought of himself as hedonistic, but around Lee there was no way he could get enough of him. Every touch satisfied and cried for more. Dirk felt the water shift, and he realized Lee was adjusting the showerhead. Water pelted his back, and Dirk wriggled his butt from the sensation. His skin was already sensitive, and the water heightened it. Lee cupped his cheeks, pulling them apart, and Dirk groaned when Lee zeroed his hot tongue in on his hole. "Love that," Dirk mumbled.

"I know," Lee responded, tongue-fucking him deep and hard. Dirk cried out and pressed back toward Lee's face. Lee ate him into near oblivion. With his fingers and tongue, Lee played his ass like an instrument.

"Lee, can't last," Dirk pleaded as his legs began to shake, his cock pressed against the tile, and Dirk found his hips moving as he humped the wall. Lee moved his hands and tongue away from Dirk's skin, and the water stopped. Dirk moved away from the wall and opened his eyes, steadying himself. He hadn't expected to feel dizzy, but Dirk's mind was still on what Lee had been doing to him. Drying himself quickly, he waited for Lee before moving into the bedroom.

The world around him had narrowed the way it always did whenever Lee touched him, but now that Lee wasn't as close to him, the sounds around him began to intrude, and Dirk heard what he thought was a car. Peering out the small window, his heart immediately raced as he saw his father's BMW in front of the house. Talk about killjoy.

"My father is here," Dirk said softly, and all the excitement and joy that they'd built together crashed to the floor around him.

"I'll wait up here for you," Lee said, but Dirk could see that some of the light in his eyes had gone out. Without thinking, Dirk hugged Lee tight. They left the bathroom, and Dirk pulled on a pair of sweatpants and a T-shirt before hurrying down the stairs as his father pounded on the front door. Dirk pulled it open, and his father hurried into the house.

"What's going on?" Dirk rarely saw his father flustered or in a particular hurry. The man was usually collected and in charge.

"There's a fag in that firehouse where you work," his father said gruffly. "I was at the church this evening for a planning meeting, and one of the board members reported that they're planning a protest at the borough. Children look up to firemen, and it makes me think that one of them is a pedophile. I want you to quit and come work with me. No son of mine is going to work with fags." His father shuddered and was already handing him papers.

"Wait a minute, Dad," Dirk said, his mouth going dry and his stomach roiling. Dirk knew he should tell his father that he was one of the gay men in his company, but he couldn't. Instead he found himself taking the papers from his dad.

"We need to protect our children, and we certainly intend to make our voices known at the next borough council meeting."

"Dad, don't you think you're overreacting just a little?" Dirk asked through his fear, trying to sound reasonable.

"No, I'm not. I saw the fag at your house a few weeks ago, and do you have any idea what you hanging around with... with... people like that will do to my reputation? It could kill my business." His father actually looked panicked.

Dirk's throat was so dry he couldn't swallow, and he could barely think. *What? People like me?* he wanted to ask, but couldn't do it. His father was a horse's ass, but he was the only father Dirk had. "You'll have to deal with it, because I like where I work, and I like the people I work with."

"How can you? None of them came to visit you in the hospital, and you were injured on the job. They're not worth your time and effort."

Dirk handed his father back the papers, but he refused to take them. "I don't want to work with you, Dad. I'll make my own way." Had he actually said that? "I like my job, and I want to keep it."

"If you think—" his father began, and Dirk stepped toward him.

"This is my life, and I will not live it for you. Frankly, I can barely stand what little time we spend together because all you talk about are whatever securities you're interested in, your latest deal, or whatever those busybodies at the church are up to." Dirk pushed the papers into his father's hand. "Thanks, but no thanks." Dirk was actually feeling pretty good. He'd really stood up to his father. Before, he'd always listened and did what he needed to do anyway.

His father sputtered, and Dirk could see the heat rising in him. Dirk expected his father to fight back, but he simply stood where he was, vibrating with anger. "This isn't the last of this," he finally ground out between his teeth.

"Actually, it is. I don't want to discuss this any longer."

"We certainly will."

"No, we won't. I don't know what's gotten into you over the last few weeks, but I don't care for it. You were always pushy, but now… I…." Dirk stared at his father, still in his tailored suit and perfect tie, and he realized that his father hadn't changed at all. It was he who'd changed. Dirk wasn't looking at the world the same way. All Dirk wanted right now was for his father to leave so he could run back upstairs and tell Lee all about it.

"What?" his father demanded.

"Nothing you need be concerned with. I'm going back upstairs because I need to be at work early tomorrow." Dirk looked toward the stairs, knowing who was waiting for him up there. "Good night, Dad."

"This opportunity won't be presented again," his father warned, and Dirk nearly made some remark about small blessings, but said nothing instead. Finally, his father walked toward the door and glared at him before leaving the house. Dirk breathed a sigh of relief and caught his breath for a few seconds before heading toward the stairs. Dirk had stood up to his father, but he worried about the cost… and there would be one, of that he had no doubt.

Climbing the stairs two at a time, he nearly barreled into Lee as he made his way down. "Where are you going?"

"Home," Lee responded solemnly as he pushed by him and on down the stairs. "You know," Lee said, turning toward him at the base of the steps, "your dad was talking about me. I'm the fag you work with, and you couldn't even stand up for me. You didn't need to tell your dad about us or that you love to get fucked, but you could at least have stood up for me. You couldn't even do that. Instead you let your dad talk about me like I was dirt, and you said nothing!" Lee hurried toward the front door, and Dirk rushed after him, nearly tripping on the stairs. "At least I really know what you think of me."

"I don't," Dirk said as he hurried to where Lee was already leaving the house. "I don't think that way about you at all." He could feel his pulse racing and his stomach dropping to his feet.

Lee stopped and turned. "Yes, you do. Actions speak louder than words, and your inaction screamed volumes. Don't blame yourself, I should have known better than to develop feelings for someone so deep in the closet."

"You don't know what it's like," Dirk tried to explain, and Lee stopped, walking back to him, chest out, eyes blazing.

"The fuck I don't. I told my folks I was gay, and they haven't talked to me since. I was nineteen years old and on my own with the people I loved most refusing to acknowledge that I existed. They actually told me I was dead to them. My parents changed the locks on the house and even their phone number. I know where they live, and I'm not welcome and never will be. But you know something? I'm still better off than you because at least I don't hate who I am. I can look at myself in the mirror each morning and be proud of what I see. So you're wrong again, Dirk, I do know what it's like." Lee turned and walked toward his bike.

Dirk knew he should go after him, but he was rooted on the spot. The engine of Lee's motorcycle reverberated through the neighborhood, and Dirk found his legs hurrying forward, but as he reached the sidewalk, all he saw were Lee's taillights getting farther away from him.

Dirk wanted to swear, but he kept his anger and disappointment inside until he got back in the house. Then he let loose with a barrage of vitriol aimed squarely at Lee. It didn't last long, however, especially once his mind took over and placed the blame squarely at his own feet. Lee had been right. Dirk hadn't stood up for him even when his father had called Lee names. Sure, he stood up to his father for something as ridiculous as a job he didn't want, but not for someone he really cared about. Once his anger slipped away, Dirk closed the door and turned off the lights before going up to bed. He wanted to call Lee and apologize, but he didn't. Lee had made his feelings crystal clear, and Dirk couldn't think of anything that he could do to make things better. He'd blown it, and that's all there was to it.

# Chapter 6

FOR WEEKS, Dirk worked as much as he could before going home to crash. Thankfully, his shifts didn't coincide too much with Lee's, but the times they did, Dirk was miserable. Actually, he was miserable even when their shifts didn't coincide. He missed Lee, but the few times he'd tried to talk with him, Lee had listened for a few seconds and then shut down. On the bright side, Dirk really seemed to have mended a lot of his fences with the guys, and they had even invited him to go out a few times. It was nice, but sort of hollow. They talked about the girls they were dating or their wives and kids, while Dirk sat at one end of the table and listened with very little to contribute.

"What's bothering you, Dirk?" Charlie had asked one afternoon as they were sitting around the table, and Dirk had almost told him. It was on the tip of his tongue to actually tell Charlie the truth, but he chickened out. On the plus side, he hadn't had much contact with his father, and Dirk was beginning to think that was probably a good thing. His father had never been particularly encouraging about anything. Dirk had thought he'd miss his father, but he didn't, not really, and if his father was going to cut him out of his life after a disagreement over Dirk's job, then maybe that was for the best.

Late summer turned into fall, the temperatures cooled, and it started to rain. At first it was just showers and the usual thunderstorms, but then a hurricane passed off the coast, and the entire department got ready for serious weather-related issues. Instead, there was just more rain. The hurricane was followed by Tropical Storm Lee, who parked himself over the area for days without moving.

"I sure as hell wish this would stop," Charlie said as he stood next to Dirk, both of them peering out the open firehouse garage doors.

"Did you see the pictures of Hershey on the news?" Dirk asked. "The water rose by the foot in a matter of minutes." Dirk watched as the rain came down in sheets, and they almost had to shout to be heard over the pounding on the pavement. A call came in, and both he and Charlie got into their gear. Dirk had finally been cleared for full duty a week earlier, and he was more than ready to ride along on calls. In the truck, lightning crackled in the air, immediately followed by a snap of thunder that shook the truck.

"In weather like this, you don't expect a fire," Frank said from next to Dirk, and he agreed, but he'd definitely seen stranger things, and sure enough, when they arrived, they found a house outside town that had been hit by lightning right down the center. The rain was doing a number on the fire, but they hurried inside and made sure everyone was out as the hosemen doused the flames. As he first entered the house, Dirk got a flashback to the last time he'd entered a burning building, but pushed it away. The shrink he'd seen in the hospital had told him this might happen. This was not the same, and he was not going to worry about that every time he had to do his job. Dirk simply would not let it affect him, he couldn't. This time, instead of a baby, he emerged with the family poodle under his arm. The fire was put out, and eventually, after information was gathered, they were recalled to the station.

Dirk was already tired after that call as well as two earlier ones, and after stripping out of his gear, he went upstairs and found a bed. After making it up, he decided to crash for an hour, if he could. With this weather, there was going to be a lot of work and very little time off for anyone.

Dirk fell asleep almost immediately, barely aware of the other guys in the room with him. Almost immediately, he began dreaming of Lee. He'd been doing that a lot lately, but this one seemed so real, he could almost touch and hear him. Dirk woke with a start and looked around, hoping he was there, but reality quickly set in, and Dirk settled back on the bed once again.

The siren went off, and Dirk went from lying down to standing up in a heartbeat. He pulled on his clothes, jumped into his gear, and dashed to the truck.

"Water rescue," the captain told them through their radios as the truck pulled out and headed toward LeTort Park.

When they arrived, Dirk saw that the usually sedate LeTort Spring Run that wound through the park was a torrent breaking over the usually scenic boundaries and had burst out of its rock-lined banks. Trees had fallen, their roots loosened by the rain, and a number of them were now partially submerged in the raging water. Clinging to one of the branches was a small girl screaming and crying while her father paced at the water's edge.

"Secure a line across," the captain barked over the near-deafening sound of the water. Dirk crossed the usually high and dry footbridge, now almost impassible itself, and got to the other side. Looking back over the water, he saw a huge man—it could only be Lee—get ready to throw the line. Dirk caught it and secured it to a sturdy tree. Lee fastened the line on his side and threw a second. Dirk tied it as well, and he saw that Lee was about to do the same when the tree the little girl clung to began to roll.

Dirk leapt without thinking, grabbing one of the branches, placing himself as a wedge between the ground and the tree. The pressure was incredible, but the tree stopped moving, and Dirk saw the other men scrambling. Men had been on their way already, but Dirk heard cries and shouts over the sound of the water. "Get her!" Dirk shouted as one of the men, Jason, arrived near him. Dirk felt Jason scramble along the tree, and a few seconds later, the girl's cries got louder. Once he saw they were clear, Dirk gave a final push and jumped back out of the way. The tree rolled with the water, turning in circles as the current carried it downstream, until a branch snagged on one of their ropes. Dirk heard the groan as the rope stretched under the now full strain of the tree and the water that the tree was backing up. "Get out of here!" Dirk called to Jason and anyone in the area as he began to move. The strain built, and Dirk got out of there.

For a second the rope held, and then a snap like the crack of a whip cut the air, and the tree continued downstream. Dirk breathed a sigh of relief that they were away. Jason carried the little girl to her parents, and Dirk smiled when he saw her father's hug. He couldn't see the man's face from where he was standing, but he didn't need to, he'd seen that expression of thankful relief many times in his career. That expression was one of the perks of the job.

Walking toward the bridge, Dirk crossed carefully back and joined the rest of the company. "Don't you ever do that again," Captain Morris told him sternly, and Dirk nodded. He knew he'd put himself in danger, but at the time he hadn't thought about that at all.

Dirk jumped when he felt a rumble under his feet. Turning, he saw that part of the bank had collapsed, and he saw what looked like Lee falling into the fast-moving water. The torrent carried him downstream, and Dirk's stomach jumped into his throat as he saw Lee tumbling in the water. Lee bobbed up again, and Dirk took off, his heart racing a mile a minute. The rain had loosened a lot of trees and wood. Not knowing what else to do, Dirk began looking for anything he could extend into the water. "Lee, move toward this bank if you can!" Dirk shouted, not sure he could be heard. Other men were right behind them, and they managed to get ahead of Lee.

"I have a rope!" Frank said from behind him.

Dirk grabbed one end and began tying it off around his waist. "Fasten the other end to a tree!" Dirk was already stepping into the current. Luckily, a small eddy had formed, and Dirk was hoping to pull Lee into the calmer water. Keeping his eye on Lee, Dirk waded further and further into the water. He knew he only had one chance at this before the water ran through a heavily wooded area with a lot of boulders and snags. Dirk's heart pounded, and he nearly lost his balance, but he kept his attention on Lee. Frank had his back; Dirk knew that without thinking, and behind him, he could hear other men arriving.

"Take it easy, Dirk," one of the men said. "He's almost there."

For a second, Dirk thought the current was going to move Lee away from him. Dirk took another step, the water swirling around his chest. He could feel his feet shifting under him, and he only had a second. Throwing himself at Lee, he grabbed hold and felt himself being tugged back toward the bank.

As the current lessened, Dirk got his feet under him and got a good look at Lee. His eyes were closed, and Dirk guided him toward the bank, keeping his head above water. Other guys trudged into the eddying water, helping Dirk get Lee onto the bank. Charlie and Frank began CPR, and Dirk stood back, water running down his face that he barely noticed. Brushing his eyes, Dirk paced back and forth. Other men arrived with umbrellas that they used to keep the rain off Lee.

More sirens sounded in the distance that Dirk pretty much ignored as he heard a cough followed by retching. Dirk saw Lee roll onto his side. On instinct, Dirk cut through the men gathered around Lee, pushing two of them to the side before kneeling next to Lee. "You scared me half to death," Dirk said softly, and Lee's blue eyes shone up at him. As far as Dirk was concerned, that was the best sight he'd seen in a long time. "I'm sorry," Dirk said before taking Lee's hand. "I'm sorry about everything." Dirk wasn't sure if there were tears running down his face or just rain, but it didn't matter, not now. "I love you, Lee," Dirk whispered as he swallowed around the huge lump in his throat.

He felt Lee squeeze his hand, and then the paramedics arrived, taking charge of the situation. It wasn't until they loaded Lee on the stretcher that Dirk looked away from his lover and saw the expressions of the men standing in a circle staring at him. Then the nerves hit him. Dirk realized what he'd said and braced himself for the fallout. He'd just outed himself and Lee in front of the entire company. He braced himself for what he'd always feared, the name-calling and the rejection. Dirk looked from face to face, but nothing happened. Then Dirk felt a pat on his shoulder.

"You did good, kid," Charlie said from behind him, and one by one, the other men nodded before trickling away to head back toward the truck.

The ride to the station took forever with Dirk shivering from the cold water. Up till then, he hadn't felt it, and as soon as they arrived, Dirk stripped off his gear before hurrying upstairs to change clothes.

"Can you come in here?" Captain Morris called from his office once Dirk was dry and changed. He walked into the office and closed the door.

"I was just coming to see you," Dirk explained as he took the chair the captain indicated.

"You're either the biggest fool I have ever met or the luckiest son of a bitch on the planet," Captain Morris said firmly, his eyes blazing, and Dirk began to squirm. "On a single call, you put yourself in danger twice, and fuck all if it didn't work out both times. You saved that little girl and one of your fellow firefighters."

Dirk shook his head. "I was just part of the team."

Captain Morris's eyes widened. "When in fuck did you get so magnanimous?" Then Dirk saw the captain's expression soften. "Like I said out there, if you ever do either of those things again, I'll kick your ass off the team so fast it'll make your head spin." Then he smiled. "But I'm damned glad you did what you did, and I'm sure the little girl's father thinks the same thing. But the risks you took were unnecessary."

Dirk stood up and glared down across the desk at the captain. "What was I supposed to do? Let that little girl get pushed under by that tree? I couldn't do that any more than I could let Lee drown. And regardless of what you say, I'd do exactly the same thing again, and you'd want me to if it was your ass that had fallen in the water!" Dirk had had enough of this crap. "Besides, what I did wouldn't have meant anything if it wasn't for the rest of the team backing me up."

"Sit down," Captain Morris said firmly. "Dirk, you're impulsive, and I'll be damned if that won't get you into trouble someday, but not today."

"Is that all? Because I want to get down to the hospital to see how Lee's doing." Dirk was becoming so impatient, his leg began to twitch.

"I've already heard from the hospital, and Lee is going to be fine. He's breathing normally, and after they're done checking him out, you can go pick him up. But there's something else I need to talk to you about."

That sounded ominous, and Dirk braced himself for what was coming. "Most of us heard what you said to Lee, and I'm assuming that wasn't some sort of misplaced brotherly show of affection."

Captain Morris leaned back in his chair, and Dirk shook his head slowly. There was no sense hiding now. He knew what he'd said, and damn it, that was how he'd felt. He might have been scared shitless that he was going to lose Lee and said what he had impulsively, but he'd meant it. He knew that the minute the words crossed his lips. He loved Lee, and he wasn't going to let him down a second time.

"What you heard was the truth," Dirk said, his eyes meeting the captain's, firm and hard, head held high, jaw set. If he was going down, he was going like a man.

"I never thought I would be saying this on my watch, but that's only because we haven't had any females in the department yet. I don't know what Lee's feelings are, but whatever happens, I expect, no demand, that both of you act professionally at all times while you're at work."

"Captain, I...," Dirk sputtered in prideful outrage.

"I'm not treating you any differently than I would a married couple or if there was a... uh... straight relationship involved. I have no problem with a relationship between you as long as you aren't working for each other, and I have no problem with you being gay. My daughter broke the news to us about two years ago, so I understand, and I won't tolerate any hanky-panky, nor any bullying or anti-gay behavior."

Dirk was floored. "Thank you, sir. I don't know what to say."

"Nothing to say. That sort of behavior has no place anymore. We watch each other's backs, and the guys haven't treated Lee any differently than anyone else, so I don't see why they would have an issue with you."

"You knew about Lee?" Well, fuck, if that didn't beat all.

"He told us at the interview. Said if we couldn't be open-minded and honest with each other, he didn't want to be a part of our company. Now if you don't have any more questions, I need to get ready for a borough council meeting. They're talking about consolidating fire companies again to try to save money, and while we're the oldest one in town and that says a lot for us, it takes a great deal of money to keep this old station operating."

"You think they'd close us?" The notion was something Dirk had never considered.

"Don't know, but I need to get ready, and they want information on everything from gasoline to the amount of toilet paper we use." The captain went back to his paperwork, and Dirk left the office, still worried about Lee but feeling better that he was going to be okay. Whether *they* would be okay was another matter.

Dirk grabbed a cup of coffee and sat alone at the table. It was still raining, and everyone else was busy making sure they were ready for the next inevitable call. Dirk hurt all over. Charlie sidled into the chair across from him with his own mug, handing Dirk two ibuprofen, the firemen's friend. "It's no big deal, you know," Charlie told him, and Dirk looked around the room.

"Then why won't anyone meet my eyes?" Regardless of what the captain had said in his office, he couldn't make the men accept him. Dirk popped the pills into his mouth and washed them down with a gulp of coffee.

"They're a little pissed," Charlie said with a smile, and he placed a piece of paper on the table with a grin.

"I get that, but...." Dirk trailed off when he looked at the sheet Charlie had shown him. "What's this?"

Charlie gloated. "It's a pool, and I won five hundred bucks."

"What kind of pool?" Dirk looked closer.

"You might have thought you were careful, but we all saw the way you both looked at each other. Even after whatever fight you seemed to have had, neither of you could take your eyes off each other, even if neither of you quite realized it. So we bet on which of you would be the first to say something around one of us. Although when your grumpiness returned, I figured I was sunk. Who knew?"

"You were betting on us?" Dirk asked loudly, and some of the other men snickered. "Aw, guys," Dirk said. "I never knew you cared."

"We don't. At least not that way," Rusty, one of the younger men, scoffed, and Dirk knew he looked uncomfortable.

"You're not my type, anyway," Dirk quipped quickly, and the others who were helping Rusty clean and dry the firesuits began razzing him something terrible. In this wet weather, keeping everything dry and ready for use was becoming a problem they usually didn't have. Dirk finished his coffee before helping the guys with the equipment.

"So after today, it looks like you and Lee are even," Rusty said once he'd gotten over being quiet when Dirk joined them.

"It's not about keeping score," Dirk replied, and then the meaning of what Rusty had said sank in. "What do you mean?"

"Lee saved your life and you saved his," Rusty explained, looking up at Charlie for some backup.

"He never told you?" Charlie asked as he hung up one of the suits so it would be ready for use.

"Told me what?" Dirk was totally confused.

"That fire that put you in the hospital, it was Lee who pulled you out. The floor had given way, and you were falling into the basement. Lee grabbed you by the arm and somehow hauled your big ass out of the hole and the house just before the place feel to pieces. You don't remember?" Charlie asked, and Dirk shook his head. "And he didn't say anything?" Charlie hung up another suit that they'd finished cleaning and drying. "I wonder why?" Charlie asked almost to himself. Dirk had been asking himself the same thing.

"Dirk, they're releasing Lee," Captain Morris called, and Dirk was up with his coat on in two seconds, dodging raindrops to get to his car. It was still raining cats and dogs when he pulled up to the hospital and saw Lee walking toward him. Dirk's stomach roiled with doubt and regret. He knew he'd treated Lee like shit, and he only hoped Lee would give him another chance, but he wouldn't blame him if he didn't.

"We need to stop meeting outside hospitals," Dirk joked. He had to say something, and the way Lee's eyes drilled into him, Dirk wasn't at all sure if that was a good sign or not.

"And you need to stop acting like an asshole!" Lee shouted at him, but kept walking closer. Dirk wasn't sure if he was going to get smacked or what. It looked like Lee was ready to ball his hands into fists. When he got close enough, Dirk felt Lee grab him and stiffened for the punch. Instead, a kiss took Dirk's breath away, and Lee showed no signs of letting him go. Lee's hold on his jacket held him in place as Lee took possession of his mouth.

"I heard what you said even if you didn't expect me to," Lee told him once they both came up for air.

"It seems everyone heard it, and while Rusty looked like a scared rabbit ready to bolt at any second while I was working with him, no one really seemed to mind." Dirk held Lee close, loving the feel of having the huge man back in his arms. "I really missed you," he admitted.

"Um," Lee rumbled deep in his chest. "I think we better take this someplace else before half of town gets a look at our business."

"I thought you wanted to be out."

"Out of the closet is one thing, but nearly flashing half the town is something else," Lee explained. Thankfully, the rain had let up, and they made it to the car relatively dry. Dirk started the engine, and they rode back toward the station.

"Why didn't you say anything about rescuing me from the fire?" Dirk kept his eyes on the road as the rain began again, getting harder and harder. Dirk turned on the radio in case there was a call. "You should have said something." Dirk glanced at Lee, who shook his head, and Dirk heard him sigh softly.

"What would that have accomplished? Yes, I pulled you out of a burning building, and you kept me from drowning."

"Yeah, but...."

"If I had told you when we first met, you might have felt guilty or grateful. You wouldn't have liked me for me, at least not right away."

"I *didn't* like you at all right away," Dirk clarified.

"I know, but my hotness grew on you." Damn, Lee was adorable when he grinned.

"More like you pestered me and wore me down." Dirk tried to sound serious but couldn't pull it off.

"More like drove you nuts. I told you right off I saw through you, and I did. I still do." Lee got quiet as Dirk carefully drove down streets where some of the storm drains were partially clogged. "Did you really mean what you said?" Lee bit his lower lip when Dirk glanced at him.

"Yes, I really did, and I'm sorry it took you nearly drowning to make me see what I felt." Dirk wanted to talk more because it sounded as though Lee had forgiven him, but now wasn't really the time. They pulled into the station and parked. Everyone seemed to have turned out to greet Lee and express how happy they were that he was okay. None of them were happier than Dirk, and he stood back and watched.

A call came in a short while later, and everyone got in their gear. He and Lee were asked to stay behind and watch the station by Captain Morris. He didn't say anything, but the look in his eyes was enough to remind Dirk of their earlier conversation.

"Let's make dinner," Lee suggested once they were in the living area. "They're going to be hungry and cold no matter what happens, and this is perfect chili weather." Lee was already pulling out a massive pot, setting it on the stove.

"Okay," Dirk agreed, and he followed Lee's instructions for browning off hamburger while Lee got the other ingredients ready. "So, what kind of chili are we making?"

"Hot and spicy, just like you," Lee answered, and Dirk returned his grin. "So I take it you've sort of come out, at least here at work."

"Yeah," Dirk said breathily as he turned down the heat. "I'm sorry about the way I acted with my dad. You were right. I should have stood up for you and not let him say crap like that in my house. He's still angry with me for disagreeing with him, and he hasn't talked to me much since. I'm starting to think the silent treatment from him is a good thing. At least he's not pestering me about my job or my friends." Dirk stirred the meat, keeping his attention there.

"You know, there are some people who will never understand for one reason or another. For some, it's beyond them to think or consider anything outside their own worldview. That was my parents. They couldn't understand how I could be different from them and why I wouldn't change who I was to fit what they expected. So they wrote me off."

"That must have been hard." Dirk took the meat off the heat, and Lee drained away the fat. "I think my dad will do something like that but only because me being gay might affect some of his 'Christian' clients. I was raised with all that, and what I can't figure out is what's so Christian about hating everyone that isn't like you. On Sunday they're praying like crazy, and on Monday they're berating someone for being who they are." Dirk realized he was on a bit of a tirade, but he couldn't stop. "I thought Christians were supposed to love each other."

"The real ones do," Lee told him softly. "I knew this lady in my neighborhood growing up. She went to church every Sunday and was the most Christian person I know. After I told my parents I was gay, I ended up at her house because I couldn't take the yelling at home anymore.

At first, I thought she would treat me the same as my folks, but she just said she'd pray for me. I thought she was a little off, but when I saw her again, she said that God had answered her prayers and told her that he made me this way, and since God didn't make mistakes that I was to live a good life and not worry about the rest." Lee began dumping the chili ingredients into the pot, putting it on to heat and stirring it with a huge spoon. "I learned a lot from her then."

"What happened to her? Is she still there?" Dirk wanted to talk to her if she was.

"She died a year ago, and I saw my folks at her funeral. They ignored me, but I stayed anyway, because of what Mary Lou had done for me." Dirk put aside the pan and slipped around behind Lee, putting his arms around his waist. Dirk rested his head between Lee's huge shoulders. "My own parents cared less for me than our next-door neighbor. I used to wonder what that said about me."

Dirk couldn't help scoffing lightly. "It doesn't say anything about you other than your parents were dipwads." Now Dirk understood why his not standing up for Lee hurt so much, because the people who should have stood by and protected Lee had instead thrown him away.

"Are you going to tell your father?" Lee asked him softly.

"Eventually. But he isn't important anymore." Dirk tightened his grip around Lee's waist and just stood there with him as he worked. It was quite a while before Dirk remembered where he was and that he probably shouldn't be doing this, but they were alone, and Lee needed him. "I will tell you this, as God is my witness, I won't deny you again. If my father asks, I'll tell him the truth, and if he badmouths you again, I'll kick him out of my house."

"Is that what you want? Because it's one hell of a thing you're promising."

"It's what I want," Dirk said with a touch of finality. "That is, if you'll have me."

Lee continued stirring the pot, and Dirk just held him. They didn't talk much after that.

The chili simmered, and when they heard the engines pull back in, the entire room smelled of spice and tomatoes, with a touch of heat. The men were indeed tired and hungry. It had been a bad one, from all accounts. A house near one of the creeks had had its basement wall give way and the entire house had become unstable and collapsed. They'd gotten everyone out, but a gas line had burst, and the place had then burned until they could get the gas shut off. Once everyone had changed, Lee began dishing up bowls. Lee sat next to him, and Dirk felt the same desire he always seemed to feel when Lee was nearby rise from deep inside him.

DIRK WENT home once everyone had eaten. Lee still had part of his shift to go, and he stubbornly insisted on finishing it out. Dirk thought of just sleeping at the station because with this rain, there wouldn't be a letup in calls, but the captain had insisted he go home for a while. "Lots of people are getting water in their basements, so make sure your home is okay and sleep in your own bed. It's going to rain for days, so we're closer to the beginning than we are to the end."

Dirk didn't have to be told twice, and after saying good-bye to everyone, he left the station. He managed to get a few seconds with Lee, and he agreed to come over to Dirk's once his shift was over. In fact, he looked a bit excited about it, which warmed Dirk's heart and got him going a little as well. Dirk was more than anxious for some alone time with him. On the drive home, his phone rang, and he answered it without taking his eyes off the road.

"Where are you?" his father's voice demanded without preamble.

"I'm on my way home," Dirk replied. He was exhausted and really didn't have the energy to deal with his father right then.

"I'll meet you there," he said and then disconnected.

Dirk concentrated on the roads, the five-minute drive home taking much longer because of the rain and detours around standing water. When he parked in front of his house, his father was already waiting. Dirk got out of the car and rushed up onto the front porch. Out of habit, he checked around, but everything seemed as dry as could be expected. His father followed him under his umbrella so he wouldn't get his suit wet. Dirk opened the door and went inside, waiting for his father, who shook out the umbrella and then set it aside before stepping into the house.

"What's so important, Dad?" Dirk asked, stifling a yawn. He was sore, and his body screamed for sleep.

"I wanted to make sure you were okay," his father explained, and Dirk narrowed his eyes, wondering just what his father was leading up to. "The little girl you rescued today was Margie Graham. Her family goes to the church. Her father called me and told me what you did for them." Dirk's father settled into one of the chairs, and Dirk sat as well, almost unable to stand he was so tired. "He also said you saved one of the other firefighters who fell into the water."

"It was a busy day, Dad," Dirk explained, his mind shifting to the realization that he had very nearly lost Lee today.

"Don't be so modest. You're a hero, and you saved lives." Dirk saw his father's eyes shift in intensity. "I'm proud of you."

At first, the words didn't sink in because Dirk had been prepared for another condemnation of his job or at least a rebuke for putting himself in danger.

"I hadn't realized how important what you did was." His father actually looked mildly contrite. "I'm still not happy about what's going on there and who they've hired."

"I don't see where that's any of your concern. The men at the station are my brothers. We watch out for each other regardless of who they are. It's part of what we're trained to do, and it doesn't matter if one of the men is gay or if one of the guys is actually a girl. You have their back because the next time they'll have yours."

"But what if...."

Dirk raised his hand to stop him. He knew he should explain things to his father, but Dirk wasn't ready. "I know who I am, and I'll act according to my beliefs and conscience, not yours." Dirk stood up and walked into the kitchen. "Can I get you something to drink?" Dirk opened the refrigerator and grabbed a beer, waiting to hear what his father wanted.

"Nothing for me, I have to get home."

Dirk returned to the living room, carrying his beer, and after saying good-bye to his dad, Dirk set the bottle on the table and wandered down to the basement to make sure all was dry before turning on the television. He sipped his beer, watched a game, and dozed.

He woke when the door opened and Lee walked inside. "Why didn't you go upstairs?" Lee asked when Dirk yawned. He tried to cover it, but he was so tired even having Lee with him couldn't wake him up.

"I was waiting for you," Dirk said, turning off the television and getting out of the chair. "Do you need something to eat?"

Lee shook his head, and Dirk felt Lee take his hand. The lights were turned out, and then Dirk was being led up the stairs. He followed, barely knowing what was happening. Lee didn't turn on any of the lights, and Dirk barely registered as his clothes were removed. He did realize when Lee helped him into bed, and he took notice when Lee crawled in after him. "Missed you," Dirk mumbled as he hugged himself tight to Lee's body, the warmth soaking clean through him.

"I missed you too," Lee's voice rumbled, and Dirk felt Lee hug him back. This felt so right. He knew they had a lot to talk about, but for right now, he was happy, and Lee sounded happy. Dirk fell asleep to the sound of Lee's breathing and rain falling on the roof.

DIRK WOKE in the morning when Lee got out of bed. Cracking open his eyes, Dirk peered at the clock and groaned. They had to get up soon, and Dirk was still so tired he could barely keep his eyes open. Dirk heard the toilet flush and water run before Lee came back to bed. It was still raining, and Dirk tried to put the work ahead out of his mind. Lee helped when he rolled over and pulled him close. "I meant what I said yesterday, I do love you." Dirk's hands roamed over Lee's wide back.

"I know. I love you too," Lee told him, and Dirk smiled, hugging Lee tighter.

"I won't deny you again. I may not be ready to tell my dad about me yet, but if he or anyone asks, I'll tell them the truth. It's time I stopped hiding, and that includes hiding from myself." The words had barely been spoken before Lee was kissing him hard.

"That's all I ever wanted," Lee said when they parted for air.

"I know that now, and I'm sorry it took me so long to realize exactly what was important." Lee was important, and Dirk fully realized now that if he wanted him in his life, they needed to be honest with each other. Lee rolled him on the bed, Dirk's legs parting around Lee's waist, Lee's cock sliding along Dirk's hip. "Make love to me," Dirk said softly.

"I intend to, for a very long time," Lee told him with a smirk, and Dirk wondered if Lee meant right now or forever. As he contemplated what Lee had said, Dirk realized it wasn't an either-or proposition: he could have both.

# STRENGTHENED BY FIRE

# Chapter 1

LEE STANTON sat in the station living area watching television during the evening shift. He'd just returned from a call, and he could hear the captain in his office working on the call report. The station was unusually quiet. If the television weren't on, the place would feel closer to a morgue than a fire station. "Find something to do," the captain called from his office, and then Lee heard heavy footsteps on the floor. "Go check on the drying hoses," he barked a little harshly, pointing at one of the men. "The showers need to be cleaned," he said, pointing at another of the guys. Lee jumped off the sofa and headed downstairs to the engine garage. He certainly was going to keep himself busy so he didn't get one of the shit jobs. Finding a soft rag, he got to work polishing the brass and chrome on the pumper they'd bought recently. The yellow engine was the first piece of new equipment the company had been able to purchase in almost five years, and they'd been raising money for most of that time. Lee looked around the garage and reminded himself that he'd meant to ask if there were funds in the maintenance budget for paint and supplies. The inside of the garage could use a fresh coat of paint, as could the entire building, for that matter. Actually, what the building needed was a renovation. The showers and bathrooms were old and really showing the wear, and the kitchen needed updating. Not that any of it was Lee's responsibility exactly, but he had eyes and he could see it, the same as anyone else. The captain had told him that once they got the pumper they needed, the plan was to raise funds to redo the building. Others worked around him, doing the same thing Lee was—keeping busy and staying out of the captain's way.

No one talked like they usually did. Instead, the same tension and quiet seemed to hang over the entire building. Greg Martin, who was working on one of the older engines, dropped a wrench, and the clang resounded through the building like nails on a chalkboard. Lee could feel the tension that had crackled around all of them for hours begin to sizzle. There wasn't a person in the station who wasn't balancing on a knife edge, and when the alarm rang, Lee practically jumped out of his skin before leaping into his gear and getting on the truck. The others rushed around with trained efficiency, and in a matter of seconds, they were ready to leave. Never in his life had he been so grateful for an emergency call. The vehicle began to move, and the siren sounded as they pulled out of the firehouse and turned onto Hanover Street.

Lee's heart pounded like it always did, and his mind shifted from worry to what he was trained to do. The tension that had been building for most of the evening receded, and he focused on the job ahead of him. By the time they arrived at the house with smoke billowing from the windows, Lee was in his normal work frame of mind and ready. The fire engine had barely pulled to a stop and the men were jumping to the ground, pulling out hoses and getting equipment ready. "There's still a boy in the house," the captain told Lee as he pulled on his breathing equipment. "First floor toward the back of the house, according to the mother." Lee nodded and walked through the spray of water already being poured on the house. He often got assignments like this, both because he was levelheaded in these situations and because of his size. Lee was massive and strong as hell. A few weeks ago, he'd been in a burning building and part of a wall had fallen, trapping a man under it. Lee had simply lifted the wall, shoving it away, and carried the man to safety.

Entering the front door of the small house, Lee was surrounded by swirling smoke and very little light. The smoke seemed to be heaviest in the area of the house that appeared to be the kitchen, and he heard crackling and sputtering from that direction, but he didn't stop, continuing down the hall of the typical ranch-style house, pushing open each bedroom door and peering inside. They all appeared empty, and the smoke was definitely getting thicker. Lee could also hear fire building in the kitchen. Through his radio, he called his position to the crew and told them what he thought was happening. "We're on the kitchen," he heard in response. "Find the kid."

"Roger, on it," Lee said as he approached the final door. It seemed to be locked, and Lee backed up before using his weight to break it in. The door flew open, and a kid who looked to be about twelve and who wore nothing but underwear jumped up out of the bed, screaming at the top of his lungs. The room appeared momentarily clear of smoke, but it billowed in through the open door, so Lee slammed it shut behind him.

Lee rushed to the bedroom window and threw it open. "I'm sending the kid out the back bedroom window. Have someone there!" Lee called through the radio, and he heard an affirmative response. A loud whoosh sounded from behind him, and Lee immediately felt heat through his fire suit. Fire had erupted somewhere in the house, and the door to the bedroom blew open. Grabbing a blanket off the bed, Lee wrapped the kid in it and threaded him out the window. He felt someone take hold, and then the kid passed out of his hands. Lee grabbed a chair from the corner and used it as a club to break out the rest of the window. Making sure the opening was free of glass, Lee climbed sideways through it and felt the guys helping him out and onto the ground.

"Get the hell away!" came through the radio in his headgear, and Lee grabbed the kid, lifting him off his feet as they ran a safe distance away. Then the house exploded in a fireball that knocked them all to the ground.

"What the fuck was that?" Lee asked out loud as he turned back toward the house, trying to stop his heart from leaping into his throat. A few more seconds and he would have been toast. "We're okay back here," Lee said, looking around at the other firefighters and the kid, who were all slowly getting to their feet. Catching his breath, Lee pulled off his breathing equipment and lifted the barefooted kid into his arms before walking around the neighboring house to the street where numerous fire, police, and ambulance vehicles now sat with their lights flashing.

"Juan!" A woman ran to where Lee was carrying the boy, tears running down her face, two small children in tow. Lee set the boy down, and he was immediately engulfed in what Lee assumed were his mother's arms. She cried and began speaking rapidly in Spanish. Lee understood every sentiment, because her relief and the expression in her eyes when she looked at him told Lee all he needed to know.

"What happened, Cap?" Lee asked once he'd stepped away. One of the guys handed him a bottle of water, and he gratefully took it. The last portions of the house standing collapsed in a hiss of smoke and steam as the flames died down.

"They were storing gasoline in cans in the basement. If I'd known, I would never have sent you inside like that." The usual lines on the captain's forehead deepened. "We didn't find out until we were able to get someone in here to translate."

"There must have been quite a bit, judging by the size of that fireball." Lee gulped from the bottle, watching as more water was poured onto the pile of wreckage that had been a house. A man rushed across the front yard and joined the family, the five of them all looking at what had once been the center of their lives. Lee sat down, his heart still racing as he finished his water. Then he threw the bottle in a trash can and helped the guys police the area and make sure the fire was completely out. The laborious task of cleaning up and moving out equipment began.

The entire time, Lee didn't allow himself to think about what could have happened if he'd have been a little later getting out of that house. Sixty seconds had meant the difference between life and death. It took a while, but they eventually certified that the fire was out. The ambulances left—empty, thank God—and some of the fire trucks loaded up and headed back to their stations. The Red Cross arrived to help the family, and eventually Lee and his fellow firefighters headed back to the stationhouse.

When they arrived, Lee took care of his equipment, checking it over carefully before cleaning it and getting it ready for the next call. Once that was taken care of, he headed upstairs and into the showers. He heard other men doing the same thing, but just like before the call, no one was speaking, laughing, or recalling the fire the way they usually did. They'd had their respite, but the tension was back almost instantly, just like they'd never left. The water felt good, but Lee didn't linger, mechanically washing himself before rinsing and drying off. Then he dressed, walked back out to the living area, and sat on the sofa.

"Stockton, you did real good," Cap told him with a pat on the shoulder as he walked past and into the kitchen. Other men wandered in, all sitting around looking at each other and then at Cap, each asking the same question: *how could that happen?* "I don't know," Cap said with a shrug before heading to his office. Lee knew he'd have one hell of a report to write up after that fire.

Footsteps reverberated like a herd of elephants on the stairs, and everyone looked up at the same time as some of the men from the other shifts wandered in, taking chairs, each of them hanging their heads. Lee watched for Dirk Krause, his boyfriend, who was the last one up the stairs. Lee knew exactly how the borough council meeting had gone by the anger and resentment that shone in his lover's eyes. "Okay," Cap said as he joined them. "Let's get this over with so we can get some work done."

"Council decided to reduce the number of fire stations in town from three to two," Dirk said from between gritted teeth. "All they talked about was the potential for saving money that some consultant came up with." Dirk was fuming, and for once the man's temper seemed to come in handy, because the others all echoed it. "It looks as though the one to close will either be Goodwill or us."

Lee glanced at the others, who all nodded their agreement with Dirk's assessment. "Did they make a decision?" Lee asked.

"No," Carter, one of the other captains, answered. "They seemed to go back and forth between one and then the other. I think we have two or three council members on the side of keeping us open, and there are an equal number in favor of keeping Goodwill open. I think the only reason they didn't decide to close us tonight is because we're the oldest fire company in town, and there are enough historic preservationists on council and in town that we got a reprieve, but I don't know if that will save us in the end or not. They kept saying that they weren't talking about cutting personnel, and that all firefighters would have a job at one of the two remaining companies." Lee knew Carter was trying to put the best face on it he could. "They did agree to decide in three months because of other issues that are before the board, so we can expect visits from council members."

A groan came up from everyone in the crowd. "Is it okay to accidentally spray them with water?" one of the guys asked, and some of the others chuckled as Captain Carter rolled his eyes.

"Not if you want to keep this place open," he answered with a bit of a smile. "We also need to figure out how much we have in the maintenance budget, because among the things cited were the age of the building and the need for renovations."

Lee watched Carter look around, and they all did the same. It was funny how he seemed to see things he'd never noticed before: the old carpeting, the scratches in the walls, places where hundreds of hands had turned the areas around the light fixtures oily and dark, the furniture that was dated and rough from heavy use. Lee sighed softly, tired and a bit defeated. He moved over when Dirk sat next to him, and though he wanted to lean against him for a bit of comfort, he couldn't do that here.

The guys knew they were a couple—that had been made plain last fall when Dirk had rescued him from the flooded spring run and kissed him in front of half the company. However, both of them had been circumspect about their behavior at work, conscientiously keeping their behavior professional. "You look beat," Dirk told him quietly, and Lee nodded.

"My shift is over in half an hour," Lee supplied, waiting to see how Dirk would react. Most nights they spent together either at his place or at Dirk's, but sometimes Dirk needed his space. Lee was fine with that, usually; he just hoped tonight wasn't one of those nights.

"I'm going to take off. There isn't anything any of us can do tonight. I'll see you at my place?" Dirk asked, and Lee nodded, trying to return his attention to what the captain was saying.

"The captains will compile a list of projects we believe we can get done to help spruce up the place and post it on the board in the private quarters. That way if we get a visit, it'll be less conspicuous."

"Cap, do you really think spruce-up projects are going to help?" Gerald, one of the younger firefighters, asked.

"I think the council's on the bubble. We need to move them in our favor, and every little bit could help," Captain Carter answered.

"If you say so, but this place needs new bathrooms, a new kitchen, roof, tuck-pointing of the brick. There are lots of things that haven't been done in years because the borough never allocates enough money, and we're paying for their cheapness now," Gerald said in a huff, and most of the other men grumbled their agreement. Lee knew he was probably right but refrained from commenting. All he wanted to do was get to Dirk's so he could forget about houses exploding and borough councils that might shut down the station. He needed some quiet time and a chance to get out of his head for a while.

"All we can do is what's within our power," Captain Carter explained, and the session broke up as the men who weren't on shift began to head out. The others looked dazed, and most of them sat or stood alone with their thoughts, while others drifted away to get their assignments for the day completed. Lee gathered his things together, praying there wasn't another call as he waited for the next shift to arrive. After turnover, he headed to his bike and rode through the lighted streets to Dirk's house. He parked in front of the house and entered through the front door without knocking.

Dirk met him in the living room, and Lee dropped his bag, yanking Dirk to him without a word before crashing their mouths together. Lee took possession of Dirk's mouth, devouring him as he tried to let work go, needing something intense to push away his day. Luckily, Dirk was up for it, and Lee got as good as he gave. "You need to eat?" Dirk asked once the kiss broke, and Lee shook his head, lifting Dirk into a fireman's carry before turning to start climbing the stairs. "Okay then," Dirk said, knowing that words weren't needed.

Lee bounced Dirk on the bed and then began pulling off his lover's clothes. A few buttons on his shirt may have come off; Lee couldn't quite tell, and fuck if he really cared. His vision and his needs centered around his lover, and once he was naked, Lee tugged off his own clothes before climbing on the bed and sucking Dirk's cock down his throat. The nearly strangled cry Dirk made was all Lee needed to hear. They could be tender and careful with each other, but tonight Lee needed rough, and all of Dirk's signals told him he was ready and willing. Vacuum cleaners had nothing on Lee when he got going, and the room filled with Dirk's cries and groans as Lee tasted and damned near devoured his lover. "Lee, coming!" Dirk cried, and Lee sucked harder, feeling Dirk explode and swallowing every drop before kneeling and flipping Dirk onto his belly without waiting.

"Need you bad, Dirk," Lee grunted, his brain completely fogged with lust and need. He had the presence of mind to find the bottle of lube from the stand, slicking his fingers before burying them in Dirk's ass. He wasn't soft or gentle, and he heard Dirk cry out as he squirmed beneath him. Then he slicked himself as he gave Dirk a few more finger thrusts before pulling out, then sinking his cock into Dirk with what he knew was a fast, eye-popping, breath-stealing movement. And only once he was buried in Dirk did some of the urgency fade away, as the feeling of Dirk's body around him helped to ground some of his nearly out of control emotions.

Lee pulled out and drove into Dirk's body, using all his weight, and then stopped, wondering if he was hurting Dirk. "Fuck me like you mean it!" Dirk growled from under him, and Lee felt the strings that held his control begin to stretch and break. His hips snapped and pounded into Dirk, the bed bouncing, Dirk's body gripping him hard and strong. "That's it!" Dirk encouraged, and Lee snapped his hips again, giving Dirk everything he had.

Without warning, Lee pulled out and flipped Dirk onto his back like he was a rag doll. Shrugging Dirk's legs over his shoulders, he drove back into his lover, meeting his gaze as Dirk growled, and Lee returned it with another snap of his hips. "Not... hurting... you... am... I?" Lee grunted between thrusts, and Dirk gripped him tighter.

"No fucking way!" he answered, meeting each of Lee's thrusts with a cry. "You're an amazing stud!" Dirk grabbed him by the shoulders and tugged him forward, their lips crashing together in a bruising kiss of lips, tongue, and teeth that left Lee breathless.

"I fucking need you," Lee growled as his hips continued moving. Dirk's expression told Lee he fully understood and would give him whatever he needed. Lee pounded into Dirk, fucking him to within an inch of both their lives. The room got hotter and hotter, sweat pouring down Lee's chest, but he didn't pause or let up. His mind still threatened to go in a million different directions, and when he couldn't take any more, he screamed as his climax slammed into his chest like a body blow. He heard Dirk cry out as well, seeing his mouth hang open as he came, shooting in high arcs onto his chest.

The last of Lee's flagging energy left his big body, and he collapsed onto Dirk's chest, breathing like a chugging freight train. Floating on waves of endorphins until his heart slowed, he barely registered Dirk encircling him in his arms. "Do you want to tell me what that was all about?" Dirk asked, and Lee nodded but didn't say anything. "If you're not ready, I understand."

"Can't... talk," Lee grunted, and continued waiting to catch his breath. Once he could remember his name again, he slowly began to tell Dirk about rescuing the kid and how the house had blown up right behind him. "They were storing ten gallons of gasoline in their basement. The entire place could have gone up at any time, and we were all fucking lucky to get out alive." Lee had found out that the others, who were in the kitchen, had gotten out and were knocked over by the explosion but hadn't been hurt. "Those kids were lucky they didn't get blown up or poisoned in their sleep."

Dirk shifted, and Lee rolled onto his side. He could feel Dirk shaking next to him. Dirk wasn't a big one to talk about his feelings, but Lee had always been able to read him like a book, and that shaking combined with the way Dirk tightened his grip conveyed his lover's fear better than any words could ever have done. "We all know that danger is part of the job," Dirk told him, "but it sucks when the danger comes so close." Lee saw Dirk's eyes close and felt him quiver. "It's okay for it to get to you."

Lee grunted softly, because he could almost hear Dirk's thoughts. "It's okay for you to feel scared as well. I know I would if our positions were reversed." Lee rested his head on Dirk's shoulder, listening to his lover's heartbeat as he wrapped an arm around his chest. He needed to feel close to someone. Lee had come close to death before. The danger came with the job—everyone in the company knew it, and so did he. But when it happened, it brought the fear and sense of mortality closer to home. "I'd be scared of losing you." Lee tilted his head up so he could see Dirk's expression, and he saw a slight smile and felt Dirk's arms squeeze him for a few seconds. "It's okay to talk, Dirk."

"I don't want to lose you either," Dirk finally whispered.

"Was that so hard?" Lee taunted with a smile before shifting so he could kiss him. "I figure I need to start rewarding you for opening your mouth and talking to me. It may come as a surprise to you, but I can't actually read your mind." Lee tugged Dirk into a harder kiss. "I think we'd better shower before we go to bed, otherwise we're going to end up stuck together."

"There are worse things I can think of than being stuck to you," Dirk told him sweetly, and Lee tried not to make too much of it even as he realized what Dirk was saying in his own way. Lee got up and waited for Dirk, who went into the bathroom. Lee heard the water running as he slowly followed behind. He was both tired and sore. Stepping under the water, Lee felt his muscles relax, and when Dirk stepped in behind him, Dirk stroked and massaged his shoulders. Lee groaned softly as the tightness and tension leached out of his muscles. Then Dirk stepped closer, his chest pressing to Lee's back as Dirk wrapped his arms around his chest. "I do love you, Lee," Dirk said from behind him. "I know I don't tell you as often as I should, but I do."

Lee turned in Dirk's arms, the water running down his head and then pounding on his sore back. "I know you do. And no, you don't say it that often, but you show it, and that's what counts, most of the time." Lee pressed Dirk back against the tile, kissing him hard.

Dirk hugged him tight, and Lee continued pressing, his skin sliding against Dirk's. He needed to feel close to Dirk for a while, and once their kiss ended, Dirk reached for the shower gel and began soaping his hands. Lee closed his eyes and let Dirk soap and care for his big body. There were times when Dirk could be one of the most caring and thoughtful people Lee had ever met... and then there were other times... Lee pushed those out of his mind as Dirk carefully washed his cock and balls, prolonging the process. Lee knew Dirk was playing with him, and that was another of the things he liked. Sometimes for no apparent reason, Dirk would act like a wide-eyed kid, as he appeared now. It didn't happen often, but when it did, it was special and rather endearing. "Feels good," Lee said softly, and Dirk answered with a lopsided grin.

"It's supposed to," Dirk said before turning him. Lee parted his legs and closed his eyes as Dirk stroked his hands over his skin, slick, smooth, and intimate. When Dirk had finished, Lee rinsed off, and Dirk stepped under the water for a quick rinse before turning it off.

"Don't you need a wash?" Lee asked, a bit surprised.

Dirk shook his head, opening the shower door and reaching for towels. "This was all for you. I'm good." Dirk stepped out, and Lee followed. They dried themselves, and Dirk did Lee's back for him. He loved that. Dirk had a special touch, and Lee reveled in it. When they were done, Dirk hung up the towels, and the two of them climbed back in bed.

"You're awfully quiet," Dirk said after a few minutes, and Lee shifted, not really sure this was the right time to bring up what was on his mind, but he decided to do it anyway.

"Do you really think they'll close the station?"

"They might. We're the oldest company in town, but the building is in rough shape. They could close it and keep the museum portion in the original firehouse open. I don't think you have anything to worry about. If they do, we'll move to one of the other two companies, and it'll be fine. They said over and over that they weren't looking to cut personnel."

Lee shifted until he was lying on his side, resting his head on his hand. "You believe them? They're doing this to cut costs, and with fewer companies, they won't need as many firefighters. They'll cut positions. Maybe not right away, but you know that's what they'll do. And I'm one of the newest hires, so that means they'll cut me. I worked hard to get this job, and I'm good at it. I put my life in danger every day, and more often than not, I'm the one they send into the burning buildings, like today. But I'm the one who's going to pay the price if they close the station." Lee could feel the tension he'd worked off earlier already beginning to return. "You know that, Dirk."

Lee saw Dirk's eyes darken, and then he sighed loudly. "I suppose you may be right, but there's nothing we can do about it." Dirk tugged him closer. "We'll figure it out when it happens, but we can't do anything right now, so go to sleep." Dirk wrapped his arms around Lee's chest after he'd settled on the bed. Lee knew Dirk was at least partially right. They might not be able to do anything about it tonight, but he wasn't giving up a job he loved without a fight. Ideas flew through his head as Lee closed his eyes and tried to sleep. But even with Dirk holding him, he found it difficult to turn off his thoughts.

# Chapter 2

THE MOOD at the station hadn't improved much over the last two days. Most guys still did their jobs, but quietly. When they did talk, they grumbled and sometimes snapped at each other. Some of the men, however, talked incessantly about what they thought might happen, spreading gloom and doom with each breath. Lee was tiring of it quickly and had joined the quiet group, trying to keep doing his job, which right now included painting the stairwell from the engine garage to the living quarters. He was making good progress and figured he'd be done in an hour, provided no one stuck their hand on the fresh paint again. "Looking good, Lee," one of the guys said as he passed without stopping to talk, and Lee barely looked up from his work. He needed to get this done.

Lee put the last roll of white paint on the wall and gathered his supplies before heading to the cleaning sink to rinse out the brushes and roller and hang them to dry. There were three or four brushes that had already been cleaned and left to drip dry. Everywhere he went in the building, the rooms smelled of paint. They'd found they didn't have much in their maintenance budget, but the captains had figured out what projects might make the most impact for the money. If nothing else, it would show anyone who walked through the station that the men cared about the place where they worked.

"All finished?" Dirk asked from behind him. "Captain wants everyone upstairs for a meeting.

"I was wondering what you were doing here," Lee said. Dirk wasn't on shift today, and Lee hadn't been expecting to see him. He followed Dirk upstairs and saw that most of the men from across the shifts had gathered. Lee wondered how he'd missed the meeting notice and checked the board. There it was, plain as day.

"Okay," Captain Morris began. "As all of you know, this station is up for closure and consolidation into the other two companies. I talked to some borough council members, and they don't want to close us. We're the oldest fire company in town and one of the oldest in the state, maybe even the country. But our facilities are in need of renovation, and the council can't afford it. Now, Goodwill is also under consideration, and they have their own problems."

"So there's hope," Lee said.

"Yes and no," Captain Morris answered. "We've done some figuring, and we need a new roof, kitchen, baths, and general building maintenance, including brickwork. Our estimate in the kitchen is thirty thousand, the bath areas forty thousand, the roof twenty-five thousand, and the other work an additional twenty thousand." As the numbers were read off, Lee could see the faces of the others in the room falling like a wedding cake in the July sun. "So to be safe, we need one hundred fifty thousand dollars, because once we start a project, there will be hidden costs."

"Looks like more chicken dinners," Steve Granger said from where he sat across from Lee. "The next one is scheduled for six weeks, so we'll be able to get started."

"How much did the last one make?" Lee asked, and Steve looked to the captain.

"About five thousand dollars," Captain Morris answered. "Which isn't bad, but in order to pay for this, we'd need to hold thirty of them. Now, the good news is that we don't need to have all the money at once, because we aren't going to be able to do all these projects at the same time. The roof needs to be done first, and then the bath areas. We can paint and work on the kitchen to get us through a little while longer."

"So what's the bottom line, cap?" Dirk asked from next to Lee.

Captain Morris cleared his throat. "I figure we need to raise between fifty and sixty thousand dollars to show the council we're serious and that we have the capability to get the rest of the money over time. If we do that, they'll probably keep us open and look at consolidating Goodwill. We also need to increase capacity for additional firefighters, because if they do close Goodwill, we will need to absorb some of their equipment and men. We can do that, there's physical room here—we just need to get our facilities in better repair." Captain Carter joined Captain Morris, the two of them standing next to one another. "We need ideas for raising money, but we both agree that we don't want to turn this into a fire-station-shaped begging bowl, and there will not be a stupid thermometer sign on the lawn. If we decide to try to do this, we are going to do it right."

"Yes," Captain Carter echoed. "So what kinds of ideas do you have?" All the men looked at one another, shaking their heads. "What we've been doing brings in a steady amount of money, but we need to do things differently and shake things up, because we aren't going to raise this kind of money selling chicken dinners the way we have." The captain looked as frustrated as everyone else in the room appeared to be. "We need to figure out what we're going to do, and we need to come up with a plan fast. We'll have another meeting on Friday, and we need to present and discuss all ideas. If you don't feel comfortable bringing it up in front of the group, give it to Morris or myself, and we'll present the idea."

The two captains left the room, and everyone looked around, but no one seemed to have anything to say. The people from the other shifts left, talking quietly with each other. Lee looked at Dirk, who shrugged and gazed back at him blankly. "You got any ideas?" Dirk asked, and Lee shook his head with a soft sigh. "Me neither," Dirk added. "I checked the schedule, and we're both on tomorrow." Then he leaned closer so the others couldn't hear. "Why don't you come by tonight?" Lee nodded slowly, his mind still churning over the fundraising issue, trying to find an answer. "You don't have to," Dirk said when Lee didn't answer.

Lee rolled his eyes. Dirk put up a big, hard front, but underneath, way underneath, he was a pussycat whose feelings got hurt more easily than Lee would expect. "Just thinking. I wasn't saying no. I'll see you after my shift ends."

"Maybe we can throw around some ideas if you want," Dirk offered, and Lee smirked.

Lee peered around the room, thankful no one was paying them any mind. "If we're at your house, there are definitely other things I'd rather be throwing around," Lee told Dirk with a grin.

That earned him a chuckle. "Then I'll see you after your shift, caveman." Dirk stood up and left the room. Lee had to keep himself from following him with his eyes. Instead, Lee listened to the other guys talking and throwing around ideas among themselves. None of them seemed to pan out for one reason or another.

"It's a lot of money in just a few months," Karl Peterson said. He was one of the old-timers, and he could usually be counted on to be the voice of pessimism in the group.

"That may be, but it's not impossible," Lee said. "Since we already have the chicken dinner planned, how can we maximize it? We'll have a lot of people showing up because we always do. I keep asking myself how we can capitalize on the traffic." Lee let his thought trail off.

"We could put together a flier explaining what we're doing and ask for donations. We usually put out a jar and get some anyway," Steve said.

"I think I can do that," Davey volunteered. "I'll get something written up and pass it to the captain before the meeting." He left the group, and Lee could almost picture him hurrying to the computer he always brought with him to work.

"I was also thinking that we might offer more than just chicken. We cook it and people take it to go. Why not prepare sides and sell them too?" Lee asked, and others nodded.

"That helps, but it doesn't bring in more people, and that's what we need to do," Lee commented, still thinking about a way to draw more people, but nothing came to mind. The small group talked for a while longer, deciding nothing, and Lee excused himself. He had chores to do; so did the rest of them, for that matter.

THE FOLLOWING morning, Lee and Dirk rode in together. This was becoming normal when they spent the night together. They'd just arrived and clocked in when the alarm sounded, so they dashed into their gear and were on the truck before Lee could give anything much thought.

It was a bad one. An old, abandoned factory outside town had caught fire, and the building was nearly fully engulfed by the time they arrived. Since it was abandoned, they weren't concerned about anyone being inside, but as they poured water on the blaze, explosions rocked the building and everyone was called back as black, caustic smoke billowed out of the building. "Evacuate the area and get any civilians out of here," came through the radio, and the trucks and all personnel backed away.

"Do we know what's in there?" Dirk asked from beside Lee once everyone was at a safe distance.

"Could be anything," Captain Morris answered before getting on the radio to call for backup and help evacuating the area. All they could do was let the building burn and keep the fire from spreading. It wasn't worth anyone getting injured. The surrounding buildings were sprayed as long as they could remain upwind and out of the smoke, and after a few hours, the fire began to burn itself out. By the time they returned to the station, everyone was sweaty and stank from God knows what.

Lee went up to the bunk area, got his bag, and carried it to the showers. Other guys were doing the same. Lee got into one of the shower stalls and closed the door before getting undressed. He took a quick shower, since there were others who needed to use it as well, and after dressing he cleaned the shower for the next person and walked out.

The sight that greeted him practically knocked his socks off. Dirk stood outside the door wearing only what looked like a pair of fire pants. They hung around his hips with just a single suspender holding them up. Others milled around waiting their turn, but Lee couldn't take his eyes off Dirk. He had this urge to pull him into the shower stall and strip off those pants to see just what he had on under them. Lee's cock liked the idea as well, because it throbbed and jumped in his now tight pants. Damn, the man looked amazing: large arms and a full chest with cut abs that disappeared into those fire pants, and the way the suspender fell over Dirk's nipple made Lee want to reach out and touch it to see if he could make Dirk squirm. Of course, he didn't, and instead he moved out of the room and let Dirk clean up, but the image stayed with him. Maybe he'd ask Dirk to bring his fire pants home once. Lee finished dressing in the bunk area as other men came and went, waiting their turn to clean up.

During that shift alone, they got three more calls and spent much of the day away from the station, catching a quick bite when they returned, only to be called out once again a few minutes later. The summer heat was building, drying out grass and woodlands. At the end of the shift, Lee had a chance to sit down and relax with a huge bottle of frigid water that felt like the nectar of the gods. No one had had a chance to talk about fundraising plans, but an idea was forming in the back of Lee's mind. He wanted to run it by Dirk, though, before he said anything to anyone else. Finally, their shift was over, and Lee rode back to Dirk's house. They hadn't talked about what was happening, but as soon as Lee stepped into Dirk's living room, the man was all over him.

"I kept thinking about you in that shower, getting all soapy, and kept trying to figure out how I could join you," Dirk said as Lee's shirt was tugged over his head. "You are an amazingly sexy man." Lee felt his belt being opened and the button on his jeans popping. Dirk's hand slipped under his boxers, gripping his shaft hard and strong. Lee grunted in Dirk's ear as a slow, firm stroke slid along his shaft and Dirk swiped a thumb over the head of his cock.

"You're gonna kill me," Lee groaned, and Dirk stroked again.

"Want you naked," Dirk growled as he shoved Lee's pants down his legs.

"Here or bedroom?" Lee grunted as he tried to get out of his boots before stepping out of the denim bunched around his ankles.

Dirk nibbled hard on one of Lee's ears, making his cock throb in Dirk's hand. "I can fill you across the arm of the sofa or over the edge of the bed, but you have two minutes to decide because I want you right fucking now!"

Lee shook as he finally managed to get out of his pants, but with Dirk stroking him like he was, he couldn't move. As soon as Dirk released him, Lee raced for the stairs with Dirk right behind him. By the time he reached the bedroom, Dirk was already nearly naked as well, and Lee saw Dirk yank off his pants. Dirk threw them to the side, and Lee began to climb onto the bed, but Dirk had other ideas, and Lee found himself bent over the mattress.

"That's it, spread those huge legs," Dirk crooned as he stroked his hands up Lee's thighs, sliding over his cheeks before spreading them wide. "That's what I want." He ghosted a finger over Lee's opening, and Lee shivered with anticipatory delight. Dirk slid a hand behind his balls and then up under him. Lee lifted himself up, and Dirk stroked his cock once before pulling it back and pressing his butt down. Lee's cock pointed down with the side of the bed rubbing against him.

"Fuck, Dirk," Lee growled as he tried to move. He got friction, but not enough or the right kind.

"No, fuck Lee, and I intend to do that soon enough," Dirk told him, roaming his hands over Lee's skin. Lee sensed rather than felt Dirk kneeling behind him, hands stroking his ass, exposing him. When Dirk licked the underside of his cock up to his balls, Lee moaned softly, pressing back into the sensation for more. When Dirk kept going, Lee whined like a child, and as soon as Dirk's tongue reached his hole, Lee was breathless. "I love it when you sing for me."

"Can't sing," Lee groaned as Dirk sucked one of his balls into his mouth.

"Sure you can," Dirk told him. "You just need the right incentive." Dirk proceeded to provide that incentive, sucking and probing with his tongue until Lee couldn't see straight. And he sang, or at least made enough noises that by the time he felt Dirk stand behind him, Lee was nearly hoarse. "Don't move."

Lee heard Dirk move around behind him, and he kept his head on the bedding. He knew what Dirk was doing, but his entire body sang with want and desire. A snick sounded behind him, and then Dirk pressed a slick finger into him, going deep before bending slightly. Stars flashed behind his eyes as Dirk found his gland, and Lee nearly bucked off the bed.

"Stay still," Dirk chided softly, and Lee shook his head.

"Can't when you do that," Lee growled and pressed back, wanting to get Dirk deeper. Dirk pulled his finger away, and then Lee felt the pressure of Dirk pressing to his entrance. He braced himself as he was stretched and Dirk entered him. The stretch nearly overwhelmed him, and he tried to catch his breath as Dirk slid deeper, filling him, connecting them together. "Fuck, Dirk...." Lee groaned loud and long as he sank deeper and deeper. When Lee felt Dirk's hips against his butt, he let out the breath he'd been holding, breathing hard to manage the sensations that washed over him. Having Dirk inside him was always like this—a rush of emotion as well as a feeling of fullness that sent him soaring.

Dirk had an amazing talent for control. He moved when he wanted, and Lee could do nothing but wait until Dirk was ready. He could feel Dirk inside him, though, jumping and throbbing. Lee stretched out his hands, gripping the far side of the mattress. He felt Dirk lean over him, stretching over his back, kissing his shoulders and neck. "Love this. Being inside you is like coming home."

Lee turned his head and felt Dirk's lips suck at his neck. He wasn't sure what to say. Dirk usually wasn't one to talk like this during sex, and while he liked it, Lee just wasn't quite prepared for it. "I love you too," Lee responded, and he felt Dirk's weight shift. Then, with near agonizing slowness, Dirk began to pull back, his cock jumping the entire time, pulsing against the spot that sent ripples throughout Lee's large body. Dirk didn't stop until he'd pulled out, and then he entered him again, driving deep as Lee groaned so hard and long he gasped for air, with Dirk continuing his slow trek inside him. "You're going to drive me insane!"

Lee groused in a voice he knew Dirk would ignore. Dirk was going to drive him insane in the best way possible. "Move, damn it!"

Dirk snapped his hips and then stopped, and Lee growled again. "You'll get the fucking of your life, but only when I'm damned good and ready." Dirk nipped at his ear before snapping his hips lightly once again. Lee could feel his cock throbbing, and he moved his hips, trying to get a bit of friction against the bedding, but it didn't work. He could barely move with Dirk's weight on top of him. No, he was at Dirk's pleasurable mercy.

"Paybacks are a bitch," Lee threatened, but all Dirk did was chuckle.

"Bring it on, big boy. I can take what you got to dish out." Dirk pulled back once again, and Lee held his breath, only to have it whoosh out when Dirk drove back into him. "Can you take what I have for you?'

"Shit yes! Now fuck me!" Lee nearly screamed. Dirk took him at his word and pulled out, driving into his body with enough force to shake him and make the bed jump slightly. "Yes!"

Lee held on as Dirk went nearly wild. His entire body shook with Dirk's force. If he could just get a bit more friction, he'd be perfect, but Dirk managed to keep that from him. His moans turned to frustrated groans, and he tried his best to move in such a way as to get what he needed. "You're not coming until I'm ready, so just relax and put yourself in my hands," Dirk told him, stroking his hands down Lee's back. "You're not going to be able to see or sit straight by the time I'm done."

"Shit...." Lee muttered as Dirk pegged his gland for like the millionth time, and he tightened his grip on the mattress as the last of his resistance and need for some sort of control fell away and he put himself fully into Dirk's care. That was when he began to really soar. Lee felt Dirk's hands on his side, driving them together as deeply as was humanly possible. It was also then that he realized he didn't need anything but his own desire and will.

"That's it, big guy, let it build," Dirk said from behind him, but it sounded like his voice was coming from everywhere. "You can feel it starting in your balls and the base of your spine." As soon as he heard the words, Lee could feel a tingle begin just where Dirk said, and as he continued talking, it built and built without any additional stimulation other than Dirk's voice in his ear.

"Jesus, Dirk," Lee cried as his climax built to the point where he had no control over his body, and he exploded as he felt Dirk sear his insides with his own release. The room echoed as their cries mingled and died away, leaving behind quiet. Lee held still, waiting for Dirk to move once again. He gasped when their bodies separated. Lee was a complete mess and unable to move. He heard Dirk walk out of the room and then return before he felt a towel cleaning him up.

"Climb into bed," Dirk whispered, and Lee made himself move. Dirk joined him, and Lee waited for Dirk to crawl next to him the way he usually did. Dirk wrapped his arms around Lee's chest. They didn't talk, and Lee closed his eyes, taking in the quiet that was broken only by the sound of their breathing and the soft beating of Dirk's heart when Lee rested his head against him. He'd once read that after making love, there was the "time for two," when the rest of the world stopped and it was only them, quiet, peaceful, and alone with their hearts. Lee loved those times, and while they'd never talked about it, he was sure Dirk did as well. "I know you're worried about work," Dirk said, breaking the silence.

"I am, and I have an idea to raise money, or at least make the chicken dinners bring in more money. But I'm wondering if it's too much or...." Lee sighed and cut himself off as he felt Dirk shift on the bed.

"Just tell me about it," Dirk said.

"Well, for one thing, I think we need to offer the whole package and see if we can get people around town to donate things and help cook. I bet if we agreed to put up signs recognizing the people who donated, we could lower the food costs, which would make the money we do bring in go further," Lee explained as he bit his lower lip.

"We've tried that in the past; sometimes it works and sometimes it doesn't," Dirk explained. "It can't hurt to try. But I don't think that's your real idea."

"No. My real idea is to do something to get more people to the dinner." Lee rolled over to face Dirk. "I noticed that most of the people who stopped by to pick up the chicken were men, and I thought we could change that." Lee could feel his excitement growing.

"How?" Dirk sounded tentative and a bit suspicious.

"I was thinking we could hold a sort of a chicken and beef... cake dinner," Lee said. "We could do the chicken dinner the regular way, but add a sitdown dinner at one of the local halls. The guys would serve the dinner, and I was thinking we could wear our boots and fire pants."

"We usually serve in our gear, or at least some of us do," Dirk replied.

"No. I mean that the only thing we'd be wearing is our boots and fire pants, maybe our hats too. Most of the guys at the station are in shape and work out. If we made it sort of a ladies' night, I bet we could sell a lot of tickets." The more Lee thought about it, the more excited he got, and Lee realized he was beginning to talk faster. "I bet we could even set up an area where the ladies could have their picture taken with a firefighter for ten bucks or something. It would be great, and I bet it would bring in a lot of money for the station." Lee stopped talking and waited. The idea had been running around in the back of his head for a bit, but he didn't realize how much he'd thought about it until he began talking about it with Dirk. He waited a few seconds for Dirk to say something, but he was quiet. "What do you think?"

"Are you nuts?" Dirk asked, and at first Lee thought he was kidding. "We could never do that. The borough wouldn't allow it, and the guys would never go for it. Besides, most of the people who support us are older couples—how do you think they'll react to this?"

Lee was surprised at how hurt he felt that Dirk didn't like his idea. "If we expect to raise enough money, then we need to get other people to support us. Has anyone ever brought it up or asked anyone?" Lee pressed defensively.

"No. Because it just couldn't be done. We're a fire company, not a Chippendales revue," Dirk snapped sharply.

"It wouldn't be like that. I'm not suggesting we become strippers or anything. But it would get the ladies in for a nice meal with some scenery." Lee pulled away from Dirk's arms. "You don't have to like my idea, but you don't have to be bitchy about it either," Lee continued, moving away. He began getting out of the bed. "I don't hear you coming up with any ideas." Lee stood up and began stomping around the room, gathering up his clothes. Maybe his idea wasn't the best, but Dirk didn't need to be an asshole about it. Lee pulled on his underwear and then his pants before shoving his arms in his shirt.

"I'm sorry," Dirk said from behind him, and Lee stilled when he felt him touch his back. Lee could count on one hand the number of times he'd heard Dirk say those words. "I shouldn't have sniped at you."

Dirk slipped his arms around his waist. "I don't think it's a good idea, though, and I don't want you to be hurt when others don't either." Dirk rested his head against Lee's shoulder. "I should have been nicer about the way I said it. Because you're right, I haven't come up with any ideas either." Dirk began to trace small, slow circles on his stomach. "Are you hungry?"

Lee nodded slowly, not trusting his voice right now. He couldn't believe how much Dirk's words had hurt, and he really didn't want Dirk to know. He'd liked his idea and thought it was a good one. Sure, not everyone would be up for it, but he bet enough of the guys would be willing to do it if there was the chance it could help save the station from closing. He knew that if they wanted to raise the money, they needed to take some risks. Lee sighed softly as he waited for Dirk to pull on his pants. He didn't talk as he followed Dirk to the kitchen.

Lee settled in one of the chairs as Dirk put sandwich fixings on the table. Lee made his sandwich and took a bite, not really tasting it. He knew he shouldn't have seen so sensitive, but he was still angry at Dirk and wasn't ready to forgive him yet, even if he was giving Lee that lost puppy look. Dirk's hand took his, and Lee looked up from his plate as Dirk squeezed his fingers lightly. Maybe Dirk was right and his idea wasn't so great. Lee took another bite of his sandwich before getting up for something to drink. "There's beer in the door," Dirk said, and Lee got two before returning to the table. He handed one to Dirk and sat back down.

Dirk looked a bit lost and stared back at him. Lee could see the hardness in his eyes and knew Dirk wasn't going to back down. In his mind, he'd apologized, which Lee knew had been hard for him, and in Dirk's mind that should be the end of it. But for Lee it still hurt. Normally he wasn't a sensitive person. He was strong and put himself on the line every day for strangers because of his job, one that he loved. Over the past six months or so, he and Dirk had steadily gotten closer. Dirk had even gotten so he actually talked about things, most of the time anyway, but sometimes he could still be the most insensitive person on the face of the earth. "You know you can still be such an asshole," Lee said, meeting Dirk's eyes. "You don't have to agree with what I say, but you don't need to ridicule it either."

Dirk looked a bit contrite, and Lee figured that was the most he was going to get. "Okay, I'll try." Dirk finished his sandwich, continuing to hold Lee's hand. Lee finished eating and debated whether he should just go home. As Lee placed his dishes in the sink, Dirk pressed his chest to Lee's back, holding him around the waist. "Come back up to bed. I really am sorry, and I'll show you if you let me." Lee let Dirk guide him back toward the bedroom.

# Chapter 3

ALMOST EVERYONE from all the shifts filled the living and dining areas of the fire station. "We need ideas," Captain Morris was saying. "We've received contributions about expanding the chicken dinners, and we're looking into those, but at most they'll bring in a thousand dollars. What we need is an expansion of our fundraising, and we need it fast."

Lee sat quietly, staring at the others around him. Over the past few days, he'd become convinced that Dirk was right and his idea wasn't any good. He hadn't come up with any more, so he sat and waited for the others. Lee was ready and willing to help with anything he could.

"There has to be something," Captain Carter prompted. "If we thought it would help, we'd sell chocolate bars."

"How about a station open house?" one of the men Lee didn't know offered. "Forget it," he followed up with. "If there was a fire or a call, we'd be sunk." A few others offered suggestions, but none of them seemed to pan out.

"At this rate, we may as well give it up and let them close us down," Captain Morris sniped as he looked around the room. "Lee, you're always full of ideas, you have to have something." Lee shrugged and looked at Dirk, who shook his head slightly. "Don't let Krause speak for you. What have you got?"

Lee nearly shook his head but figured he might as well take a chance. They hadn't come up with anything, and his idea wasn't any worse than any of the others. "Well, first thing, I think we need to hit the local merchants harder for donations to lower food costs."

"We've tried that a few times with mixed results," Captain Morris answered.

"I know. So this time, we go in teams of two, and we wear our uniforms. Let them see who they're saying no to," Lee suggested. "I bet we get a lot more donations. If we want to keep the station open, we need to flex a little muscle, so to speak."

"We'll give that a try," Steve, who was in charge of the chicken dinner sales, said from off to the side. "I'll need volunteers," he added, and a few men held up their hands.

"Anything else, Lee?" Captain Morris prompted.

"Yeah," Lee said without looking at Dirk, because he could almost feel him scowling beside him. "In addition to flexing our muscles to get donations, I think we need to flex them in other ways too. I think we should add something entirely new to our chicken dinner evenings. Think of it as sort of a ladies' night." Lee paused a second to get his thoughts straight and then stood up. He felt out of place, but with so many people here, it was easier to talk. "We try to get one of the halls for an evening and sell tickets for the dinner."

"We tried that and it didn't really work. Most people want to get their food and go home. That's why we put up a tent for those who want to stay and mostly serve in to-go containers," the captain explained.

"That's where the ladies' night comes in. Like I said, we rent one of the halls and do a served dinner, with us as the servers," Lee said, and a rumble went through the room, but quickly quieted. The mood seemed positive, with guys looking at each other and nodding. "The thing is that if we really want to pack the place, I figure we have to goose it, so my idea is that as we're serving, we wear just our fire pants, boots, and hats. My thought was to bill it as a chicken and beef... cake dinner. We'd charge more than for the standard takeout dinner...." Lee gave up as the voices in the room began to rise around him.

Looking around, Lee expected to hear angry voices, but he really didn't. Instead, he heard things like "I need to go on a diet," and saw a few of the guys flexing slightly. "Are you serious?" Captain Carter asked, and Lee nodded, figuring he might as well go for broke.

"We could find a photographer who could take pictures. Say ten bucks for a portrait with your favorite hunky fireman. That would bring in extra money, and I bet we wouldn't interfere with our regular sales because we'd be appealing to a different audience," Lee explained, feeling more confident when he saw the other faces around the room. "I know it's probably a bit risqué, but like you said, Captain, if we don't take a chance, we won't raise the money." Lee sat back down as people around the room talked over one another. Most of them seemed interested in the idea, if nothing else.

Lee sat back with a pleased smile on his face and turned to glance at Dirk. He glared back at him, eyes narrowed. "I thought you weren't going to bring that up," Dirk whispered in a harsh tone.

"I wasn't, but no one else had any ideas. And look, they seem to like it." Lee nearly beamed as he turned his glance to the rest of the room. Almost everyone seemed excited.

"So I take it you want to pursue this?" the captain asked, and most heads in the room nodded. He began doling out tasks to people so they could see if what Lee proposed was feasible. Lee could hardly believe that the rest of the station seemed to like his idea. "Lee, I'm going to ask you to get volunteers willing to act as servers," the captain said, and Lee nodded. "We assume you'll be one." Lee grinned and turned to Dirk, but his chair was empty. Other guys made their way over, particularly the younger, single ones, eager to impress the ladies.

"I can also try to line up the photographer," Lee volunteered, and the captain nodded with a bit of a smile. Then Lee looked around the room to see where Dirk had gone, but he was nowhere to be seen, and other guys were crowding around Lee to ask questions.

"I think it's a great idea," Vanessa, one of the female firefighters, told him, and Lee smiled. "If we can pull this off, I'll get the rest of the women to help with ticket sales." She seemed tickled, and Lee put her down to help.

Captain Morris whistled, and everyone paused where they were. "Just to make this official, let's have a show of hands for those who want to give Lee's idea a try." Most of the hands in the room went up. A few didn't, and Lee knew that if Dirk was anywhere nearby, he was probably voting in the negative. "Okay. Then we have a lot of planning to get done in five weeks. Lee will act as overall coordinator, so talk to him. He's going to need plenty of help."

The energy in the room was amazing. People were excited about something for the first time since they'd heard about the possible closure. Lee made notes about who was willing to volunteer for what, and after the meeting broke up, he sat at the table making a list of everything he could think of that would need to get done. They had to find a hall, sell tickets, arrange for the food, do promotion, get tables, chairs, and dishes, and all the other things to make the dinner seem special. He added centerpieces to the list.

"You're going to need music," Vanessa said from over his shoulder. "Also, the photographer is going to need space and a place to work. And

I'd suggest a screen with a projector so you can run a slideshow of the station over the years. There are tons of pictures at the historical society, and I bet we could get them to let us make copies." Vanessa took the chair next to his. "I'd also see what you can put together in terms of entertainment, and definitely find a place with a bar."

Lee sighed, becoming anxious that he hadn't seen Dirk around for a while. "There's a lot to do," Lee said as he looked at the list, which kept getting longer by the second.

"Yes, but you've got plenty of help, and whatever you do," she leaned closer, "ask for it. Don't try to do everything yourself. We're all in this together, and we as a group will determine if it's a success." She nodded for emphasis, and Lee smiled. "What's got you worried?"

"Dirk hates the idea," Lee said, glancing around one more time.

Vanessa scoffed and then laughed out loud. "He's the most pigheaded man I have ever known. Great firefighter but as stubborn as a mule. He'll come around, and if he doesn't, there are plenty of fish in the firefighting sea, if you know what I mean." Lee narrowed his eyebrows and shook his head in confusion. "You don't think you and Dirk are the only guys at the station who prefer hoses to plugs, do you?" As much as he tried not to, Lee couldn't help laughing along with her. "I have to go, but call if you need anything." She patted him on the shoulder as she stood up. "By the way, I'm looking forward to seeing you serve dinner," she added with a wink before walking away.

Lee continued working for a while on his list before wandering away to see where Dirk was. Unlike Lee, Dirk was on his shift, so he couldn't have gotten very far, and Lee found him in the engine garage. "Where did you go?" Lee asked as he approached.

"I needed some air," Dirk said huffily without looking up.

"Find some?" Lee retorted quickly, and Dirk threw down the rag he'd been using on the fire engine running board.

"Until you came down, yeah," Dirk huffed barely above his breath. "I can't believe you brought up that idea."

"What? No one came up with anything else, and in case you didn't notice, most people liked it. You told me the other night you were afraid no one would like it, but that was bullshit, and I bought it." Lee stepped closer, clenching his teeth. "You're angry because my idea was good and everyone liked it."

"Don't be ridiculous," Dirk said. "I'm glad they liked your idea."

"Then what's your problem?" Lee asked, so confused his head spun. "Everything worked out. They liked the idea, and it may bring in a lot of money for the station. I don't understand why you're angry."

"Because I asked you not to bring that up, and you did anyway," Dirk growled. "I thought we'd agreed, and you did what you wanted anyway." Dirk's tone softened slightly.

"So that's it. You're pissed off because you don't like the idea, and I shouldn't do what you don't like? Well screw you, Dirk," Lee hissed between his teeth as he heard others moving around. "You don't get to control my life." Lee turned to walk away but stopped and faced Dirk once again. "You know, instead of being a dick, you should be supportive and helpful, if not for me, then for the station and the team." Lee walked away, his heart racing and his spirit flagging. He climbed the stairs, grabbed his list off the table, and stopped by the captain's office before leaving the station. Most everyone was talking about the dinner, and they said goodbye, offering help of any kind. As he passed Dirk, all he got was a scowl, and Lee shook his head as he walked away, heading for his car. He climbed inside and started the engine before pounding the wheel with his fist. "You're such an asshole!" Dirk Krause could be the most exasperating man on the face of the earth. "Fuck you!" A stream of expletives followed, and once he'd let it out, Lee drove home, but his insides kept roiling.

LEE SPENT the night alone that night, and for the next week. He'd been busy both at work and making plans for the dinner. Though he hadn't been avoiding Dirk, he had to admit he wasn't searching him out either. Lee was definitely still angry with him, and he was determined that he wasn't going to be the one to come forward, not this time. He was right, he knew he was, and Dirk had to learn he needed to treat him as an equal and not like someone he could push around. Lee broke the pencil in his hand just thinking about it. "Hey," Vivian, another of the women in the company, said from across the table, "what did that ever do to you?" Lee took a deep breath and dropped the pieces of pencil. "Trouble in paradise?"

That made Lee scoff. "Being with Dirk has never been what you could call paradise," Lee lamented. But it had been good most of the time. And damn it, he missed him.

"I can bet, but I'd also guess it was probably intense, and in his own way, he told you how he felt." Vivian didn't appear to be guessing. "He never talked to me about much, but I've known guys like him. They're hard as hell on the people who care for them." Vivian peered over his arm to look at what he'd been doing. "How's the dinner coming?" she asked, and Lee was grateful she changed the subject. Lee had spent enough time thinking about Dirk, and he really wasn't interested in talking about it.

"I have the hall. A friend of mine is on the board at the expo center, and they had the Saturday we were interested in open. The place is clean and relatively new. There isn't much as far as decoration, but there's a huge set of doors, and I thought we could probably drive the antique engine inside. It'll actually fit in the building and make a great backdrop for the stage area. Cap also said we could use some of the antique hand pumps and fire extinguishers as well. There's a lot of space, and I don't want the room to seem empty." Lee showed her his drawing for how everything would go.

"How many people are you planning on?" Vivian asked and Lee shrugged.

"Not sure. I can seat up to 1,500 without the trucks and about 1,200 with them, but I can't plan the room configuration until we have an idea of the number of people to expect." Lee looked to Vivian, who smiled at him. If he were into girls, she would definitely be the one. Vivian was an eyecatcher, there was no doubt about it, and Lee knew half the men in the station would give anything to have her looking at them with those huge blue eyes of hers. She was also smart and tough.

"I have the tickets being printed, and they'll go on sale just as soon as I can pick them up from the printers."

"You don't think twenty dollars is too much?" Lee asked. When they'd settled on the price, Lee had thought it was too expensive, but he'd been overruled.

"It's fine. Remember, it's a fundraiser, and everyone will know that. I also have a surprise for you. I dropped the poster off to be printed." Vivian handed him a rolled-up piece of paper. "This is the sample." Her eyes danced with mischief, and Lee wondered what she'd done as he unrolled the sheet.

"Jesus," Lee gasped. "Where did you get that picture?" He was looking at a picture of himself from the waist up, bare-chested, wearing only his fire hat. He wasn't sure how he felt about being plastered all over town, but how could he complain? He'd been the one to dream up this shindig.

"I gave it to her." Lee turned around and saw Dirk standing behind him. Vivian stood up and walked away, giving Lee a quick smile before leaving the room. "She came to my house a few days ago and read me the riot act." Dirk sat next to him at the table. "She walked in, and instead of saying hello, slapped me on the side of the head. When I asked her why, she told me that on the farm where she grew up, the first thing you learned was when you wanted to get the attention of a jackass, you kicked him. 'I could kick you, but I figured a good slap upside the head would work,' was what she said."

Lee began to laugh. He could so see Vivian doing that. "What else did she say?"

"That you were working your butt off for the good of the station, and if I was any kind of boyfriend I'd be here helping you instead of letting my pride get the better of me," Dirk answered. "Only she wasn't that nice when she said it, and there was at least one threat to my manhood involved." Dirk shivered a little, and Lee wondered exactly what Vivian had told him. "Suffice it to say, she told me to pull my head out of my ass and get down here to help you. Then she asked for the picture."

"When did you take it?" Lee asked, because he couldn't remember posing for a picture like that."

"I took it in July when you were coming over to see me. You came right from work, and it was so hot, you'd taken off your shirt, but left your hat on because of the sun." Dirk scooted closer. "You look drop-dead sexy like that, and I had to get a picture." Dirk bumped his shoulder. "I should have been more supportive," Dirk admitted before looking at the drawing of the hall. "So what do you still need?"

"What don't I? The venue has tables and even chairs, but we need dishes and cutlery, tablecloths, and napkins. I also need to find a photographer." Lee was beginning to wonder if he could pull this off. "I found some places that rent stuff, but they want a lot of money, and I'm trying to keep the budget tight so we can make as much money as possible." Lee looked at his list and was about to make another round of phone calls.

"Are you still on duty?" Dirk asked, and Lee shook his head.

"Then let's go. I know someone who might be able to help." Dirk motioned toward the door, and Lee picked up his pad, following Dirk down the stairs to his car.

They drove downtown and pulled up in front of Cafe Belgie. Lee had been there a few times, but never with Dirk. "What are we doing here?"

"I met Darryl and Billy a few weeks ago when they had a bit of a kitchen fire. Nothing too bad, thankfully, but they probably have contacts that may be able to help us." Dirk finished parking the car, and they got out and walked into the restaurant. There were a few customers at tables, but the dining room was largely empty. Lee supposed that was normal for the middle of the day. "Is Billy or Darryl here?" Dirk asked a server as he came out of the kitchen.

"Billy will be right out," he said and stood for a second watching them. Lee nearly smiled when he realized they were being checked out by the waiter. The kitchen door opened, and Lee saw a man about their age, maybe a little younger, come out.

"Can I help you?"

"Hi, Billy. I'm Dirk Krause. I was one of the firefighters who was here a few weeks ago." Dirk smiled.

"Is there a problem?" Billy asked, looking around, and Lee swore he heard him sniffing.

"No. But we need some help," Dirk said, and Billy motioned them to a table.

"Would you like some coffee?" Billy asked, and before they could answer, he was already retrieving a pot and some cups. He poured them each a cup and then sat down at the table. "What can we do for you?"

Dirk looked at him, and Lee nodded and began. "We need to raise some money because the borough is thinking of closing our fire station. We're planning a fundraiser, and we need things like tablecloths, dishes, and cutlery. We've looked into renting them, but they want a fortune, and we'd just be spending all the money we're hoping to bring in." Sometimes things seemed to conspire against his best intentions, and this was one of them. "Dirk said you might be able to help." Lee looked around the restaurant and wondered what they could do. They obviously didn't have the dishes and supplies for over a thousand people.

"What sort of dinner are you doing?" Billy asked, and Lee explained what they were serving and the concept for the evening.

"Okay," Billy explained. "First thing, when you have tickets, we'll take ten because I'm not missing this for the world." Billy's eyes danced and he grinned. "You two running around in your boots and fire pants? There's no way I'm missing that!"

"Missing what?" a man in a chef coat asked as he approached the table. Billy explained about the dinner, talking so fast Lee could barely understand him. "I said we'd take ten tickets. I figured we could get the guys to go along." Billy turned back to them, and Lee saw the chef smile indulgently at Billy. "Sorry, this is my partner, Darryl. He's the chef here." Billy went on to explain what they needed.

"If you want my advice, I suggest paper plates unless you want to do dishes for days. They make disposable plates with a plastic coating so they feel heavier, more like real plates, but you don't have to wash them, and they'll be cheaper than renting everything. I suggest the same for the utensils. Use disposable. But rent real glasses, especially if you're planning to have a bar of any type."

"Don't know if we can," Lee said, and Darryl nodded as he sat down next to Billy.

"The liquor laws here," Darryl shook his head, "are antiquated at best. Let me do some checking with a friend at the Liquor Control Board—they may have a temporary license provision for civic groups. I'll also give you the name of our restaurant supplier. He should be able to get what you need at a pretty good price." Darryl leaned back in his chair.

"Peter, it's Billy." He was already talking on the phone. "Some of the firemen are doing a benefit, and I think they need your help. Could you meet with them?" Billy listened for a minute. "Does tomorrow work?" Billy asked Lee, and he nodded. "About three?"

"Barring a fire," Lee answered.

"Three it is, at the Union fire station on Louther," Billy told Peter. "They're looking at the good disposables you have, so you might bring samples. They're looking at about 1,200 people." Billy listened for a few seconds. "Good, thanks. We'll see you soon." Billy laughed lightly. "Don't worry, I already reserved tickets." Billy listened for a few more seconds and then hung up. "He'll be at the station tomorrow at three, and he thinks he has things that'll work."

"Thank you," Lee said as some of what had been threatening to overwhelm him slipped away. There were so many details he was trying to nail down, including decorations, and trying to figure out how much to order of anything was a constant headache. Looming over everything was the thought, *what if everyone did all this work and no one came?* That alone was enough to make his stomach do flip flops.

"No problem. Glad we could help," Billy said, and he stood up. "I'm looking forward to seeing both of you in a few weeks." Billy glanced around the dining room and then excused himself. Lee finished his coffee as Darryl got up as well.

"Let us know if you need anything else," Darryl said, shaking hands with both of them. "You guys saved my business. I'll help any way we can."

"Thank you," Lee said, and they left the restaurant. "That was a big help," Lee added with a sigh of relief. "This whole thing is kind of overwhelming." Lee walked toward Dirk's car. He expected Dirk to say some kind of "I told you so," but he didn't. "I need to get my things from the station," Lee explained once they were in the car.

"Do you want to come back to the house?" Dirk asked.

"Yeah," Lee answered, and Dirk started the engine.

Lee grabbed his things from the fire station and then got on his cycle, riding through town to Dirk's house. He parked behind a familiar car and climbed the steps to the porch, hearing the raised voices of Dirk and his father through the front door. "It's an illness, and I found a place that can cure you," Dirk's father was saying. Lee didn't knock, pulling open the door and striding inside. The conversation stopped almost immediately, especially when Lee loomed over Dirk's father, arms crossed over his chest. He saw the older man swallow hard. Lee didn't say anything, letting his size speak for him.

"Dirk is just fine the way he is, and he doesn't need any of your closed-minded, bigoted crap. He's a good man who works hard and puts his life on the line helping others. If you can't see that then, you're full of it." Lee glanced at Dirk, whose expression seemed pinched and worried. Dirk and his father hadn't been talking much lately, and Lee had thought they might have come to some sort of understanding. Obviously he was wrong.

"Dad, I think you should go," Dirk said, and Lee looked from him to Dirk's father and then back again. Lee growled deep in his throat, scowling at Dirk's father, who seemed to get the idea. He stood up, dropping a few brochures on the coffee table before leaving. At one point

Lee saw him turn, and Lee growled under his breath, clearly signaling that it was time for him to go. Lee didn't relax until he heard the front screen door close. "He was waiting for me when I got home," Dirk explained.

"Your father is a total ass," Lee said, watching through the window as Dirk's dad's car pulled away. With a father like that, it was no wonder Dirk tended to be stubborn and occasionally a complete asshole—look at the role model he had.

"Yeah, but he's still my dad," Dirk commented softly, and Lee turned away from the window, sitting next to Dirk on the sofa.

"Thank you for helping today," Lee said, changing the subject. "I really appreciate it."

Dirk turned away from looking out the window, and Lee caught his gaze. "You're welcome. But don't expect me to be one of the waiters running around half-naked. I'll help you with the planning and things, but I'm not doing anything else."

Lee swallowed. "Why not?"

"Because I still don't think this is a good idea for the station. It was your idea, though, and everyone else seems to like it, so I'll help where I can, but I'm not doing that." Dirk's eyes firmed up, and Lee knew there would be no talking him into it. Not that it was required. Dirk being willing to help was enough, and if he wasn't comfortable acting as one of the waiters, Lee cared enough about Dirk to respect that. He didn't understand and figured there was more to it, but he could be wrong. At least Dirk was willing to help and support him.

"I can live with that," Lee said, taking Dirk's hand. "And I appreciate your support."

Dirk smiled slightly before admitting, "You should have had it all along."

Lee felt the same way, but he wasn't going to push it. Dirk pressed him back on the cushions, both of them laughing until Dirk kissed him hard. Lee deepened the kiss by placing his hands on Dirk's cheeks, light stubble pressing into his palms. He stroked lightly, letting the roughness play along his skin. Lee loved the small reminders of just what a virile man Dirk was, and none worked as well as the way Dirk kissed, hard and strong, but with an emotional intensity that rarely surfaced at other times. Dirk slid his hands under Lee's shirt, stroking his skin as he pushed the shirt up his chest. "Love how big and strong you are," Dirk murmured after he broke the kiss, and before Lee could say anything in return, Dirk latched onto one of his nipples, tongue swirling, lips nibbling, and Lee's eyes rolled to the back of his head.

"God, Dirk," Lee groaned, arching his back into the sensational, wet heat. "You make me want you," Lee said with a growl as he pressed back against Dirk, using his strength to take charge of the situation. Standing up, Lee pulled off his shirt, dropping it on the floor before tugging Dirk to his feet. "Let's go upstairs," he added before practically pulling Dirk along behind him.

In Dirk's bedroom, Lee didn't wait. He pressed Dirk onto the edge of the mattress, pulling off his lover's shirt and shoving him back onto the bed. "Pushy much?" Dirk quipped.

Lee growled again. "You made me wait for a week before you pulled your head out of your ass. So yeah, I'm pushy. I missed you," Lee admitted before taking Dirk's mouth in a bruising kiss that had them both fumbling and gasping for breath. Stroking Dirk's skin, Lee teased his fingers over the skin of his belly as Dirk held his breath and pulled in his stomach, trying to encourage him to go lower. Chuckling lightly, Lee opened Dirk's belt and parted the fabric of his jeans, pulling them down his hips before smiling into Dirk's now clouded eyes. "Just so you know, you're going to pay for that week."

"I am?" Dirk gasped, and Lee ghosted his lips over Dirk's straining, cotton-clad cock.

"Oh, yeah," Lee said. "I intend to make you wait while I drive you so crazy, you're going to beg me to fuck you, and even then I just might not give you what you want." Lee licked again, swirling his tongue around the head of Dirk's cock, sucking and licking wickedly as Dirk's hips flexed and thrust, trying to get more friction that Lee wasn't going to let him have. Lee felt Dirk's hands on his head, pressing him down, and he stopped, looking into his lover's eyes. "Stretch your hands over your head. You're being punished, remember? I could just leave you like this." Lee moved closer to Dirk's chest, inhaling the deep, rich scent, laden with desire, musk, and a hint of sweat. Lee licked a line up from Dirk's navel before blowing on the wet skin, watching as Dirk shivered.

"Lee, don't you dare," Dirk groaned, and Lee smiled before lightly flicking a nipple with his tongue.

"Then be good, and I'll consider it," Lee joked. He had no intention of stopping, and Dirk knew it too. Dirk lifted his arms over his head, and Lee climbed onto the bed, massaging the strong muscles of Dirk's shoulders as his nose filled with the heavenly scent of a rugged, strong man. Lee slowly ran his hand from Dirk's wrist down over his forearm, and then up to his shoulder and along his chest. A pebbled nipple ticked Lee's palm as he continued stroking. He heard Dirk sigh as he knelt near Dirk's head, letting his hands wander over Dirk's skin.

"If I've been bad and this is my punishment, then maybe I should be bad more often." Dirk smiled up at him, and Lee bent forward, kissing his lips lightly.

"I'm having mercy on you, ya dumb ass," Lee said with a wink before stretching his arms to reach all the way down Dirk's chest and stomach, slipping his fingers beneath the elastic of Dirk's underwear. He felt Dirk's breath hitch, and Lee wriggled his fingers along Dirk's now straining cock before pulling back once again. "Maybe you spoke too soon."

"Lee," Dirk whined, and he ignored it as he continued working Dirk's skin and muscles.

"Roll over, Dirk," Lee said, and Dirk complied while sliding up so he could be more comfortable. Before Lee settled between Dirk's legs, he tugged down his briefs, dropping them on the floor. "You have great legs," Lee commented as felt the powerful muscles pass under his hands. When he reached Dirk's butt, he worked the cheeks, resting his fingers near Dirk's entrance, and Lee felt Dirk tense and groan softly. "Like that?"

"Uh-huh," Dirk groaned, and Lee worked the other cheek before kissing each one and then licking down between them. Automatically, Dirk spread his legs, and Lee licked across Dirk's entrance as the unique musky flavor of his lover burst on his tongue. Lee heard Dirk groan. He knew this drove Dirk out of him mind, and as he probed the puckered flesh, he felt Dirk press backward. Spreading Dirk's cheeks Lee probed his opening, sucking and licking his skin. "God, Lee!"

"I know," he soothed, and continued probing as Dirk bucked and whimpered. Lee continued rimming Dirk until he could feel his muscles relax, then he probed deeper, opening his lover more and more until Dirk felt completely pliant beneath him.

"Fuck me, Lee," Dirk begged softly. "I want to feel you deep and hard." Dirk damned near waggled his butt at him, and Lee found the bottle of lube and slicked himself up before positioning himself at Dirk's entrance, waiting. "Lee!" Dirk cried as he backed toward him. Lee was ready for it, and backed away as well, and once Dirk was prone on the bed again, he pressed forward, entering his lover's body in a single, swift movement, plunging into Dirk's steamily hot body.

Dirk groaned deep and loud as their bodies joined together. Lee tried to take it easy, but control was something in short supply right now. "Did I hurt you?" he asked once he felt his hips pressing to Dirk's butt. Lee swallowed hard, trying to regain some type of command over his body and desires.

"No," Dirk said, and pushed back to emphasize the point. Lee gave him a minute to adjust before withdrawing. Every time they were together like this, Lee told himself to take his time, and every time he found himself so turned on he was unable to do anything but fuck Dirk into the mattress. This time, he forced himself to move slowly, pulling out in what seemed like slow motion before snapping his hips. "Jesus!" Dirk cried, and Lee grinned. He knew just how to angle himself to hit Dirk's special spot, which he did repeatedly.

Dirk vibrated beneath him, and Lee leaned forward, kissing and licking Dirk's shoulder as he drove into his body. The bed shook, and Dirk grunted, his entire body moving along with the bed. Wanting to see Dirk's face and watch him as he came, Lee pulled out and flipped Dirk onto his back. After positioning Dirk's legs on his shoulder, Lee drove back into his body, watching as Dirk's eyes clouded with lust and desire. Few things in life were more beautiful and sexy than Dirk when he looked at him while making love. Lee loved the way Dirk's mouth hung open just the slightest bit and the way he shuddered each and every time Lee hit that one magic spot. Or the way he arched his back, trying to milk that slight little bit of extra sensation. Lee knew Dirk would never admit it, but the man was a hedonist through and through. Lee continued snapping his hips, feeling every inch of his lover's body around him. Whenever he stopped, Dirk's body pulsed around him in time to their beating hearts. "Lee!" Dirk groaned when he waited too long.

"Too slow?" Lee asked as he snapped his hips. "Is this what you want?"

"God, yes!" Dirk cried. "You weren't the only one who went without for a week. Now fuck me into next week." Dirk sounded a bit like a whiny kid, but Lee was losing his last remnants of control, so he gave his body free rein. Closing his eyes, he reveled in the feel of Dirk's body, the small grunts he made whenever he slammed into him, and the warmth of Dirk's skin where he held on for dear life. "Yes!" Dirk once again arched his back as Lee gave him what he wanted.

"Come on, Dirk, I want to see you come for me," Lee called as he stroked Dirk in time to his thrusting. He was trying to keep his mind on what he was doing, but he knew his hands were fumbling. Lee was determined to wait for Dirk, even though his body was screaming at him to climax. Tightening his grip, Lee stroked hard, watching as Dirk's eyes drifted closed and his stomach tightened. He was familiar with every movement his lover made, and the tension and energy had Dirk stretched as tight as a drum.

"Just a little more Lee, please," Dirk begged, and Lee stroked harder, lowering his hips just a little. Dirk began to shake, his entire body stretching completely taut. Lee felt Dirk's cock begin to throb and pulse as he came, his voice filling the room with groans and cries. Then Dirk became quiet and didn't move, his chest rising and falling with each breath. Lee didn't want to move. He knew Dirk was in that floaty place, and he wanted him to remain there as long as possible. Lee's cock jumped and bounced inside Dirk's body, but still he didn't move.

Dirk opened his eyes, smiling up at Lee, and Lee began to move once again, digging his fingers into Dirk's side. He knew he'd probably leave marks, but he couldn't help it. Lee's body screamed, and his climax built quickly. Dirk's eyes shone up at him, that crooked smile, sweaty body, and hair plastered to his head combined to drive Lee over the edge. With a final, massive thrust, Lee pressed into Dirk's body and held still as wave after wave of pleasure washed over him. Lee could barely breathe as he poured himself into Dirk's body.

# Chapter 4

"LEE," DIRK said from behind him as he was working to finalize more details for the dinner. There were only two weeks left to plan, and the pressure was beginning to mount. "Cap wants to see you." Lee turned from his list and saw the serious look on Dirk's face. There was no way that could be good, and he began running things through his mind to see where he might have messed up. Not being able to remember anything, he stood up and walked to the office.

"Close the door," Captain Morris said, and Lee complied before taking the seat the captain indicated. "There are people on the borough council all up in arms over this dinner, and it will be discussed at tonight's council meeting. I'd like you to be there to answer questions. We aren't doing anything wrong, and there really isn't anything the council can do to stop us. We're breaking no laws or ordinances. But according to the council member who called me, some of the members are receiving complaints from a few constituents. This will probably be nothing more than lip service, but we need to be there to defend what we're doing."

Lee's head swam. "It's only two weeks before the dinner, and I have a ton of things to get done yet. We don't have time for this."

"I know, but we have to do it if we want the council behind us—and we do. They're the ones who approve our operating budget, and we're trying to avoid being consolidated out of existence, so we need to play nice." Captain Morris looked as thrilled about the prospect as Lee felt, but Lee nodded his assent and left the office. Regardless of the meeting, he had plenty to do. Sitting back at the table, he tried to work. His phone rang, and he answered it absently.

"Lee," a familiar voice said, "this is Peter Christopoulos. I wanted to let you know that I have the plates, utensils, and napkins you needed. I ordered enough for 1500, and you can return unopened packages. I also arranged for the rental of 1500 glasses." Lee heard papers rustling in the background. "The tablecloths were a little more difficult, but I got those too."

"You're a godsend," Lee said.

"It's no problem. I even got my cheap boss to kick in a donation, so I applied that to the bill already," Peter said. "I'll be there with Billy and Darryl, and I'm looking forward to seeing you again." Lee could almost hear an excited smile. "Everything will be delivered to the expo center by truck the morning of the dinner, so you won't have to store it and then haul it over again."

Lee could hardly believe it. "Thank you."

"You're welcome. Call me if there are any issues."

"I will," Lee said excitedly before disconnecting the call. At least something appeared to be going right. Lee placed the phone on the table and held his head in his hands.

"You okay?" Vivian asked as she pulled out the chair next to his.

"Yeah," he answered after glancing at her. "How are ticket sales?"

"Pretty good. We've sold about four hundred so far," Vivian answered, and Lee groaned. He'd really been hoping for more. "Don't worry," she added patting his back. "We still have two weeks, and sales will pick up the closer we get."

"I certainly hope so, or else we're going to be eating chicken until the day we die," Lee said. Vivian was probably right, but this whole thing with the borough council had him on edge.

"Don't worry. This is how it always works. Actually having sold that many tickets already is a good sign. Trust me. We've got posters up all over town, and the merchants have been really supportive," Vivian said as she peered over his shoulder. "What else have we got to do?"

"Mostly wait and hope, which is driving me crazy. I can't place the final food order until next week. I just found out the supplies are being delivered, so we're taken care of there. We need decorations for the table, and I forgot to budget for them, so I've been trying to figure out what to do but can't come up with anything."

"I know," Vivian said before turning to the other men in the room. "How many of you have old fire hats sitting around that you'd like to get rid of?" Almost everyone raised their hands. "Bring them in for Lee. We'll use them as decoration, and if you agree, we can raffle them off. Tell everyone else as well. We need as many as we can get." Vivian smiled at Lee, satisfied with herself. "Don't worry. Everyone is helping and pulling their weight. You're not alone in this, so just relax a bit."

That was easy for her to say; she wasn't the one who was going to need to answer questions from the borough council. But he didn't say anything. Lee figured the captain didn't want everyone to know what was going on either. Everyone in the station was getting excited about the dinner. He'd had no shortage of volunteers for everything from serving to cooking the food. Some of the men had said their wives would help set up the room as long as they could have a front-row seat for the evening. Lee had even managed to get a photographer lined up who had agreed to donate his time, and all they needed to pay were the direct costs. In return, he'd asked if he could bring an assistant to book appointments for portraits and things like that. He'd even be able to print the pictures on site for people so they wouldn't have to wait. It was perfect, and guaranteed to help sell pictures.

"Is everything okay?" Dirk asked, and Lee tensed slightly when he felt hands on his shoulders, Dirk's fingers lightly kneading the muscles.

"It will be, I guess," Lee said, and quietly explained what was going on. "I know you're on shift, and I'll be fine," Lee added once he'd filled Dirk in. "I'm just nervous." The alarm rang, and the room instantly filled with activity. "Cap, do you want me to go?" Lee asked as he met him coming out of his office. He wasn't on duty, but had come in to work on the dinner.

"Yeah. Punch in," he said firmly. "This looks like a big one. It's the old Thorngood Mansion." Captain Morris hurried away, and Lee grabbed his gear, shrugging into the last of it as the truck pulled out of the garage. They roared through the streets, dodging cars through heavy traffic. By the time they arrived, the other companies were already on the scene, and they were directed to the homes behind the huge building to keep the fire from spreading. The mansion was located at the back of a park with homes behind it. The old place had been empty for years. Flames shot out of the roof, and black smoke billowed out of the now broken windows.

Lee helped evacuate the homes closest to the fire, and then he and his team poured water on them in case of stray sparks while the rest of the company joined the others trying to put out the massive blaze. The fire was so intense that from where he stood hundreds of feet away, he could feel the heat radiating off the burning building. Lee wetted down the back of the homes as well as the yards and heard the roar of the flames and hissing where water met them.

Minutes became hours in the heat of the day. Add to that the scorching from the inferno behind them, and Lee was soaked to the skin inside his fire suit. Every time he moved, he felt sloshy, he'd sweated so much. Finally, after hours, the flames began to die and the heat from the fire abated. They got the word to wrap up what they were doing since thankfully, the mansion fire had been put out, and they headed back to the station. With another station acting as the lead on this fire, they were able to return to their station first. Lee had never been so grateful to be back in air-conditioned comfort in his life.

In the station, Lee cleaned up in a bit of a hurry before returning to work on his preparations for the dinner, and once the rest of the company returned, Lee punched out and headed for home so he could get ready for the council meeting that evening.

LEE FINISHED dressing, checking himself in the mirror to make sure his uniform looked perfect before leaving the apartment. He walked the four blocks to the borough hall and found Captain Morris waiting for him in the hallway. Tamping down his nerves, Lee followed the captain into the room. They found a seat toward the front and waited for the meeting to begin. He looked through the agenda and didn't see anything about the dinner on the list. Captain Morris was doing the same, and they shared confused looks but said nothing.

People wandered in, and the room began to fill. Lee looked around a few times, and eventually the council members entered and took their places, along with the mayor and borough officials. The meeting began with the Pledge of Allegiance, and Lee had to try to remember the words since he hadn't said it since elementary school. The floor was opened for citizen questions and comments. An older man with gray hair walked to the front of the room. "I'd like to know why our fire company is holding an unwholesome fundraiser."

"I wouldn't say it's unwholesome," the council president said and then looked in their direction. "Captain Morris and Lee Stanton from the Union Fire Company are here this evening, and I believe they can answer your question."

So this was how it was—they wanted to distance themselves. Lee stood up and moved toward the podium. "I'm Firefighter Lee Stanton, and we're raising money to pay for maintenance projects for the station."

"But why this?" the old man asked. "We're a good Christian community and—"

"Excuse me, sir, but religion has nothing to do with it. This is a civil matter, not a church matter, and we leave religion at the door," Lee said firmly. "You are free to believe what you like, that is your business, and I am free to do the same." Lee was already feeling a bit frazzled. After dealing with Dirk's father for months now, he had little patience for people who felt their beliefs trumped everyone else's. "But our station is up for closure partly because the borough does not have the money to perform the upgrades and maintenance we need. There will be no 'unwholesome activity', as you claim. We are having a chicken dinner that will be served by the firemen from Union."

"You're calling it Chicken and Beefcake," the man said, exaggeratedly appalled.

"That's right. The male waiters will be shirtless. That is all. The servers will be volunteers, and it's all in good fun." Lee tried to keep his answer light.

"I for one don't think it's appropriate," the mayor said from his place with the council members. "Are there any ordinances being violated?" he added, looking toward the borough lawyer.

"No," the lawyer answered succinctly. "The fire companies are largely autonomous. The borough pays firefighter salaries, benefits, and a portion of building maintenance. Money for the equipment is raised by the companies themselves."

"I still don't believe this is the kind of behavior we should be endorsing," Gerald Spitzer, one of the council members, added, picking up the theme. "However, I'm also curious about what you plan to use the money for."

"Maintenance projects on the building—primarily new bathrooms, initially." Lee looked at the captain, who smiled and nodded his encouragement.

"Why would you do that when your station is up for consolidation?" Councilman Spitzer asked.

Lee had already been told by Captain Morris earlier in the day to address all questions and answers to the president of the council, regardless of who asked. Lee stood tall and answered, "Because we're the oldest fire company in the borough and one of the oldest in the state and country. If we raise enough money to help make the repairs to the facility, we're hoping to influence your decision about consolidating us into the other companies."

"Well, your actions may very well influence our decision," Councilman Spitzer told him threateningly. Lee felt defeated and was about to step down from the podium when he heard the door at the back of the room open, and he saw Dirk stride down the center aisle. Lee stepped away from the podium and took his seat next to Captain Morris, wondering why Dirk was here.

"Sorry I messed up," he whispered, and Captain Morris smiled.

"You didn't. Spitzer was never on our side, and the mayor is a blowhard," the captain whispered as Lee watched Dirk stop at the front of the aisle.

"Do you have something to say?" the president of the council asked.

"Yes, I do," Dirk answered before striding to the podium. "There are a few facts that I believe haven't been brought to light yet. First, I think it's important to point out that the event is being held at the expo center, which is outside the borough and out of your jurisdiction, and it is being held outside of working hours. All firefighters are working on this fundraiser on their own time, which is also outside your jurisdiction."

"You're not helping your case," Councilman Spitzer warned. "We'll still decide which fire company to close."

"Not anymore," Dirk said levelly. "I consulted with an expert on the borough's own historic preservation law, and because the Union fire station is within the boundaries of the Carlisle Historic District, you will have legal difficulties trying to close it."

"Whose opinion is this?" the borough lawyer asked.

Lee noticed that Dirk didn't answer the question as he continued. "The reason you can't is because you have willfully withheld the funds needed to properly maintain the property, or at least that's what the fire company is going to argue when we sue you if you decide to try to close us." Dirk sounded so self-assured, and Lee thought it was totally hot. He also looked amazing in his pressed and creased dress uniform, confident as he put the asshole portion of his personality to good use. "We already have top-notch representation ready and available. So I have just one question for you. Are we done here?"

Lee saw the president of the council and a few other members trying to hide their smiles. "Yes, I believe we've spent enough time on this topic. Good luck with your fundraiser," the council president said.

"Thank you," Dirk replied before adding, "We have tickets with us if anyone would like to purchase them." A few people in the audience snickered, and Dirk walked to the back of the room as the president continued the meeting, calling the first item on the agenda. Lee waited a few minutes, and then he quietly left his seat and walked down the side aisle toward the back. Dirk was standing just outside the now closed door, and Lee grinned at him.

"What were you thinking?" Lee asked. "You pissed off the council something terrible," Lee added, not really caring.

"Actually, I pissed off a few members—the others are happy the decision has been taken out of their hands," Dirk explained, and the door behind them opened again as Captain Morris came out and then closed the door behind him.

"I'm not sure whether to smack you or hug you," Captain Morris said.

"From you, I'd rather be smacked," Dirk sniped, and the three of them laughed quietly.

"Where did you dig up that information, anyway?"

"A friend of a friend happens to be a judge, and he was most helpful. It seems his former legal partner was one of the men who wrote the statute," Dirk smirked, "and he wasn't happy about how they were using it." The door opened and closed again. This time a woman came out, walking up to Dirk.

"I'd like five of your tickets if you have them," she said, and Dirk reached into his pocket, withdrawing a stack of them. "Will you take a check?" she asked, already searching in her pocketbook. "I loved how you put them in their place." Dirk told her who to make the check out to, and she wrote it and handed it to Dirk, and he gave her the tickets.

"Thank you. We'll see you at the dinner," Dirk said with a warm smile, and Lee saw her blush as she placed the tickets in her purse. With a nod and a smile, she rejoined the meeting, and as a group, the firemen walked out of the borough hall.

"You know the council is going to give us grief for years over what you said," Captain Morris said once they were on the street.

"That's what Lee said, but I was right, and they're useless. They decided they were going to try to close a historically protected fire station rather than allocate the money needed for its maintenance and upkeep." Dirk shook his head.

"You do realize that you've tied their hands, and Goodwill is now most likely going to be the station that will close," Captain Morris said, and Dirk nodded.

"I know," Dirk replied. "I'm not happy about that either, but the goal was to keep Union open, and while we may have done that, we still need to raise the money. Our needs haven't changed, just the reason. Now we need to raise the money so we can have a proper station. Plus, the council could still decide to fight and try to close us."

Captain Morris motioned for them to go outside. Dirk opened the door, and they followed. Once the door closed, Captain Morris's eyes hardened. "Look, you two, you may have won that round, but Dirk's little grandstanding play may have made all our lives a lot harder. The council is the group that passed the historic preservation ordinance, and they can change it. Also, that's the group that approves our operating budget each year. We have friends on the council, but also some challenges, and you made those challenges harder for the next time." Captain Morris's eyes blazed, and Lee saw Dirk's happy expression fade. Lee almost instinctively moved closer to Dirk but had to keep quiet. This was a work issue, not a personal one. Not that he ever liked anyone berating his lover.

"Sorry, Cap," Dirk said softly.

"I know your instinct is to go into any situation with everything you have. That's what makes you a great firefighter, because you always give it your all. But here, you have to play politics, and that's going to be tougher from now on." Captain Morris descended the concrete stairs, and Lee looked alternately from Dirk, who looked as contrite as Lee had ever seen him, to Captain Morris, whose posture was rigid. "I can tell you one thing," he added, and then turned around. "This dinner had better be a huge success or else we're never going to hear the end of it, and every time we want something, they're going to bring it up for the next decade." Captain Morris sighed and looked about to walk away. "Come on, you two. We've got work to do."

Lee slowly descended the stairs with Dirk behind him. Lee got into his car and drove home. He'd barely gotten inside when he heard a knock on his door. Opening it, he saw Dirk, still in his uniform, hat in hand. "I didn't mean to make things harder for you. I was trying to help." Dirk stepped inside, and Lee smiled, pulling him into a hug. "You aren't angry?"

Lee squeezed tighter. "No. You came in there, guns blazing, trying to help me. You talked to people and did some research, all to help. I know sometimes you can be...."

"An ass," Dirk mumbled, and Lee chuckled, running a hand down Dirk's back.

"Well, yes, but this wasn't one of those times." Lee lifted his head off Dirk's shoulder. "Sometimes I don't understand you at all. You'll fight me over the stupidest things, and then come charging in like a white knight whenever you think I need you." Lee didn't wait for an answer, instead capturing Dirk's mouth in a time-stopping kiss. Reaching around, Lee grabbed Dirk's butt through his uniform pants, pressing their groins together, hard. "You looked so sexy standing up there like you owned the world. It was one of the hottest things I have ever seen in my life." Lee kissed Dirk again and felt his lips part. Without waiting for a further invitation, he surged his tongue forward, taking complete possession of Dirk.

Part of Lee could hardly believe Dirk had stood up for him like that, but Dirk seemed to be surprising him a lot lately. Or maybe this was the real Dirk, and Lee was finally seeing the core of the man he'd fallen in love with months ago. Some guys became firefighters for the adrenaline rush, and some because of a need to help others. Many of the guys had some of both; after all, their job was one of self-sacrifice, and Lee had fallen in love with Dirk when he realized he was one of the men who truly wanted to help others. But to see those protective instincts used on him was a bit heady. "Aren't you on shift?" Lee asked when his head swam from lack of air, forcing him to break the kiss.

Dirk nodded. "I need to get back pretty fast, but I had to see you first." Lee knew Dirk's pride wouldn't let him admit he had been afraid. Lee had known for a while that he had the ability to make Dirk happy, just like Dirk could do the same for him. But these few moments had shown him just how much influence he had.

"I'm glad, because I wanted to see you too." Lee kissed Dirk once again and then released him. "Go on and get back to work. I'll meet you at your place when you're done with the shift." Dirk nodded before turning to open the door. "Don't worry, whatever happens, we'll deal with it." Dirk stepped out and was about to close the door when Lee stopped it. "I really appreciated you being there. It meant a lot," Lee admitted, and he saw Dirk smile before closing the door.

Changing out of his uniform, Lee went over his list for what seemed like the millionth time. But right now, all he could do was sell tickets and stay hopeful. If this wasn't a success, it could cost the station a lot of money and grief. It wasn't long before he was pacing the small room, wondering just what he could do to get the word out and publicize what they were doing. He'd sent notifications and press releases to every newspaper and radio station in the area, but hadn't heard a thing. Granted, there were still two weeks to go, but after today the stakes had been raised, and this had to work out well. Lee kept comforting himself with the fact that they'd already sold over 400 tickets. But that wasn't enough to make the event the overwhelming success he knew it had to be.

Lee didn't allow himself to think of what would happen if the event flopped and the council called him to answer their questions, which they were likely to do after today. This had to work, it just had to. Lee checked the clock, finding he still had hours to wonder, worry, pray, and silently will people to buy tickets. The benefit had to be a success, because failure now could mean a whole lot more than losing the fire station. Lee fully realized that with the way Dirk had inadvertently raised the stakes, both his and Dirk's jobs were on the line. If the fundraiser failed or even appeared to fail, once the fire stations were consolidated, Lee knew both he and Dirk would somehow be consolidated out of their jobs. "That may happen anyway," Lee said to the empty apartment. At least he hoped to go out with a bang.

# Chapter 5

LEE COULDN'T lie still no matter what he did. For the last three nights, Dirk had done his best to wear him out, two, sometimes three times a night, and still Lee knew he'd nearly driven Dirk out of his mind. "I'm going to tie you to the bed and gag you," Dirk growled before throwing his arm over Lee's chest and tugging him a little closer. "You've done everything humanly possible to make this work, so please just relax and go to sleep. You won't be any good to anybody if you're dead on your feet. And I can't fuck you again because you've worn me out and Mr. Happy is dead."

"Sorry," Lee grumbled, but Dirk just held him tighter.

"Go 'sleep," Dirk slurred, and Lee closed his eyes, eventually falling to sleep, only to wake as soon as the sun began shining in the bedroom windows. Dirk was sound asleep next to him, snoring softly. Lee tried to move away, but Dirk tightened his grip, rolling next to him without waking, so Lee lay beside him for a long while, thinking and trying to keep his nerves at bay.

When Dirk got warm and rolled over, Lee carefully pushed back the covers and slowly got out of the bed. He pulled on a pair of shorts and then went down the stairs as quietly as he could. After starting the coffee maker, Lee sat at the table and waited as the rich coffee scent filled the room. Lee filled a mug when the pot was full and sat back down, going over in his head all the things he needed to do. "Lee," Dirk said from where he was standing naked in the doorway. "Turn on the radio."

Still feeling a bit blurry-headed, he reached over and flipped on the radio Dirk kept in the corner of the kitchen. A rock station was playing, and Dirk walked in the room, his bare white butt shining at Lee as he leaned over the counter to change the station. "What are you listening for?"

"Shhh," Dirk said and turned up the radio.

"This morning in local happenings," a female voice said, "it seems the Union Fire Company in Carlisle is holding a Chicken and

Beefcake Dinner. They're raising money to make repairs to the station, and apparently the firemen themselves will be acting as waiters. You can also have your picture taken with a hunky fireman. I know I'll be the first one in line. So, ladies, if you've ever wanted to be waited on by shirtless firemen, now is your chance." She sounded like an excited teenager. "Call 244-5623 for tickets, or you can buy them at the Carlisle Convention Center. The dinner starts at six, and they stop serving at ten, so stop by and get an eyeful of Central Pennsylvania's best beefcake. I know I will." The announcer moved on to the next story, and Lee stared wide-eyed at Dirk as he slowly felt himself smile.

"If that doesn't sell tickets, I don't know what will," Dirk said, grinning, and Lee stood up, leaving his mug behind as he engulfed a very naked and extremely hot fireman in his arms.

"That announcer would be so jealous right now," Lee quipped before Dirk kissed him hard and deep.

"Yes, I bet she'd give anything to be in my place right now," Dirk said, and Lee scoffed lightly.

"I'm the one with his hand on bare fireman butt right now." Lee cut off Dirk's reply with a kiss and felt his lover's body react, a thick, long cock sliding along Lee's hip. He closed his eyes as Dirk's firm lips battled with his for dominance. Skin to skin, hands over quivering muscle, Lee let himself be guided back upstairs. As soon as they reached the bedroom, Dirk's alarm began to blare, and Lee groaned, not wanting to look at the clock but knowing it was already getting late.

"Damn it," Dirk swore as he slapped at the clock, silencing it. But the damage was done. They both knew what that meant. They needed to get to the station, Dirk for his shift, and Lee to start the preparations for that evening. Reluctantly, Lee stepped back, groaning softly at the sight of Dirk hard and ready. Lee wanted to press him back onto the bed and pound into Dirk until they both screamed, but he knew that wasn't in the cards, and his mind was already turning over all the things he had to do.

"I'm sorry," Lee said with a deep sigh as he closed his eyes and ran his hand over his face.

"Hey. It's all right, but when this thing is over, you're mine, and I don't want you to even think about going into the station tomorrow. We both have the day off, and we're going to spend it in bed." Dirk prowled closer, his cock wagging with each step. "Now go get cleaned up before

I forget myself and make us both late." Lee didn't want to move at all, but he did anyway, walking into the bathroom to shave and shower.

Lee was both thankful and disappointed that Dirk didn't join him in the shower, but they would never have made it into work if he had. That didn't stop Lee from wishing for a momentary distraction before the activity wound up around him.

After showering, Lee dressed and made sure he had everything he needed for the evening. He hadn't pressed Dirk about helping to serve the dinner. Dirk had made his feelings clear earlier, and he'd been so supportive that Lee didn't want to ask for more. Besides, he knew that part of being in a relationship was respecting the other person's feelings, and Lee was willing to respect Dirk's wishes even though he really wanted him to be there.

By the time he was cleaned up and dressed, Dirk was nearly ready as well. Together they went to the kitchen, and Lee dumped his coffee before pouring a fresh mug. The last thing he needed was caffeine, but there was no way Lee could start the day without his coffee. "It's going to be fine," Dirk said as he slid the pot back into the coffee maker. "Do you know how many tickets have been sold?"

Lee shook his head. "Vivian has refused to tell me. All she says is 'enough' whenever I ask her. Three days ago we'd sold over 700, but she refuses to tell me anything more. We have enough food for 1500, and I hope to God we don't end up with only 700 people. We'll be eating chicken until we turn into one." That was Lee's biggest fear—that they would have so much food left over that it ate into the profits. "The room will be set up for 1000, and I'm hoping people will come and go so others can take their place if needed." Just talking about it made Lee's nerves kick up again, and he set his mug on the table.

"Go on and find out. I'll lock up here and come to the station in a few minutes," Dirk told him. "You're going to worry yourself to death." Lee got up, and after giving Dirk a kiss, left the kitchen, gathering his things before getting into his car and heading toward the station.

Excited conversation filled the station as Lee walked in. They had the expo center from nine o'clock on, and some of the men were getting the antique engine ready to move. It was always kept in running condition because, even though antique, it was still an official fire vehicle. The grills were being loaded into trucks, as was the other equipment that was going to be used as decoration. "If you brought hats, put them in my trunk. If you want it back, put your name in it. Otherwise we'll raffle them," Lee told the guys, and Jimmy came out carrying a box.

"These are hats, and there are three more boxes. As far as I know, they can all be raffled, but I'll check when I get them over there," Jimmy said with a smile before placing the box in the back of a truck and going to get another. The activity around him was chaotic, and yet Lee could see all the things that needed to get done were being done. The weeks of organizational and logistical planning were paying off.

"Vivian's inside," Jimmy called over his shoulder as he lowered the box into the bed of the truck. Everything looked in hand, and Lee went inside where Vivian seemed to be waiting for him.

"Before you ask, we've sold about 900 tickets. It's not as many as we were hoping for, but not bad either. I have to make the rounds of the merchants yet, so we might have sold a few more, but that should be about it for advance tickets. We'll sell some at the door," Vivian told him, and Lee knew she was trying to make him feel better. Lee had been hoping for more, but 900 people wasn't bad, and he wasn't going to complain. "We have been getting calls this morning, so…."

"It's okay, Vivian. Go ahead and make your rounds, and I'll see you at the expo center." Lee gave her a hug, and she returned it. "You've been a godsend."

"Hey," she said, giving him a pat on the back. "This is a success if we don't sell another ticket, so I don't want you to worry about anything. And have a good time, because if you're having fun, they'll be having fun." She squeezed him one more time and then backed away. "Now let's get going."

"Yes ma'am," Lee teased as he grabbed his notebooks and headed out to the expo center.

Lee met the representative, Chuck, and they opened the doors. The room looked huge and empty. Lee stood in the middle of the space and wondered just how they were going to get everything set up. A horn sounded, and Lee looked out the wall of windows to see the antique fire engine slowly making its way across the parking lot. Chuck helped him open the large doors, and together they guided the engine inside. "Perfect!" Lee cried, and Captain Morris turned off the engine.

"You didn't think I was going to let anyone else drive this baby, did you?" Captain Morris said as he got out of the truck.

"It looks great," Lee said, and Captain Morris cranked the main ladder up toward the ceiling to make it look more impressive. "Beautiful," Lee said with a smile as he and the captain stepped back to take a look. Other guys began to arrive along with their wives, and Chuck showed them where the tables and chairs were kept. Part of their deal with the center was that they would set up and clean up the tables and chairs, so guys began moving tables and setting them up. Each round table was set up with ten chairs. "Let's set up a hundred tables and leave this area nearest the side empty. If we need additional tables, we can easily set them up, and if we don't, there will be room for people to move," Lee told the assembled group, and the men immediately began setting up tables. "The plates, tablecloths, utensils, and glasses should be here soon." *He hoped.* Lee found himself looking out the windows constantly as he worked, hoping the truck would get there soon. Then he saw it pull up, and to his surprise Billy from Café Belgie got out and walked inside.

"I have your stuff, and I thought you might need a little food service expertise, so I'm here to help," Billy told him with a grin.

"The ladies are here to set the tables," Lee said.

"Then you guys set up the tables and get the chairs around them. I'll start bringing in tablecloths, and we can get to it."

They worked for hours setting up tables and placing the chairs. Then the next group came, covering each table with a cloth before setting ten places with utensils, napkins, and glasses. The plates would arrive with the food, and Billy directed much of the operation. Jimmy spent time at one of the sinks, cleaning and drying each of the fire hats before setting one in the center of some of the tables. They didn't have enough to put one on each table, but they gave the room some color. One of the florists had donated a number of small arrangements, and the vases were set in the centers of the other tables. "We need to return the vases at the end of the night," Lee told Jimmy, and he promised to make sure they got picked up.

"Where's Dirk?" Jimmy asked as he and Lee carried what looked like the last table and set it in place. "I know he's not on shift today."

Lee extended the legs and they set the table in place. "He's got things he needed to get done," Lee answered.

"Is he one of the servers?" Jimmy asked, moving a stack of chairs into place to begin placing them around the table.

"No," Lee answered, and Jimmy peered up from what he was doing. "He doesn't want to do it, and I'm respecting his decision." Lee smiled, and Jimmy nodded as they stepped back from the table. The others were finishing up as well, and a few minutes later the team stood together and looked across the room at a sea of white tablecloths, flowers, and helmets.

"It's very festive looking," one of the ladies noted, and Lee had to agree. It looked bright and fun.

The excitement was already beginning to build as the other men began to arrive. The grills were lit two hours before service was to begin, and they began cooking chicken out behind the kitchen, placing the nearly cooked chicken in trays and then in a low oven with pans of water to finish cooking and keep warm. The scent drifted into the room, reminding Lee that he'd missed lunch completely. Some of the others had as well, so the first pieces of chicken off the grill were immediately devoured.

The photographer arrived and set up in one of the corners, and an hour before service, Billy and Lee gathered all the firemen who had agreed to act as servers in the back of the room. "I thought I'd share with you guys some of the tricks of the trade. You'll never serve all these people carrying a handful of plates at a time. So I got some trays." Billy picked up one of the restaurant-size serving trays. "Place five to six plates on the tray." Billy placed his hand in the center and lifted it over his head. "This is entertainment, and tonight you're the show. So when you serve, do it with flair." Billy twisted his hand, bringing the tray down. "Serve from the left and clear from the right, and if you have to do something, give it a bit of panache." Billy pulled Lee to stand next to him. "Flex a little, and when you serve, remember, chest out, stomach in." Billy demonstrated, and some of the guys laughed a little because Billy was such a slight man, but he made his point when he stood tall and handled the tray with ease. "Take a few minutes to practice," Billy added with raised eyebrows.

Lee took a tray, and the other guys did as well. They held them over their heads the way Billy had showed them and brought them down. Almost immediately, seven trays fell to the floor, with most of the others following right behind. "It's not as easy as it looks," Harry, a beefy firefighter standing next to Lee, mumbled under his breath as he retrieved his tray from the floor. They tried again and had better luck the second time.

"The trays are big, and you need to get used to them. They'll also be heavier with food on them, and as the evening goes on, they get heavier and heavier, so you need to pay attention at all times. Don't be afraid to steady the tray with your other hand. Remember, you'll be serving drinks as well. Use the smaller tray for those, and when you make a trip, fill all the glasses you encounter. I suggest you divide the room into stations and manage yours, but help the people around you as well."

"Are you going to be serving?" Jimmy asked Billy, and he chuckled.

"Are you kidding? I have my ticket, and I'm trying to figure out which station I'm going to sit at." Billy grinned at them, and to the men's credit, not a one of them blanched or looked away. Instead, they returned Billy's smile, and in that moment, Lee had never been prouder to be a member of the Union Fire Company. Lee had always thought that the guys tolerated Dirk and him being gay. It seemed to be one of those things no one talked about and everyone sort of ignored. But now he realized he was truly accepted, and Lee swallowed hard.

"We need to get changed and ready. We open the doors in forty-five minutes," Lee said, and the guys hurried away. Excitement continued to build as some of the retirees arrived. They'd volunteered to sell raffle tickets and help staff the photography station, and some of them were going to answer questions about the antique equipment. The ladies who'd helped set up took their places, handing Lee their tickets. "You didn't need to pay for tickets."

"Nonsense. We're paying guests now, and we get to watch the show," Jimmy's girlfriend said. As Jimmy turned around, one of the women wolf whistled.

"Just practicing," came from the table amid a chorus of giggles. It was definitely going to be some night. Lee was acting as master of ceremonies, and after changing into his boots, hat, and fire pants, complete with suspenders, he walked into the dining room and saw the other men dressed and ready. They looked good, and he smiled as he peered out into what looked like a packed lobby.

"We're opening the doors in ten minutes, and it looks like we're going to get a crowd right off the bat, so let's make sure we have plates set up and ready to go so we can start serving right away. Don't forget to smile and have fun, because the more you have, the more they'll have." Lee looked over the men. They looked fantastic, and Lee felt a jolt of excitement coming off all of them. They looked good, and they knew it. "Answer all questions you can with honesty and a touch of humor. Do you all know where your stations are?"

"Yes!" they answered in unison, a chorus of deep voices.

"Then get your trays full, because I'm going to open the doors." Lee unlocked the set of double doors and blocked them open. Applause and a few whistles greeted him. "Are you ready?" Captain Carter was greeting people as they entered, looking smart in his dress uniform. He began taking tickets, and the first guests entered the dining room. They gave them a few minutes to begin filling tables, and then the other men fanned out around the room to more applause and catcalls.

Lee helped direct people to tables and answered questions. After ten minutes, there were several hundred people in the room, and a steady stream continued to come in. The sounds of conversation ramped up, and Lee watched the men walking among the tables, serving the food and talking to people. He saw Harry standing by one of the tables flexing his muscles as a cry of delight came up from that end of the room. It was a group of ten men, including Darryl and Billy. One of them was in a wheelchair, and he rolled over to Lee.

"Lee, it's good to see you again," Peter said with a smile, and Lee shook his hand.

"The miracle worker," Lee told him with a grin. "We couldn't have done this without your help," Lee said. "You were a total godsend." Lee leaned down and hugged him. When he stood up, Peter had an ear-to-ear grin.

"You're welcome," he said, looking a bit starry-eyed before rolling back to the table with the rest of the guys.

People young and old continued to pour through the doors. The room began to fill, and the guys continued serving. Stepping out in the lobby, Lee saw a line at the ticket booth, and he threaded his way through the people and around to the side before knocking on the door. Vivian opened it and broke into an immediate grin. "We've sold over two hundred tickets already tonight, and they keep coming in. At this rate we could sell another six to eight hundred tickets." She bounced on her heels and then hugged Lee around the neck. "Looks like you've got a hit on your hands."

"Thanks," Lee said and left the booth, heading back to the dining room. The men were moving around the room much faster than they had been, and Lee could see they were having trouble keeping up. They needed more servers, but everyone was busy. Lee walked to the kitchen, where platers were keeping up. Food was going out, but not quite fast enough.

"We need help, Lee," Jimmy said. "I'm just carrying food, and if we stop to chat a minute, we're behind."

"I'll see what I can do," Lee said and reached for his phone. But before he could place the call, Harry caught his attention.

"We're going to need more tables," Harry told him, and Lee nodded and hurried out back.

The grills sizzled with heat and chicken. The men were turning meat, and some of them were feeding more charcoal into the grills that were going cold before they too were put back into use. "We need some help inside if you can spare anyone." Two of the guys walked over, and Lee led them inside. He showed them where the tables were, and they began carrying them into the dining room and placing chairs around them. Lee spread tablecloths on them as soon as they had chairs around them and quickly set utensils and glassware. The table was taken almost before they could move to the next one. One of the other men took over for Lee, and he reached for his phone again.

"Dirk," Lee said when he got Dirk's voice mail. "We're swamped and we need help," Lee said as he watched the guys hurrying as fast as they could. He hung up and wondered just who else he could call. All the men they could spare were here. The room was filling, and more people kept arriving. When they had put out every table that space allowed for, Lee pressed the two men as waiters, and they began helping with the food.

Lee knew he had to give people an excuse to get up and move around. No one was getting their picture taken, and the firefighter scheduled to be in the booth was serving. Lee looked around and saw one of the girls he'd gone to high school with, so he approached her. "Sheila, could you give me a hand a minute?" Lee asked, and she looked up from the table, her blue eyes widening as she nodded. Lee led her to where the photographer had set up. "Can we take your picture?"

"With you? Yeah!" she answered with a grin, and Lee lifted her into his arms. She giggled and laughed, mugging adorably for the camera as the photographer flashed a picture. Lee paid for the picture and handed it to her when the photographer's assistant had printed it. Sheila gushed and hurried back to her table to show everyone, and soon Lee had a line of people.

"Don't forget your raffle tickets. You can win great prizes, including some of the fire hats on the tables. You don't need to be present to win," came through the loud speaker, and Lee saw ladies heading for the raffle table. People seemed to be having a good time. The firefighter who was scheduled for pictures returned, and Lee stepped away.

"Ladies, Carl will be happy to take care of you," Lee said before hurrying to the front of the room to help people find seats. Some tables had emptied, and they were being reset, so he directed people there, but it wasn't enough. Guests were lingering, and others were standing as they waited for a place to sit. Lee didn't know what to do, and he was thankful whenever people got up so he could seat more people.

"How's it going?" someone said from behind him, and Lee turned to see Dirk. Lee's mouth fell open, and his mind flashed back to the day he'd seen Dirk dressed almost identically as he waited his turn to use the shower.

"I'm glad you're here. We've run out of places for people to sit, and the tables aren't turning very fast. There aren't places to set up more tables, and what are you doing here anyway?" Everything seemed to rush out of him at the same time.

"I got your message and called the captain—he told me what was happening," Dirk said as he walked over to the microphone. "Everyone, please take a look out the windows. Two of our fire engines have just arrived, and we'd like to invite you to take a closer look if you like."

Instantly, a number of people got up, freeing up space. The tables were reset, and a large number of the people waiting were seated. From then on, the tables seemed to turn more regularly, and soon no one was waiting long. The lines stayed steady at the photographer's, and Lee took his assigned turn. One little old lady actually tweaked his nipple as they snapped the picture, while other ladies kissed him on the cheek. It was all in fun, and it was raising money for the station. As Lee tired and waited for his replacement, he saw Dirk waiting in line. He paid his money, and then Lee stood next to his lover, who'd once again placed Lee over himself, and the photographer snapped a picture. Dirk asked for one more, and this time, Dirk turned and whispered "I love you" into Lee's ear just before the picture was snapped. Lee knew he wanted that picture as soon as the flash died, and he paid for it, leaving Dirk to get it as he took a turn getting mauled by the ladies.

"A huge success," Vivian said when she came to stand next to Lee, and he turned and smiled. "They've finally stopped coming, and we've sold between fifteen and sixteen hundred tickets."

"The kitchen is beginning to come to the end of the food," Lee said as he watched servers bring out still more plates. He noticed that they were moving slower, and there were now empty places at the tables. Lee still wished they could have arranged for a temporary license to sell beer, but the red tape had been a mile long. If they decided to do this again, he'd have to start earlier. Lee took a minute to watch and breathe, listening to the sound of multiple conversations that quieted when an announcement was made that the raffle was going to begin. They called names, and occasionally someone in the crowd would jump up excitedly to claim their prize. A few of the helmet winners got in line to have their picture taken with a fireman while they wore their prize.

Once the prizes were given away, the crowd really began to thin, and Lee took a trip out to the grills. Some of them were dark and cooling as the last pieces of chicken were cooked. "We did good!" Lee called, and he was greeted with weary smiles. "Go ahead and start cleaning up as soon as you can. We're coming to the end of service. Don't forget to get your own dinner, and there are drinks in the kitchen."

Lee went back inside, walking more slowly than he had all night. Dirk met him as soon as he entered the dining room. "I had some of the guys quietly start breaking down the tables and putting away the chairs. Most people are lingering and talking."

"Thanks," Lee said, stifling a yawn.

"You did well," Dirk told him. "Really, and you were right. This was a fantastic idea, and you pulled it off almost without a hitch."

"Thanks, Dirk," Lee said, trying not to yawn, but failing miserably.

"No. Thank you, from me and everyone at the station. This was not only a huge success, but it probably enhanced basic teamwork more than any amount of fire training ever could." Lee felt Dirk's arm around his waist. "I also need to tell you I was wrong. This was more fun than I've had with my clothes on in quite a while. I shouldn't have let my pride get in my way and given you such a hard time."

Lee didn't know what to say, so he kept quiet. He was simply happy that Dirk was there and had come to help when he needed him most. "Let's get this place cleaned up so we can get home and in bed."

"Best idea I've heard today," Dirk said with a leer before moving toward the tables that needed to be cleared. Lee checked on the progress of all the teams. Cleanup was in full swing as the last people began packing up. With calls of goodbye, Lee closed the doors, and the cleanup began in earnest.

Tables banged against the floor as they were tilted onto their sides and hauled away. The dirty tablecloths were placed in the bags the service had provided and loaded in the truck that Lee needed to park behind Café Belgie before going home. Slowly and steadily, the room was cleared. Captain Morris came by after his shift and drove the antique fire engine back to the station. The other antique items were carefully packed and hauled back as well.

"How'd we do, Viv?" Lee asked when he stopped into the ticket booth where she and one of her helpers were still counting money.

"It looks like we've taken in just shy of forty thousand, all totaled. The raffle brought in a ton," Vivian said as she bundled the last of the bills. "We also got a number of straight donations, so I'd say this was an amazing success, and no one can possibly say otherwise. Regardless of what the council wants to do, we have nearly forty thousand votes of support, and they can't ignore that no matter how hard they try." Vivian looked almost as tired as he felt, but also excited and happy. "We've got just a half hour here and then we'll be done. I'm going to get the deposit ready, and then we'll drop it at the bank night drop on our way home." Lee had no idea what to say. So many people had come together to make this happen. "Did you keep a list of who donated what?"

"Yes, and I was thinking that we need to have the guys write thank-you notes to everyone. I thought about printing them and having everyone sign, but I think a handwritten note signed by some of the guys would be better."

"If we make the effort, then we'll be more likely to get donations next year," Vivian agreed and went back to work. Lee left and went out back where the last of the grills were being loaded and hauled away. The kitchen was being cleaned as well, and the dining room cleanup was nearly done. The photographer was packing up the last of his equipment, and Lee thanked him.

"We booked a lot of appointments, so if you decide to do this again, let me know. I'll work with you any time." They shook hands, and the photographer began carrying his equipment out to his van.

Everyone seemed to finish at almost the same time. Lee and Chuck walked the building to make sure everything was left as it should be. Then he said goodbye, and Lee got in the truck, with Dirk following behind. It took a bit of machinations with vehicles, but at nearly midnight Lee parked his car in front of Dirk's house, dead tired and ready to fall into bed. After getting out of the car, Lee trudged up the walk and onto the porch. The front door opened, and Dirk stood in the doorway, still wearing his fire pants. His feet were bare, and he'd taken off his hat, but Lee couldn't tear his eyes off him. "You know, it was seeing you like this that gave me the idea for the dinner."

"I didn't know," Dirk said, stepping back so Lee could go inside.

"Yeah. You were waiting for the shower with just one suspender holding up your pants." Lee reached out and slipped one of the suspenders off Dirk's shoulder. "I knew you were wearing clothes under them, but it was still one of the sexiest things I have ever seen." Lee stepped close enough to feel the heat from Dirk's chest on his skin.

"There's something I've wanted to ask you," Dirk whispered, and Lee felt Dirk splay his hand on his chest. "Move in here with me," Dirk said. "You spend most of your time here, and when you're not, I miss the hell out of you. I don't sleep very well when you aren't here."

"Is that the only reason?" Lee asked in a voice just above a whisper.

"We aren't girls," Dirk protested.

"I know that. But I want to hear it, Dirk. I deserve to hear you say it." Lee touched Dirk's cheek. "Because I love you with everything I have. You are the last person I want to see when I go to bed and the first person I want to see when I wake up. I know you've told me you love me, but what do I mean to you?"

Dirk was quiet for a long time, and Lee wondered just what Dirk was going to say. "Everything," Dirk answered, and Lee realized that sometimes a single word said it all. Lee stared into Dirk's amazingly deep eyes, not wanting to move for fear of breaking the spell. Dirk slipped a hand from his chest, and then Lee felt it slip into his. The lights turned off, and then Dirk led him slowly to the stairs without saying a word.

They climbed the stairs with the clomping of Lee's boots the only sound. When he reached Dirk's bedroom, Lee somehow got his boots off while Dirk waited for him. When he turned around, Dirk stood in front of the bed, and Lee moved close. "You are sexy as hell, Dirk," Lee muttered as he took him in, wondering just what Dirk was wearing under those pants. Reaching out slowly, Lee pushed the second suspender off Dirk's shoulder, and it fell to his side. Dirk's fire pants hung on his hips for a second before crumpling around his legs, and Dirk stepped out of them. Like a Greek sculpture, Dirk's muscles moved and flowed as he came closer, cock swinging slowly back and forth with each and every step. Lee stood rooted in place, his legs shaking slightly as Dirk continued moving closer. Then Lee was gathered into Dirk's arms and tugged close. Their lips met in a kiss that started off amazingly fierce but softened and deepened until Lee rested his weight against Dirk, letting his lover support him as his mouth was devoured, lips tugged, and tongue sucked. Lee whimpered loudly when Dirk pulled away.

"Let's get you out of these," Dirk told him, and first one of his suspenders slipped off his shoulders followed by the other, and Lee's pants slid down his legs just like Dirk's had, except he'd been wearing shorts under them for the dinner. But they didn't stay in place for long, and quickly joined his pants around his ankles. Lee stepped out of the pile of clothes, and Dirk was right there, chest to chest, lips to lips, hands cupping his ass hard, fingers working the flesh while Lee was kissed fiercely. He could feel every inch of just how Dirk felt sliding along his hip, and Lee reciprocated with every ounce of his being. This was the man he loved with all his heart, and even though Dirk had shown him and even told him he loved him from time to time, Lee knew without a doubt what Dirk felt for him and would always feel for him.

"Will you move in with me and be with me always?" Dirk asked breathlessly.

"Yes," Lee answered before kissing Dirk again. "Yes, I will," Lee added. "Now that wasn't girly, was it?"

Dirk shook his head, and Lee felt Dirk grip his cock firmly. "There's nothing about either of us that's girly," Dirk told him, stroking lightly. Lee's head bobbed back as he thrust into Dirk's hand.

"I love you, Dirk," Lee moaned as Dirk tightened his fingers around him. Nothing ever felt like Dirk touching him, no matter where he did it. The sensation abruptly ended, and Lee snapped his head up and his eyes open.

"I love you too, and if you get into bed, I'll show you just how much." Dirk pulled back the covers, and Lee slid under the sheets with Dirk right next to him. And Dirk kept his promise, taking the next hour or more to show just how much Lee was loved, using hands, mouth, and every other part of his body imaginable. Lee was filled, slowly, completely, and their bodies rocked together in the dark, with Lee crying out his love as he came, and Dirk following right behind. Lee barely remembered Dirk cleaning him up. He was so tired that all he could concentrate on was the fact that he'd done it—he'd made the fundraiser a success—and that Dirk had asked him to move in. The last thing he remembered before falling to sleep was the press of lips gently against his forehead and a whispered "I love you" from his fireman. Life was perfect.

# BURNISHED BY FIRE

# Chapter 1

DIRK CHECKED the clock in the station for what had to be the millionth time today. Just four hours to go and his shift would be over, without another one for nine whole days. It had been slow, with no calls, and combined with the cold outside, they were left with limited things to do. Dirk had been manufacturing chores for himself for the past two hours. All he had to do was get through the rest of the day and he was home free. Dirk moved back so he could inspect the chrome on the engine he'd been polishing. It looked fine. In fact, it had looked fine when Dirk started, but he'd needed something to do.

"Hey, just a few more hours," Lee practically sang from behind him, and Dirk grinned. They had both been acting like schoolkids for the past two days.

The alarm sounded, and Dirk threw his rag aside, hurrying to where his gear stood ready. Within seconds, both he and Lee were suited up and on the truck as it pulled out of the station. "Business fire downtown," one of the guys said as he spread the word. That meant one thing: an old building that would burn quickly, probably with apartments on the upper floors. If it wasn't a false alarm, this could be a bad one. Dirk looked over to where Lee sat and saw the same realization on his lover's face.

The drive wasn't long. Traffic through town was already being diverted. Dirk jumped off the truck, looking up as smoke poured out of second- and third-story windows. Dirk groaned as he put on his breathing equipment and communications gear, ready to receive instructions. When he was done, Dirk saw that Lee was doing the same. "Not sure how involved the building is," the captain said through their earpieces. "Seems like mostly smoke, but there are probably people trapped in the upper floors. Go up the side stairs and carefully check around. The building is wood frame and old, so for God's sake, don't take any chances." Dirk acknowledged the captain's instructions as he started climbing the stairs. Lee pointed, motioning that he'd continue up, and Dirk nodded, entering the second floor.

Dense smoke packed the air, and Dirk used his heat-sensitive glasses to see through the murkiness. They showed something glowing hot at the far end of the hall, and he began pushing open doors, making quick sweeps of rooms before continuing on. The apartments were small, and Dirk searched two quickly. In the third, the door didn't want to open, so Dirk kicked it in. The rooms were filled with smoke, and Dirk went carefully, searching for any residents.

"Dirk, have you found anything?" Lee asked through the radio.

"No," he answered before pushing open the bedroom door. "You?"

"No. I'm almost done here."

Dirk saw no one in the room and left, then went to open the next door. "Lee, get down here. Three young children, second apartment on the left," he called through the radio, knowing the team on the outside would already be arranging for medical support. A man, presumably the father, was trying to help them, but he was coughing and no use at all. Dirk told him to get out and pointed toward the door. "We have them. Go!" he yelled when the man hesitated. The kids couldn't be any older than four or five. Dirk scooped up the youngest of the three and began carrying her out. He met Lee coming down the hall and transferred the girl to him before returning to the apartment. "Make sure the father gets out too." The heat at the end of the hall was growing more intense, and just before he entered the apartment again, he saw open flames. They looked to be spreading fast.

Dirk rushed back into the bedroom and lifted both remaining children. He had no idea if they were breathing, but he tucked each one under an arm and hurried out into the hall. The flames were already licking down the walls, and Dirk could feel the heat building inside his suit. Lee came over to him, and Dirk handed him one of the kids. "Get the hell out of here. The place is going to go up," Dirk warned, staying behind Lee as they made their way toward the stairwell. As they were descending the stairs, they were met by other men who took the kids from them. Dirk could hear breaking glass. Turning around, he saw flames shoot out of the doorway they'd left seconds before.

Dirk raced for the ground floor behind Lee with the roar of flames right behind them. As they moved, the sound dissipated slightly, and once they reached the outside, they continued moving away as glass blew out of windows, with flames following right behind. The crews were already spraying water, but it seemed to be having little effect. The building was made almost entirely of old, dry wood, and it was set to burn fast and hot. Crews were dousing the neighboring buildings to keep the fire from spreading, and Dirk followed Lee to where the rescue crews were working on the children. Now away from the fire, Dirk pulled off his helmet and breathing gear.

"How are you? Any breathing issues?" one of the paramedics asked as he rushed over.

"No, John, I'm fine. The mask worked like a charm. How are the kids?" Dirk took a deep breath of fresh air as he waited for the answer.

"All three were alive when you and Lee got them out. We're transporting them to the hospital. It's too soon to tell for sure, but they looked okay. You and Lee did great."

"There was still an apartment I didn't get into. Is there anyone else missing?" Dirk asked, turning to one of the police officers.

"We don't know. No one seems to really know anyone else. We're still trying to get in touch with everyone," he answered, and Dirk nodded his understanding before looking to Lee, who was doing the same thing. They'd both heard that story before. Eventually they would know if they'd missed anyone, and then they both would have to deal with it. Dirk simply hoped today was not one of those days. After thanking the officer and paramedic, Dirk walked to where the captain was directing operations.

"You two head for the truck. You did good work," he said, and they followed his instructions. He and Lee had become the men who most often went into the burning buildings. They both seemed to have developed, probably out of necessity, a way of instinctively reading what a burning building was going to do.

It took a while, but the crew got the fire under control. The flames diminished and then went out, leaving the building a soggy, dripping mess. Word came down that there were three people unaccounted for, and Lee volunteered to take a look inside. Dirk watched as his lover entered the charred shell and then watched the door until he came out again a half hour later, pointing and explaining what he'd found.

Dirk hung his head. It was obvious he hadn't gotten to someone in time. Once Lee was done, he walked over to where Dirk waited and sat down next to him. "There was nothing you could have done. They were in the apartment closest to where the fire seems to have started."

"I could have gone there first," Dirk protested, but Lee shook his head.

"If you had, they would probably still be dead and so would those kids, as well. They have a chance because you got to them in time. Think about that instead. I know it's hard, but it's what we have to do."

"Was it bad?" Dirk asked.

"There wasn't much left of the apartment or the bodies. The fire was so fast and hot, I doubt they had any chance at all. Poor fuckers." Lee sighed, and they sat quietly until the captain came to get them.

"Let's pack up and head home. The fire marshal will investigate the cause, but we pretty much know where it started." He patted them both on the shoulder. "Don't beat yourselves up. You did great work, and three children are alive because of you."

Dirk stood up and walked toward the engine. No matter how many times people told him it was okay, he still always wondered about the ones he hadn't gotten to. He knew Lee was thinking the same thing, but it was too late now. They didn't save everyone, they never could, and this was simply one of those times. He'd experienced this before and he would again. But that didn't make it any easier.

"Come on. Let's get back and we can commiserate over ice cream— the cure for everything," Lee said, and Dirk nodded. They'd been seeing each other for almost eighteen months now, and it still surprised him how much Lee knew about him, not that he didn't know just as much about Lee. What he found hard to believe was that he was interesting enough for anyone to want to know that much about him. "Captain says as soon as we have our cleanup done, we can clock out and start our vacation." Now that was a bit of good news.

The ride back to the station was quiet. It always was when they lost someone. Everyone took it hard. They celebrated when they saved people, and commiserated when they couldn't, but today, because there had been both, they simply kept quiet.

At the station, after the short ride, Dirk climbed off the truck and stripped off his gear. He cleaned it and made sure it was ready for use again before heading upstairs for a quick shower and the obligatory paperwork. He wanted to get this over and done so he could put it behind him and maybe have a chance to relax with Lee.

The shower and paperwork went faster than he expected, and Lee was waiting for him when he was done with both. He'd driven them in at the start of the shift, but Lee drove them home. Dirk didn't feel much like talking, and Lee knew him well enough to let him have his peace, at least for a while.

"You know that I'll let you brood until we get home and then I'm going to slap you out of it," Lee told him, and Dirk growled from deep in his throat before turning to look out his window again. There were times when Lee drove him crazy. He also knew Lee was right—if you took things to heart, you became ineffective. "Besides, we're on vacation. It may be cold here, but when we get to Florida, it's going to be warm, and once we get on that ship, we'll be sailing to even warmer places." They pulled up in front of the house, and Lee cut the engine before leaning over to him. "I packed the small bathing suit you like so much."

Dirk growled again as he turned toward Lee. He knew he was being baited, and damned if he wasn't rising to it, in many different ways. "Damn you," Dirk swore before grabbing Lee's cheeks, kissing him hard. Lee gave as good as Dirk did. He always had. That was one of the things Dirk loved about the man. He was as strong as Dirk and could take and give what Dirk needed. Dirk felt Lee's tongue duel with his until the car filled with moans that got louder and louder.

"If you want to take this inside, I can do my best to make you forget everything, including your name," Lee told him, and Dirk nodded before opening the door. They both retrieved their bags from the trunk and carried them inside before placing them in the laundry room, where they would stay until they got back. Dirk then climbed the stairs with Lee on his heels, and somehow he managed to make it to the bedroom before he was tackled. They bounced on the bed, with Lee landing on top. "I promised you forgetting," Lee told him before yanking up Dirk's shirt and clamping his lips around a nipple.

Dirk squirmed and hissed at Lee's perfectly rough play. That was how he liked it: hard, rough, and with as much intensity as he could get. "Lee," Dirk growled.

"You keep those hands behind your head, and I'm going to blow your mind," Lee told him as he worked open the belt of Dirk's jeans, pushing his underwear out of the way before fishing out Dirk's cock. The cool air felt good on him, but he didn't have much time to think about it because Lee swallowed him whole, sucking like his life depended upon it.

Dirk's consciousness narrowed to where Lee's lips wrapped around his cock and Lee plucked and pinched his nipples, driving him wild. He closed his eyes, thrusting his hips forward, the temptation to hold Lee's head almost overwhelming, but he kept his hands where they were. "Damn, Lee, I love your mouth," Dirk groaned, and he heard Lee hum his response before sucking still harder.

Lee stroked down his stomach and then along his thighs. Dirk spread his legs and thrust upward. Lee must have been waiting because Dirk felt Lee slide his hands under him, his fingers ghosting over his hole. As he settled back onto the bed, one of Lee's fingers breached his body, and Dirk cried out, thrusting again. Lee plunged his digit deeper, locating the spot inside him and making his head spin. Dirk was so far gone by this point, he could barely think of anything other than what Lee was doing to his body. He grunted and groaned, and Lee sucked him halfway to heaven.

Lee let his lips slip from Dirk's cock, and Dirk groaned loudly even as Lee stroked him hard.

"Let it go, Dirk. Give me what you got," he coaxed before sucking him deep once again.

Dirk couldn't take much more, and he thrust with complete abandon as he gave himself over to the pleasure Lee offered and let go of the doubt and self-recrimination that had been running through his head since they'd returned from the fire. Everything was silent in his head except for how Lee was making him feel. Dirk groaned and whimpered under Lee's ministrations, already going out of his mind with desire. He felt Lee curl his finger, repeatedly massaging the spot inside him, and Dirk howled as he came hard, shooting down Lee's throat, his back arching on the bed.

Dirk could barely breathe or think as the tension left his body. Slowly, he opened his eyes to a smiling Lee, who crawled up his body and then kissed him hard. Dirk hugged Lee close, returning his lover's kisses. "What about you?"

Lee shook his head. "I'll let you make it up to me tonight once we're at the hotel." Lee nuzzled Dirk's neck and began sucking up a mark.

"What's that for?" Dirk asked, but the only answer he got was a soft, slurpy kiss on his neck followed by a sly, smirky smile.

"Now that you're feeling better, I hate to remind you," Lee winked playfully, "but we have a reservation at a hotel in Baltimore, so get your last things packed because in half an hour, we're leaving for a fabulous vacation of sun, sand, sex, surf, sex, lounging on the deck, and sex." Lee climbed off the bed. "So I suggest you get ready, hot stuff."

Dirk got himself together and began putting the last of his things in his bags before closing them and carrying them downstairs, where he set them by the door next to Lee's. "So what's the plan?" Dirk asked as he wandered into the living room, where Lee was looking through a set of papers.

"You have your passport and all your things, including your kit?"

"Yes," Dirk answered, rolling his eyes. "What's the plan?" he repeated.

"We're at the hotel tonight, and our plane leaves at eight tomorrow morning from Baltimore. We fly to Orlando, and the cruise company will transport us to Port Canaveral, where we'll board the ship and our fun begins."

"I can't believe we're actually doing this," Dirk said as he sat next to Lee on the sofa. "I never would have thought of a cruise."

"I wouldn't, either, but Marshall had a package deal and he was able to get us in the group, so we'll even get a hundred dollars in onboard credit, which will probably pay for a few drinks," Lee said as he leaned against him. Dirk kissed Lee gently. "I think we'd better get the car packed so we can get this party started."

Dirk nodded, taking one more kiss before putting on his coat and braving the wintry evening. He got the bags loaded while Lee closed up the house and made sure he had all the tickets and paperwork. Once Dirk was done and the car loaded, he made a trip around back to check that everything was locked up and secure. By the time he was done, Lee was getting into the car. "Ready?" Dirk asked as he slid the key into the ignition.

"You bet," Lee said with a grin.

Dirk put the car into gear and pulled away from the house, heading toward the highway. Tonight they were going to be in a hotel with a hot tub, pool, sauna, steam room—the works.

"Does your father know we're going to be gone?" Lee asked.

Dirk felt the pressure inside shoot skyward. "God, no. He still hasn't stopped pestering me about you moving in, and that was months ago. The last thing I want to do is actually talk to him about anything unless I have to."

"I really thought, given time, he'd start to come around," Lee said softly, and Dirk squeezed Lee's thigh as he stopped at the light, waiting to make the turn onto the freeway.

"I know. I did too. But he's being a stubborn ass, and the last time he called, he was still singing the same old song." The light changed and Dirk made the turn, accelerating up the ramp. "Let's not talk about my father, work, or anything un-fun for the next week, okay?"

"You got it!" Lee said with a grin as Dirk merged into traffic.

# Chapter 2

THE DRIVE to Baltimore and then the flight and trip across Florida to the port went off without a hitch, and to top it off, Dirk had seen an alligator sunning itself along the way. How cool was that? As they approached the port, the bus wound around and pulled up alongside the biggest ship he'd ever seen. "Good God," Dirk said softly, before letting out a whistle. "I had no idea the thing was going to be that gigantimous!"

"When it was built, *Freedom of the Seas* was the largest cruise ship ever built," Lee explained as he too leaned across to get a better view out the window. They sat on the bus for a few minutes as their luggage was unloaded, and then they were instructed to get in line for boarding. It was quite a process. The bags had to be X-rayed, and then they stood in a line where they signed papers, had their pictures taken, presented credit cards, and received the SeaPasses that would act as their credit cards, room keys, and identification. "Have a good cruise," the lady said as they walked away, holding onto their carry-on bags.

They wound through the port building's hallways and eventually found themselves on the gangway and then aboard the ship. Dirk could hardly believe it. They were here and ready to start their vacation. "Staterooms aren't quite available yet," one of the crew members explained, "but please go up to the Windjammer on eleven and have some lunch. By the time you're done, they should be available." She motioned them inside, and they found the elevators and pressed the call button.

They rode up in the glass elevator car to the eleventh deck and followed the other passengers into the large buffet. Lee found a table and they set down their bags. "Go ahead and get something to eat. I'll sit with the bags."

Dirk thanked him and got some lunch before returning to the table. "They have everything you can think of," Dirk told Lee as he set down his plate.

"A waiter came by and I ordered something to drink," Lee explained as he got up. "I'll be right back." Somehow Dirk doubted that. The place was huge and there was food everywhere. He began to eat, and the waiter returned with water and coffee. When Lee got back to the table, he was carrying two plates and had a boggled look on his face.

"What do you want to do first?" Lee asked as he began eating.

"I say we change into bathing suits and hit the pool deck or maybe the FlowRider thing," Dirk said. "I wanna get wet and then lie in the sun."

"Sounds like a plan, but we have to watch the time. There's a muster drill at four, but other than that, the day is all ours." Lee looked like a teenager when he said that, and Dirk couldn't help returning his smile. For months, they'd both worked hard, taking extra shifts so they could start their lives together on a solid financial footing. It was paying off, but had been exhausting for both of them. Dirk wanted to reach across the table to squeeze Lee's hand, but he wasn't sure how it would be received, so he simply smiled at him and ate his lunch, anxious to get started on the fun.

Excitement seemed to be everywhere as they finished eating. People hurried around them, talking spiritedly. Dirk couldn't hear what anyone was saying, but the anticipation had everyone on an excitement high that he found contagious. "Look at the other ships," Lee said as he pointed around the harbor. "There's a Disney ship and a Carnival ship. Those things look small compared to what we're on." Lee grinned as he took a bite of his chicken. "This is going to be great."

"There you are," Marshall, the travel agent who'd booked the cruise for them, said as he approached their table. "We sort of lost track of you two. The rest of the group is meeting on the helipad for sail-away if you want to join. That way you can meet everyone. We had to travel in two groups, and some people came down yesterday."

Dirk looked at Lee to see if he was interested. He didn't particularly care if they met everyone or not. All he wanted to do was relax in the sun for a while. "Maybe we'll see you there," Lee said with a smile that Dirk knew was pure placation.

"I'm in stateroom 6519 if you need anything," Marshall said.

"I'm sure we'll be fine," Lee said. "We've booked excursions at Coco Cay and St. Thomas. On St. Maarten we're going to get off the ship and find the nearest beach. You have a great cruise, and enjoy yourself too. Don't let everyone run you ragged."

"I'll try not to," Marshall said, moving away from the table, and Dirk went back to his lunch.

"You have no interest in the sail-away thing, do you?" Lee asked, and Dirk rolled his eyes before shaking his head. "I didn't think so." Lee reached into his bag and began fishing around before removing a small bottle and handing Dirk a blue pill. "Bonine," Lee explained as he swallowed one.

"You get seasick?" Dirk asked, and Lee shrugged.

"Don't really know, and I'm not interested in finding out," Lee explained. "I doubt it, but I'm not really interested in ruining the trip by woofing all over the place."

Dirk looked at the little pill before handing it back. "I'm fine." Lee put the pill away and packed up the things he'd pulled out. "Do we need to carry our dishes someplace?" Dirk asked, looking around.

"No. It looks like they clean things up." Lee stood up and lifted his bag. "Let's go have some fun," Lee told him with a boyish grin that Dirk found both infectious and sexy as hell. "Hopefully, we can drop the bags in our stateroom."

They left the buffet and threaded their way out onto the pool deck. The warm, fresh breeze was wonderful, and Dirk immediately realized he was wearing too many clothes. He stripped off the sweatshirt he'd forgotten he had on, shoved it into his bag, and immediately felt more comfortable.

People were already swimming and relaxing in the bubbling whirlpools. Waiters roamed among the deck chairs with frozen tropical drinks in souvenir glasses. A live calypso band played on a small stage near the main swimming pools. It seemed like a tropical party, and they'd been invited. "This is going to be so cool," Dirk said with a huge grin as he stopped and watched a group of kids already playing in the kid's pool decorated with spouting figures and a waterfall.

"Shit, what's he doing here?" Lee said from behind him, and Dirk turned, following Lee's gaze.

"What are you...?" Dirk saw who Lee was looking at and nearly dropped his bag. "What the hell?" Dirk asked softly, seeing his relaxing vacation flying away on the wings of one of the birds gliding over the ship as his father made his way toward them. "Fuck!"

"What are you doing here?" his father asked, teeth clenched, without so much as a hello.

"We're on vacation," Lee answered with a surprising amount of pleasantness—much more than Dirk knew he could muster at the moment. Another man who Dirk didn't know appeared to have followed his father and was standing patiently behind him. Dirk's father seemed to realize he was there and turned to the other man. "Karl, this is my son, Dirk, and his… friend, Lee. They're on the ship as well."

They shook hands. "It's nice to meet you," Karl said pleasantly. "Phillip didn't tell me his son was on the ship. We're on our way to lunch. Would you care to join us?"

"No, thank you," Dirk answered, trying to keep his expression blank while his father glared daggers at him. "We just finished."

"Then I'm sure we'll see you around the ship," Karl said pleasantly and began to move away.

"I'll be right there," Dirk's father called, and Karl nodded before heading toward the buffet. As soon as he was far enough away, Dirk felt as well as saw his father's intense gaze shift to him. "Karl is a client of mine," his father whispered tersely. "A very good client, and I will not tolerate him seeing the two of you *cavorting* together on deck."

Dirk clenched his fists. "For one thing… Dad, I'm this cruise to have fun, and I fully intend to, whether you're here or not, and if you don't like it, that's too bad. You may not like me or who I am, but that's your problem, not mine. And as for Lee and me cavorting…." Dirk had to stop himself from laughing like a lunatic. "We'll act any way we please, and if your client sees it, then he sees the truth." Dirk looked toward where Karl had gone. "You don't want to keep the important people in your life waiting," he added, tilting his head in Karl's direction.

"If I had known, I would have forbade you from coming," his father spat.

Dirk moved closer to his father, puffing out his chest to make himself appear larger. "If I had known you were going to be onboard, Lee and I wouldn't have come. But either way, you can't forbid me from doing anything." Dirk looked around, but no one was paying attention, thank God. "You need to cool off, Dad. So I suggest you either go have lunch with your client, or I can cool you off right here and now." He looked toward the swimming pools. He'd had enough of his father's controlling nature. *Forbid him?* His dad couldn't forbid him from doing anything.

Thankfully, his father turned away and walked toward the stern of the ship, and Dirk strode toward the rotating doors that led back inside.

"Dirk," Lee said from behind him, and Dirk punched the button for the elevator before turning around. "You're scaring people." Dirk huffed and tried to let go of some of the anger. "We're on deck eight," Lee prompted once the elevator arrived and then pressed the button. They rode down alone, the elevator car stopped at their deck, and they stepped off. Dirk followed Lee as he searched for their cabin. Lee slid his card in the door and opened it. Dirk followed him inside and dropped his bag on the bed.

"Son of a bitch!" Dirk swore as soon as he heard the door click closed behind them. "Of all the ships, he had to end up on ours."

Dirk sat on the edge of the bed, still fuming. He felt Lee sit beside him. "There are over three thousand passengers on this ship. It's not as though you're going to see him all that much." Dirk knew Lee was trying to make the best of the situation, but he wasn't ready to let go of his anger yet.

"Forbid me," Dirk muttered. "Like he could stop us from taking a vacation. The arrogant son of a bitch." Lee began moving around the cabin and opened the closet doors. Dirk knew he was just ignoring him and letting him get it out.

"There's a safe and shelves in here," Lee told him before closing the closet and opening the bathroom door. "This is pretty nice." His voice carried out of the bath. "There's no way we can both take a shower in here without needing a shoehorn, but otherwise it's good." Lee stepped out of the bathroom and closed the door. "Are you about done, or have you decided to let your father ruin your vacation?"

Dirk huffed, but stood up and began rummaging through his bag for a bathing suit. "Okay. You've made your point, and no, I'm not going to let him ruin our vacation." Dirk pulled off his shirt and began taking off his jeans. "What are you waiting for?" Dirk asked when he saw Lee just watching him.

"Taking in the show," Lee quipped before rummaging in his bag. Dirk chuckled as he finished changing, shucking his pants and then pulling on his new bathing suit. They'd been clued in to pack anything they needed for the first day in their carry-on bags to hold them over until their luggage arrived. Once he was done, he watched Lee finish changing, stroking Lee's butt playfully before it disappeared into his suit. "Let's go," Dirk said, feeling better and ready to try to forget his father and have fun. "You know, the room isn't what I was expecting,"

Dirk commented as he waited for Lee to get his deck shoes. "Everything is small, but incredibly well organized." Dirk grabbed his SeaPass off the small desk, then began pulling open some of the drawers and storage spaces. "There's even a sofa under the window." Dirk pulled the curtains and saw the view to the shopping arcade in the center of the ship. "We'll have to check out everything."

"I think we'll have plenty of time." Lee moved behind him, and Dirk pulled the curtains closed. "We're on vacation," he whispered, and Dirk smiled, tugging Lee closer before kissing him a bit more possessively than he intended.

"Wow," Lee mumbled when Dirk gentled the kiss, and Dirk smiled. Lee's responsiveness was one of the things he loved about his huge, strong lover.

"Let's go before we never leave the room," Dirk warned, and Lee grinned, backing away before heading for the door. "I got towels," he said as he opened the bathroom door and grabbed two from the rack. Throwing them over their shoulders, they left the room and walked down the passageway to the elevators. "So what do you want to do first?"

"FlowRider!" Lee answered confidently, glancing at the deck numbers for the elevators. "We can probably walk up." Dirk agreed, and they began climbing the stairs. It was only three decks up, and then they stepped out into the warm Florida air. They walked the length of the ship and climbed two more decks, following the signs to the very back of the ship. People were boogie boarding and looked as though they were having a great time. Lee and Dirk had to sign liability waivers and then got wristbands so they could surf.

"Have you done this before?" Dirk asked over the sound of the surf machine, wind, and people.

"Nope, but it looks like a blast," Lee answered like the huge kid he was. They got in line, and Dirk watched the people in front of them. When it was Lee's turn, he followed the attendant's instructions and managed to boogie board for a while until he fell off the board and the jets of water pushed him up to the top. He got up, grinning, and handed Dirk the board. "It's way cool," he told him, and Dirk took his turn.

The attendant explained what he needed to do, and Dirk jumped onto the board, skimming over the water. At first he just tried to stay on the board, but once he got the hang of it, he tried moving from side to side. It was an unbelievable rush. Dirk had seen people getting up on their knees, so he decided to try it and ended up wiping out. Getting out of the water, he handed the board to the next person in line and then walked to where Lee was already in line again. "They do surfing too," Lee explained to him, pointing out the boards. "That would be fun."

"Damn right," Dirk agreed.

"Good. Because I already paid for lessons, Tuesday at five," Lee told him with a grin. "Happy vacation!" Then it was Lee's turn again, and he took the boogie board and began his run. Dirk took his next, and then they got back in line. As he was waiting for another turn, Dirk saw his father standing at the edge of the viewing area. When his father saw him, he motioned Dirk over, but Dirk simply turned away and ignored him.

"This is our last run, and then we need to get back to the cabin to get dressed for the muster-drill thing," Dirk commented, keeping one eye on his glowering father. Lee took his turn, and then Dirk made a run, managing to roll over and get back on the board this time. He tried again, but wiped out. Handing off the board, he walked to where he and Lee had set their towels and began drying off.

"I want to talk to you," a familiar voice said from behind him, and Dirk sighed.

"I don't want to talk to you," Dirk began. "This is our vacation, so we're going to pretend you don't exist. Whatever you want can wait until next week," Dirk said civilly before slipping on his deck shoes and following Lee out of the area toward the elevators.

Back in their cabin, they dressed, finishing just as announcements were made about the mandatory muster drills. Dirk followed Lee down to one of the lounges, where they lined up and waited. They watched some quick demonstrations and were given safety information. Dirk saw his father at the far side of the room and ignored him once again. The captain made an announcement, and then they were dismissed. "Let's just explore for a while," Lee suggested, and they strolled down the promenade. Most of the shops as well as the casino were closed and wouldn't open until after they left port, but Lee and Dirk wandered through and then down to the decks where the theater, ice rink, and photo shop were located. "They have everything," Lee explained. "I signed us up for all the shows. We don't have to go, but I was told that it's best to get reservations ahead of time."

"You thought of everything, didn't you?" Dirk asked affectionately.

"I tried," Lee said with a grin as they continued walking. "How about a stop in the gym for a workout, steam, soak, and then sauna before we go to dinner? It'll give us a chance to check out what they have. I understand from what I read online that they have a boxing ring and punching bag on board."

"Wonderful, let's go," Dirk said, anxious to work off some of the latent anxiety, pressure, and nerves so he could really start to relax. Lee was already leading the way to the stairs.

THE WORKOUT was great. It felt amazing to push a lot of weight, and Dirk worked all thoughts of his father from his mind. His arms and shoulders ached, but that was a good thing, as was the time he and Lee spent on deck in the whirlpool. They'd been sitting there when the ship began to move and the hot water flowed back and forth with the movement of the ship. The steam room was next, followed by a near nap in the sauna. Now he and Lee were showered and dressed, walking back toward the cabin. Dirk was relaxed enough that he didn't care about much of anything except food. "We're at the late seating, so why don't we go up to the buffet for a small snack to tide you over, as long as you don't pig out."

"Yes, Mother," Dirk quipped, but he knew Lee was right. It would be all too easy to eat their way through the trip.

Their luggage had been delivered outside the cabin, so they unlocked the door and brought it inside. After taking a few minutes to unpack and slide the suitcases under the bed, they left to get food.

Dirk's stomach growled loudly as they entered the buffet, but he limited himself to a small steak and some salad. Once they'd eaten, they left right away to avoid temptation before wandering the promenade, checking out the shops and bars and just enjoying an hour together before going in to dinner. Their SeaPass cards showed their table number, and Lee and Dirk were directed to a table for ten at one side of the dining room with a view out one of the large porthole windows. They'd just sat down when other couples began to arrive. They both stood and introduced themselves, shaking hands with Brian and his wife Heather as well as Vince and his wife Cindy. Everyone sat down and the waiter was just pouring water when the last people at their table arrived, and Dirk found himself sitting right across the table from his father. How in the hell could this happen? His father's client sat across from Lee, and Dirk tried his level best not to grind his teeth.

"Is this really your son?" Cindy asked, and Dirk graciously nodded his head.

"My son and his friend booked the same cruise and we didn't know," Dirk's father explained. Dirk had seen his father charm clients for years, and he knew that was the mentality at work now. He laughed and engaged with each person at the table except Dirk and Lee, whom he largely ignored.

The waiter was handing out menus when a single lady joined them, taking one of the two empty chairs. "I'm Sarah," she said as she took her place. Dirk watched his father say hello and then talk to Sarah. Maybe she'd keep him interested for a while. Dirk smiled as he picked up his menu.

Rolls were chosen and passed out, and then the waiter took their orders. The food descriptions looked amazing, and Dirk had a difficult time choosing between the chicken and a stir-fry. "You can order both," Lee told him.

Dirk did, as well as an appetizer.

"What do you do?" Heather asked. She seemed about Dirk's age and had a bright, intelligent expression.

"Both Lee and I are firefighters," Dirk answered.

Heather lifted her water glass, and Dirk noticed that most of the attention around the table had focused on them. "Have you ever saved anyone's life?"

"Yes," Dirk answered honestly. "Actually, Lee saved me from falling when the floor of a burning home collapsed, and I once saved Lee from drowning during a flood." Dirk couldn't help smiling at his lover.

"Dirk's being modest. He saved three young children yesterday," Lee explained before turning to him. "I found a text message I missed as I was turning off my phone. All three are going to be fine."

Dirk was still bothered by the people he hadn't gotten to, but that was good news at least. "Thanks," Dirk said as he glanced over at his father, who seemed engaged in conversation with the woman next to him.

"So you're both real heroes," Vince said from next to his wife. "You must have some amazing stories," he prompted expectantly. Dirk looked at Lee and took a deep breath. They both had stories, but many of them were not for the dinner table.

"There was the time we got a call from a woman who said that her house was full of smoke. She was advised to get out of the house." Lee paused briefly. "When we arrived, she was standing in front of the house, and she had to be about ninety. Dirk talked to her, and since I was geared up, I went in. I quickly found the fire in her oven, which was pouring smoke everywhere. I turned it off and carried the remnants of what had probably once been a plastic container outside. The lady took one look and cried, 'My lunch! I was wondering where I put that.'" Everyone around the table chuckled as Lee paused. "Then she looked at Dirk, serious as a heart attack, and said, 'What am I going to eat now?'" Everyone chuckled again.

"Was she all right?" Brian asked.

"We had the EMTs look at her and found out she hadn't taken her medication. We got her pills, and once she'd taken them she was fine," Lee explained. "We got her something to eat, and then she was upset about the mess."

"Is she okay now?"

"Yes. We see her around town every now and then. For ninety, she's amazing, and she remembers Dirk. Whenever she sees him, she assures him she took her pills. I really think she has eyes for him," Lee teased, and everyone chuckled again.

The waiters refilled their glasses and brought the appetizers, then everyone ate and talked about the food. It would have been a great meal for Dirk if his father hadn't spent much of the time glaring at him for some unknown reason.

"You must be very proud of your son," Cindy said to Dirk's father.

Dirk wanted to see how he answered that question. His father had tried to get him to work with him at the investment office. For whatever reason, Dirk's father hated that he was a firefighter. Maybe it was the hazards of the job, because those efforts had intensified after Dirk had been injured. He wasn't convinced that was it, though. Dirk suspected he didn't measure up to his father's image of what was successful. And somehow his father saw that as a failure on his part.

"Of course," his father said. "Although as a parent, I'm concerned because of the danger."

Dirk wanted to call his father on the bullshit answer, but ate his salad instead, feeling Lee's hand pat his leg. Thankfully, the conversation moved on to other people, and they talked about what they did.

"It's fine. Just don't worry about your dad," Lee whispered softly, and Dirk nodded. He'd often wondered why his father got to him the way he did. They hadn't had a good relationship since his mother died, and it was obvious Dirk couldn't measure up to his father's expectations. He certainly wasn't willing to do what he felt was necessary to get into his father's good graces—become a clone of his father. He would never give up Lee and go to work as an investment advisor—in other words, become as miserable and self-centered as his father. Dirk knew he'd been lucky enough to find Lee and have him actually look deep enough to see him.

Their appetizer dishes were taken and the main courses were served. Dirk ate quietly, listening to the table conversation and offering an occasional contribution. He found out his father's client was a doctor whose wife had passed away a few years earlier. This trip was the first vacation he'd taken since his wife's passing. "I thought it would be easier if I went as part of a group," he explained, and Dirk wondered how his father had agreed to come with him. Maybe he had a heart after all.

Once the main courses were done, Phillip and Karl excused themselves and left the table. Dirk immediately felt better. Sarah followed behind them, leaving Dirk and Lee and the other two couples.

"Does your father have a clue that you're a couple?" Heather asked.

"Heather," Brian scolded lightly.

"It's okay," Dirk said. "Yes, he knows, but he doesn't approve. We talk as little as possible and really did end up on the cruise together by chance." Dirk could only figure they'd ended up at the same table because they were part of the same tour group and had the same last name.

"Would anyone like dessert?" the waiter asked as he passed around the dessert cards for the evening. Dirk was tempted by the crème brûlée, but decided to pass.

"I'm fine, thank you," Dirk told the waiter when it was his turn. He'd already eaten plenty, and the coffee would be enough. Lee asked for a piece of chocolate cake, and the others ordered as well. The small group continued talking until they'd eaten their desserts and finished coffees. Then they all said good night and left the dining room, thanking their server on the way out.

Outside the dining room, Dirk and Lee took the stairs up to the crowded promenade and walked toward the front of the ship. "Would you like a drink?" Lee asked, and Dirk nodded, then followed him toward the Champagne Bar.

Dirk saw his father sitting in one of the chairs, talking to Sarah. He motioned to Lee, and they headed on down the way instead. "Let's just go back to the cabin," Dirk suggested, and they continued walking, arriving at their door a few minutes later. Lee slid his card in the lock before pushing open the door.

"Look, Dirk," Lee began once the door was closed, "are you going to let your dad ruin this vacation? You scowled at each other at dinner, and we had to bypass a drink because he was in the bar. What are you planning to do, hide in here for the rest of the trip?" Lee placed his hands on his hips, his elbows damn near reaching across the cabin. "This has got to stop. So your dad is onboard, so what?" Lee wasn't yelling, but Dirk could tell he was upset.

"He's an ass and drives me crazy," Dirk said.

"Well, remember it wasn't too long ago that everyone had you pegged in the asshole category too." Lee moved closer and pushed Dirk onto the bed. "You're still an ass, but just less often." Lee loomed over him, and Dirk was already excited. "So get this notion out of your head that your father matters one iota to your happiness, because you know damned well he doesn't."

"Sometimes I wish we could have a real relationship," Dirk admitted.

"I know. But it's up to him to accept you for who you are. So let him see the real you. The man who rescues children from burning buildings and men from floodwaters, rather than the one who doesn't want to sit across from him at dinner and won't sit in the Champagne Bar because he's there." Lee rested his hands on Dirk's knees, meeting his gaze. "Because I have to tell you that I don't like that Dirk very much myself." Lee leaned in close, the pressure on Dirk's legs increasing as did the heat. "I like the take-charge, resourceful Dirk who knows what he wants, and I love the hot Dirk who's strong, confident, and not afraid of anything."

Dirk shuddered at the heat in Lee's stare. "I'll try," Dirk agreed, and Lee continued moving closer, taking his lips in a hard kiss as he pressed him back onto the bed. Dirk held Lee tight as their kiss deepened. "You're mine tonight, Dirk," Lee growled after breaking the kiss. Lee stood at the foot of the bed, pulling off his shirt. "And I want you naked," Lee told him, fire blazing in his eyes as he opened his pants and slipped them down his legs.

Dirk toed off his shoes and pulled off his clothes. Lee set them on the chair and then prowled onto the bed, running his hands up Dirk's legs. "I love the way you shake for me," Lee said, his hands gliding over Dirk's thighs and then up his stomach and chest. "Remember this the next time you're with your father. Remember how hot you are and how I make you feel. Then you won't care what the bastard thinks."

Lee took command of his lips, possessing Dirk's mouth with his tongue as he settled his weight on Dirk's body. *Damn, Lee's skin felt good, his lover's thick cock grinding along his.* "I'm going to fuck you until you scream," Lee whispered into his ear, and Dirk shuddered. "So roll over and let me take care of you," Lee told him as he slid down Dirk's body. Dirk felt the bed shake as Lee got up, and Dirk rolled onto his stomach and waited. He felt Lee grab his ankles and tug. Dirk and the bedding slid to the end of the bed. "That's what I want," Lee cooed, and Dirk felt him stroke up his thighs and over his ass.

"Lee," Dirk groaned with a touch of warning, wishing he'd do something other than just talk.

"Spread your legs for me," Lee said, tapping the inside of Dirk's thighs with his warm hands. Dirk opened wide, giving himself to Lee without reservations. Lee stroked up his thighs, and Dirk moaned when Lee skimmed his balls with the lightest touch. Continuing on to his ass, Lee stroked his butt, spreading him wider. Then Lee skewered him with his tongue, and Dirk arched his back, crying out at the surprising intensity.

"Fuck, Lee," Dirk groaned.

"You like that, don't you?" Lee said before blowing warm air on his wet skin, and Dirk shuddered again, his muscles going wild at the gentle, erotic stimulation. "I'm going to drive you out of your mind," Lee told him, and he proceeded to do just that. Dirk could barely breathe by the time Lee had rimmed him until he couldn't see straight. All Dirk could do was beg and plead for more, less, anything. His skin was on fire, and still Lee used his tongue and fingers until Dirk writhed on the bed, grasping the edges of the mattress to steady himself. There were times when his head felt so light he thought he was going to float away, and the only thing that seemed to keep him grounded was holding on.

"Damn, Lee, just fuck me already!" Dirk groaned. Lee simply chuckled and slowly slid two wet fingers into Dirk's body. "God," Dirk sighed, but then Lee withdrew his fingers and used his lips and tongue on

Dirk's opening once again. Not that Dirk was complaining, but his cock was already leaking and throbbing on the bedding, and he was going to come damned fast.

Lee pulled away, and Dirk heard a snick, then he felt Lee lick his way up his back and settle his cock between his cheeks. "You're going to get what you wanted. Hard and fast," Lee told him, and Dirk felt Lee's cock against his opening. Without further warning, Lee pressed inside his body. The stretch and burn had him hissing, but Lee gave no quarter and pressed deeper, filling him. All Dirk could do was force his muscles to relax and ride the wave of sensation.

Lee pressed his hips to Dirk's ass, his cock throbbing inside him. Lee worked his arms beneath Dirk's chest, lifting him up, and Dirk arched his back. Their kiss was totally sloppy and completely hot as his impressively strong lover manhandled him into whatever position he wanted. Dirk never would have guessed all those months ago, when he and Lee had begun their roller coaster of a relationship, that he would adore giving up control, but when it was Lee, he was willing to trust, and he hadn't been disappointed yet. Lee held him tight, snapping his hips slightly, and Dirk nearly howled as sensation pounded into him and continued until Lee lowered him to the bed.

"You ready?" Lee asked, and Dirk nodded. Lee snapped his hips, driving deep and hard into Dirk's body. They were out into the ocean and the ship was rocking slightly back and forth. Lee snapped his hips in time to the movement of the ship, and soon Dirk didn't know what was Lee and what was the ship. He simply knew his world was being rocked. Lee pulled from his body, and Dirk held his breath at the emptiness until his lover slammed back into him. Again and again, Lee pounded his ass in the best way possible, until Dirk knew he wasn't going to last much longer. The rocking of the ship and the way his body quaked every time Lee pounded into him had him rubbing his throbbing cock against the bedding constantly. "Don't come until I say so," Lee hissed into his ear.

"Or what?" Dirk asked feebly.

"I'll spank this ass until it's nice and rosy," Lee replied as he rubbed Dirk's butt before spearing it once again with his thick cock. "I know you're not into that, so you hang on for me." Lee settled into a steady pace, and Dirk forced himself to breathe. Lee's fucking had him wound tight, and his entire body begged for release. But he found the strength to hang on. "Come for me, Dirk," Lee hissed from behind him. It took two more thrusts of Lee's cock, and then Dirk plunged into orgasm, howling into a pillow so he wouldn't wake half the ship. Lee followed right behind him, throbbing and filling his channel.

Then, everything stilled. Lee rested against his back, and the only thing Dirk remained conscious of other than Lee was the slow rocking of the ship.

# Chapter 3

THE NEXT two days were incredible. Dirk rarely saw his father during the day, and he wasn't at dinner. Lee said he might have switched tables, but Dirk wasn't complaining. The few times he had seen him, his father was with Sarah, which was a bit surprising. Today, the ship was scheduled to dock at St. Thomas, and Lee had booked an expedition to go sailing and snorkeling. "What are we supposed to do when we get off?" Dirk asked as he helped Lee pack the bag they would use while they were ashore.

"There will be someone at the dock to meet us, so don't worry," Lee said, moving closer. "Do you need more stress relief?"

Dirk was about to say yes when the captain made an announcement that the ship had docked and passengers were free to go ashore. "Definitely later," Dirk said before he picked up the bag, leaning in for a kiss before heading for the door. Lee was right behind him, and they left and walked happily to the stairs. They descended to deck two, where they got in line to get off the ship. They had to scan their SeaPass cards to get off, and then they were out in the sunshine. A number of people held up cards for the various excursions, and Dirk found theirs and lined up where the guide indicated. "This is going to be great." Dirk could barely contain his excitement. He had never snorkeled or spent time in the tropics, so he was interested in experiencing everything. Looking around, he watched as others got in line and the guide checked everyone's tickets.

"I just have a few more," the guide explained. "And here they are," he added before leading them to a bus. Dirk and Lee were the first ones on and they sat in the very back, with everyone filing on after them. Dirk watched as the seats filled, and he saw the last people get on were Karl, Sarah, and his father. Dirk could feel his teeth start to grind, but he stopped himself. He was going to take Lee's advice and just let it go. Maybe he and his father would find they had something in common besides yelling at each other. The bus started to move, and Dirk watched as they turned onto the road.

"He's driving on the wrong side of the road," Dirk told Lee, getting concerned they were going to be in some fiery accident.

"They drive on the left here," Lee explained, and Dirk shrugged, watching the tropical scenery as it passed outside the window. The ride to the far side of the harbor wasn't too long, then the bus parked and everyone filed off.

"Hey, Dad," Dirk said once he stepped off, approaching his father. He was determined to be friendly. "I didn't know you snorkeled." The expression on his father's face instantly told Dirk that this particular activity had not been his father's idea.

"This is my first time," his father explained.

"Cool, mine too," Dirk responded, plastering a smile on his face as he looked around for Lee.

Lee came up next to him, and Dirk saw his father's expression darken further, but he said nothing. "Have you been snorkeling before?" Dirk asked Karl and Sarah, making conversation while they waited.

"No," Sarah answered a bit nervously. "I'm not a real water person, but I understand they have vests to help you float, and the brochure said we could see fish, coral, and a shipwreck." She smiled, and Dirk had to give her credit for guts and determination.

"They'll also have people in the water with us," Lee explained. "You have nothing to worry about except having fun."

"I snorkeled a number of years ago, and it was very easy," Karl added, and that seemed to reassure Sarah even more.

"If everyone will follow me," the guide called. "Please have your tickets out, and we'll take them as we board the boat." Everyone lined up and began to step onto what looked a bit like a pirate ship. They were even flying the Jolly Roger. Some of the crew were dressed as pirates, as well. It was a bit campy, but fun nonetheless.

Dirk and Lee found a place to sit and stowed their bag under the bench. Once everyone was on board, the crew cast off the lines and the ship motored away from the dock. "Ahoy, mateys," came through the loudspeakers. "We'll be voyaging to Shipwreck Cove this afternoon. Your scurvy crew will be there to help you fit snorkels and masks, so relax and have fun. We'll be putting up the sails once we're out of the harbor, and after snorkeling, we'll open the bar."

It wasn't long before the motor quieted and the crew hoisted the sails. The craft skimmed over the water with just the sound of the wind and waves. Birds flew and dipped overhead from out of the bluest of blue skies as they moved. "This is what I was hoping for," Lee told Dirk, moving a little closer. Dirk nodded, extremely content for the moment to sit next to his partner.

Dirk watched as people moved around the boat, talking excitedly. The crew passed out cards showing the various types of fish so people could get familiar with them. "You really shouldn't act like that," his father said quietly as he approached. Dirk realized how close he and Lee were sitting to each other, and he moved slightly closer to Lee, daring his father to say anything more. He then turned away from his father and looked out over the water.

"I think that's where we're going," Dirk said, pointing to an island on the horizon. "Do you think we'll actually land?" There appeared to be a lighthouse of some type on top of the island, and Dirk thought it might be interesting to hike to the top for the views.

"We anchor offshore," one of the crew members answered, and Dirk thanked him. "The island itself in uninhabited, and it's a kind of bird sanctuary." He continued mingling with passengers, and Dirk turned back, watching as the island got larger.

The crew began handing out masks and fins. It took a couple of tries to get fins that fit Dirk's long feet, but he finally found a pair. The crew demonstrated how to use the equipment as well as the safest way to get off and back onto the boat. They also handed out vests and showed them how to inflate them.

"You can snorkel close to shore, but don't touch any of the rocks or coral. You'll damage them and you could get cut. Also, don't get too close to shore or the waves will push you against the rocks. Stay where the water is smooth. In deeper water," the guide said, indicating as he stood on top of the pilot house, "there's a shipwreck, and fish often congregate around it. We'll be here for little more than an hour, so take your time and see whatever you'd like to see. We'll be watching you from the boat, and there will be guides in the water. So have fun." He jumped down and began assisting people into the water.

Dirk helped Lee get his vest fastened, and then Lee helped him. They lined up, and when his turn came, Dirk jumped into the water and got his fins on and mask in place while he waited for Lee. "Let's see the shipwreck before going closer to shore," Lee suggested, and once they were ready, they headed for where the guide had indicated.

The water was incredibly warm, and Dirk floated easily with his mask in the water, seeing the dim sandy bottom as he propelled himself through the water by kicking his legs. A shape loomed, and he continued forward, breathing through the tube. With every breath, he kept expecting to get a mouthful of water, but he only got air. Dirk saw Lee point, and he followed him, gliding right over top of the wreck. He swore he could reach out and touch it, even though it was well below them, fish darting in and out of holes and swimming quietly around the hunk of metal. After a while, Lee began to swim away, and Dirk followed, heading toward the shore.

The bottom got closer, and instead of sand, he saw rocks covered with plants and coral. Brightly colored fish in blues, yellows, and reds swam and darted beneath them. Dirk realized it had been a long time since he'd felt this comfortable and relaxed. The warm water cradled him, and all he had to do was kick his feet to make a strange world flow under him. This was awesome! Dirk lifted his head and realized he was getting close to shore. He turned around and began heading toward the point to see what was there. He saw a few others doing the same as he got oriented, then he looked under the water once again.

Movement ahead caught his eye, something stirring up the water, feet kicking frantically. A figure went under the water and came up again. Dirk lifted his head and saw what appeared to be a woman floundering in the water. Her vest had deflated, and she was trying to blow it up while keeping herself afloat. Dirk paddled toward her as fast as he could. "Are you okay?" he asked, and she went under again. Dirk went under as well and grabbed her arm, guiding her back to the surface. She was foundering heavily now, kicking and flailing her arms. Dirk could instantly tell she was panicking. "Calm down, I have you," Dirk said, and he held her to him. "I'm a strong swimmer and you're going to be fine." Dirk turned onto his back and got the woman turned around and up against him as a wave crashed into him.

*Fuck, they were too close to shore.* Dirk held onto her and swam as hard as he could. He knew he had to get away from the breaking waves or the water would beat both of them onto the rocks. "Kick your feet for me if you can," he told the woman, and he felt her legs move against his. "That's it," he praised as they began to move. Another wave broke this time, right where they were swimming, and then moved on. As long as they kept moving, they would be fine. Dirk's heart raced, but he kept his actions calm and smooth as he continued kicking, holding onto the woman.

Her panic had subsided and she was helping him now. Lee appeared at his side, moving along with them. "Everything's fine. Dirk's got you," Lee told her, and the woman nodded. As they approached the boat, Dirk's legs burned and his arms ached, but he continued until he heard splashing and someone else appeared with a buoy.

"Take this," a crew member said, but the woman clung to Dirk, so he took it for additional buoyancy and brought her over to the ladder.

"You're okay now. I've got you. All you need to do is grab the ladder and climb it," Dirk told her, and Lee helped her hold the ladder. The woman slipped from his arms and shakily went up the ladder, where people helped her onto the deck. Dirk followed her up, collapsing onto one of the benches, breathing deeply. He felt Lee place a towel over him before sitting down next to him.

"Are you okay?" Lee asked.

Dirk lifted his gaze off the floor. "Yes," he said with a smile. "I'm fine, a little tired but nothing else." In fact, his blood was racing and he was full of adrenaline, one of the aftereffects of excitement like this. He could always think clearly during a rescue, but afterward, his brain sometimes seemed a bit overwhelmed.

"Thank you," a woman's voice said, and Dirk looked into Sarah's smiling face. "You saved my life."

"I'm glad I could help," Dirk answered with a smile. At the time, he hadn't even realized who he'd been helping. He'd simply leaped into action when he was needed.

She leaned forward and gave him a hug. "Your father must be so proud of you. I know I would be if you were my son," she whispered into his ear before letting him go. Dirk wanted to say that he wished that were so, but he simply nodded and smiled as she carefully made her way across the deck. Others were getting back on board, and the boat began to fill. The bar opened, and Lee left him for a few minutes before returning with glasses of rum punch and handing him one.

"Go ahead. It's pretty good, and you could use it," Lee told him, and Dirk drank it down. The fresh fruit juice tasted good, and Dirk finished the glass without thinking.

Once everyone was on board, the crew unhooked the lines and motored away from the island before raising the sails once again. Word seemed to travel through the boat about what had happened, and Dirk found lots of people patting him on the shoulder or asking to shake his hand as they rode back toward the dock. The crew broke out small sandwiches, cookies, and fruit along with additional drinks, adding to the party mood.

"You were great," Lee told him after bumping his shoulder lightly.

"Did you see what happened?" Dirk asked.

"I saw the two of you fighting the current, but I didn't see what happened before that," Lee answered. "I was following a rather large fish, and I thought I might have gotten a glimpse of a sea turtle, but it didn't come close enough for me to be sure. When I came up, I saw you fighting with the surf and was on my way to try to help as you got out."

"Young man, that was amazing." Dirk looked up as his father's client, Karl, sat down next to him. "How did you know what to do?"

"It's what I'm trained to do," Dirk said modestly. He'd learned from Lee to accept gratitude more graciously. When he'd started his career, he'd eaten up every accolade he could get, but he'd also learned that for every success, there could be a failure, and those stuck with him longer.

"It was still impressive," Karl said, shaking his hand. "No wonder your father is so proud of you." Karl stood up and walked back to where he'd been sitting, and Dirk looked at Lee, trying to figure out if he'd heard right. Dirk had never gotten the impression that his father had been proud of anything he'd done in his life. As he thought about it, he figured that impression must be based on something his dad had said to make Karl think they were the perfect Christian family. That would be like his father. Everything had to appear just the way he wanted it, regardless of whether the appearance reflected reality. With his father, it was all about what other people thought, not what his son thought or felt; that was immaterial.

As they sailed, the sun came out from behind a cloud, shining brightly on the water. Dirk fished in the bag beneath their seat for his sunglasses, and after putting them on, laid back and let the warm sun shine on him for a while.

"Do you have any idea how sexy you look right now?" Lee whispered into his ear, and Dirk grinned without moving. "You were always a hero to me, but right now you're glowing."

"Are there times you wish you could turn off the job?" Dirk asked without opening his eyes. "Even on vacation...."

"Sometimes," Lee answered. "But I can't turn it off any more than I can turn off the way I care about you. It's part of who we are... even when we're on vacation." Dirk heard Lee chuckle and then felt him settle back on his seat as the wind carried them back to port. Dirk loved the sound of just the wind and water, and he wondered what it would be like if he and Lee learned to sail and they could be out in a boat, just the two of them, with nothing but the water and wind.

Dirk opened his eyes when he heard the engines start and saw the crew pulling down the sails as they began coming into the harbor area. He and Lee got their things, and once the boat was tied up, they disembarked. As Dirk stepped off, the crew members shook his hand and thanked him for all his help. Once they were back on dry land, they made their way to the waiting bus and rode back to the port area.

It was still early, so they wandered in and out of the port shops, buying a few souvenirs, before getting back on the ship and heading up to their cabin. "Let's get something to eat, then we can relax on the pool deck for a while," Lee suggested.

"Good idea. I'm starved and could use some time doing nothing," Dirk said as he changed out of his wet clothes and into shorts and a T-shirt. Lee did the same, and soon they were ready to go. Together, they hit the buffet and then returned to the cabin, swapping shorts for bathing suits and grabbing towels before heading up to the pool deck.

They managed to find deck chairs in the solarium area, and Dirk stripped off his shirt, spread out on the chair, and closed his eyes. Lee rubbed some sunscreen onto Dirk's back, and then Dirk got up, slathering the rest of himself before lying down once again. This was the life. Neither he nor Lee had anything they had to do or any place they needed to be. Dirk closed his eyes and let the sun warm his skin.

"Dirk." He lifted his head and saw his father standing next to him.

"What do you want to give me grief about now?" Dirk asked, already closing his eyes again. "If you're here to bitch, complain, berate, or just be a pain in the ass, go away and leave me alone. You can do that at home."

"Sarah told me what you did, and I wanted to thank you for helping her," his father said. Dirk rolled over, pulling off his sunglasses.

"That's what I do every day, Dad. It's the part of my job that I like most," Dirk explained, surprised and pleased that he and his dad were talking without yelling at each other or his dad simply issuing orders.

"Well, thank you," his dad said again before walking away. Dirk watched him go, wondering just what was going on. Turning his head toward Lee, he saw his partner staring back at him, looking just as surprised as he was.

"Huh...," Dirk said, not having any idea what else to say. Closing his eyes, he decided to leave whatever had just happened alone. Maybe he'd find out later what was going on, or maybe it was exactly what it appeared to be—his father simply saying thanks. He was getting tired of trying to find ulterior motives and hidden meaning in everything his father did or said. It was wearing him out, and like Lee had told him on many occasions, it wasn't worth his effort.

THEY GOT ready for dinner after spending the late afternoon and early evening either on the pool deck or back at the FlowRider. The lesson had paid off, and Dirk was getting so he could surf pretty well, and now he was really starting to have fun with it. Lee was doing pretty well, too, and all Dirk had to do now was figure out how to install one in the backyard. When the ship pulled out of port, he and Lee stood by the railing watching the lights of St. Thomas get farther away as the sun set over the ocean.

"We've got plenty of time," Lee told him as they rested in the cabin. Dirk had his eyes closed and his head resting on Lee's shoulder. He'd thought of starting something a little more active, but being quiet and alone with Lee was enough for now. Dirk had never thought something as simple as being held for a while would feel as good as it did. He turned his head and shifted his body slightly.

They lay side by side for a long time, just kissing. In some ways, it felt strange to kiss, and Dirk kept expecting the kisses to lead to something else, but neither of them escalated the contact, both of them seemingly content to simply be together for a while. "We can probably start getting dressed for dinner," Lee told him, and Dirk was thankful that tonight wasn't one of the nights they needed to dress up. He slowly got off the bed and stripped off his shorts and T-shirt before pulling on a pair of jeans and a fresh shirt.

"Is this okay?" Dirk asked, and Lee patted his butt.

"More than," Lee told him with a smile that said "after dinner you're all mine," and Dirk turned around.

"I'm glad you approve," he added before tugging Lee into his arms. He thought about kissing him, but rested his head on Lee's shoulder instead.

"I know. You keep seeing what would happen if you hadn't gotten there in time," Lee told him, and Dirk nodded his head against his lover's shoulder.

"What's wrong with me? I saved her and she's fine. I know that," Dirk said softly into Lee's ear. "Then I see the people I didn't get to in the fire just before we left."

"Hey," Lee told him, squeezing tighter. "That was only a few days ago, and you need some quiet time to process it. This isn't the first time that's happened, and it won't be the last. You know that, and so do I. It goes with the job. But that doesn't mean we have to like it or that we don't feel it. Everyone goes through this in their own way, and each time it's different. Are you feeling guilty because you didn't get to them in time? Because you couldn't."

Dirk stood quietly in Lee's arms, trying not to think about it too hard. "But what if…?"

"Dirk, you can what-if yourself to death. You didn't get to them because the fire got there first, and you saved three children instead. You did get to Sarah in time, and she may be at dinner tonight, laughing and having a good time because of what you did. Let yourself accept that." Lee tightened his grip.

"Why don't you ever get like this?"

"I did. You remember about three months ago, when that house collapsed on that family? I kept wondering why I was only able to bring out the baby. Yes, I saved her, but she has no mother and father because of me. I beat myself up over that for a long time, until the captain smacked me on the back of the head and reminded me that she was alive because of me and that I had done all I could." Lee gently lifted Dirk's head so they could see each other. "Don't make me smack you on the back of the head for being a doofus. We do what we can, and you know that. Concentrate on what's important and how I feel about you."

Dirk nodded slowly, accepting Lee's reassuring kiss. "I think I needed this vacation more than I thought I did."

"Hey, the job sometimes gets to all of us, and pretending it doesn't isn't being truthful with yourself or with me. I know you have a huge heart, no matter how much you try to keep it hidden from everyone else."

Lee kissed him again and then moved away. "Let's go to dinner, and afterward maybe we can find a place on this ship to go dancing. We're going to have fun and take your mind off all this for a while. Okay?"

Dirk nodded and smiled. "I'm being stupid, aren't I?"

"No. But I think you're letting your feelings get all muddled up. You aren't responsible for the world, only you." Lee turned away, opened the closet door, and got his shoes. "I think that's enough of me playing amateur psychologist for a while. Let's go have dinner before that stomach of yours starts making noises so loud they think the ship is sinking." Lee laughed, and Dirk gathered his things, and a few minutes later they were walking through the ship toward the dining room.

They were the last to arrive at the table, and Sarah stood up and gave Dirk a hug before he could sit down. "I wanted to thank you again for what you did today."

"You're welcome," Dirk said. "I'm glad I could help." He returned her hug and watched as she took her place next to his father. Dirk sat, and the others around the table asked what had happened. Dirk gave them an abbreviated version of the events, and then, thankfully, the waiters came around with menus and took drink orders. Sarah ordered two bottles of wine and glasses for everyone at the table as a celebration. When the bottles came, Dirk noticed that his father took a glass, and that he looked happy. It had been a long time since Dirk had seen his father happy.

"Here's to Dirk for saving my life. Thank you, darlin'," she said with a smile, and everyone at the table raised their glasses. Dirk sipped the wine and looked over at Lee, who was grinning back at him.

"Now doesn't this make up for the rest?" Lee asked, and Dirk nodded slowly. He knew he had to let go of the fear and doubt that had been plaguing him for days. He had to stop thinking about failing. Lee wound an arm around his neck and drew him closer. "It was a wonderful thing you did."

When Lee released him, Dirk looked across the table to where his father sat, expecting a scowl or recriminating look, but his father wasn't even paying him any attention. He and Sarah were talking, and his father, the man who seemed to have time for nothing but business, was completely and totally enthralled, hanging on her every word. Dirk wasn't sure if he should be grateful for his father's distraction or not, but he decided to be happy for him regardless.

The waiters took their orders, and dinner began with a lot of conversation about what everyone had seen and done that day, as well as their plans for the next day on St. Maarten.

"You okay, Dirk?" Lee asked about halfway through the meal. "You haven't said much." The conversation around the table continued.

"I'm fine."

"You've been watching your dad through the entire meal," Lee whispered just loud enough for Dirk to hear.

"I'll tell you about it later," Dirk muttered with a nod, and Lee turned his gaze back to the table as the dinner conversation continued. Dirk paid attention and even participated, but for some reason he couldn't seem to stop watching his father. Thankfully, everyone seemed to be in a bit of a hurry, so dinner ended a bit earlier than it had the previous few evenings, and they left the dining room.

"Come with me," Lee told him, and Dirk followed him down a deck to where he could hear the beat of music. Lee pulled open the door to one of the clubs and led them inside.

Dirk saw a live band playing on a small stage, a dance floor, chairs, and a bar to one side. There weren't many people and most were just sitting around, listening and drinking. "Let's find a place to sit," Lee told him, and they filed around the edge to a table in one of the corners. "We haven't been to a club in a long time."

"Do you really think we should dance together?" Dirk asked, and Lee began to laugh.

"Look at us. We're both huge. No one will say a word," Lee said as a server approached, and Lee ordered two beers, handing the waiter his card to pay for them. "And if they do, you can growl at them." Their drinks arrived, and Lee drank part of the beer while Dirk downed his entirely. Then Lee stood up and took his hand. "Come on." He led Dirk to the floor and they began to dance.

Dirk was not particularly graceful or a very good dancer, but Lee was amazing. He might have been big, but he moved with ease, and the things he could do with his hips made Dirk's mouth go dry as he watched him, body flowing, taking Dirk along with him. He noticed a few people get up and leave the club, but Dirk also saw a number of people join them on the dance floor. Dirk let the music flow over him, trying to move like Lee, but it was no use, he couldn't, so he simply had fun.

After a while, the music slowed, and Dirk expected Lee to sit down, but instead he pulled Dirk into his arms. "This is what I've wanted all night," Lee told him as they moved together. Dirk felt Lee rest his head on his shoulder and sighed contentedly.

"This is nice," he whispered as they swayed back and forth on the dance floor. Dirk didn't know of much else to do, but Lee seemed happy, and he was more than pleased to simply sway and move to the soft music with Lee in his arms. Now this was his kind of dancing.

"So what was up with you and your dad? You were staring at him all through dinner," Lee said softly.

"You really know how to sweet talk a guy while you're dancing," Dirk teased and then became quiet for a while as he thought about what Lee had asked. "Do you think my dad is interested in Sarah?"

Lee chuckled against his skin as they continued swaying slowly. "It's possible," Lee answered, and Dirk shivered when he felt him lightly kiss his neck. "Does it bother you that he likes her?"

Dirk thought about it for a minute and actually stopped moving. "No. Should it?"

Lee began swaying once again, and Dirk followed him. "Babe, it should only matter if it matters. Your dad has been alone for a while now. I think it's kind of nice that he likes her. Who knows, he may turn out to be less of an…" Lee paused.

"Asshole," Dirk supplied, and he heard Lee chuckle.

"Yeah. I can tell you from experience that people in love are much happier, and it's easier to accept things when you're happy than when you're a miserable old codger who thinks he'll be alone for the rest of his life." Lee began to laugh. "Let's not spend our dance talking about your dad, okay?" Lee stopped moving and looked into Dirk's eyes. "Be as happy for him as you wish he was happy for us."

Dirk shook his head and began dancing again. That was his Lee, always a really nice guy. It was a huge part of the reason he loved him. Lee didn't take any of Dirk's crap, but he could also be the kindest, most understanding person Dirk had ever known, and this was obviously one of those times. "Are you ready to go back to the cabin?" Dirk asked, but Lee shook his head.

"Let's just dance for a while," Lee said before holding him a little tighter, pressing his body to Dirk's just a little bit more. "We never get to spend time together, just the two of us, with nothing to do. This is our time and what we came on vacation for," Lee reminded him as he once again rested his head on Dirk's shoulder, his warm breath blowing lightly on Dirk's neck. As they danced, Dirk hazarded a glance around the room and saw other couples dancing, and at least one of the other couples was two men. Dirk closed his eyes again and let himself go, relishing the time with Lee in his arms. Dirk placed his head on Lee's shoulder and let the scent of his lover surround him as time seemed to slip away.

The music changed again, becoming faster. Lee stepped back, and they returned to their table, where they watched the others for a little while. It became obvious that another slow set wasn't coming soon once the DJ packed the dance floor with young kids shaking everything everywhere. "I don't think I can do that," Dirk commented, his eyes widening.

"I don't think I want to," Lee agreed. "Let's go back to our cabin."

Dirk agreed, and they left the club, making their way to their cabin. "It's been quite a day," Dirk commented as he got undressed. He stepped into the bathroom to clean up and take care of business. When he came out, the bed had been turned down and Lee was lying on it naked, his massive tree trunk thighs spread for Dirk, chest muscles rippling each time he took a breath. Dirk dropped the towel he'd been carrying, his cock going from tired to throbbing in an instant. "Damn," Dirk moaned as he climbed into the bed. The lights in the room went out, but Dirk didn't need to see. He followed the trail of hot skin to Lee's lips as he pressed their chests together. Dirk knew every inch of his massively powerful lover, and while there were times when their lovemaking could be extremely athletic, today Dirk wanted quiet and reassuring. That was exactly what Lee gave him—slow, tender lovemaking that seemed to touch Dirk's soul. Lee moaned and writhed as Dirk entered him, making small sounds that seemed to echo off the cabin walls. Dirk held his lover tightly around the chest, his hips pressed to Lee's cheeks as he slowly emptied and filled his Lee. There was no one in the world Dirk loved more than this man, no one. Lee was the center of Dirk's world. He realized that now, and joined with him, Dirk felt complete, like he was where he should be.

"Roll over," Dirk whispered to Lee, and he knelt on the edge of the bed to let Lee get comfortable before slowly joining their bodies together again. Dirk loved the way Lee's warmth and tightness felt around him and there was always the urge to turn up the heat, but this time, the slowness seemed to heighten everything. There was no rush to the end, no burning need to finish. All Dirk wanted was to be with his Lee for as long as possible. Dirk leaned forward and kissed Lee's shoulder lovingly. Their bodies moved together in a gentle rhythm that bit by bit, drop by drop, to the gentle rhythm of the ship, built to a tower of passion that toppled over, crashing into both of them at the same time. Dirk came deep in Lee's body as he felt his lover fall to pieces around him. It was amazingly beautiful.

# Chapter 4

THE NEXT day, they had a great time on St. Maarten. They bought a few presents for friends back home and then spent the rest of the day lying on the beach, just the two of them. Dirk finally felt totally relaxed, and he hadn't thought about failing to rescue people, his job, or anything else except maybe how Lee had looked in that small bathing suit that clung to his hips and butt like a second skin. Come to think of it, half the beach had probably been thinking the same thing.

"So what do you have planned?" Dirk asked as he pulled on a pair of shorts after changing from their day on the island.

"Nothing. Let's go up on deck and see if we can scout out deck chairs."

"How about hitting the gym first?" Dirk asked.

"Good idea," Lee agreed, pulling out the bag, and they shoved in workout clothes before gathering the last of their things and heading for the workout area.

The gym was packed with people. Every piece of cardio equipment was in use, so after changing, they scoped out the free weights. Dirk grabbed a flat bench, and they took turns doing presses before moving on. They worked out for about an hour, pressing and pushing massive amounts of weight. Dirk spent the time he wasn't working out watching Lee's muscles work beneath his tight T-shirt. By the time they were through, Dirk ached and he was half tempted to pull Lee back to the cabin for a different kind of exercise.

"Is that your dad on the treadmill?" Lee asked as he ran a towel over the back of his neck after finishing his last set. "I didn't know he worked out."

"He doesn't," Dirk quipped, motioning toward the treadmill next to him. "I think he's either trying to impress Sarah or just keep up with her." Dirk watched his father for a few minutes and began to get concerned. "Go over and make sure he's okay." Lee looked at him like he was crazy. "He's not breathing right. He may be pushing himself too hard."

"Okay. I don't see it, but I'll check," Lee said after rolling his eyes, and he walked to where Dirk's father was walking. Lee stood near him for a few minutes and appeared to be talking to both his father and Sarah. Then he returned to where Dirk was waiting. "He's fine. Your dad didn't sound winded, but he did slow the treadmill down a little." Lee shook his head. "No matter how many names you call him or how much you fight with him, you still care for him."

"Of course I do, he's my dad," Dirk said softly as they moved toward the locker room. "He's a total asshole, but he's still my dad... and before you say it, I know I get it from him."

"As long as we're clear where your assholeness comes from," Lee told him as he pulled open the locker room door. Dirk swatted Lee's ass, and he chuckled, hurrying inside.

"I'm not an asshole," Dirk protested.

"Most of the time... anymore," Lee quipped as he opened one of the locker doors and began pulling off his sweaty clothes. "You were a real asshole when I met you, though," Lee told him. Dirk was thankful that the locker area was empty as he took another half swipe at Lee before pulling off his own clothes and then grabbing a towel from the stack. They each stepped into showers to rinse off before using the sauna.

Lee closed the sauna door behind them, and Dirk sat on one of the middle benches and leaned back as the heat surrounded him, water droplets from the earlier shower running down his chest. "Why don't you lie down and relax," Lee told him, and Dirk shifted, lying on the warm bench and closing his eyes. He heard the wood creak as Lee shifted and just the occasional ting from the heater as it cycled on and off. Dirk sort of zoned out for a while, not paying attention to anything. He didn't fall asleep, but went into a kind of daze where most of the tension left his body. Dirk opened his eyes and looked around. He'd heard the door open and close a few times, but he hadn't paid attention.

Lee must have left, and Dirk figured he'd had enough, especially with the way one of the other guys was looking at him. After leaving the sauna, he showered quickly to cool off and then pulled open the door to the steam room. He saw Lee sitting on the tile bench, so he sat next to him and looked straight into his father's eyes. "Hey, Dad," Dirk said and closed his eyes, half expecting his father's usual discourse about him and Lee, but the room remained quiet and Dirk kept his eyes closed as the steam hissed, filling and warming the small room.

"You and Sarah seem to be getting along," Lee said softly, and Dirk tried his best to keep his eyes closed and pay no attention.

"I like her," his father confessed, and Dirk got the feeling he was speaking to him. "She's bright and funny."

"You know, it's okay to like her, Dad," Dirk said. "There's nothing wrong with it at all."

For the first time Dirk could remember, he saw doubt in his father's expression. "But what about your mother?" his father asked barely above a whisper, like the question was painful.

"What about her, Dad? She's been gone three years," Dirk said, and the steam room door opened and closed. "Let's go talk somewhere," Dirk offered as the man who had entered sat down. Dirk waited to see if his father would accept or push him away. He half expected his dad to shake his head and get up and leave, but he didn't.

"Okay," he agreed, and Dirk glanced at Lee, seeing a small smile on his face.

"Then we'll meet you in the Champagne Bar in half an hour," Dirk offered, and he saw his father look at Lee and then back at him. Dirk met his gaze with one of steel. If his father wanted to talk, he could do it with both him and Lee, or he wasn't going to talk at all.

"Half an hour," his father said before lifting himself off the seat. After straightening the towel around his waist, Dirk's dad left the steam room. The other man in the room moved closer, and Dirk got up to leave as well. Lee followed, and they headed for the showers. He had half an hour to get ready to hear whatever his father had to say.

Dirk showered and dressed. He and Lee stopped off at their cabin to drop their bags before walking through the promenade to the Champagne Bar. After taking a seat in the comfortable chairs around one of the tables, they ordered drinks and waited for his father. "You're nervous, aren't you?" Lee asked as their drinks arrived.

"Yeah. We haven't talked much in years, and when we have, it's been to yell. What if this turns into another of those kinds of talks?" Dirk asked with a sigh, and when the waiter brought his beer, he took a large drink and then sat the glass on the table.

"It seemed to me like he had something on his mind," Lee commented as he sipped from his glass.

"I've thought that too, but each time it turned out what he wanted to talk about was some part of my life that he didn't like, or to tell me about something he was determined that I was going to do. Do you remember the time when we'd first met, when he tried to fix me up with the daughter of one of his clients and tried to get me to come work with him? What he does would bore me to tears, but working with him would be like hell."

"I only offered because I was scared for you," his father said from behind him, and Dirk swore under his breath as his father walked around the table and took a seat. "You're my son, and you'd just gotten out of the hospital because part of a building had collapsed under you. I was scared and I blamed you, your job, everything." His father settled in the chair, and a waiter came over. His father ordered a soda, and they waited for the server to leave. "I didn't understand or want to accept that you were gay. I kept deluding myself that you were going through some phase, but I know you weren't, and I'm sorry."

Dirk wasn't sure what he should believe, but he glanced at Lee, who nodded slightly, so Dirk decided to give his father the benefit of the doubt.

"We've been angry with each other for so long, I didn't know how to be *not* angry with you." His father paused as the waiter set down his glass and then left again. "We've been going after each other for so long, and I really want it to stop. I know that I can't and shouldn't control your life. Your job and who you love are your own business, and they should be up to you."

"Dad, I'm gay, and I love Lee. You know that isn't going to change, and I'm not going to tell you someday that I've changed my mind. Do you really believe you can accept me and Lee together? That you'll accept him as your son-in-law?" Dirk saw his father swallow before he picked up his glass once again. "Because that's what you will have to do if you want to be a part of our lives," Dirk said. "That's right, not my life, but our lives. We're together, and I'm not going to hide him from you or anyone else."

Dirk stopped. He'd placed his cards on the table, and now he had to see if his father would be part of the game or walk away from the table. "It's hard to get used to," his father began. "To see the child you raised and had so many hopes for—"

"He's still the same person," Lee said. "Every day Dirk goes to work means there are people who'll get another chance at life, because Dirk is a hero. And when he was growing up, I bet you and his mother always told each other that what was important for Dirk was for him to be happy." His father nodded. "Then let him be happy. I make him happy, and he makes me happy. We're building a good life together, and we wish you could see that."

"I think I'm starting to," his father said, and Dirk reached for his beer, taking a gulp to cover his surprise. "Love doesn't necessarily come in the package you expect; I get that now, and I realize what a fool I've been."

Dirk emptied his glass and set it on the table. "What changed your mind?"

"I guess you could say Sarah did," his father said, obviously uncomfortable. "You can see I like her. She's got this way of making everything seem fun. She even laughs at my jokes, and no one has done that since...." His father looked at the floor.

"Since Mom?" Dirk supplied.

"Yeah. There hasn't been anyone since your mom."

"That's when everything started to go to hell with us. You got all absorbed in your work and started getting preachy," Dirk reminded him, the pieces he'd been overlooking for years falling into place.

"I threw myself into what I had left," his father explained. "But that's not it, either. I've been alone and miserable, and I've taken most of that out on you."

"You know, it's okay to move on with your life. I'm actually happy that you might have found someone who interests you." Dirk smiled, and it was his father's turn to look surprised.

"You aren't mad?" he asked.

"No. There's one thing being with Lee has taught me, and that is everyone deserves to find love, even a couple of assholes like us." Dirk actually saw his father smile slightly. "I get the feeling that we aren't so much talking about how you think I might feel, but rather how you feel about her. She's a nice lady, and you really seem to like her. I think Mom would approve of you moving on with your life, so what's the problem?" Dirk motioned the waiter over and ordered another beer for both him and Lee. He figured they were going to need them.

"Well," his father said nervously, and for a second Dirk tried to think of the last time he'd ever seen his father nervous or unsure of himself. "Damn the torpedoes" was more his speed. "I really like her, but Sarah isn't like your mother. She has her own job and…." Dirk wanted to interrupt, but he kept quiet and let his father finish what he wanted to say. "Sarah has her own very definite ideas about things, and I'm not sure they fit with mine."

"What? Is she a Democrat?" Dirk teased, knowing his father's political leanings.

"Well, yes, but that isn't it. She's so different from your mother. She has her own career and her own business. She's very successful, and she doesn't believe in some of the more traditional types of things I do." Dirk waited for his father to get to the point.

Dirk's father shook his head and huffed softly. "She's Jewish," he said, looking extremely uncomfortable.

"So?" Dirk challenged. "What the hell does that matter? Do you care for her, or is this some shipboard thing that you want to write off when you get off the ship?" Maybe his father really was a supreme asshole.

His father shook his head, clearly a bit shocked.

Dirk scooted to the edge of his chair. "Anyone you let into your life is going to require change on your part. They'll have their own likes and dislikes, and they won't be the same as Mom's or yours, and yes, they may have their own religion. But that doesn't mean they're wrong—just different. You have to decide if she's worth changing your life for." Dirk looked at Lee, who was grinning at him. "Lee was for me. It took me time to see that at first, but I know it now, and I'd do anything for him."

"But, son, you're young. I'm old and set in my ways," his father protested, and Dirk grinned.

"You're not too old to fall in love, and the religion of the person you care for is no big deal. I don't know what you and Sarah have talked about for after the cruise, and what happens then is for the two of you to decide. But do what you think will make you happy. And maybe a little chaos and excitement in your life will do that. It certainly won't hurt to have your horizons broadened."

"You're really okay with this?" his father asked before rising from his chair.

"I only want you to be happy, Dad," Dirk said. He watched as his father walked toward the entrance to the bar. "We'll see you at dinner tonight." Dirk's father nodded, and as soon as he was gone, Dirk collapsed back into his chair. "That was not a conversation I ever expected to have with my father. What the hell happened to him?"

Lee chuckled softly. "I think he's in love and as confused as any other man in love. God, I know you confused the hell out of me when we first met. I also think those feelings might have opened his eyes and maybe his heart just a little." Lee lifted his glass and drank the last of the beer before setting the empty glass on the table. "I think maybe we'd better get some food in our stomachs."

Dirk got up as well. "I wasn't planning on drinking this early in the evening, but I think I needed it."

"We both did," Lee agreed, and after leaving the bar, they headed to the elevators for a ride up to the buffet.

THE NEXT few days were unbelievable. He and Lee did everything they'd ever wanted to do on a ship at least twice: rock climbing, basketball, dodge ball, ice skating, everything the ship offered. They watched shows and spent time on the pool deck and in the whirlpools. But tonight was their last dinner on the cruise, and tomorrow he and Lee would head home. There was something bittersweet about the end of the vacation. Truthfully, Dirk was ready to go home, but he didn't want to leave the fun behind, either.

"Let's get ready for dinner, and then after we eat I'll make you forget everything for the rest of the night," Lee said as he moved closer to him in the cabin, and Dirk forgot all about buckling his belt. "It may be our last evening on board, but that doesn't mean we can't make it memorable." Lee leaned closer, licking the base of Dirk's neck. "You know, I could suck a mark right here," Lee mumbled, and Dirk stretched his neck as Lee licked and sucked the spot at the base of his shoulder. "You can think about that for later." Lee lifted his mouth from his neck and kissed him hard.

"I love you," Dirk said once their kiss had ended. "I know I don't say that often enough, but I do." Dirk tugged Lee into a hug. "I don't know what I'd do without you."

Lee hugged him right back. "I'm right with you. You may be a pain in the ass on occasion, but you're my pain in the ass, and I love you too." Lee squeezed him once and then released him. "Now we'd better get to dinner or we never will." They finished getting dressed before leaving the cabin and heading to the dining room. The others were already at the table by the time they arrived, and Dirk noticed everyone looking at his neck and then sharing looks.

"I think we all know why you were late," Cindy said, to her husband's chagrin. But obviously she was only saying what everyone else was thinking, judging by the looks the couples shared with each other.

Lee snickered and bumped his shoulder, but neither of them said a word. Let everyone think what they wanted. Dirk felt happy and lighter than he had in a long time. "Did everyone have a good day?" Dirk asked, and the conversation went around the table with everyone telling what they'd done.

"We spent the day on the pool deck," Sarah said when it was her turn, looking happily at Dirk's father, who actually took a second to smile at Dirk. He wasn't willing to hope that everything had changed between them so quickly, but it was a start, and Dirk would give things with his dad another chance.

Animated conversation seemed to be the order of the day throughout dinner. Dirk had expected it to be somewhat subdued with the cruise drawing to a close, but it wasn't. The excitement about their various adventures during the trip continued through the entire meal, and when the meal was over, everyone exchanged handshakes and hugs before leaving the dining room. He and Lee even made plans to meet Vince and Cindy for dinner in the coming weeks once they found out they lived on the other side of Harrisburg.

After they left the dining room, Dirk and Lee strolled along the promenade, taking a final look inside the shops. "Would you like to have a drink before going to the cabin?" Lee asked, and Dirk shook his head.

"If you'd like one, we can stop," Dirk offered, but Lee kept moving. People appeared to be lining up on either side, so they hurried on through. It looked like they were getting ready for a parade, so Dirk and Lee picked up the pace, taking the stairs to their deck as they heard the music starting. Dirk had no interest in the parade. In fact, the only thing he was interested in right now was Lee.

At their door, he slid his card in the lock. The unlock light turned green, and they entered, then Lee pressed him against the door as soon as it clicked closed. Dirk couldn't move at all with Lee's huge wall of muscle in front of him and the door pressing to his back, but there was nowhere on earth he'd rather have been right then. The sensation from Lee's kisses exploded in Dirk's brain. Dirk managed to wrap his arms around Lee's neck, and he was lifted off his feet. Lee walked backward through the cabin to the bed, carrying him the entire way. As soon as there was room, Dirk wrapped his legs around Lee's waist, and he felt Lee's powerful hands on his butt. Their lips didn't part as Lee lowered him to the bed, and when they did, both of them gasped for air.

Lee pulled off his shirt, then shucked his pants and shoes in record time. Wearing only a pair of black briefs, Lee tugged off Dirk's clothes, practically ripping his underwear from his body. "Up on the bed, legs spread apart," Lee growled as he heaved a breath. "I promised you'd forget everything and you will."

Dirk scooted until his head reached the pillows, his gaze never leaving Lee's smoldering eyes. Dirk waited, not moving, but he could feel Lee's gaze burning onto his skin. Dirk swallowed, wondering what Lee was planning. He actually jumped slightly when Lee laid his hands on his ankles. Slowly, Lee stroked up his calves and thighs. Dirk closed his eyes, holding his breath as Lee got closer to his throbbing cock. But he never touched it, skimming along his hips and then up his stomach and chest, stopping just long enough to pluck his nipples before moving on.

Lee caressed along the side of his neck and up his cheek before gliding his fingers over Dirk's lips. Dirk opened his mouth, and Lee slid two fingers inside, Lee's rich flavor tingling on his tongue. "You're a beautiful man, Dirk," Lee told him before swiping his tongue over his left nipple. "And I'm going to show you just how much I love you."

Lee slowly pulled his fingers away, brushing them along Dirk's lips before taking his mouth in a kiss that stole Dirk's breath. Dirk wrapped his arms around Lee's back, hugging him close as their kiss went on and on. Their legs entwined, and Dirk stroked down Lee's back, sliding his hands into his lover's briefs, cupping his rock-hard butt. Dirk heard Lee moan softly into their kiss, and he followed suit as he felt Lee wrap his hand around his cock, squeezing tightly. Without thinking, Dirk thrust into the tight grip, wanting more, but Lee gripped him tighter, not allowing his cock to move.

"You can touch me all you want, but you can't touch yourself. I'm in charge of your body tonight," Lee told him, and Dirk nodded. "You can ask for what you want, but you can't take it." Dirk swallowed and nodded again. "Good. Now roll over, because I'm going to eat that hot ass of yours until you beg me to stop."

Dirk shook with anticipation as he complied with Lee's instruction. "Like this?" Dirk asked, and Lee lightly tugged on his hips.

"That's it, butt in the air," Lee said as he stroked Dirk's skin, skimming his thumbs over Dirk's opening. Damn, that felt hot and good. Dirk loved when Lee touched him there, but he was the only person he'd ever trusted enough to be this open with. "I love how your tight hole throbs for me." Lee ran his tongue over Dirk's sensitive skin, and he groaned both because of the sensation and as a way of begging for more. "I know what you want, and I'm going to give it to you, but only when I'm ready."

"Damn, Lee, you can be mean," Dirk fake-groused, and Lee skimmed his opening with his fingers, circling the delicate skin. Dirk pushed his butt backward, trying to get a little more sensation, but Lee was in complete control, and all Dirk could do was moan softly and wait, the anticipation driving him wild.

"Not mean," Lee corrected, spreading Dirk's cheeks wide before blowing on his wet skin, making his skin and muscles throb and ache. "Loving on you deep and long," Lee told him before licking his tongue over Dirk's skin. Dirk tried not to whine and moan like some little hussy, but he couldn't stop himself. In minutes, as he always seemed to, Lee had turned him from a strong man into a completely wanton hedonist. His entire body shook as Lee continued his relentless assault with his tongue, probing, licking, sucking—whatever Lee was doing to him made Dirk's blood boil.

Lee gripped his cheeks before probing his opening deep and hard. Dirk arched his back, thrusting himself backward in an attempt to get Lee to go deeper. "Good God!" Dirk swore breathlessly as his legs began to give out. Lee's attentions stopped, and Dirk stilled, waiting to see what was next, wondering how he was going to be able to stand it. Dirk gasped as he felt Lee stroke along his throbbing length. Then Lee swirled his tongue around Dirk's opening before trailing his tongue over his balls and down his shaft, sucking the head lightly before making the return trip. Dirk gripped the pillow he was resting his head on, giving up the last semblance of control. He knew he was moaning steadily, but he didn't care. Lee made him feel so damned good.

Dirk felt Lee breach him with a finger, and he wriggled his ass for more. "I know you want more, but you need to wait a minute," Lee told him, stroking his cheeks after the finger slipped away. "Roll onto your back," Lee told him, and Dirk turned over, gazing at Lee as he prowled onto the bed. Lee spread Dirk's legs with his knees, and Dirk watched as Lee grabbed the bottle of lube from the drawer in the bedside table. There was a soft snick, and then Dirk saw Lee coat his fingers before teasing them into his opening. Dirk hissed softly at the slight stretch as Lee scissored his fingers inside him. "You're hot as hell, you know that," Lee said. Leaving his fingers deep inside Dirk's body, Lee kissed him hard, probing Dirk's mouth with his tongue as he probed his ass with his fingers. "What do you want, Dirk?"

His head spun, and he tried to form an answer. Lee hadn't even removed his briefs and Dirk was already about to explode.

"You want me to fuck you? Spread you wide on my thick cock and make you ride me until you can't stand it anymore?"

"That," Dirk gasped as Lee twisted his fingers inside him. He could barely think and Lee actually wanted him to talk. Lee shimmied out of his briefs using one hand, keeping his fingers within Dirk's body. After a twisting motion that had Dirk's head throbbing, Lee pulled out his fingers and got into position. Dirk met Lee's gaze as his lover slowly pressed into his body, stretching him almost beyond belief. "Fuck...," Dirk hissed as Lee went deeper and deeper. He didn't stop, and Dirk panted as he was stretched and stretched. Dirk's head throbbed and he clutched at the sheets, every muscle clenching as he tried to keep from being totally overwhelmed.

"I know," Lee soothed as he sank further, his hips settling against Dirk's ass. Then and only then could Dirk breathe. He wanted to swear and curse, but he didn't have the energy. Muscles throughout his body spasmed, and he tried to control them. He'd just managed a start when Lee slowly pulled out, and Dirk's head went in a million different directions all over again.

Slowly, Dirk regulated his breathing as Lee moved inside him. He saw him shift, and then Lee was kissing him again, snapping his hips in small movements that massaged the spot in his passage over and over again. Lee seemed to know just how to touch him, both inside and out. After another sloppy kiss, Lee loomed over him, thrusting deeply as his slicked hand wrapped around Dirk's cock. Dirk moved with Lee, meeting his thrusts. "That's it," Lee said, and Dirk felt him still, "thrust into my hand."

Dirk did, and Lee tightened his grip. His cock slipped out slightly, and when he relaxed, Lee went deeper. Damn, he wasn't sure what he liked best, but he kept thrusting, fucking Lee's hand as he fucked himself on Lee's cock. Harder and harder, faster and faster, Dirk closed his eyes and let instinct take over. Each movement felt so good he could barely think what to do next. "Not gonna last," Dirk warned, and Lee gripped him tighter.

"Don't, come for me. I want you to come on my cock and pull me right along with you."

Fuck, that was hot, and Dirk let go, but he wasn't quite there. He could feel Lee throbbing inside him and he needed just a bit more pressure. Lee swiped his thumb over the head of his cock, and Dirk was almost there. Lee did it again, and Dirk notched higher and higher until he could no longer take it. Clamping his eyes closed, holding his breath, Dirk came in a blinding flash that sent him spiraling into an orgasm he hoped he never recovered from.

Dirk floated on a cloud of endorphin-fueled magic. He heard and felt Lee as he came, and then he was surrounded in a blanket of warmth. Slowly, the clouds and fog that surrounded him abated, and he held Lee tight, kissing his lover tenderly as he waited for his brain to begin working again. After a while, how long Dirk couldn't say, Lee got up and then returned with a towel that he used to clean them both. Then the lights snapped off and Lee climbed back into bed, holding him. Neither of them talked or did anything other than be together for a few moments as the ship slowly rocked back and forth. "Love you," Lee whispered, and Dirk echoed his sentiment as sleep overtook him.

THE FOLLOWING morning was a mad rush. They got up early and headed to the buffet for breakfast before meeting at their designated location. When their group was called, they lined up and filed off the ship, getting their SeaPass card scanned for the last time. Once down the ramps and in the terminal, he and Lee spent the next half hour in line for customs and immigration before getting their luggage and heading out for the bus ride to the airport.

The walk along the pier beside the ship was definitely bittersweet. At the bus, Dirk handed over their bags for the driver to load. Lee got on the bus, and Dirk took one last look around.

"Son," he heard from behind him and saw his father wheeling his bag toward him. Dirk took his father's suitcase and gave it to the driver. "I want to thank you for listening the other day. You were right about a lot of things." Dirk knew that for his father, this was definitely uncharted territory. "Sarah lives in Chambersburg, and she and I have decided to continue seeing one another. I don't know where this could lead, but we both want to give it a chance."

"That's good, Dad," Dirk said with a smile, nodding slowly. "I hope you make each other very happy." Dirk turned to get on the bus, but stopped when he felt a hand on his shoulder.

"Do you think it's too late for you and me?" his father asked quietly.

"Dad, it's never too late as long as you accept that having me in your life includes Lee," Dirk answered honestly.

"I know that. It was obvious to everyone who saw you how you feel about one another, and I would have seen that a long time ago if I'd have allowed myself to," his father told him, and Dirk smiled before turning to get on the bus.

He found Lee toward the middle and slid into the seat next to him. "Did you talk?" Lee asked.

"Yeah, and things may be different. We'll have to see," Dirk said hopefully as he watched his father talking with both Karl and Sarah. All three of them got on the bus, and his father moved past him with a smile. Once the bus was full, the driver pulled out and they headed back the way they'd come a week earlier.

"I think I'm going to make an appointment with the department psychologist," Dirk told Lee. "I want to talk over some of what I'm feeling. The vacation was good, but I need to deal with it." He'd been burying things like this for years, and maybe it was catching up with him. He needed to find out and deal with it, and not just for himself, but for Lee too.

"I'll go with you if you need me to," Lee told him, and Dirk smiled, because he'd never doubted that for a second. Dirk bumped Lee's shoulder and settled back in his seat as they rode the rest of the way to the airport.

# Epilogue

IT WAS good to be home. Their flights had been on time, and they'd arrived home as the sun was setting. There had been a message from the captain to call the station when they got in, so after unloading the bags, Lee began unpacking while Dirk called the station.

"Dirk," the captain said, sounding happy. "Did you and Lee make it back in one piece?"

"Yeah. He and I had a good time. We'll both be in for our shifts tomorrow," Dirk said as he watched Lee move through their bedroom, throwing the dirty clothes in a basket and then putting the clean clothes away.

"Is there any chance you could come in for a few hours? We're really understaffed right now. Some of the guys are down with the flu."

"Give us an hour," Dirk told him before hanging up the phone and turning to Lee. "Looks like the vacation's over. Captain says they're really shorthanded and asked if we could come in for a few hours."

Lee didn't look too happy. "Will you get extra clothes together? I'll finish putting this away so we can come home to a clean house." Lee was already moving faster, carrying the basket down the stairs. Dirk got everything into the car, and they arrived at the station with time to spare. They parked and unloaded their gear, greeting everyone as they carried it inside.

"It's about time you got back," one of the guys teased as they put the gear away and settled at the table after signing in and poking their heads into the captain's office.

"What'd we miss?" Lee asked, and the stories started. They were just getting to the part where one of the newbies lost control of a hose when the call bell sounded. Dirk hurried to get into his gear, with Lee right behind him.

"Welcome home," Dirk told him, and Lee grinned.

"You ready to save some lives?"

"You betcha," Dirk answered without hesitation. Leaning over, he kissed Lee quickly before pulling on his helmet and heading for the truck, with Lee—his lover, partner, and the man he knew always had his back—right behind him.

# HEAT UNDER FIRE

## FIRE

# Chapter 1

CARS PASSED by again and again, twenty-five, twenty-seven, thirty-two miles per hour. God, he hated traffic duty with a passion. Justin Briggs reached absentmindedly for the cup of coffee in the console. He had to do something to stay awake. The speed limit was thirty, and his job was to make sure that people drove sanely and carefully where South Hanover Street narrowed from four lanes to two.

The Borough of Carlisle had gone on a "road diet" a few years ago and narrowed both main streets through town to one lane each way. The purpose was to try to slow traffic, reduce trucks coming through town, and add bike lanes. While it had done all that, it had also created a drag-race scenario where the road narrowed, and the chief was determined to nab the offenders, especially since his wife had been involved in an accident a few weeks earlier right in front of where Justin was sitting in his cruiser.

So, here he was, babysitting the chief's new pet peeve and watching car after car pass by just below the speed limit. Granted, he was parked in the ambulance garage parking lot, where he could clearly be seen. The chief wasn't as interested in giving out tickets as he was in making sure drivers slowed down and stopped acting like idiots on the roads of their town.

Justin, on the other hand, would have liked nothing more than to give out a few tickets just to alleviate the boredom. He'd been sitting here for days, spending his entire shift watching cars pass, burning gas to keep the air-conditioning going. He tried not to fall asleep, but it was getting harder and harder.

He heard the car before he saw it—the low rumble of a gunned engine. Justin pointed his radar gun at the oncoming car, but the guy barely slowed even once he clearly saw Justin's vehicle. The white Charger weaved around a slower vehicle right in front of Justin. He flipped on his lights, sounded the siren, and took off. Cars got out of his way as he chased the other car through town. The idiot made no effort to slow and just kept going. Justin called in for backup, keeping the other vehicle in sight. Finally, the idiot pulled off, and Justin slowed behind the vehicle, waiting for another patrol car to show. Once it did, Justin slowly approached the car. The driver's window lowered, and a pair of huge blue eyes surrounded by long blonde hair batted up at him. "I'm sorry, Officer," she tittered. "I was listening to my music and got all caught up."

"License, proof of insurance, and registration please, ma'am," Justin said, keeping his attitude all business.

"Of course," she said, still batting her eyes. She reached into her purse, and Justin tensed until she pulled out her wallet. She handed him her driver's license and then leaned over to the glove box, making sure her endowments were on clear display. Justin paid no attention—she didn't have anything he wanted to see. He took the registration once she handed it over and then walked back to his car.

"Everything okay?" Marty asked as he walked over from the other car.

"Yes. Just a blond bunny who thinks she can do what she wants then bat her eyelashes and shake her boobs to get out of it," Justin said.

"You gonna let her?" Marty asked.

"Heck, no. She can shake her boobs at the judge if she tries to fight the ticket," Justin said, opening his car door so he could run her information.

"I'd let her off if she was clean otherwise," Marty said.

"Yeah." Justin smiled. "But you think with your dick." He punched up the program on his laptop and scanned the barcode on her license—Brenda Patterson—before letting the computer do its thing.

"Like you don't," Marty said from outside the car, and Justin nodded his agreement, because that was easier than getting drawn into a discussion of how what Brenda was displaying didn't do the least bit for him. It wasn't like he was deep in the closet or anything; he just never talked about his sex life at work. Hell, he didn't talk about his personal life at all if he could help it. He figured it was safer that way. Justin didn't like lying or deception of any kind. His entire life was built on openness and honesty. He'd had enough deception and tricks growing up, and he didn't need or want them now.

His computer returned the results that Brenda had a clean driving record. Somehow, Justin doubted that greatly, and he pulled out his book of citations and began filling one out. "I don't think you need to stay around," he told Marty. Justin could tell the other officer was itching to get a closer look at the bombshell in the Charger, but he banged on the car door.

"Okay, but I'll keep an ear to the radio in case you need backup." Marty winked and then moved away from the patrol car.

Justin finished making out the citations and then got out of his car, following standard procedure to keep an eye on everything and everyone. As he approached the car, he saw Brenda once again smiling and batting her eyelashes at him—that is, until he handed her the ticket. Then she scowled and narrowed her eyes. The woman went from Barbie to harpy in the blink of an eye. Justin ignored her scowl and mutters, explaining all the information.

"Ma'am, you broke the law and endangered other drivers and pedestrians along the way. Now, I suggest you slow down and take your time." Justin backed away from the car. "Drive safely," he added before heading back to his cruiser. Inside, he made a series of notes in his book and then turned out his lights and drove back to his post for a few more hours of watching cars go by. He parked and set up the gun again before settling back in his seat and radioing in that he was back on station.

About an hour later, a speeding car heading out of town caught Justin's attention, and he flipped on his lights and pulled out to follow the car. He'd just gotten behind the driver and was about to radio in the call when a long screech, like nails on a blackboard, crawled up his spine. Justin looked up from the car in front of him and saw a school bus facing him on the freeway overpass. It took him a second to realize the bus was hanging over the edge of the overpass, and by then, he'd already disengaged from the speeder, who had sped up again and was heading up onto the freeway.

"Bus accident on I-81 South," Justin radioed in. "Don't know number of people involved. Need emergency services. Bus hanging over overpass, need South Hanover closed both ways. On my way to assist at the scene." Traffic was already stopping on the surface streets. Justin needed to get up to the freeway, but the lane to the on-ramp was clogged, so he went up an off-ramp and turned so he went the wrong way down the freeway shoulder, siren and lights blaring so he could get to the bus.

It was teetering on the edge, and as soon as he stopped his car and got out, he could hear children on the bus, screaming. Cars on the highway were slowing, and Justin got the first cars to hold. He knew he was backing things up, but he needed to help those kids. "Stay there," he told the drivers, and they held still, effectively closing the freeway. The bus screeched, and Justin saw it move slightly.

"It's all right, kids," Justin yelled, and the screaming subsided. "I want you all to slowly move to the back of the bus. Don't move fast or suddenly, but slowly walk to the back of the bus." He saw the kids begin to move inside and heard sirens approaching from what seemed like all directions, but he kept his eyes on the kids. "That's it. Keep walking slowly," Justin encouraged as the back wheels of the bus settled back down onto the pavement. "Good, now all of you stay where you are. We're going to get you out, but it will take a few minutes. No one move," Justin said. "Is the driver with you?" he asked the kids through an open window.

"No," a small kid about seven answered. "He's in his seat with red stuff all over him."

"That's blood," one of the other kids said, and a few of the kids began to cry.

"It's okay, you're going to be all right. We're going to help you, and then we'll get the driver out too. I promise," Justin said, trying anything he could to calm them down. Other emergency vehicles arrived, and Justin continued working to keep the children calm. "Is anyone hurt besides the driver?" Justin asked.

"I hit my knee," one little boy said.

"I hit my head."

"My arm hurts."

"Is anyone bleeding?" All the kids he could see shook their heads. "Is anyone else bleeding?"

"Timmy's hiding under the seat," one girl said.

"Make sure he's okay," Justin said, and he waited a few seconds as the girl's ponytailed head disappeared.

"He's just scared," she reported. "He told me so."

"Very good. Please don't move around, and we'll get you all out as fast as we can," Justin said, then turned around to the gathering group of vehicles.

"How many are hurt?" Rockland Sparks asked him, and for a brief second Justin's composure failed him. *Damn, why did he have to be the one who responded?* Every time the EMT was around, Justin got completely tongue-tied. Rock, as everyone called him, was just that: built solid, with arms that stretched his shirt sleeves. Justin swallowed and opened his mouth to respond, hoping like hell some sort of sound came out.

"The driver," Justin said, closing his eyes for a brief moment to clear his head and moisten his dry mouth. "The children seem to be okay. A few got banged up a bit, but they say they're okay for the most part."

"What's the status?" the chief asked gruffly from behind him.

Justin turned away from Rock to face the chief, wondering which man made him more nervous. "When I arrived on the scene, the bus was teetering on the edge. I got the children to all move to the back, and the bus has stabilized for the moment. The driver is injured, but the bus is too unstable to get inside, and if we take the children out, the weight will shift and the bus will go over the edge," Justin reported quickly, still a bit in awe of the chief and desperately wanting to do good and be noticed.

"Any fuel leaking?" the chief asked.

"I smelled nothing when I was by the bus," Justin answered as still more sirens sounded and additional fire trucks and a massive tow truck arrived.

"Good. Keep the kids settled," he said, and then he hurried away. Justin saw him consult with the various chiefs. Justin hurried back to the bus with Rock just behind him. Great, just what he needed—tongue-tied and dry-mouthed. Taking a deep breath, he put it out of his mind and focused on the task at hand.

"We're going to get you out really soon," Justin told the kids. "Just sit still and everything will be fine."

Rock walked as close to the front of the bus as he could, peering into what was left of one of the driver's windows. He looked for a few minutes and then turned back to Justin, the expression on his face saying everything. The driver was most likely dead already. Justin and Rock continued talking to the kids, and eventually Justin heard the beep, beep, beep of a truck as it backed up.

"We're going to hook the tow truck to the bus to stabilize it so we can get the kids out, then we'll pull it back onto the road," the chief said from behind him. "You're doing great," he added and then left again.

"What's happening?" one of the kids asked as the tow truck got closer.

"We're going to get you out real soon—stay where you are," Justin said, and he heard Rock telling the kids the same thing from the other side of the bus. The beeping got louder and then stopped. Men got out of the huge truck and lowered a cable from the winch on the back. One of the men walked it to the bus and took a few minutes to attach it to the frame. Then a second cable was lowered and attached. "Okay, tighten them," the one man called, and the lines were tightened. The bus began to move, and the kids screamed inside.

"Stop!" the operator called and the winch went silent.

"Okay, get those kids out. The concrete of the overpass railing is starting to go," the chief said, and Justin opened the back door of the bus, reached for the first child, and lifted a little girl in a pink dress to the ground. As soon as her feet touched the road, she burst into tears, and an emergency worker led her away.

Justin was already reaching for the next child when the bus shuddered and scraped. He lowered another girl and reached for the little boy after her. "Go to the ambulance," he told each one, not waiting for the emergency workers any longer. He had to get these kids out of there.

"Just hand the kids to me," Rock said from next to him, so Justin lifted the kids out of the bus and handed them to Rock, who got them away from the bus. Kid after kid came out. Justin's arms burned, but he kept working. Finally, the last one appeared in the door, and Justin lifted him down.

"Anyone else in there?" Justin called, looking down the right and then the left row of seats. He saw nothing and was about to move away when he heard a small cry. "There's someone in there," Justin said, and he was about to climb inside when Rock stopped him. "Someone has to go—you're too big," Justin told Rock.

"Get a rope," Rock called, and one of the firemen, a huge guy who looked like he was about to bust out of his uniform, hurried over. "Lee, fasten it around his waist. That way, if the bus starts to go, we can hopefully pull him out."

"Okay," Lee said, and he fastened the heavy rope around Justin's waist.

"Be careful, and no sudden moves," Rock said as Justin slowly climbed up into the bus.

The nearly empty shell creaked and groaned with each movement, and as Justin got closer to the front, he could almost feel the tension the tow-truck cables were under. It seemed to run right though his body. "Where are you?" All Justin heard was a low whimper, and he followed the sound. Seat by seat he got closer to the front, and the floor under him moved a little more. "Please talk to me."

"Here," a small voice said, and then Justin heard crying.

"Can you move? If you can, stand up and slowly walk toward me."

"I can't," the child said and then began to cry again. Justin felt the floor move under his feet and knew he was reaching the bus's pivot point. His weight was going to start to shift the bus, but he had to continue, one row of seats and then another, the bus creaking ominously with each step.

"Are you okay?" Rock asked from behind him. "We have you," he added, and Justin nodded, his throat completely dry. He took another step and reached the third seat. A small boy of about five or so clutched the seat behind him, his legs encased in braces.

"You're going to be okay," Justin said as he reached for the little boy.

"My crutches went over there," he said and pointed to the well by the front door.

"We'll get them later," Justin said, lifting the featherlight kid into his arms. He turned and slowly retraced his steps toward the back.

"Mama will be mad if I lose them," the boy said in a small voice as the bus began to shift under their feet.

"Hurry," Rock cried. "The overpass railing isn't going to last much longer." The bus moved and shifted violently. Justin felt the rope around his waist pull tight, and he began to run, clutching the boy in his arms. The bus began shifting sideways and Justin wondered how much longer the cables could hold. "The tow truck is being pulled," Rock shouted, and Justin kept going as fast as he could, climbing uphill as the bus tipped forward still more. Justin reached the door as the bus moved further. Without thinking, he jumped and hit the pavement, letting his legs buckle and using his body to shield the boy as they rolled. Someone lifted the kid from his arms, and then Rock lifted Justin off the concrete and moved toward safer ground. Justin heard a whir and looked up as the winch released its tension. The concrete railing gave way, and the bus tumbled over the precipice in a crash and rumble that felt like it shook the entire world.

"Did everyone get out?" Justin asked before leaning his head against Rock's chest and closing his eyes.

"Yes," Rock said. Justin's eyes got heavy and he closed them. The last thing he remembered was Rock holding him tight. Everything else blurred and then went dark.

Justin woke a few minutes later resting on something much softer than the concrete. He opened his eyes and stared into Rock's eyes. He opened his mouth to speak, but nothing came out. Just the impression he wanted to make on the man who filled his dreams.

"It's all right," Rock told him in a rich, resonant voice that went through Justin like a hot knife through butter. God, he wanted to listen to that voice for the rest of his life. "You got pretty scraped up and bruised, but you're going to be fine."

"Then…," he began, finally finding his voice again. "Then why did I pass out?" Justin lifted his head and the world stayed in one place.

"Stress. It happens sometimes," Rock explained, and then he helped him up. "You're going to be fine, and so are all the kids you got off that bus before it tumbled off the overpass."

Justin looked around at the kids standing together. "What about them?"

"We're transporting them to the elementary school, where their parents are waiting for them," the chief said as he appeared at Justin's side.

"Sorry, sir," Justin said as he stood up, making sure everything was working.

"Nothing to be sorry for," the chief said. "Now, if you're done lying down on the job"—he winked at him. *The chief actually winked*—"we could use your help transporting the kids to the school."

"Sure," Justin said, and the chief walked away. "Thank you for everything," Justin stammered to Rock. "Umm, I have to get back to work." God, he was such an idiot. It always worked out this way. Every time he saw a guy he might be interested in, he stammered and sounded like a moron. "I'll see you," Justin said and hurried away. The kids were being loaded into squad cars, and Justin helped three of them into the backseat of his patrol car. Once he made sure they were belted in, he slowly drove off the freeway and down the ramp.

"Can you put on the siren?" one of the boys asked.

"I will when we get to the school," Justin answered, and that seemed to satisfy the boy. He drove through town and pulled up to the elementary school, where a group of parents were waiting. He turned on the lights and siren and pulled up to the group, then turned everything off again and let the kids get out. The children were immediately engulfed in their parents' arms, with plenty of crying, more hugging, and then some more crying. Another car pulled up and more kids got out. After more hugs, the families drifted away, many thanking him for his help before departing.

The other police cars left, and soon it was just Justin and one extremely nervous family. "He's going to be fine. They said he was fine. Just a scrape," the man said as he held his wife. "Marky is going to be fine."

"I know," she said, "but what if he hadn't been able to get off the bus?" She blew her nose in a tissue. "He can't walk on his own very well." She buried her head in her husband's shoulder. Justin was about to say something to them, but an ambulance pulled into the drive and stopped near them. Rock got out and walked around to the back. When he reappeared, he was carrying the last little boy Justin had just gotten out of the bus.

"Marky," the woman cried, rushing forward. Rock set him on his feet, but she scooped the boy into her arms. "I was so scared." She rocked him back and forth as she hugged him.

"I'm okay, Mommy," he said, and she stopped. "That man saved me." He pointed at Justin. "He jumped out of the bus just before it fell, boom! Then we falled, but I'm okay—he says so." Marky pointed at Rock, who smiled.

"You saved my son?" the woman asked, and without waiting for an answer, she hugged the stuffing out of Justin. "You saved him."

"It's okay, Jane," her husband said gently, and she transferred her hug to him.

"Don't be sad, Mommy. I'm okay. I lost my crutches, though. They went boom in the bus," Marky said. His mother laughed through the tears and hugged him again.

"We'll get you new crutches and new anything else you want, as long as you're okay," she said. "Thank you, thank you both for saving my son." She was crying again, and Justin felt his throat constrict. The woman carried her son toward the car with her husband behind her. Marky leaned over her shoulder, waving to both of them before they bundled him into the backseat. Justin watched as they drove away.

"That's why I became a cop," Justin said softly. "Not to watch traffic, but for times like that." Justin took a deep breath and turned to Rock after checking his watch. He was officially off duty, and he wanted to ask Rock if he might like to grab a bite to eat or something. The hours he'd spent at the accident scene had felt like a few minutes. But now that he was away from the chaos and things had slowed down, he was starved. Justin caught Rock's gaze, and he was sure the other man was looking at him with interest. Maybe if he just asked him, he'd say yes. Justin was about to say something when his mouth and throat went completely dry. He tried to speak, but he knew he must have looked like a ridiculous largemouth bass in a police uniform when nothing at all came out. He tried again, but now he was so nervous and flustered he couldn't stand it. He'd been able to talk to Rock before, but that was about work and stuff, and he hadn't thought about it. Now that he wanted to ask him to go to dinner, nothing seemed to work and he felt like an idiot. Trying to leave some of his dignity intact, if that was possible, Justin walked hurriedly toward his car, making a hasty retreat.

JUSTIN CLOSED the door and tossed his keys on the table before removing his equipment belt. His entire body felt lighter as soon as he unsnapped the heavy belt. He rarely noticed the extra fifteen pounds or so he carried until he took it all off. The vest came next, and he held his arms away from his body, letting his skin breathe. He wanted to sink into a chair and do nothing, but his equipment had to be taken care of. He went through his routine to see it was all cleaned and properly put away and cared for before wandering into the kitchen. He lived in a small apartment above an antique store downtown. He loved the old building. It had character, and his landlords had been thrilled to have him move in. It seemed their last tenant had been difficult, and they'd had to evict him. Justin refused to let his thoughts wander all over the place, and his stomach brought his attention to dinner.

In the kitchen, Justin reheated a quick dinner—spaghetti with meat sauce he'd made on his last day off—and settled in front of the television to try to forget his idiocy. He couldn't understand it. He could talk to anyone in the course of his job. He had no problem there, but in a personal situation with someone he was interested in, he clammed up, his heart raced, and his voice completely escaped him. It truly sucked, and it didn't only happen with Rock. When he'd been in college and first started to explore being gay, instead of having fun, he'd ended up a monk because he couldn't talk to guys who interested him. Soon he'd given up altogether and concentrated on his schoolwork and training, which served him well because he'd been able to snag the one rookie opening the Carlisle police had had in three years.

"Fuck," Justin grumbled as he slumped in his living room chair. He'd been able to talk to Rock when they were working together, and he'd thought that his problem might actually have gone away. No such luck—as soon as he'd thought Rock might be interested and decided to try to talk to him about it, everything had gone to hell. Maybe he was meant to be alone.

His buzzer sounded, indicating that someone was down at the door to see him. Justin never had visitors, and it took him a few seconds to realize what he was hearing. He got up and opened his apartment door, then trudged down the stairs, expecting to find some kids playing tricks or someone selling something. As he reached the bottom of the stairs, he saw Rock through the window in the door. Excitement raced through him, and he swallowed, making sure his mouth was wet before pulling open the door.

"What's wrong with you?" Rock asked, and Justin stared at him wide-eyed as anger rolled off the other man in waves. "We worked great together, and then you just left like you couldn't get away from me fast enough back there. Is it because I'm gay? If that's it, I ought to beat the shit out of you right now to prove how big a man I am, you little shit." Well, that answered that question. Now Justin tried to figure out how to make his mouth work.

Justin opened his mouth and something that sounded like "no"—at least to him—came out. He stood there helpless, shaking with frustration.

"You don't have anything to say? I should have figured that you were just a bigoted coward," Rock said before turning and marching briskly away.

Justin reached for the door to slam it closed. Anger built inside him. He might be many things, but he was nobody's coward. He'd fucking rescued a kid from a bus just before the damn thing tumbled off an overpass. He was no coward, and he certainly wasn't a bigot. He stepped through the doorway, raced up behind Rock, and yanked the man to a stop, turning him at the same time. He opened his mouth to say something, but again, the words wouldn't come. *Fucking hell*, he thought. This was his one and probably only chance. Rock had actually come to his place, and if he couldn't bring himself to say something, or do something, the chance he'd longed for would be gone forever.

Rock stared at him like he was an idiot, and Justin knew he looked like one. When Rock stepped away, Justin knew this was his last chance. He reached out, grabbed Rock's cheeks, and kissed him with all his might. He might not be able to get his freaking vocal cords to work, but his lips certainly did, and Justin let them do the talking for him. Rock didn't react right away, and Justin ended the kiss, gazing quickly into Rock's eyes before realizing he'd probably only made an even bigger idiot out of himself. He stepped back and then turned around as the notion sunk in that Rock probably already had a boyfriend, and he'd just been kissing another man right on the sidewalk where everyone could see them. At least he wasn't in uniform, but still, probably not the smartest thing he'd ever done.

*Well, screw it*, he thought while he turned around, striding back toward his building. Inside, Justin slammed the door closed and climbed the stairs. At least Rockland Sparks wouldn't be calling him a coward again anytime soon—stupid, maybe, but not a coward.

At the top of the stairs, Justin went inside his apartment, then closed the door behind him before flopping back into his living room chair with a huff. He'd been completely stupid to kiss Rock like that, and he was probably lucky the huge man hadn't punched his lights out—not that Justin couldn't defend himself. What bothered him most was how Rock's lips had tasted and felt. His own lips still tingled from the touch. At least once, just once, he'd gotten to kiss Rockland Sparks. He curled his lips into a slight smile.

# Chapter 2

TWO WEEKS later Justin was back in his usual location near the ambulance garage, watching traffic go by. This assignment was driving him out of his tree with boredom. He'd received a few accolades for rescuing the kids from the bus, but over the past two weeks, his life had mostly been completely normal. In other words, as dull as dirt. One good thing about traffic duty was he got to spend time watching the men from the ambulance company come and go. He'd seen Rock any number of times, but every time he turned away and pretended he hadn't seen the man for fear of complete embarrassment. For his part, Rock had stayed away as well, which was probably good.

Justin heard his call number through the radio less than five minutes before the end of his shift. "Please respond to a fire at the old Masland Carpet factory. The building is fully engulfed. Assistance is required for traffic control." *So much for having an evening to myself.*

Justin acknowledged the call and pulled out. After turning on his lights and siren, he hurried through town. He saw the clouds of deep, black smoke long before he reached the scene. He parked near the fire vehicles, and the fire captain explained what he needed. Justin got into position, cordoning off the south end of the road, while one of the other officers did the same to the north. With the road closed, Justin got out of his car and headed up to where the firemen looked to be planning strategy. "Is there anything I can do to help?" he asked.

"Not really. We've been told the building's empty, which means we can concentrate on putting the fire out. But now we're getting reports of chemicals inside, so we're trying to figure out what's in there," he explained before turning back to his men.

Justin figured he'd been dismissed and walked back to the intersection where his car blocked the road. Hearing more sirens approaching, Justin moved his car to let an ambulance pass and saw

Rock behind the wheel. His heart sped up like it usually did, and he was determined to speak to the man if he got the chance, even if he had to write down what he wanted to say. He moved his car back and used the radio to request barricades.

He was just finishing up when he heard explosions from inside the building. The firefighters pulled back as more acrid-looking black smoke billowed out, and flames shot from the windows. "Everyone back!" came the cry.

"You too," the fire chief yelled, pointing at him, and Justin extended the perimeter further away from the building as more explosions sounded, followed by what seemed to be the deep rumble of parts of the roof falling in. "We'll have to let it burn and try to keep it from spreading," the fire chief said, and Justin stayed back, away from the firefighters.

He got a call that the barricades he'd requested were on their way, and he went to meet the truck.

Justin instructed the driver where to place the barricades, and the driver and another officer began setting them up in front of his vehicle then moved around to the street that ran behind the factory. Justin checked in with the other officers to make sure the barricades were all set up and the public far enough away to remain safe. Then he settled near his car to wait.

"So, what was with the other week?" Rock appeared near his shoulder, and Justin started slightly, his hand jerking to his weapon and then stopping. Justin could feel his heart speeding up, so he took a deep breath. He was not going to let this happen yet again. He could talk to Rock; he'd done it before.

"Sorry," he said, his voice pitched a little higher than usual, and he cleared his throat.

"So what was all that about? And why have you ignored me for weeks, looking away whenever you saw me?" Rock asked.

"Sometimes it's hard for me to talk to people," Justin said, feeling better now that he'd gotten the first words out. His mouth was still as dry as cotton, but at least he was talking.

"You were able to talk to me while we were at the scene. Is this just some sort of way to blow me off? Because if it is, just say so," Rock said. "Otherwise, I don't get you at all."

Justin looked at the burning building, forcing his concentration away from Rock. "Sometimes I have trouble talking to people I like." There, he'd said it, and he refused to look anywhere but at the burning building. "I can talk about work and stuff, but…."

"Talking to guys gets you tongue-tied?" Rock asked, and Justin nodded. "Is that all it was? Shit, I thought you hated me or something." Rock laughed, and Justin wondered if he was laughing at him. He crossed his arms over his chest and glared at the EMT before returning his attention to the burning building.

"Is that all it is?" Justin snapped, his anger overriding his caution and self-consciousness. "I get tongue-tied around guys I like, and you think it's funny. Try having your guts tied in knots every time you try to speak to a guy."

"You're talking to me now," Rock said levelly with a slight smile before turning away

"Hey, Sparks," the other EMT called from near the ambulance, and Rock walked toward him. They conversed, and Justin watched the firefighters as they approached the burning building once more, spraying water on the fire since the explosions and pops from inside the building seemed to have stopped. Justin returned to his vehicle, guiding traffic on the main road to move the gawkers along.

Justin's throat began to ache as he continued working in the heat. During a break in the traffic, he went to his car and got a bottle of water, chugging from it to lubricate his throat. He felt better and went back to work. After a few minutes the sensation was back, more forcefully now, and he began to cough. Then he saw wisps of smoke blow past him. Justin turned around and realized the wind had shifted and was blowing fumes from the fire right over him. He moved out of the way and radioed for help, now coughing constantly and almost unable to speak.

Justin moved away from the road to where he smelled fresh air and breathed deeply, trying to get the crap out of his lungs, but every deep breath resulted in more coughing. Justin continued coughing, and it got steadily worse until he was doubled over and barely able to breathe.

"I got you," he heard Rock say, and then strong hands helped him move across the grass. "Someone bring some oxygen and have them get that road closed," Rock shouted. Justin heard more shouting as orders were given and people took charge, and then a mask was placed over his mouth. "Breathe slowly and naturally," Rock said, cradling his head as

Justin did as he was told. "You got some fumes, and we aren't sure what's in them." Justin tried to move, but Rock settled him on the ground. "Just relax and breathe for me."

Justin heard more yelling from the fire chief. "Get those houses evacuated. If that wind shifts again, we'll have more injuries."

Justin swallowed and his throat burned, but at least he could breathe more clearly. And if he was careful, his cough stayed away. *Thank God.*

"Does your throat hurt?" Rock asked.

Justin nodded. He wanted to speak but gave up and nodded again. He felt like such an idiot, and unfortunately that was becoming a common emotion for him whenever Rock was around.

"Okay, we'll stay here for a while until you can breathe better, and then I'm transporting you to the hospital. I want someone to look at your throat. These chemicals may have burned you," Rock said, and Justin looked up at his face, admiring his angled jaw, his bright blue, caring eyes, and for the love of God, the way his chest stretched his uniform whenever Rock breathed. This was definitely no time to be crushing on the man. "I think you're going to be okay, but I want to be sure."

"What happened?" the fire chief asked, and Rock explained.

"It seems whatever is in that smoke is particularly harmful," Rock explained. "Make sure your men are using breathing gear and that they don't get too close. The smoke could actually burn their skin if they're exposed for too long." The ground rumbled and shook as part of the building came down.

"Everyone get the hell away," the fire chief bellowed, and the cry was taken up. Justin watched as everyone once again pulled back from the building.

"You're far enough away here that you'll be fine. I'm going to call in that I'm taking you to the hospital, and then we're going for a ride," Rock told him, and Justin rolled his eyes. "See, with that mask on, you have an excuse not to talk to me." Justin swore, but the mask swallowed the sound, which was probably just as well. "Now, now, that's not nice." Rock flashed a smile, and Justin looked away. "Is it me? Do you not like me?" Rock asked. "Whenever I talk to you, you look away."

Justin lifted the mask and looked away. "Not you. Don't know why," Justin said, and then he lowered the mask again.

"So you haven't ever been able to talk to guys you like?" Rock asked. Though he was extremely uncomfortable with the conversation,

Justin nodded his answer anyway. "But you could talk to me when we were helping those kids." Justin rolled his eyes again. "Ah, I see, you weren't thinking of me as attractive then."

Justin lightly whapped Rock on the arm. "It was work," Justin said after lifting up the mask. He was talking to Rock now, and everything was okay.

"You know, if you haven't been able to talk to guys you liked before, but you can talk to me now, I wonder if that kiss you gave me a few weeks ago has anything to do with that?" Rock asked, whispering into Justin's ear. "You're a really good kisser, Justin, and maybe if you're really good, I'll show you just how good a kisser I can be."

Justin gasped and then began to cough again. Rock held him steady until it passed and then helped him up and guided him toward the ambulance.

Inside the back of the ambulance, Rock got him onto a gurney and strapped him down. Then they took off, and Justin heard Rock explaining to the driver what was happening and where they were going. "Contact Chief Wallace and tell him Officer Briggs is being transported with smoke inhalation and possible burns to his throat." Justin couldn't hear the response, but Rock seemed pleased. Justin closed his eyes and concentrated on breathing and trying to relax his throat so it would feel better. It wasn't working particularly well. "Is your throat still sore?" Justin nodded. "Does it feel like it's getting worse?" Rock asked, and Justin shook his head. But it hurt and protested whenever he swallowed. "We're almost there, and we'll get you right in," Rock said, and Justin nodded slowly, closing his eyes and trying to ignore everything around him.

"Feel stupid," Justin said, and then he put the mask back in place.

"No way. That smoke could have gotten anyone—all it took was a slight change in the wind. Before that fire's out, there will be more people hurt the way you were. I can guarantee it," Rock told him as they turned a corner and began to slow down.

Justin figured they were pulling into the hospital, and his suspicions were confirmed when the ambulance stopped and Rock went into action. He opened the back door of the ambulance. "I don't want you to walk, so just relax and we'll do the driving."

Justin flashed him a quick smile, and then Rock and the ambulance driver got him ready. Soon he was rolling into the hospital, overhead lights with covers decorated with clouds flashing in and out of his vision. Then they stopped and Justin was transferred to an emergency room bed. A nurse talked with Justin, and then she fiddled with cords and crap until they had him settled.

"I have to get back, but I'll see you later," Rock said, and Justin nodded, raising his hand. To his surprise, Rock took it, squeezing lightly before letting go and leaving the room. Justin wondered what that was for and figured it was Rock's way of giving comfort, but part of him hoped for something more.

Doctors and nurses came and went, asking questions, and Justin did his best to answer. His oxygen mask was replaced with one that was more comfortable, and after a while he was taken down for tests and brought back again. People came and went, and Justin fidgeted and wondered when in hell someone was going to tell him what was going on. Oh, they'd informed him what they were doing, but he wanted to know when he could go back to work. Granted, he would probably be back on traffic duty, but that wasn't so bad compared to lying in a hospital bed staring at the ceiling.

The curtain slid open. "Officer Briggs, I'm Dr. Stanton," the emergency room doctor said. "We have the results of your tests, and you have chemical burns on your throat and lungs. Luckily, they don't appear severe, since your exposure was limited. However, I am going to admit you overnight for observation. Sometimes with internal chemical injuries, the damage can show over time, and we don't want to take any chances. Tomorrow we'll run some additional tests, and I suspect they'll show no additional damage, but we need to be sure."

"When can I go back to work?" Justin asked.

"Hopefully in a few days, but we need to be sure you don't have any permanent damage to your lungs," the doctor answered, and Justin nodded, his throat still aching. "I'm going to have the oxygen removed, but I want you to take it easy and give your lungs a chance to rest. They'll heal faster, and you'll be back on your feet in no time. One of the nurses will be in to get you ready to move to a room."

"Thank you," Justin said, breathing carefully and gently.

"You're very welcome," the doctor said, pulling the curtain aside. It fell back into place, leaving Justin alone.

Over the next half hour or so, a nurse helped him change into a gown and then got him settled on a bed before wheeling him up to a room. He tried to figure out where he was going, but gave up and let the orderly do the driving. He was wheeled into a room, and the bed clunked as the orderly put on the brakes after getting the bed in place. "Thank you," Justin said, and the orderly left the room. A nurse came in, followed by Marty, looking concerned.

"How are you doing?" Marty asked as the nurse took Justin's temperature.

"They think my throat and lungs were burned from the crap in that smoke," Justin said, relieved when he didn't start coughing. "Would you take care of these for me?" Justin asked and pulled his belt out from under the bedding. They'd had a lockup for his weapon, but he needed to take care of the rest of his equipment.

"Sure," Marty said and wrapped up the belt. "So what did they say?"

"He's going to be with us just overnight," the nurse said, turning to Marty and flashing him a bright smile, which Marty returned with equal wattage. Marty was a good-looking man, especially in his uniform, which accentuated his shoulders and chest. Not that Justin was the least bit interested, because, well, that would be just wrong—like dating your brother or something. "He's going to be fine," she added, but Justin got the impression that he was superfluous to the conversation at the moment. The energy between the two of them filled the room. "I'm Stacey," she said. Marty introduced himself, shaking her hand. Justin coughed slightly, and Stacey returned her attention to him. "I'll have them bring up some dinner for you," Stacey told him. "It'll be things easy to swallow because we don't want to irritate your throat."

"Thanks," Justin said tiredly. "How are things at the scene?"

Marty sat in a chair near the bed. "Still pretty bad," Marty answered, but he was watching Stacey, who was straightening Justin's bed and sort of futzing around the room. Eventually she said good-bye to both of them and left.

"She likes you," Justin said, and Marty grinned like a high schooler. "So anyway…," Justin prompted.

"The place is still burning, and they've evacuated the blocks around the factory complex. Three civilians were brought in with inhalation injuries after you, and everyone is out for blood. I wouldn't want to be the guy who owns that place. He's going to be investigated within an inch of his life by us and the fire marshal. That building was supposed to be empty," Marty added with a touch of anger Justin knew wasn't directed at him. He and Marty had gone to school together, and while they hadn't been close friends in high school, their shared past had helped a friendship bloom quickly once Justin had joined the force.

"I'm going to be fine," Justin said. He'd been given some pills, and he wondered if one of them was to make him sleep, because he could barely keep his eyes open.

"I know, and I'll stop by after the rest of my shift. The chief asked me to come up and check on you." Marty stood up, the leather he was wearing creaking as he moved. "Get some rest, and I'll see you later."

Justin nodded and said good-bye, his eyes already sliding closed.

He woke some time later, the large clock in his room reading almost seven. "You're awake," a now familiar, deep, rumbling voice said from next to him. Justin rolled his head on the pillow and saw Rock sitting in the chair beside his bed. The usual nerves and jitters shot through him, but he tamped them down hard, driving them back as best he could. "You're not still too shy to talk to me, are you?" Rock asked lightly.

"Not shy," Justin countered. "I don't know why this happens," he added carefully. He kept expecting the jitters and dry mouth to come back, but thankfully they stayed away. He'd talked to Rock before and he'd even kissed him once. Justin kept reminding himself there was nothing to be nervous or get weirded out about.

"How are you feeling? Does your throat still hurt?" Rock leaned forward, and Justin heard the rustle of paper. "I brought you something that might help." Rock placed a milkshake on the bedside table. Justin's mouth watered and his stomach rumbled.

"Thank you," Justin said as he reached for it. Rock placed the straw through the lid, and Justin brought it to his lips, sucking some of the cold sweetness down his throat. The first swallow hurt, but after that, each one felt better and better. "That's good," Justin said after taking a few more swallows and setting the cup back on the tray.

"I'm glad," Rock said, and Justin stared at him. "There's nothing to be nervous about."

"I know. But each time I try to talk, it's like the first time we ever talked," Justin admitted. "I know it sounds dumb, but it's what happens." He swallowed hard, and pain welled in his throat as it began to constrict and tighten, his mouth going dry once again. He reached for the cup and took another drink of vanilla shake. "I always thought if I could get up the nerve to talk to someone just once, it would get better," he said before taking another drink. "But it seems to be the same, no matter what." Justin hated feeling like he had no real control over his body's reactions. He took another sip and set the cup back on the table. "I hate it. It makes me feel like a freak." Justin looked away, and the jittery feeling passed. "It's easier to talk to a wall than it is to someone I find attractive."

"So you do like me," Rock said with a chuckle.

"Well, duh. If I didn't, I could talk to you just fine," he said, facing the wall because it was easier and his throat hurt less.

"How long have you had this issue with talking to guys you… like?" Rock asked, and Justin tried to remember.

"As long as I can remember, I guess," Justin answered. He'd often tried to figure out how this whole thing started, but whenever he thought about it, his memories around it seemed muddled and rather blank. "Can we talk about something else?" *Anything else.* "Were many other people hurt?"

"Smoke got in a few people's homes, and we treated them at the scene. A few we transported. The entire area has been evacuated, and the fire isn't showing any signs of burning out yet. The place is so hot, the fire chief has said it may be tomorrow before they have everything out. The chemicals aren't helping, and that has everyone up in arms."

"I suppose," Justin said, reaching for the cup.

"Is there anyone you need to call?" Rock asked.

"Yeah, I should call my mother," Justin said softly.

"You don't sound happy about it," Rock noted. Justin shrugged and figured there was no better time than right now. "I'll find your phone," Rock said, already digging through Justin's clothes until he found what he was looking for and handed Justin his phone.

Justin dialed the number and waited. "Hi, Mom," he said when she answered.

"Were you involved in that huge fire? They said on the news that a police officer was injured," she said frantically, and he felt terrible. He really should have called her earlier.

"Yes, that was me. I'm in the hospital, but I'm fine. Got too much smoke, and they're just making sure I'm okay. They're keeping me overnight for observation, and I should be able to go home tomorrow." He didn't want her to worry because when she got worked up, she could be a tornado of chaos to everything around her.

"I'm on my way," she said. "I assume you're at the hospital in Carlisle?" she asked.

"Yes, but…." He didn't get a chance to say anything more because his mom ended the call. "Damn," Justin said softly as he hung up the phone. "My mother is on her way."

"Do you want me to leave so you can spend time with her?"

Justin reached to Rock and grabbed his hand. "Don't you dare," he said, and then he thought better of it. He liked this guy, and it seemed Rock liked him, even if he hadn't actually said so. Did he really want to subject the man to his mother? Rock would probably never speak to him again. Granted, he had a hard enough time talking to him, so at least that problem would be solved. "I mean, you don't have to."

Rock began to laugh. "Your mother must be something else. Remember, I've seen you rescue a kid from a bus perched on the edge of a freeway overpass, and you were cool as a cucumber. But it's your mother that has you scared. This is someone I have to see." Justin rolled his eyes without saying anything and then reached for the cup again, his mouth drying. As he drank, he saw Rock watching him a bit strangely. The quirky smirk slowly fell from Rock's expression. "You were serious about…." Rock settled back in the chair without saying anything more, and Justin rested back on the bed. He'd already had enough of this conversation.

Rock took his hand once Justin put the nearly empty cup back on the tray. He liked that Rock was touching him. It felt nice, and he couldn't remember another man touching him that way, like just holding hands really meant something. "Have you ever done anything like this before?" Rock asked, lightly teasing Justin's palm with one finger. Justin swallowed, thankful the pain was subsiding, and shook his head. "Have you ever…?" Rock asked, and Justin shot him a look. He didn't know Rock well enough to discuss things like that with him. The state of his… experience… in that way wasn't Rock's business, at least not yet. "You haven't, have you? Not being able to talk to guys you like has kept you from getting close to anyone, hasn't it?"

"Rock!" Justin snapped. "That's not a question to ask." He had no trouble saying that.

"Have you noticed you have no trouble talking when you're angry?" Rock asked.

"Is that what you're doing? Trying to make me angry so I can talk to you?" Justin asked. "Because it's working." He pulled his hand away.

"There's no need to be touchy," Rock said calmly. "I'm just trying to figure you out."

"Is that so?" Justin crossed his arms over his chest.

"Sure. You're pretty fascinating," Rock told him. "And hot too," he added with a wink. "I'm trying to see the real you, and if getting you flustered or angry is the only way to get you to talk, I'm okay with that." Rock tilted his head slightly to the side. "Besides, I'm a hell of a lot bigger than you, so you can't intimidate me with your cop voice."

Justin turned away, huffing softly as he returned to staring at the wall.

"Honey," his mother cried from the doorway, and Justin turned in time to see her breeze into the room. "How are you, sweetheart?" she asked, setting her purse on the foot of his bed on her way around so she could lean over and give him a hug, carried along by the fumes from her perfume, Emeraude, the same thing she'd worn, or bathed in, as long as Justin could remember. "Who's this?" his mother asked, stopping mid-hug as she saw Rock.

"Mom, this is Rock. He's the EMT who helped me when I got too much smoke," Justin said. "Rock, this is my mother, Arlene." They shook hands, hers dwarfed in Rock's.

"So, honey, I thought when you got out, you could come home with me for a few days. I have your room all made up just the way you left it, and I can make you your favorites," she said, and Justin glanced at Rock, willing the ground to open up and swallow him whole. She always acted as though he were twelve years old.

"I'll be fine at my apartment. I inhaled too much crap, and they just want to make sure I'm okay before going back to work. I'm not helpless or an invalid. I appreciate your offer, but I don't want to put you out, and I'll be fine." Justin patted her hand, and she sat on the edge of his bed, stroking his forehead.

"Are you sure, honey?" she asked, pursing her lips into a pout that had always made Justin's father give in to whatever she wanted. Justin was sure that was why he'd eventually left.

"I'm fine, Mother," Justin said firmly, hoping that would somehow disabuse her of the notion that he was a teenager and needed his mommy. He gave Rock a sort of "help me" look, but the fucker had a silly grin on his face. "Thank you, though."

"I have to go," Rock said, "but I'll see you soon." He reached over and took one of Justin's hands, holding it in his for a few seconds. They shared a smile, and then Rock let go and started for the door.

"What was that?" Arlene asked. Rock stopped, and Justin felt his throat go dry again. He reached for the shake and drank a bit. "Are you…. Are you being… *dirty*"—she whispered the word—"with him?"

Rock stopped dead in his tracks and walked back to the bed. "We certainly were not," Rock said haughtily. "I held his hand, and we shared a kiss once." Rock took Justin's hand again. "I like your son."

"He's a boy," she countered, and Rock glared at her. Justin was beginning to get a bit of a headache from snapping his head from one to the other.

"Your son is a man, all man, and he's more than capable of making his own decisions." Rock leaned closer. "Dirty or otherwise," he whispered, shaking his head. "Look." Rock turned his full attention on Justin, and mother or not, that gaze burned into him. Justin was very thankful there were blankets over him, because he got so hard he thought his dick was going to explode. "I'll see you later." Rock took his hand again. Justin heard his mother click her teeth, which meant she was really getting herself worked up. He figured it was probably a good time for Rock to go, but the big man didn't move. His mother began making more noise, and Rock leaned down and kissed him forcefully before pulling away again. "I'll call you real soon." Justin nodded. At least this time he had a reason to be speechless. Then Rock turned and strode out the door, with Justin watching his primo butt swing slightly with every step.

"I don't like you behaving that way," Justin's mother said, and he turned his head toward her when Rock disappeared from view. Her eyes blazed, but her face was as calm as ever. "That's not how a man should behave."

Justin's mouth went dry again, and he reached for the cup, drinking the last of the shake before setting the cup back on the tray. Why in hell was he feeling this way now?

"I like him, Mother, and I've already told you I'm gay, so what's the big deal?" he asked softly. "You act like me liking another guy is a surprise to you," Justin said, and he realized it was. "It shouldn't be."

His mother's expression didn't change, and he wondered what she was up to. There was one thing Justin could always count on with his mother—she would do what she had to in order to get what she wanted. "This is not the way I want my son to behave," she said decisively.

"I'm not a child, Mother. I'm an adult, and I get to make my own decisions about my life. We've talked about this before."

"But you're my little boy," she said softly. She reached for her purse, fumbled with it, and came up with a tissue.

"No, I'm not. I'm my own man, and I should be leading my own life, not being your little boy," he said, his throat aching. He wanted to stop talking. It was wearing him out, the pain in his throat and mouth getting worse. "You have to understand that." Justin swallowed. "You don't treat any of the girls like this, but you act like I can't take care of myself," he said firmly.

"None of your sisters turned out deviant," his mother said, and Justin shifted on the bed so he could see her better. Her tone was as soft as ever, but the edge in her voice cut like a knife. Justin swallowed hard. "None of your sisters...," she began, and then she turned toward the window.

"What, Mother?" Justin pressed, wondering what it would get him.

"Nothing," she said, turning around. "I'm going to go and I'll see you soon." She dabbed her eyes with the tissue, and Justin wondered if the tears were real or part of her manipulations. He'd seen and been on the receiving end of her tears enough times they no longer had power over him. They had when he was a kid, but not now. "I'll call you soon," she said and then abruptly strode from the room, leaving Justin to wonder what in the hell was going on. He thought about it for a while, but nothing came to mind. There was nothing he could do about his mother; she was the way she was.

The room was quiet, and rather lonely, if Justin were honest. He found himself wishing Rock were still here with him. That was what he wanted—to spend time with Rock, his own little idiosyncrasy be damned.

# Chapter 3

JUSTIN GOT released from the hospital the following day with instructions to take it easy and give his lungs a rest. Marty came to pick him up, and for two days, Justin stayed in his apartment, watching television and squirming for some sort of activity. His throat had stopped burning and returned to normal, and he was breathing clearly without the slightest hint of a cough. But the thought of spending another day doing nothing was driving him crazy. He was scheduled to go back to traffic duty tomorrow, but today he needed something to do, so he packed a bag and decided to drive to the gym. He wouldn't do anything heavy or strenuous, but he desperately needed some sort of normalcy right now. His mother hadn't called since her hospital visit, which was unusual, and his usually chatty sisters had been quiet as well. Pushing it all from his mind, he finished packing his bag and headed down the building's back stairs and out to his car.

The drive to the gym at the edge of town was quick, and he parked just outside the door. He walked inside, scanned his membership card, and walked past treadmills, elliptical machines, and the free weight area to the men's locker room. The gym had been open a decade, according to the anniversary sign that hung from the ceiling girders, but nearly everything looked and smelled as clean and bright as if it were new. In the locker room, with its natural maple lockers, Justin changed into workout clothes and headed back out to the workout floor. Justin wasn't sure what he wanted to do, and settled for a walk on a treadmill. He usually ran or lifted, but he'd promised he'd take it easy. He stepped onto the machine and programmed it with what he wanted, and the belt began to move.

"I hope you aren't stressing your lungs."

Justin couldn't help smiling even though his throat and mouth went dry like they usually did. "I'm taking it easy," he said, fighting nervousness. He wished to hell he knew why this kept happening to him. But he'd promised himself he wasn't going to let this crap bother him, so he pushed on. "I didn't know you worked out here," Justin said, raking his gaze over Rock's chest, which stretched his T-shirt to capacity, and down to legs that bulged from strained shorts. God, the man was a walking wet dream.

"I just joined a week ago. I was working out closer to Harrisburg, but it was too long a drive, so I transferred here," Rock said as he programmed his treadmill and began walking. Justin turned his attention back to his own workout. "How did things go with your mother at the hospital? I didn't mean to get you in trouble."

"It wasn't you," Justin said more easily now.

"She sort of made me angry," Rock prevaricated.

"I got that part." Justin looked to see if anyone was close to them. "Is that why you kissed me?" Justin asked the question and expected the dry mouth to come back in spades, but everything was okay, which was a bit of a surprise. He relaxed and continued his leisurely walk.

"No. I kissed you because I wanted to and because I was relieved that you were okay," Rock answered. "I don't tend to be shy."

"I got that part too," Justin said with a chuckle and released the breath he'd been holding. He kept expecting his mouth to go dry, but everything felt good, normal.

"When do you go back to work?"

"Tomorrow," Justin answered. He saw Rock nod, and then they both lapsed into silence for a while. Rock seemed to be keeping an eye on him, glancing at him every few seconds and then at Justin's treadmill display. "I'm not overdoing it," Justin said after what he figured was the fifth time Rock had checked.

"I know. I was wondering something and wasn't sure how to ask. I was wondering if you'd like to get something to eat when we're done here," Rock asked.

Justin waited for his mouth to go dry and his throat to constrict, but nothing happened; everything was normal. Maybe he'd gotten to the point with Rock that he was over it. He wanted to jump for joy. "Yes, that would be nice."

Justin took a deep breath and then released it. His lungs felt a bit tight, but there was no cough and he felt pretty dang good. He continued walking and talking to Rock like a normal person. Once or twice he peeked down at himself and was pleased he'd worn shorts that weren't too tight, because watching Rock was turning him on to no end.

After they'd walked for about half an hour, Justin slowed the treadmill for a cool-down and then stopped it. Rock did the same, and they wiped down their equipment before heading together toward the locker room. A bout of nerves hit him when Justin realized they were going to be changing together. He certainly wanted to see Rock naked—he'd been curious about what the gorgeous man looked like without his clothes for months—but they ended up in different areas of the locker room. Justin gave Rock his privacy and hurried to the individual showers with their stone tile walls and floor. He showered and dried himself in the stall before pushing the curtain aside and stopping in his tracks. Rock stood by the sinks, a towel wrapped tightly around his small waist and pulled tight over his butt, his wide shoulders and back on display, and Justin looked his fill until Rock saw him and flashed a quick smile.

Justin smiled back and then walked to the locker room, where he finished drying off and then got dressed. He usually wasn't a shy person. He showered at the station all the time, but he suddenly felt a bit self-conscious and didn't want that to trigger another episode, as he'd come to refer to them in his mind.

Once he was done, Justin wandered through the gym toward the front door, chatting with a number of the guys he knew.

"I heard you got hurt," one of the men sitting on the edge of the flat bench asked between sets.

"Yeah. Got too much smoke in that big fire a few days ago," Justin said.

"I heard you rescued a bunch of kids from that bus accident," Russ, another of the guys said, while yet another walked up to him and shook his hand vigorously.

"Yeah, he did. One of them was my little Sally," the huge man said, clapping Justin on the back. "You need anything, just say the word."

"Thanks," Justin said with a smile. He'd never ask for anything—it was against most departmental rules—but it was nice to be appreciated. Rock came out of the locker room, and Justin let the guys get back to benching, watching as one pressed half the weight of a small car, and then followed Rock to the parking lot. "Where do you want to go?" Justin asked, relaxed and refreshed from his workout and shower.

"There's that new café toward town. I've never been, but it looked good," Rock suggested, and Justin agreed before opening his trunk and putting his bag inside.

"I'll meet you there," Justin said, and Rock slid into the seat of his convertible. Justin watched him put on sunglasses and pull out of the parking lot. Justin followed, pulling into the café parking lot and parking his blue Camry next to Rock's red Mustang. Justin got out, looking over Rock's car with a bit of envy. "Beautiful wheels," he said, running his hand over the saddle leather headrest.

"It's my dream car. I've wanted one since I got my license. Finally got it last year. After lunch, you can take it for a spin if you want," Rock said with a grin.

They walked into the restaurant and sat at an available table. Justin pulled a menu out of the holder and looked it over.

"I'm starved," Rock said, looking around for a server, but they saw no one. The place was very quiet, too quiet, and Justin felt the hair on the back of his neck stand up. He cast a detailed eye over the place, but didn't hear anyone, not even in the back. The soda machine against the wall kicked on, the soft whir of the condenser breaking the quiet.

"Something isn't right," Justin said, all his senses on alert. "There's no one here." Justin got up and wandered to the cash register, which was powered on but closed. The feeling of wrongness intensified as he continued looking around. He pulled out his phone and called the dispatch. "Jane, I'm in the Sunnyside Café, the new place out on Ritner Highway. The place is open, but no one's around. It seems strange and I get the feeling something isn't right."

"Aren't you supposed to be off?" Jane asked.

"Yeah. I stopped in for lunch and I'm getting a really bad feeling." He knew it probably sounded stupid, but the feeling wouldn't go away.

"I'll send someone by," Jane said skeptically.

"I'm serious. It's almost eerie in here," Justin explained. He disconnected the call and continued slowly looking around. He was a bit reticent about poking around in the back. He wished he had his weapon, but he knew it was best to wait, so he sat back at the table with Rock and continued watching and listening.

It only took a few minutes for a police vehicle to pull into the lot. Marty and Phillips, one of the more senior officers, got out, and even from this distance Justin could see they were having a laugh, most likely at his expense. They pulled open the door and walked inside.

"What's got you spooked?" Phillips teased. "You know bad service isn't illegal."

"There's no one here," Rock answered with a glare at the older officer. "The place seems deserted; listen instead of flapping your gums." Rock refused to break eye contact with Phillips, and everyone became quiet. "No one cooking, no banging of pots and pans, nothing at all. There hasn't been a sound since we arrived." Rock was obviously angry, and didn't take kindly to being teased. Or was he angry for Justin? The thought made Justin want to smile.

"We'll check it out," Phillips said, obviously figuring he'd humor them. He and Marty looked around the restaurant, checking out the restrooms before walking into the kitchen.

"Jesus Christ," Justin heard Marty call, and then he returned to the dining room looking a bit green. "You're the EMT, right?" Marty asked, and Rock nodded. "Can you take a look?"

Rock followed Marty, and Justin followed him. In the kitchen were two people, a man and a woman. The woman was on the floor, and the man was slumped over the work station. "What happened?" Justin said. "Did you call an ambulance?"

"Yes," Marty said.

Rock looked them both over. "They're alive, but barely. Turn off all the gas. This could be carbon monoxide poisoning, and we need to ventilate this room right away," Rock ordered, and he pointed toward the back door, which was closed. Phillips opened it, and fresh air blew into the kitchen. It was hot, but at least it was clean.

"I found the shutoff," Phillips said.

A siren sounded in the distance, getting louder and louder. Marty left the kitchen, and when he returned the EMTs were right behind him. Rock, of course, knew both of them, and Justin stood back, as did Marty and Phillips, while they got both people on oxygen. A second ambulance arrived, and both people were placed on gurneys and loaded into the ambulances.

"We believe it's carbon monoxide poisoning," Rock explained, "and we may have found them just in time. They didn't have much longer." Rock began wandering around the kitchen. "The stove is older than the hills, and I bet it's the source of the problem."

"You're probably right," Phillips said, no longer a hint of teasing in his voice. "We'll have it checked out." He left the kitchen, and Justin heard him calling the service that would close up the diner, along with someone from the gas company to check out the stove. Once he was done with that, Justin and Rock both gave him their statements and left, still needing to get some lunch.

"We can go to my place," Rock offered. "I'm not the best cook, but I have the stuff for sandwiches." Justin readily agreed. He was starving and knew Rock had to be as well. Rock gave him the address, and Justin followed him through town to a small house at the edge of the historic district. Justin found a place to park and crossed the street.

"Nice place," Justin said as he approached where Rock was waiting for him in front of the stone house.

"It was a mess when I bought it," Rock explained. "The siding was old and half peeling off the house. It had to be replaced, and when I got it off, I found the stone underneath. It appears the main portion of the house is from the late eighteenth century, but it had been updated so much that no one really knew. I've stabilized the exterior and started work inside." Rock unlocked the door, and Justin stepped into what appeared to be a construction zone.

"Wow," Justin said as he looked at nearly bare walls.

"Yeah, I found deep-welled window shutters behind drywall, and a fireplace that had been closed over at some point. I found a plasterer, and he's working to restore the walls in here." Rock led Justin into the dining room. "I finished this room a few months ago."

"Amazing," Justin said as he admired the simple but elegant architecture. "This isn't what I was expecting at all. I sort of pictured you as a condo guy."

"Nope, I really love working with my hands. I've done most of the work, with the help of some specialists and friends. It's sort of a labor of love." Rock led him into the kitchen, which was small, but almost fully modern. Almost, because one wall was a huge stone cooking fireplace. "I tried to keep everything original that I could."

"Have you ever used it?" Justin asked, staring at the fireplace that he could almost stand up inside.

"No. But I wanted to keep it."

"Don't blame you," Justin said, watching Rock open the refrigerator and pull out lots of sandwich stuff, then set it on the counter.

"You realize you've been talking to me for most of the afternoon without an issue," Rock said as he pulled out the bread. Justin had just been thinking about that, but hadn't wanted to say anything for fear of jinxing things.

"Yes, I know," Justin said, "but things have been pretty exciting."

"So you don't have a problem taking to me when you're angry or excited," Rock said with a wicked smile. "I think I like that." Rock began building sandwiches, dealing out the fixings like cards. Justin leaned against the table and simply watched. Rock wasn't doing anything particularly unusual, but each movement seemed special, like it had meaning, even if it was something as basic as making a sandwich. Eventually Rock handed him a plate with a huge sandwich on it. Before he began to eat, Rock opened a cupboard and pulled out a blender. He then grabbed some fruit from the freezer, throwing in pieces from plastic containers before adding juice and probably protein powder before turning on the machine.

The resulting concoction was bright orange, and Rock poured it into two glasses and handed Justin one. "Let's go into the living room," Rock said, leading the way with his plate and glass in hand.

Rock sat on the sofa. Justin wasn't sure where he should sit, but because of the placement of the coffee table, he sat next to Rock. The smile he received told him that was the right choice. He settled down to eat and ended up nearly inhaling the sandwich, in spite of its huge size. He hadn't really realized just how hungry he was until he took that first bite.

Rock must have been hungry as well, because both plates were empty in a short time. Rock leaned back with his glass, sipping his frozen smoothie, and Justin followed suit, closing his eyes for a few seconds. He opened them when he heard the sofa squeak. Rock had moved closer. He absently set his glass on the table, his gaze meeting Justin's. Justin placed his glass next to Rock's and was then engulfed in Rock's huge, strong arms.

"Is this okay?" Rock asked, and Justin swallowed, at a loss for words in the best way possible as Rock kissed him.

Up till now, the two kisses they'd shared had either been fueled by panic and desperation or used to make a point. This one was gentle, with an undertone of passion and need that went straight through Justin's body. He returned the kiss, but felt reticent—not because he didn't want to kiss and be kissed but because he wasn't quite sure what to do. Rock, of course, had been right. Without being able to speak to guys he liked, Justin hadn't had much opportunity to act on his desires other than alone in his bed after dark. And for a long time, whenever he'd done that, he'd experienced the same dry mouth and nervousness he did when he tried to speak to someone of interest. Thankfully, that had subsided. Why these things flashed through his mind when Rock kissed him confounded him.

"Is something wrong?" Rock asked. Justin shook his head, afraid to try to speak, and instead pulled Rock back into a kiss.

Rock pressed firm lips to his and took charge, nibbling lightly on his lower lip, almost languidly tracing Justin's lips with his tongue in a way that made Justin want to scream for more.

"Have you been kissed much?" Rock asked.

"No," Justin said roughly, dry throat be damned, and he returned the kiss, taking Rock's searing lips with his own. Justin's passion rose along with the beating of his heart and the thrumming of his blood in his ears. Justin pushed Rock back against the cushions, signaling what he wanted.

Rock fell back on the cushions, pulling Justin along with him, holding Justin tight, their kisses deepening and filling with energy. Justin's entire body tingled, and his hips flexed on their own as his cock throbbed.

"Relax," Rock told him, breathing hotly on his lips. "I want the same thing you do, but I want to do it right."

"I'm doing it wrong?" Justin asked. His throat tightened and his mouth went Sahara dry.

"No, you're not doing anything wrong," Rock said with a smile. "But is here where you want to do this?" he asked and then worked his way out from under Justin. Justin sat up, flustered, confused, and stared at the floor. "Hey," Rock whispered, and Justin lifted his gaze. Rock extended his hand and tugged him to his feet before leading him up the stairs and into a back bedroom with a huge king-size bed. Rock said nothing, but tugged him close, holding him with what felt like all his strength. "This is where I want you to have your first time—in my bed."

Rock propelled him toward the mattress, and they tumbled onto it. "Are you sure?" Justin asked.

Rock chuckled and lifted the hem of Justin's shirt, tugging it over his head. "Oh, I'm sure," he said, tossing Justin's shirt over his shoulder with complete abandon. "I've watched you sitting out in your patrol car." Rock nuzzled Justin's neck while he let his hands roam over Justin's chest. Justin arched his back when Rock nibbled and sucked lightly on his skin. He tried to get at Rock's shirt, but couldn't as Rock held him in place.

Rock shifted, his weight disappearing. Justin watched as he tugged off his shirt. He gazed openmouthed at Rock's massively powerful chest, with muscles that looked like plates of armor and a stomach cut with deeply grooved lines. "Jesus," Justin said and swallowed. Without thinking, he lunged, tackling Rock, and they went sprawling on the huge mattress. Rock laughed, and Justin straddled Rock's hips, staring down at him, wondering what to do first.

Justin ran his hands over Rock's skin, cupping powerful pecs in his hands as the muscles twitched and danced under his palms. Rock pulled him forward into a kiss. Their chests pressed together, skin to skin, and something inside Justin snapped like a rubber band pulled too tightly. This was not only good, but felt right, perfect. Rock stroked his back, and Justin held Rock around the neck, closing his eyes as the immensity of what he was about to do washed over him.

Justin felt Rock unfasten his belt, and he held his breath as his pants were opened. He expected Rock to simply push them away, but instead he returned to stroking Justin's back, only now going lower, teasing the skin just inside his pants. Justin groaned softly, and Rock became more bold, which was exactly what Justin needed. Rock slid his hands inside Justin's pants, cupping his butt as he intensified the kisses to the point where Justin could barely think and his mind clouded with lust and unbelievable passion.

"Do you like that? Like being touched there?" Rock asked as he lightly squeezed Justin's butt, teasing the skin a bit with his fingers.

"Yes," Justin answered. He wanted it all, everything, and somehow he wanted it all at once. He couldn't seem to make his hands settle. He wrapped them around Rock's neck, but then pulled them away to stroke up his side or to feel the muscles of Rock's chest twitch and move.

Rock smiled and pushed Justin's pants lower. When Justin lifted his hips, Rock moved the pants lower, down his legs. Justin kicked and shifted until his pants fell on the floor with a dull thud. He was naked with another man, and it was perfect—well, almost perfect.

Rock used a leg to press Justin's apart slightly and then rolled them on the bed. "I think I like you like this best of all," Rock told him. "You look good in your uniform, but you look even better naked in my bed." Rock kissed him demandingly. "What is it you want?"

"You naked," Justin growled, forgetting about everything but Rock.

Rock sat up and stepped off the bed. Justin watched as he opened his pants and then turned around. He pushed them off his legs and damn if the tightest, most perfect bubble butt didn't wave slowly in front of Justin's eyes. He knew Rock was doing that slight rocking motion with his hips on purpose, and he growled again as Rock stepped out of his pants before straightening up and turning around.

Rock stood beside the bed, tree-trunk legs spread slightly apart, cock thick and heavy, pointing nearly to the ceiling. Justin blinked a few times. He'd imagined Rock naked plenty of times, but his imagination had fallen short, in so many freaking ways. Rock slowly climbed back on the bed, prowling like a cat as he approached. Rock raked his gaze over him with such intensity, Justin could feel its heat. "You're an amazing-looking man," Rock said, and then he kissed and licked his stomach. "I bet you have no idea how hot you are," Rock said, and Justin shrugged. He knew he looked good. He worked hard to stay in shape, but it had always been for the job because, well, why work out for guys you can't even talk to?

"I'm not the one who's as big as a house," Justin said, and Rock sat up, straddling Justin's hips, and damn if he didn't flex, puffing out his chest and pumping his arms as he burst into a smile. "That's what I like," Justin said, "humility." Rock grinned and flexed again before lifting Justin and drawing him into a kiss. Justin felt a shift in the mood as they kissed. The playfulness disappeared, driven away by passion.

Rock lowered Justin onto the bed, kissing him once again before licking and sucking on the skin of Justin's neck. "I like tasting you," Rock said, latching onto one of his nipples. Justin arched his back and grasped the bedding. He'd had no idea that could feel so good. He'd touched his own nipples, but it didn't feel anything like the zing he got when Rock touched them. Rock continued his tasting, kissing and licking down Justin's stomach before tilting his head slightly upward. Then he ran his tongue along Justin's cock before sucking the head into his mouth.

Justin hissed, and Rock sucked him deeper before taking all of him. "Oh God," Justin moaned as Rock bobbed his head. Justin gasped and flexed his hips slightly. He wasn't sure if Rock would like that or not, but the big man sucked harder, so Justin continued thrusting until he could hardly stand it any longer. Rock seemed to know he was close because he slipped his mouth away and grinned up at him like a cat before licking a trail up Justin's body to his lips. They kissed and Rock sucked on Justin's tongue like he had on his cock.

"I want you like that," Justin said, and Rock settled on the mattress next to him.

"Take your time," Rock said, and Justin knelt on the mattress beside Rock, looking him over, his mouth watering like he was a starving man at a smorgasbord. He wasn't sure where to start. "Hey, do what you like, because if you like it, I'll like it. I promise."

Justin nodded and leaned over Rock, circling one of his nipples with his tongue. Rock was slightly salty, but hot and a little slick with perspiration. Perfect. He went slowly, probably a bit timidly at first.

"It's okay to touch," Rock told him, and Justin laughed. He'd been acting like a schoolgirl. Justin climbed onto Rock's body, pressing their chests together, legs entwining. They kissed hard, with Rock holding him tight. They kissed for quite a while, and then Justin shimmied slowly down Rock's body, kissing and tasting his skin as he went. Rock was amazing, all hard, sculpted muscle—strength personified, and yet gentle and caring. Justin hadn't known what he was expecting—maybe for Rock to try to use his strength—but he hadn't, and that in itself was an immense turn-on. Rock cared about him, not just himself.

He ran his fingers down the ridges in the center of Rock's stomach, and the muscles twitched and jumped with each breath. Justin licked Rock's hot skin and felt the muscles quiver with each touch. "That's incredible," Justin said to himself.

Rock's cock bounced and jumped against his belly, and Justin watched it move in time to the way he touched Rock's skin. If he kissed, Rock's cock jumped, and when he looked it throbbed and bobbed slightly. "Please, Justin," Rock pleaded softly. Justin smiled and lightly stroked his fingers up and down Rock's hot, smooth shaft. "Yes." Justin loved that he could make Rock, big strong Rock, plead for him. "You don't have to if you don't want to, but...."

Justin lifted Rock's hefty cock, opening his mouth and then closing it again. He stroked slowly and forcefully, enjoying the weighty pleasure of holding Rock in his hand. This was the first cock other than his own he'd ever touched. Part of him had always thought he was some sort of loser, but maybe he was meant to wait for this man—for Rock. The heavy shaft with its rosy head felt wonderful in his hand, and he watched Rock and listened to every sound he made. It was majorly heady to hear the huge man gasp just from a simple touch.

Justin leaned closer, opening his mouth once again, and slowly closed his lips around the head of Rock's cock. The rich, salty flavor of the other man burst on his tongue, and he sank his lips further, sucking slightly. Rock rested his hands lightly on his head, but didn't push or rush. Instead, he lightly stroked Justin's scalp, moving along with him rather than forcing anything.

"That's it," Rock encouraged, his words trailing off to a growl when Justin took him deeper. God, Justin loved that chest-rumbling sound, and he took more, being careful not to choke. He didn't want to damage the mood. "You're so hot around me," Rock said softly, and Justin used his tongue to lightly tickle the underside of Rock's shaft and heard him gasp softly.

He wasn't sure how good he was at this, but he liked it and threw himself into sucking Rock as best and as hard as he could. The small sounds that came from his partner only encouraged him, and he took Rock as deep as he could before backing off to tease him once more with his tongue.

"Is that okay?" Justin asked after a few minutes, and Rock tugged him up, kissing him hard.

"It's more than okay, it's perfect," Rock told him. "I want to taste you too."

Justin nodded, and Rock guided him around, spreading his legs. He took Rock into his mouth once more and gasped around the shaft as his own cock sank into Rock's moist heat. God, he could hardly move or think as Rock sucked him hard, and he had to force himself to return the favor. Once he did, the sensation of sucking and being sucked threatened to overwhelm him. He loved the way Rock would flex his hips slightly and his cock would jump in Justin's mouth. He also loved the way Rock seemed to be able to anticipate him, and he'd suck him deep at just the right moment. Soon, Justin began to understand some of that same connection. He'd thrust lightly, and Rock would react. It almost felt like his movements traveled through Rock's body and returned to him magnified with excitement.

Rock's movements became ragged, and Justin felt his own control waver. Then Rock paused, and all movement ceased. Justin released Rock's shaft and turned around. Rock guided their lips together, flexing his hips. Rock's cock slid alongside Justin's, who thrust his hips as well. Their heat and excitement slicked the way, and soon Justin felt his ecstasy build from deep inside him. He knew his own body well enough to know he wouldn't be able to last long.

"That's it," Rock said in his ear, and Justin arched his back, snapping his hips as he rubbed his cock against Rock's smooth skin. "I want you to come for me. I want to see your face and feel your heat on my skin," Rock said breathily. Justin had never given any thought to dirty talk, but he found it turned him on. "That's it, baby, come for me. Make me feel what you do. Show me how turned on you are."

Rock grabbed Justin's butt, pressing them together more firmly, kneading Justin's cheeks while he increased the friction between their bodies.

Justin continued snapping his hips, the tension inside him building to where he could no longer hold it. "Rock!" he cried when he could no longer contain his passion, and he came, his cock throbbing between them as his entire body quivered with unleashed desire. He took a deep breath and collapsed on top of Rock's body. Rock rubbed his back slowly, and Justin raised and lowered slightly with each shared breath. Once he'd caught his breath, he opened his eyes and kissed Rock as deeply as he could.

Rock rolled them on the bed without breaking their kiss, and Justin held Rock tight, stroking his back as he felt the other man thrust against him. Sliding his hands down Rock's powerfully smooth back, he cupped the firm butt cheeks and held on, driving Rock's passion the way Rock had driven his. Soon he heard Rock's breathing turn ragged.

"That's it, I want to see you," Justin said, and Rock lifted his head, arching his back and thrusting faster. Justin stared, completely enthralled, as Rock's passion and desire showed clearly on his face. Even without feeling Rock's release, Justin knew the exact moment Rock tumbled over the edge by the bliss written on his face.

Justin didn't move. If the world could pause, he'd be happy to stay right where he was for a long time. Rock held him in his strong arms, breathing softly in Justin's ear. "You're a real fireball," Rock whispered. Justin wasn't so sure about that, but he hummed his approval and rested his head on Rock's shoulder.

"When's your next shift?" Justin asked, hoping it wasn't for a while.

"Tomorrow morning," Rock answered.

"Me too," Justin said without lifting his head, taking in the soft caresses as Rock languidly stroked up and down his back. He soaked in the attention like a sponge. His mother had never been particularly demonstrative to him when it came to affection. She'd been completely different with his sisters, hugging and laughing with them, but almost always serious with him.

Rock paused in his attentions, and Justin lifted his head. "Is something wrong?" Rock asked. "You seem so tense all of a sudden."

"No. Just thinking about things I should let go," Justin answered and lowered his head back to Rock's shoulder.

"Good." Rock hummed from deep in his chest, and Justin closed his eyes, content and happy, at least for now.

# Chapter 4

CARS ONCE again passed in front of Justin's patrol car, and he'd never been so happy for it. He was ready to go back to work, although getting out of Rock's bed to go home and change before his shift had been hard as hell. He and Rock had thoroughly worn each other out, coming at least three times before turning in, and Justin had fallen asleep almost as soon as they'd showered and Rock had pulled him close. He'd held Justin the entire night. Justin had never been able to sleep with anyone else. Even as a teenager on school trips and in college, he'd always had to have the bed to himself or he'd spend the night nervously staring at the ceiling. That hadn't been the case with Rock.

His phone ringing pulled him out of his thoughts, and without taking his eyes off the road in front of him, he picked up the phone and placed it to his ear.

"Justin, it's Chrissy," his oldest sister said.

"Morning," he told her with a smile.

"You're in a good mood," she observed.

"Yup, and I'm not going to let anything spoil it," he said without thinking, and that was his first mistake.

"Well, Mother is extremely upset, and frankly, so am I," Chrissy said. "That little display in the hospital was totally unnecessary."

Justin kept his cool, refusing to let her upset him. "I didn't have anything to do with that. Rock got a little carried away. He wasn't too happy about the way Mom was treating me." Warmth spread through him as he thought of Rock.

"Mom came to the hospital to make sure you were all right because she cares about you. She returned and hasn't left the house since. She's so upset, she wouldn't answer the phone, and I had to go over and check up on her." She whined like going to Mom's was a huge imposition rather than something she did anyway so they could talk about everything and nothing. Not that Justin wanted to go to his mother's for afternoon coffee like his sisters did, but still, it would have been nice if his mother made an effort toward some activity that included him. "I found Mom sitting in her sunroom staring out at the backyard. She was traumatized, Justin," his sister added, pulling him out of his ruminations.

Justin sighed and rolled his eyes. "Don't be dramatic," Justin said. He was beginning to get a little tired of the over-the-top emotions that seemed to run through his mother and sisters.

"I'm not. Lynanne feels the same way," Chrissy said, as though their middle sister was any less dramatic or manipulative. "You need to go see her and apologize at the very least, and you need to go alone, without… the man you were kissing." Chrissy sounded like she'd just eaten a bad shrimp but couldn't spit it out, and Justin could imagine her narrow face contorted in distaste.

"I work all week, and I have to take it easy because of my lungs," Justin explained. "I'll stop by to see Mom, but I have no intention of apologizing for anything." Justin peered out the window. "I have to go, I'm at work," he said in a mock hurry. "Bye," he added quickly and then hung up the phone, setting it on the seat next to him. Being a cop did have its advantages. He continued watching traffic, pulling over a few speeders and hazardous drivers before breaking for lunch.

He decided to leave his cruiser where it was and walk to lunch. After calling in to let them know he was off duty but available if required, he headed to the restaurant. He took the closest available table, and the waitress brought him a menu.

"How are you, Justin?" she asked as she poured him a cup of his usual coffee. He'd known Shawna since high school. "I ran into your mother the other day at the grocery store, and she said you and I should get together."

Justin stifled a groan and stopped himself from rolling his eyes. "Shawna, you're a really nice girl, but I think my mother neglected to pass on some vital information—I'm gay." He didn't say it particularly loudly and didn't want to hurt her feelings, but he wasn't going to lead her on either.

To his surprise, Shawna chuckled. "I figured that out a while ago," she said and then continued laughing. "I don't know what your mother is up to, but she's on some sort of tear. I figured you should know that she's trying to fix you up with anything in a skirt."

Justin rolled his eyes. "I'm sort of seeing someone, and I don't think Mama's taking it too well," Justin explained with a huge sigh of relief. The door near him opened and Rock walked in. He looked around, smiled when he saw Justin, and walked toward his table.

"Is that him?" Shawna asked, and Justin grinned. "Lucky little shit," she whispered, reminding him of the way she'd been in high school. Justin's grin lasted until well after Rock sat down and Shawna had moved on to another table.

"How was the first day back? No issues breathing or coughing?" Rock asked.

"Nope," Justin answered with no issues talking, either—that was nice. He knew full well Rock knew that information. If he hadn't had any breathing issues last night, he certainly wasn't going to today, unless he'd had to chase a suspect through town on foot. He'd gotten quite a bit of exercise with Rock.

"Good," Rock said before leaning over the table. "I was hoping I hadn't worn you out."

"Nope, you'll have to try harder next time," Justin said happily, as, on cue, his phone rang. "My sister," Justin said and then answered the phone. "Hi, Lynanne." Justin kept his voice as light and happy as possible. "How are you?"

"You know very well how I am," she began, already under a full head of steam. "Mother is beside herself, and I just hung up from Chrissy and she told me everything."

"Good, so I don't have to repeat myself," Justin quipped.

"Look, you will—" She was really building up to something, and Justin cut her off.

"That's enough!" Justin snapped into the phone, keeping his voice low and letting his tone convey his irritation. "You can stop being Mama's mouthpiece and parroting what Chrissy thinks. I used to wonder why the three of you thought alike, but I think I know now. You share a brain. Put you, Chrissy, and Mama together and you'd have one."

"Justin!" she cried with all the drama she could muster.

"I don't know what you've got in that mind of yours, or why you feel you need to be involved in this, but I've had about enough."

"The way you're behaving with… with… that man is wrong, and you know it," she said in her superior tone. "And you're killing Mother by behaving this way."

Justin sighed, and he could feel his resistance begin to waver the way it usually did under the joint onslaught of his mother and sisters.

"You've never met him and yet you're ready to judge both him and me?" Justin looked across the table to Rock, and his resolve built again. If he wanted to have Rock, or anyone, in his life, then he needed to be able to stand up to his family and for what he felt was his right. "I think you should pay more attention to yourself and my niece and nephew. Jerome and Felicia need you to spend your time and effort on them." Two could play the guilt game. "I'll talk to you later; I'm on duty," Justin lied, before disconnecting the call.

"It sounds like you're in the middle of a firestorm," Rock said, taking a menu from Shawna.

"Not really, just the usual with my mother and sisters," Justin said. He wasn't going to tell Rock that the drama all seemed to revolve around the kiss Rock had given him in the hospital. Because while that might have started the whole thing, the central issue was who was going to control his life, his mother and sisters or he himself. "They're like a group of hens cackling and clucking together at all hours of the day." He half expected Sarah, his youngest sister, to call, but his phone remained blessedly silent, at least for the moment. "Have you heard anything more about the people from yesterday?" Justin asked to change the subject.

"They're both going to be fine. It seems we got to them just in time. The doctors thought there might have been permanent brain damage and it may be too soon to tell if there are long-term effects. But the last I heard they were responsive and talking, so that's a good sign."

"I saw the chief this morning, and he said something pleasant as we passed, so that's a good sign too," Justin said. Things had been going his way for the past few weeks. He'd gotten the department some good press and gotten to know Rock. His sisters and mother be damned—he was happy.

Shawna returned and took their orders, winking at Justin before scooting away. "What's that about?" Rock asked.

"We were friends in high school, and my mother, in her feeble way, tried to play matchmaker. We both got a laugh out of it before you got here." Justin lowered his voice. "I think she's a bit jealous."

Rock looked blank for a second, and then the huge man blushed. "No—"

Justin nodded slightly. "Come on. Half the girls in this town have to be batting their eyes at you whenever you walk by."

Rock shrugged. "Never noticed."

"I guess I didn't either." They shared a chuckle at their joint obtuseness. Shawna brought their lunches, and they ate. Justin kept a sharp eye on the clock, needing to eat quickly before going back on duty. He wolfed his food and then reluctantly motioned Shawna over for the check.

"I know," she said and set it on the table. "You have about five minutes to get back or Jane will get all pissy." Everybody knew everybody in this town.

"Thanks," Justin said, and he grabbed both checks and headed to the register. He paid, and Rock left the tip. They left the restaurant and walked together back toward the ambulance garage. Justin wanted to kiss Rock good-bye when they parted but knew that was a bad idea when they were both in uniform.

"Will I see you tonight?" Rock asked, and Justin couldn't help smiling.

"My shift ends at seven," Justin said.

"Mine ends at eight, so I'll meet you at your place about nine with pizza," Rock offered, and Justin accepted, never one to turn down pizza.

"I'll see you then," Justin said with a wide smile before getting back in his cruiser and calling in that he was back on duty.

"You just made it," Jane told him, and Justin echoed in the affirmative before going back to work. He had hours to sit, broken up by speeders and lane shifters who tried to rush the light. By the end of his shift, Justin was tired and damned cranky. The car had been hot, and even with the engine and AC running, the sun had beaten through the windshield all afternoon. Justin drove his cruiser back to the station, checked in, and picked up his own car for the drive home.

Once there, he sluggishly climbed the stairs and unlocked his apartment. He was tired, cranky, and a sweaty mess. After dropping his keys on the table, Justin kicked off his shoes and padded in his sock feet to the bathroom, where he stripped out of his uniform and turned on the water for a shower before stepping under the spray. God, the water felt good, and Justin's body reacted almost immediately, his cock pointing toward the ceiling, especially when he thought of Rock. Justin washed quickly and stepped out of the shower, drying himself and then hurrying to his bedroom to dress. He didn't want to be tempted to take care of things on his own when Rock was going to be over in a few hours.

After dressing, Justin cleaned up the bathroom and put his uniform in the dirty clothes hamper to be laundered. He got a small snack and settled in the living room to wait for Rock. He was halfway through an episode of *Big Bang Theory* when his buzzer rang. It was too early for Rock, but he got up and opened his apartment door in time to see his mother coming up the stairs with a man he didn't know behind her. "I buzzed so you'd know I was here," his mother said. He held the door and both of them walked into the apartment like they owned it.

"I wasn't expecting you," he told his mother. The least she could have done was call.

"This is Dr. Weston," his mother said, ignoring what Justin had said. "He's here to help you."

Justin stilled. "Help me? How? I don't need any help."

"Yes, you do, son," Dr. Weston said. "I'm here to help you recover from these deviant urges." He stood eye to eye with Justin. "I helped you before, and I can help you again." The doctor didn't bat an eyelash, meeting Justin's gaze. "Now I want you to sit down and relax."

"Helped me before? How? When?" Justin took a step back, his anger building quickly.

"That doesn't matter now," Dr. Weston said before turning to his mother. "He just needs to be reminded about what we talked about before and he'll be just fine." The doctor turned back to him, and Justin knew he wasn't letting this man anywhere near him, but he had to find out what in hell he meant.

"Remind me of what?" Justin asked.

"He helped you when you were younger," his mother said. "And look what happened. You were a good boy for such a long time."

"He helped me how?" Justin asked. The doctor moved closer to him, and Justin turned. "You move a muscle and I'll take you out in two seconds. I'm not a kid any longer and I don't know what you think you helped me with, but you aren't coming near me again." Justin turned back to his mother, anger blazing. "You better talk fast, Mom, because you've got about ten seconds before I throw the both of you out of here."

The doorbell rang again, and a few seconds later he heard Rock's heavy steps on the stairs. A knock sounded on the door, and Justin called for Rock to come in. He opened the door, carrying a pizza box.

"I know I'm early. Do you want me to come back?" Rock turned to leave.

"No, please come in. These two were just leaving."

"I'm not going anywhere!" Justin's mother pronounced. "I want Dr. Weston to look at you."

Justin turned to Weston. "What kind of quack are you?"

"I'm a psychologist," he answered, straightening himself up. "I'm not a quack," he added self-righteously.

"No?" Rock said as he set the pizza on the counter. "Well, why don't you tell me what you're practicing? So I can inform the Pennsylvania Board of Medicine. I'm sure they would be interested in you." Dr. Weston went slightly pale. "You see, I've heard about you, and I'm sure Justin here would like to know exactly what you did to him."

Rock backed Dr. Weston up until he collapsed into a chair.

"Now see here. You've done enough damage to my son," Justin's mother said to Rock.

"Mother," Justin said, stepping in. "I think it's time you went home. Rock and I will find out exactly what happened when Dr. Weston 'helped' me and what you allowed him to do. Based on what he tells us, I may or may not give you a call… ever." Justin pointed toward the door. "Go home now." Justin could barely contain his anger. "Go, Mother! I can't look at you right now." Justin was shaking, he was so angry, and he watched as his mother's defiance turned to defeat before his eyes. She turned slowly and walked toward the door.

"I did what I thought was best," she said softly and then left the apartment followed by their glares.

Justin watched her go, unable to feel anything but anger before turning to this "doctor." "So, what was it you did to me?"

"Every treatment was fully authorized by your mother," Dr. Weston said.

"I don't care. You aren't authorized to do anything right now except spill your guts. Now!"

"I think I'll be going now," the doctor said, and Rock glared at him, crossing his arms over his chest.

"You're not going anywhere. You have a lot of explaining to do and you'd better start now," Rock growled. "Bygones can be bygones and confession is good for the soul, so start talking."

"Yes. You're going to tell me what I want to know," Justin said. "You've already admitted to plenty."

The doctor looked confused, and Justin figured it was time to press any advantage they might have, but Rock beat him to it. "You've already admitted to using questionable and unapproved treatment methods on patients too young and impressionable to know better. Those methods could cause permanent harm and would definitely result in the loss of any license you might have to practice." Rock was laying it on thick, and Justin kept quiet. He could already see the doctor's leg twitching nervously. "So start talking."

"Your mother came to me. She said she'd caught you with a neighbor boy and she wanted help in curing you," Dr. Weston explained.

"And of course you were happy to oblige," Rock said and then glanced at Justin before turning back to the doctor. "What did you use— aversion therapy? Shock treatments?"

"Mostly hypnosis. Justin was incredibly responsive," the doctor explained, and to Justin's surprise he seemed to be warming to his subject. "But you can't affect someone's inner desires or make them do something they know is wrong. That's the safeguard. I told his mother that." Dr. Weston looked at Justin. "But she insisted that you needed to be cured, so I gave you a suggestion that whenever you thought about someone you were attracted to, your mouth would go dry and you wouldn't be able to speak to them."

"That shouldn't have worked over time," Rock said.

"No, it shouldn't, but I was able to reinforce the suggestion through multiple visits," Dr. Weston said proudly. "And from what your mother told me, it seemed to work. She saw instances where you couldn't talk to people, and she was very happy. I figured the effect would decline over time, especially when you became an adult," Dr. Weston explained, clearly nervous again now that he realized what he'd said.

"You broke every ethical rule of your profession. You're supposed to help people, not cause harm, and that's what you did. You gave his mother control over a part of who he was," Rock said, anger simmering in his voice.

"But it really shouldn't have worked, not for long anyway," the doctor explained.

"Did you also have me forget our sessions?" Justin asked, and the doctor nodded. "Get out," Justin yelled. "I've listened to and seen enough of you. Get out of my apartment and stay the hell away from me or anyone in my family." Justin stepped closer to the doctor. "And if I ever get wind of you 'helping' anyone the way you helped me, I'll do whatever I have to get your license pulled. You understand?"

The doctor nodded. Now it was his turn to be speechless. Justin stepped away, and Dr. Weston grabbed his bag and made a beeline for the door, closing it behind him. Justin heard his rapid footsteps on the stairs.

"Jesus," Justin sighed softly. "My own damned mother. How could she do that to me?" He flopped in one of the nearby chairs. "I knew she was manipulative—she's always been that—but this is damned near evil."

Rock leaned forward and took his hand lightly. "She thought she was doing the right thing for you," Rock said softly.

Justin's frustration and anger boiled over. "How can you defend her? She tried to change me, to impose her will over mine! That's deplorable." Justin jumped to his feet, pulling his hand away from Rock's as he moved. "There's no excuse for what she did. None at all, and for you to take her side... it's... it's...." Justin held his head in his hands, thinking it was going to explode at any second. "God, I don't know what it is. There isn't a category to put what she did in. But for you to say she had her reasons, like what she did makes any kind of sense...." Justin wandered through the apartment and then turned to stare at Rock. He'd been so hopeful, but maybe Rock wasn't the person Justin had thought he was. His own mother certainly wasn't.

"I'm not saying your mother was right, just that at the time she might have had her reasons," Rock said evenly. "I didn't mean to upset you. I'm just—"

"You don't want to upset me?" Justin said, cutting Rock off. "Okay, she did what she thought was right when I was a kid and made me a freak whose throat closed up whenever I tried to talk to a guy I liked. Fine, I was a kid, but that doesn't explain her trying to get Dr. Quack to give me a booster of the insanity." Justin flung his arms around. "No, I can't deal with this. Maybe you better go," he said softly, trying to contain his rage. "I need to be alone." Justin went into the kitchen and opened the refrigerator door, all the while listening as the chair creaked when Rock stood up. Justin didn't hear footsteps for a few precious seconds, and he hoped Rock was going to try to comfort him.

But Rock left, closing the door softly behind him, and Justin was alone. It was what he'd just said he wanted, but the apartment seemed empty and silent. The only remnant of anyone else was the box of now-chilling pizza still sitting on the counter. Justin ignored it and pulled a beer out of the refrigerator—hell, he grabbed one in each hand, then kicked the door closed.

He flopped down on the sofa and cracked open the first beer, downing it in a few gulps before opening the other. If his life was going to change in a few seconds, and everything and everyone he knew turned out to be a lie, then he might as well tie one on and try to forget about it for a few hours.

The second beer went down almost as smoothly as the first. Justin placed the cans on the coffee table and got two more, then opened the third and took a gulp. His phone rang, and he picked it up, looking at the display. It was Chrissy, and he sent it right to voice mail. She could bitch to someone else. Justin was done with both her and Lynanne as well as his mother. The old bat could rot in hell for what she'd done to him. He was through with the lot of them. After a few seconds, his phone chimed that he had a voice mail. He ignored that and the ensuing calls from Lynanne, his mother, and two from Rock. After the second one, he turned off the phone, drank two more beers, and went to bed.

# Chapter 5

JUSTIN WOKE with a splitting headache and a desert-dry mouth. God, he needed to remember not to drink, especially when he was feeling depressed. It didn't make the issue go away, and he felt doubly bad in the morning. Justin got out of bed and set his feet on the floor before standing up carefully. Thank God the room stayed in one place. He'd been up in the night and had taken some aspirin and drunk a big glass of water before going back to bed. That was probably the only reason he felt remotely human this morning. Justin shuffled to the bathroom, showered, and brushed his teeth—twice. Then he shaved and went back into his bedroom to dress. By the time he'd had his coffee and was ready to leave, he almost felt normal.

He drove to work and parked in the lot before heading inside to get his traffic duty assignment. He was really hoping it had changed. He wasn't sure he could sit outside the ambulance garage knowing the way he'd treated Rock and that the man was inside working. "Same old place," Jane told him, and Justin sighed. He wasn't looking forward to this. "What's got you looking like a beaten rug?"

"Nothing," Justin said.

"Don't give me that crap," Jane told him. She always gave Justin shit, but he really liked her. She was a feisty black lady and she didn't take crap from anyone, including the chief. "Girlfriend troubles?" Justin shook his head. "Boyfriend troubles?" she pressed, and Justin's eyes widened. "Well, there was a fifty-fifty chance," she said. "So what did you do?"

"Me? He...." Justin paused. "It's a long story. Maybe I'll tell you the whole tale over a beer sometime."

"But you still did something wrong," she said, boring her gaze into him.

"No, I didn't, and how would you know?"

Jane rolled her huge eyes. "You're a man. Of course you did something wrong."

Justin smiled slightly. "He's a man too. He could have done something wrong."

"True," Jane said as she continued working. "But the chances are since you're both men, it's likely you both acted like asses." Jane backed away from the dispatcher window and answered a call before returning. "Think about it and you'll know I'm right."

"Well…," Justin prevaricated.

"Ain't no 'well' about it," she said, slipping into her down-home speech to make her point. "Think about what happened, and I bet once you look at it from the other side, you'll realize you were an ass." Another call came on. "Now go on, I have work to do. But I'm holding you to that beer and the story."

Justin nodded and left, heading out to his cruiser. He pulled out of the lot and drove through town before parking in what was beginning to feel like his spot. Traffic was heavy, so everyone was going fairly slowly. He thought about radioing in for another location for a few hours, but it wasn't long before traffic thinned as people got to work, and speeds picked up.

One thing about traffic duty—he had plenty of time to think. "Damn it," he said after watching traffic for a few hours. Jane had, of course, been right. He had been an ass. He'd treated Rock really badly.

A car pulled into the garage parking lot, and Justin watched it for a few seconds before letting it pass out of his sight. Another followed close behind, and this one Justin knew well. He watched in his rearview mirror as it stopped and Rock got out. He saw Rock look his way and then join his coworker for the walk inside. Turning his attention back to the traffic, Justin sighed and wished the clock on the dashboard would move just a little faster.

He was never so happy for lunch in his life. He walked up to the diner, but sat alone. Shawna was all business, and Justin realized he must have been giving off stay-away vibes, because everyone certainly was doing just that. After lunch, he returned to his car and called in that he was returning to duty. Jane acknowledged his call, and he'd just settled back in his seat when his phone rang.

He picked it up and was about to ignore Chrissy's call, but figured he might as well get it over with. "What is it?" he said as he answered.

"Is that any way to answer the phone?" she asked, but her tone seemed light and teasing, something he hadn't heard from her in a while.

"If you're calling to talk about Mom, I don't want to hear it."

"She told me what happened," Chrissy said. "And I'm sorry."

Justin nearly dropped the phone. "You're what?" Chrissy was never sorry about anything.

"Look, I don't believe being gay is right. The bible says it's not, but you're my brother, and when we were growing up you were such a nice kid."

"I'm still a nice person. The fact that I like men instead of women doesn't change that," Justin said, watching traffic outside his window.

"That's what Sarah said. Mom called all three of us over and told us what you did. I know she was trying for sympathy, and… I'll admit, I was ready to give it to her, but Sarah was ruthless. She grilled Mom like there was no tomorrow and got her to admit what she'd tried to do last night and what she did when you were a kid. Sarah went ballistic." Justin smiled. *Way to go, Sarah.* "She told Mom that if she'd done that to her, she'd have done a lot more than throw her out of the apartment."

"Did you call just to tell me this?"

"Well, yes, I guess." She seemed to be searching for words. "I know it isn't going to be easy for me, but I want you in my life. You're my brother, and I need to stop treating you like a kid. We all do."

"Well, it's about time," Justin groused.

"Is that necessary?" Chrissy asked.

"Think about it," Justin said, and he heard Chrissy sigh softly.

"Okay, maybe you have a point. But I do have to ask what you're going to do about Mom," Chrissy said.

Justin thought for a few seconds. "Nothing at all. If she wants some sort of relationship with me, then she'll have to come to me, hat in hand, and issue a heartfelt apology. Then she and I will have a long talk about her role in my life. Maybe then, just maybe, I'll decide she's worth being in my life."

"You don't mean that," Chrissy said, sounding aghast.

"Yes, I do. What she did was deplorable and beyond decency. It was cruel, thoughtless, and manipulative as hell. It's what she does, and I'm not going to put up with it any longer. After Dad left, you, Lynanne, and Sarah got all her attention, and I was left out. Well, I'm not going to let that happen again…." Justin paused. "Fuck… fuck, fuck!" he yelled, probably denting his sister's delicate sensibilities. "That's exactly what I did let happen."

"What are you swearing about?" Chrissy asked.

"Nothing you can help with," Justin said, getting his thoughts together. "Remember I never had the close relationship with Mom you girls had. I was the boy, and she never paid much attention to me other than to tell me what I was doing wrong. So leaving her behind isn't that hard. It isn't difficult to lose something you never really had." Justin knew he had to get off the phone very soon.

"You're serious?" Chrissy asked.

"Yes. So tell Mom what I said, and if she's upset, then she needs to either live with it or do something about it." Justin put the car into gear and flipped on his lights. "I have to go." He disconnected the call and threw the phone on the seat before pulling out into traffic and pulling over a familiar speeder who batted her eyelashes a few times until she got a good look at him.

"Not you again," she said, and then she began looking in her purse for her license. At least this time she hadn't waved her chest in his face.

THE REST of his shift was more of the same, and then, finally, it was over. In a week, he'd transition to nights for a while. He really hated working that shift, but at least he wouldn't be on traffic detail. Back at the station, he checked in with dispatch and was about to go home when he saw Marty getting ready to leave as well. "Can I ask you something?"

"Sure," Marty answered as they headed for the door. "What's up?"

"Well, you've dated a lot. What do you do when you really mess up bad? You know, say something hurtful and stupid?" Justin patted Marty lightly on the back and chuckled. "I'm sure you've done that more than once."

"Yeah, twice this week alone," Marty said. "I usually try flowers, or something cute if we're up to that stage, but flowers first. Why? What did you do?" Marty stopped walking. "I didn't know you were dating a girl."

"I'm not," Justin said truthfully. "Not a girl, anyway." Justin didn't talk about his relationships, mainly because he hadn't had any, but he wasn't going to keep Rock a secret. That is, if he could get Rock to forgive him after the way he'd acted.

"So you're dating an older woman?" Marty asked, clearly a bit confused.

"I'm dating a guy, Marty. Or at least I was until my mother dumped a whole sackload of shit on me and I took it out on him," Justin explained and waited for Marty's reaction. "He's one of the EMTs who helped at the bus incident, and we sort of connected after that."

"You're gay?" Marty asked.

"I think that's obvious if I'm dating another guy," Justin said lightly, trying to put Marty at ease somehow. He didn't want to lose his friend, but was prepared if it came to that. "Is it a problem? Because I can just go." Justin walked away, heading out the door.

"No, newbie, it isn't a problem," Marty said as he hurried after him. "It's just a surprise, that's all. Don't get your panties in a twist," he added as he caught up. "You know some of the other guys aren't going to like it."

"So? If they try anything, Jane will send them all over town," Justin quipped.

"She knows and she's okay with it?"

"Yes. She's a smart lady."

"Okay, then. So what did you do to piss off this boyfriend of yours?" Marty asked. "Only answer that question if there's no bedroom parts. Your being gay is one thing, but I don't want to hear about any horizontal hulas."

Justin shook his head in amazement. "It's a long story, and when I tell Jane I'll tell you. For now, let's just say I opened my mouth and shoved my foot down my throat." Justin walked toward his car, and Marty hurried to his as thunder sounded in the distance.

"Then try chocolate," Marty shouted before pulling his car door open. Justin raised his hand in thanks and got in his car as well. He pulled out of the lot and drove through town. As he was pulling into the parking lot of the florist, the sky opened up, and he waited for a few seconds before making a dash for it.

The rain pounded the windows and the roof of the shop as Justin looked around. The place was filled with bouquets and arrangements—some real, some artificial—as well as other things, and Justin was completely lost.

"Can I help you?" a woman asked as she came around the counter. "Is there a problem?" she added, and Justin remembered he was still in uniform.

"Only with me, and I hope you can help me. I need something that says I messed up really bad and I'm sorry," Justin explained. He had no idea what to get—flowers, or, really, romantic stuff of any kind, which was completely foreign to him. His sisters had gotten things from boyfriends and the like, but he wasn't quite sure if it worked the same way for guys.

"If it's a girlfriend, then roses always make a statement," she said, and Justin looked at her name tag.

"Well, Linda, um...." He hesitated, and then he forged on. "The person in question is another guy. I'm hoping he'll still be my boyfriend after what I said, but I really don't know." Justin shifted nervously from foot to foot. He hated telling strangers his business, but he needed good advice.

"Does he like sports?" Linda asked.

They'd never discussed it. In fact, as he thought things over, Justin realized he didn't know much about Rock. He'd talked quite a bit about his own family, and Rock had even stood up for him when he was in the hospital, but he'd never really asked about Rock's family, and information hadn't been volunteered. Justin made a point to ask Rock about himself. That is, if Rock forgave him for acting like a complete ass. "I believe so," Justin said, remembering that at the gym, Rock seemed to watch the sports channels.

"We have some sports-themed arrangements that the guys seem to like," Linda said, and Justin followed her. "Or you could just bring a bouquet of simple cut flowers." She must have seen the confusion in Justin's expression.

"I think I'll do that," Justin said, and Linda helped him pick one out and wrap it. Justin paid and then left the shop, feeling better as a plan of action formed in his mind. After leaving the florist, he dodged raindrops getting to his car and hurried home. Justin showered and changed clothes before grabbing the flowers and driving to Rock's historic house.

Justin found a parking spot just up the street and got out of the car. He reached for the flowers and then closed his car door before walking up the sidewalk. Three houses away, he stopped as another man knocked on the door to Rock's house. It opened, and Justin saw Rock and the other man hug before they stepped inside. He heard the door close, and all the energy went out of his step. He wasn't going to interrupt whatever they were doing. No, he'd screwed up royally, and Rock had found someone else. Justin turned around and walked back to his car.

He drove home feeling like a complete idiot. Maybe Rock had been seeing this other guy the whole time. Justin didn't really think so, but that was always a possibility. Thankfully, the rain had stopped, and Justin drove home and parked. He climbed the stairs carrying the flowers, and once inside, placed them in a plastic pitcher before pulling out his phone after it chirped to remind him that he had messages. He decided it was time to listen to the voice mails he'd blown off.

Justin quickly passed through the ones from his sisters and mother—there was no point in listening to them—but he stopped as soon as he heard Rock's deep voice. "I didn't mean to upset you, please call me," the first one said. He deleted it and listened to the second. "I know you need time to think, but I'm not your enemy. Please return my call." Both of them sounded more concerned than angry, and Justin ticked himself up an additional two notches on the idiot scale.

He wanted to phone Rock back, but after what he'd seen at Rock's house, he didn't think there was really much point. Still, he owed Rock a call, so he returned Rock's voice mail, left a brief message, and hung up, feeling like complete shit. He'd brought this on himself. He might want to be angry with Rock, Chrissy, his mother, and everyone else, but the only person he could blame for this particular mess was himself. There was nothing more he could do, so Justin grabbed a beer out of the refrigerator and settled on the sofa.

His heart jumped when his phone rang, and he answered it right away. "Hello," he said hopefully.

"Jus, it's Sarah." His youngest sister's bright voice lessened some of the gloom that hung in the room. "How are you doing?"

"Don't know," he answered truthfully. "I heard you laid into Mom big-time."

"She was way out of line," Sarah explained. "She'll come around. You just need to give her time."

"Doesn't really matter," Justin said calmly.

"If it doesn't, then why do you sound like death warmed over? And don't tell me you're fine, because I can tell and you know it," she added sharply. "Or is it more than Mom?"

"She's part of it," Justin said and took a drink from his beer. He'd much rather get drunk again and go to bed than have this conversation. But he knew if he didn't talk to her now, Sarah would come over and pester him into telling her anyway. Then she'd clean everything and put things away so he could never find them. He didn't mind the cleaning part, but not being able to find the forks could get difficult.

"Then what's the rest? What did you do? Mom told me about the man at the hospital. Is he your boyfriend?" Sarah's questions came fast and furious.

"I thought maybe he was, but I acted like an ass and sent him away," Justin explained. "He showed up after Mom arrived with that doctor, and I was so angry that once Mom left, and he seemed to take her side, I thought my head was going to explode, so I told him to go. Now, before you tell me what I should do, you should know I stopped at the florist on my way home from work and bought flowers. I went to his place and saw another guy going in. So…."

"So you figured like a dope that he'd already found someone else. What did he do, call Dial a Hunk? Please… the guy you saw was probably a friend. He was probably trying to figure out what happened, just like you, and called a friend for some advice. That's what a normal person would do. Did you call him?"

"Yes, I left a message, but he hasn't called me back."

"Then don't worry about it. He'll probably call once his friend leaves, and you two can talk it out."

"But what if he doesn't call?" God, he sounded like a teenager.

"Then he doesn't call, and you find someone else, if that's what you want," Sarah told him, and he could almost see her rolling her eyes. "Do you like him?"

"Yeah. He's a nice guy," Justin said quietly. Rock was more than that. He was someone Justin felt comfortable with. "I'll call you later," Justin said as he reached for his beer once again. He needed to get off the phone so he could wallow in self-pity alone.

"Okay, but stop with the beer. It won't help," Sarah said. "Don't think I don't know you're sitting in the living room eating God knows what, drinking a beer, and figuring out if you should just have a few more before going to bed. The beer doesn't do anything except make you fat."

"Thanks for that," Justin said, looking down at the flat stomach he'd worked so hard for.

"Anytime." Sarah laughed and then hung up.

Justin sighed and hung up as well, placing the phone on the coffee table along with the half-empty can of beer. She was right; that wasn't going to help. He pushed himself up and got a bottle of water from the refrigerator and sat back down. He watched television until it was time to go to bed, his phone silent all evening.

# Chapter 6

JUSTIN WENT to work the following day and found his assignment had changed. Oh, he was still on traffic duty, but he'd been given a different section of town to patrol, so he wouldn't be parked outside the ambulance garage all day watching to see when Rock came and went. He thought about calling again, but he'd already left a message once and that was enough. He'd been stationed on the north side of town to control the speed of people coming into town from one of the car shows out at the fairgrounds, which meant there would be plenty of activity and he'd have a lot to keep him busy. In fact, Justin had just gotten done writing a ticket and was about to call in that he was going to lunch when a souped-up white car driven by a kid with more money than brains zoomed by him without making any effort to slow down.

Justin turned on his lights and siren and called in that he was in pursuit. "The driver is heading east on Harrisburg Pike, speeding up and weaving in and out of traffic," Justin said, giving a description and the license number as he sped up.

"Copy that. We'll have other units intercept. Contacting Middlesex police as well." The area was a patchwork of municipalities. Justin continued driving as fast and safely as he could, but traffic was heavy, and he hoped this driver didn't kill himself or someone else. "Middlesex police are responding," Jane reported. "Stay with them."

"Roger that," Justin said. His main concern right now was public safety. This guy was driving like a maniac, and Justin wondered what he was on. The white car swerved and turned onto one of the country roads heading north. Justin reported his position and made the turn, then sped up to try to keep the other car in sight. The car flew over the pavement, and as Justin crested a hill, his wheels momentarily left the ground. Justin barely noticed as the chase continued.

"Vehicles are heading to intercept on Cavalry Road," dispatch said, and Justin acknowledged the call and kept going. Hopefully they could get this guy in a vise move. Up ahead, Justin saw the white car cut around another vehicle. The other car swerved and the driver overcompensated. A car was coming the other way—Justin heard brakes squeal and the crunch of metal. "I have an accident on Arsenal ahead of me," Justin said.

"Stop and render assistance," he was instructed, and Justin slowed. He heard dispatch speaking to the other cars, and they had the suspect in sight and were in pursuit.

"I need medical assistance," Justin said as he approached the accident, and dispatch acknowledged the call. He stopped his car and got out. A man from the first car was already getting out. "Is everyone okay?" Justin asked.

"Yeah," the driver said, and Justin peered in the car.

"Is there anyone with you?"

"No," the man answered. "I'm fine, just shaken up."

"I've already called for assistance. Sit down if you need to. Help is on the way." Justin was already on his way to the red Mustang, which was more heavily damaged. The air bags had deployed and deflated. "Are you okay?" Justin asked, rapping lightly on the driver's side window, and he heard someone moan inside. Justin tried the door, but it wouldn't move—too damaged. He hurried to the other side of the car and managed to get the passenger door open. He leaned across the seat and found himself staring into Rock's eyes. Rock looked at him for a few seconds, moaning again softly. "I've already called for help," Justin said, trying to remain businesslike, but he could hardly breathe. "Can you move at all?"

"Legs are trapped," Rock said faintly. His face was bloody, probably from where the airbag hit him, or broken glass. God, he hoped that was all it was. Sirens sounded in the distance.

"We're going to get you out of here as fast as we can. I promise." Justin wanted to smooth the hair away from Rock's face, and he was finding it very hard to remain dispassionate, especially when Rock kept moaning softly. The sirens got louder, and Justin backed out of the car, looking at the other driver. "Are you still okay?"

"Yes, I'm not hurt. Is he okay? The guy in the white car swerved around me, and I had no place to go," the man said.

"I saw the whole thing," Justin said. "It wasn't your fault." *It was the asshole driving like a maniac trying to outrun the police.* Ambulances, fire trucks, and more officers arrived. Justin informed everyone what had happened and the state of things, and they went to work. Justin got a statement from the uninjured driver, Terry Lofton, while the fire department used the Jaws of Life to pull apart Rock's car. Finally, they got him out and onto a stretcher. He looked like hell, and it took all his willpower for Justin to continue doing his job.

"Do you need to go to the hospital?" one of the paramedics asked Mr. Lofton, and he declined.

"I'm fine. Just shaken up," he said again.

"Do you need a ride or to make a call?" Justin asked.

"My wife is on her way," he said. One of the officers let a woman through, and she hurried to her husband, engulfing him in a hug. "Is there anything more?"

"Not for now. You can call for a report number for the insurance company later tonight. A tow truck is on its way, and we'll have the vehicle taken to a holding area, unless you need to get some things out of it now." Justin said. Mr. Lofton retrieved a few things from his car, and the relieved woman led her husband away.

"How is he?" Justin asked one of the paramedics.

"Not good," he answered. The back door of the ambulance was still open, and Justin climbed in. Rock filled the stretcher, but he was quiet, and his eyes were closed. Justin willed them to open so he could tell Rock he was sorry for everything. "You need to step out. We're going to get him transported."

Justin backed out of the ambulance, and the paramedic closed the doors. A few moments later the ambulance began to move, its sirens screaming and fading into the distance.

"Is that him?" Marty asked, and Justin turned around. He hadn't even noticed that his friend was there.

"Yeah, how'd you know?" Justin asked.

"By the way you were looking at him. Sometimes it's hard to remain objective when you stumble across a victim you know," Marty told him. "Go on and head back to the station. You need to get your report written up. I'll stay here and make sure everything is cleaned up and towed away." Marty flashed him a quick smile and returned to the scene, and Justin heard him calling in to ask where the tow trucks were.

Justin got in his cruiser and drove back to the station. Inside, he found a desk and a computer and began typing up his report. It took a while, and he had to stop a few times when he wrote the part about the condition he'd found Rock in. He finished the report and sent it to the captain before gathering his things and leaving the station to go home, but his car headed the other way almost on its own. Justin ended up at the hospital. He parked in the lot and headed inside. It didn't take him long to find out that Rock was still in Emergency, so he headed over there and inquired at the desk.

"He's being admitted and moved to a room," she told him. "The computer hasn't been updated with the number yet, but it should be soon if you'd care to sit."

Justin thanked her and sat down, waiting for a while before he got up again and walked around the area. He sat again, paged through a few magazines, and once again got restless.

"Sir, I have the room number for you," the woman said, and Justin jumped up, striding to the window. "He's in 412."

"Thank you," Justin said and hurried away down the halls and into the main portion of the hospital. In the main lobby, he called the elevator and rode it to the fourth floor and strode down the hallways toward room 412. At the open door, he paused before going inside. He wasn't sure what he was going to find. When he went inside, Rock lay still on the bed with monitors hooked to him showing all his vitals.

Rock didn't move when he came in, and Justin settled in the chair next to the bed. No reaction at all. A nurse came in and checked the machines.

"How is he?" he asked her.

She shook her head. "I'm sorry. I really can't discuss his condition."

She finished up what she was doing and left. Justin didn't know what he should do, and after sitting for a while—something he didn't do very well—he wandered down to the cafeteria and got something to eat. When he returned, he found two other men in Rock's room. Justin recognized both of them. One was Lee, the firefighter from the bus accident, and the other was the man he'd seen going into Rock's house. These two were clearly together.

"Excuse me," Justin said quietly as he stepped into the room.

"Hi, Justin," Lee said softly. The man was even bigger than Rock, if that was possible. "This is my partner, Dirk. We heard about Rock and rushed over."

Dirk nodded his greeting and glared daggers at Justin.

"Knock it off," Lee said softly to Dirk. "There are two sides to everything, and you don't need to get all pissy on Rock's behalf." Lee and Dirk moved away from the bed, but Justin didn't move any closer. He wasn't sure if he should stay or simply leave. "Have they told you anything?" Lee asked.

"No. Just that they're admitting him." Justin moved closer as Lee nodded. "I came up after I wrote up my report."

"How did you know he was hurt?" Dirk asked rather menacingly.

Justin ignored the tone, and Dirk, and continued looking at Rock. "I saw the accident. I was chasing a suspect who caused another car to swerve into Rock's." Justin swallowed hard. "I was at the scene and found him."

"Jesus," Lee muttered, and Justin even saw Dirk's expression soften slightly.

"I think it was the EMTs who probably saved his life. They got him out of the car really fast and stopped the bleeding." Justin walked to the side of Rock's bed and lifted the hand that didn't have an IV attached. He ignored the others in the room and concentrated on Rock. "I'm sorry I was such a fool. I got you flowers yesterday and was going to bring them to you, but I saw Dirk going into your place and thought you were seeing someone else. So I went back home." Justin wiped his eyes with the back of his hand.

"See, I told you," Lee said softly, and Dirk grunted.

Justin shifted his gaze to Dirk. "I called and left a message, but he didn't call back."

Dirk looked away, and Justin saw his shoulders raise and lower. He thought Dirk might be crying, but when Dirk turned around, he was laughing. Lee jabbed Dirk in the side with his elbow. "What's so funny?"

"Rock was using the bathroom and dropped his phone in the toilet. It was completely fried, and he was supposed to get another one. But when you do, they erase your voice mail account, so your message was probably lost."

"And that's funny?" Lee hissed.

"No, but the part about Rock peeing and texting at the same time and then 'plop' is." Dirk turned to Lee. "Come on, you know the man can't multitask to save his life, and a cell phone doesn't stand a chance around him. He's had three already this year."

Lee suppressed a smile. "I don't think now is the time to discuss it."

"At least it explains why he didn't call me back," Justin said, lightly stroking the back of Rock's hand with his thumb. "I wish he'd wake up."

"They probably gave him stuff for pain, and with the loss of blood, his body is going to need to rest," Dirk said in a reasonably human tone. "I can't believe you thought I was seeing Rock," he said, changing the subject. "He's talked about you for days, and when you sent him away, you hurt him."

"Dirk," Lee said.

"He needs to hear this," Dirk said and turned back to Justin. "Rock is one of those guys who listens to both sides of everything, not like me. He should have been a judge. Sometimes it's a pain in the ass, but it also means he's good at his job because of his empathy. For the past two days he was hurting because he knew you were hurting."

"Did he say what happened?"

"No," Dirk answered. "He wouldn't."

"I didn't mean to hurt him," Justin said.

"I know," Rock whispered from the bed, and Justin felt him squeeze his hand. "You needed time to think."

"Rock," Justin said softly. "You're going to be okay."

"I know," he said before closing his eyes again. "Did you get the guy who caused the accident?"

"Yes, we got him. He was running because the car was full of drugs. They found a bunch of cocaine when they pulled him over," Justin explained before moving closer. "I'm sorry for what I said."

"I know," Rock said, keeping his eyes closed. Relief washed over Justin, and he turned to the other two men, who each had an arm around the other's waist.

"Is there anyone I should call for you?" Justin asked Rock, who rolled his head on the pillow but didn't say anything more.

"We should go," Lee said, and Dirk nodded. They walked to the other side of the bed and both said good-bye to Rock before leaving the room. Justin pulled the chair closer and continued holding Rock's hand as he settled in the chair and closed his eyes.

Justin dozed, waking when he felt Rock move. He turned toward the bed, and Rock's big, deep, beautiful eyes shone back at him and then attempted to flash a smile, but it shifted to a grimace.

"I'll get the nurse," Justin said and pressed the call button.

"You're awake," the nurse said as he came in. "How are you feeling? Is there pain?"

"Yeah," Rock said.

"How is it on a scale of one to ten?" he asked.

"Eight," Rock answered.

"Okay, I'll be right back," he said and left the room for a few minutes before returning with a syringe. He shot some of it into Rock's IV line before checking his blood pressure and taking his temperature. "Is that better?"

"Yeah, five," Rock said, and the nurse nodded.

"We'll give it a few more minutes," the nurse said and then retrieved a computer on a wheeled cart. He typed and entered what Justin figured was updated vitals data. "Is it better?"

"Still five," Rock said, and the nurse injected a little more. Justin could see the tension drift out of Rock's expression. "Better."

"Good," the nurse said, and then he entered more information into the computer. "You're probably going to sleep for quite a while now. So relax. The more rest you get, the better you're going to feel."

"Both my legs hurt," Rock said.

"They were cut pretty badly, and one's broken," the nurse said.

"You're going to be okay," Justin said, taking Rock's hand once again. The nurse smiled and left the room. Justin sat back in the chair and watched as the medication took over. Rock's eyes drifted closed, and soon he was asleep. Justin stayed for a while more and then left the room as well. There was nothing he could do for him now. Rock needed his rest, and Justin still had to work in the morning. On his way out, Justin stopped at the nurse's station. "Would you tell Rock if he wakes up that I'll be back in the morning to see him?"

"Of course," the nurse said, and Justin left the hospital.

It was dark when he walked across the lot to his car. He got in and drove home, stopping at a drive-through on the way for something else to eat. He parked in the lot and carried the bag of food up the stairs. His door was unlocked, and he heard the television from inside his apartment. Justin pushed open the door slowly and saw his mother sitting on his sofa. "What are you doing here?" Justin asked. He'd already been reaching for his gun.

"I wanted to talk to you, and since you weren't taking my calls, I figured you'd have to come home sometime," she answered without a hint of contrition.

"Then you need to talk fast, because I'm tired, hungry, and I need to go to the hospital first thing in the morning," Justin explained, already making his way to the sofa where he opened the bag and began eating.

"You could have some manners. I raised you better than that," his mother told him.

"How'd you do that? Use hypnosis while we were asleep? Have subliminal messages added to our *Sesame Street* videos?" Justin asked with all the sarcasm he could muster.

His mother blanched, and Justin wondered just what his mother had resorted to when they were growing up. She certainly hadn't spared the rod—or in her case, the wooden spoon—at least not on him. "I came here to talk to you, but if you can't be civil I'll leave." She stood up, and Justin returned to his dinner, paying her no attention. "I'm leaving."

"Bye, Mom," Justin said without looking at her. He'd had enough of her games to last a lifetime, and this was another one. "Please close the door on your way out."

She took a few steps, but didn't leave. "I waited for you for almost two hours," she said.

"I told you to talk fast, and your time is running out. Say what you wanted to say or leave, but don't think for a minute you have any authority here. You don't. You blew any influence or credibility you had when you brought that doctor here. So say your piece, because I have to finish eating and then go to bed." He could see his mother wavering, and finally she walked back into the room and sat down on the very edge of the chair.

"I did what I thought was right," she said. "Is it so bad to want your son to grow up normal, like everyone else?"

"No. But you didn't do that. You brought in some quack to subvert who I really was, and you knew what you were doing. Besides, he didn't do anything to change me. All he did was make me uncomfortable with who I was," Justin explained.

"But you stayed away from other men and were good for such a long time," his mother said a bit plaintively.

"Because I couldn't talk to people I found attractive. That didn't stop me from feeling the way I did. It only made me self-conscious about meeting other people. So, yes, I worked hard at other areas in my life, but it didn't change the way I felt or the way I still feel." He tried to make her understand, but also knew he wasn't going to change her mind about anything. She was many things, and stubborn as a mule was at the top of the list.

"Mom, I'm gay, and I've always been gay and will always be gay. You, my sisters, or all the doctors in the world are never going to change that. So you can either accept it or not—that's up to you. If you do, that's great. If you don't, then we'll see each other on holidays and other family gatherings, and that's all." Justin put down the hamburger he'd been holding and stood up. "But understand, no matter what you decide, I will not tolerate any disrespect from you or my sisters, and that extends to my boyfriend. You will treat him with respect and as you would any in-law, or otherwise you aren't welcome in my life." His mother went pale. "That's the way it is, and if you can't accept that, there's the door and be sure to leave your key." Justin pointed and waited. After a few seconds, his mother stood up, placed her key on the table, and quietly left the apartment without saying a word.

Justin swallowed hard and sat back down. He'd known he was foolish to believe that the result with his mother would be anything else. But he refused to dwell on it and ate the rest of his late dinner before locking the door, turning off all the lights, and getting ready for bed. He had to be up early if he wanted to visit Rock before starting his shift. Not that he slept much. He thought about Rock, and his mother leaving, for most of the night. Justin had thought he was prepared for her rejection— he certainly should have been—but the reality was harder to take than he'd imagined it would be. Finally, at some point during the night, he fell asleep.

# Chapter 7

"THE DOCTOR said I can go home tomorrow," Rock said as Justin sank into the chair beside Rock's bed. He'd been in the hospital three days now, and Justin could tell Rock was itching to go home.

"That's good," Justin said with a yawn. He'd just switched to the night shift, and he was still getting used to it. Visiting Rock before and after his shift wasn't making it easier, but the visits were important to him. "Call me and I'll come pick you up."

"You need to sleep. I can get Dirk or Lee to bring me home," Rock said, but Justin shook his head.

"No. I want to do it." Justin still felt guilty for the way he'd treated Rock, and he wanted the other man to know how he felt, even if he wasn't ready to declare his feelings yet. Justin checked his watch and stood up. "Get some sleep and call me in the morning when they say you can go." Justin leaned over the bed and kissed Rock.

"Are you still feeling guilty about what happened?" Rock asked before their lips touched.

"Yes, a little," Justin admitted.

"Is that why you're doing all this?" Rock asked, and Justin closed the small distance between their lips, pressing Rock's head back against the pillow. Then he stopped and glanced quickly at the doorway before sliding his hand beneath the blankets. He easily found Rock's shaft and gripped him firmly in his hand before squeezing. When Rock moaned softly, Justin kissed him hard, taking possession of the other man's mouth while he stroked. Rock squirmed slightly on the bed, and Justin kissed him harder.

Rock turned his head toward the door, and Justin brought his attention back to him. "Just watch me," he whispered, and kissed Rock again, stroking fast and sure, just the way he liked it himself. Justin swallowed Rock's groans while he squirmed on the bed, thrusting his hips. "That's it, give it to me," Justin whispered, and Rock closed his eyes, gripping the bed with his fists. The bed shook slightly, and then Rock's dick throbbed in his hand and Justin felt Rock coming, all over his hand.

Rock collapsed back against the bedding, and Justin heard him breathe deeply. His eyes closed, and a gentle but incredibly contented smile formed on Rock's lips. "Does that answer your question?" Justin whispered, and Rock nodded slowly and opened his eyes, his gaze showing complete content. Justin wiped his hand on the bedding before leaning over the bed once more, this time kissing Rock very gently. "Go to sleep, and I'll pick you up in the morning."

"Okay," Rock said, already half asleep, and Justin grinned as he left the room and walked down the hall. He rode the elevator down and strode out to his car. He drove to the station, changed into his uniform, and checked in for duty. Then he got in his cruiser with Marty, and the two of them headed out for night patrol.

"Sure makes a difference from traffic duty," Justin said. "At least we get to drive around."

Marty grumbled incoherently and sipped from his cup. "I hate starting a new shift. I always feel like shit, and then when I come off it, I feel like shit again." Marty took another drink from his mug, and Justin hoped he acted less pissy pretty soon. While he knew what Marty meant, there was no use complaining about it.

"At least we don't have to spend the night alone in the cars," Justin said, and Marty nodded again. For night patrol, they were always paired up for safety.

"So how's Rock doing?" Marty asked.

"He gets out of the hospital tomorrow," Justin answered and told his friend all about his encounter with his mother. The night was fairly quiet, and he turned down street after street, watching for anything suspicious, but neither of them saw anything. They got a few calls during the night, but most turned out to be false alarms. However, it did break up the night, and by the time the sun was peeking at the horizon, they were talked out, tired, and ready to get the hell home. They had a few hours left on their shift and decided to spend them near a place where they could get coffee, then at the end of their shift, they headed to the station and eventually home.

Justin trudged up his stairs and into the apartment, barely coherent as he cleaned up and fell into bed. Soon he was dreaming about annoying buzzing noises. Justin swatted his hand over his head, thinking it was a bug, but it didn't stop, and he came to enough to realize what was going on and reached for his phone. "Hello," he said groggily, willing his mind to clear.

"It's Rock. They're going to release me from the hospital." He paused. "I woke you up. Look, I'll call Dirk, and he can come pick me up."

"No," Justin said, sitting up and checking the clock. He'd managed to get about three hours' sleep. "I'm up and I'll be there as soon as I can."

Justin got up out of bed and wandered to the bathroom, cleaning up quickly before dressing and heading out. He drove through town and out to the hospital. He made his way up to Rock's room and found him sitting on the side of the bed. "Are you ready?"

"The doctor released me a few minutes ago, and it looks like my ride is here." An orderly came into the room with a wheelchair, and Rock shifted up onto his crutches and into the chair. Justin walked along as Rock rode through the hospital. When they reached the lobby, Justin pulled the car up, and Rock carefully got inside. The orderly took the chair back inside, and Justin put the car in gear.

They rode through town to Rock's house, and Justin found a place to park right out front. "What did the doctor say you could do?"

"I'm supposed to take it easy, and my leg will be in this thing"—he pointed to the plastic cast in his lower leg—"for about six weeks."

Justin helped Rock out of the car, holding his crutches for him as he maneuvered and got himself up. "Is your leg still painful?"

"It aches," Rock said as he used the crutches to lift himself up and slowly made his way to the door. Rock fussed in front of the house, trying to get his keys, and Justin dug them out of his pocket for him, then unlocked the door and helped him inside. "What a pain in the ass the next six weeks are going to be. The doctor said I could go back to work in a week, but what am I going to do?"

"I don't know," Justin said. He set Rock's keys on the counter. "Right now, you're going to get in bed and put your leg up. Then I'm going to get you something to eat, and you can rest."

"I've been doing that for three days," Rock said even as he made his way down the hall toward the bedroom. He looked tired, and Justin knew Rock was just venting a bit of his frustration. Justin couldn't blame him. Rock was an active guy, like him, and being on crutches and confined to bed was never a fun proposition. Rock opened the bedroom door and went inside. By the time he sat on the edge of the bed, Justin could see how tired he was already.

"Let me help you get undressed," Justin said, and Rock groaned as he nodded. Justin carefully took off Rock's shirt and helped him with his pants. It was quite an undertaking, and by the time he got Rock down to his underwear and into bed, a pillow beneath his foot, his eyes were already closing. "I'll be back in a few minutes," Justin told him, and all he got for an answer was a soft moan. Justin left quietly and drove to the nearest drive-through. He got something for both Rock and himself and returned to Rock's house.

When he entered Rock's bedroom, the other man hadn't moved. Rock opened his eyes, though, and propped himself up, and Justin helped him get situated. Justin left to get some orange juice and returned to find Rock wolfing down his breakfast. "Your appetite's definitely back; that's a good sign."

Rock nodded as he finished his egg sandwich, and Justin was thankful he'd bought an extra, because Rock ate that one too. Once they were done, Justin cleaned up and threw the papers in the trash.

"I'll leave you alone to get some rest," he said with a yawn, and Rock scooted over, patting the bed next to him.

"Stay," Rock said.

"Are you sure?"

"You're exhausted, and I want you here," Rock told him.

Justin toed off his shoes and stripped to his boxers before gently climbing into the bed next to Rock. Justin wasn't sure how much sleep he was going to get. Having Rock this close to him didn't, in Justin's mind, encourage sleep. His body wanted something else, but he pushed that aside and closed his eyes. Both of them desperately needed rest.

Eventually Justin did fall asleep, and he woke hours later, holding Rock around the waist. "I could get used to you doing that," Rock said.

"What?" Justin asked, trying to give Rock some room so he wouldn't hurt any of Rock's wounds.

"Holding me like that. Sleeping with you. Take your pick," Rock answered and yawned.

"You're still tired?" Justin asked and began to get out of the bed. "You need to rest, and I'm going to need to get ready for work."

"You don't go in until tonight, right?" Rock asked, and Justin nodded before allowing Rock to pull him back onto the bed. "Then stay with me for a while. I missed you."

"I'm sorry," Justin said yet again.

"Don't be sorry—make it up to me," Rock told him, and Justin shifted on the bed, pulling him close. Rock kissed him, a deep, passionate, forceful kiss full of need and want.

"I don't want to hurt you," Justin said, and Rock shifted slightly, burying his face against Justin's skin. Instead of giving Justin an argument, Rock licked and sucked on his skin. Justin groaned, his body reacting instantly to Rock.

"Want you," Rock said, and even flat on his back, he was strong enough to move Justin's body. Rock cupped his butt, and Justin moved where he was guided. Soon he was straddling Rock's chest. Rock pushed Justin's boxers as low on his hips as he could and fished out Justin's cock before guiding it to his mouth.

Justin threw his head back as Rock sucked him deep. He had to be careful not to put too much weight on Rock's body, but, damn, he could barely think. Rock filled the room with deep-throated humming sounds, and Justin quickly became fascinated by the way his cock looked moving past Rock's lips. "Jesus Christ," Justin cried as Rock hollowed his cheeks, sucking him deep, hard, and not letting him go. Justin gasped, only to have Rock suck him deep again.

Rock held his butt, digging his fingers into Justin's flesh, and Justin loved every second of it. "Not gonna last," Justin whined, and Rock eased away.

Justin's cock slipped from Rock's mouth, and when Justin tried to shift, Rock held him in place. "I want everything you have to give," Rock told him. "Now, and for a long time to come." Rock took him to the root in a single movement, sucking hard, bringing Justin to the brink, and then backing away. "You're mine, Justin—I want you to know that—just like I'm yours." Rock took him deep once again, but just like before, kept him hanging on the edge. "I want you to say it. I want you to tell me you're mine." Rock sucked him deep and held still.

Justin whined and squirmed, hanging on the very edge. "I'm yours, Rock. If you'll have me, I'm yours."

Rock moved his head, bobbing and sucking as Justin spilled himself inside a lover, *his* lover, for the first time in his life.

Justin could barely breathe, and he certainly couldn't move, but he didn't want to collapse on top of Rock, so he forced his legs to do what he wanted and climbed off Rock before collapsing on the bed, breathing like he'd just run a race. Rock rolled slowly onto his side and tugged

Justin close until they rested chest to chest. "That wasn't just the sex talking. You're mine. I knew that the minute you stepped into that bus to search for that last child. I wanted you then."

Justin closed his eyes, resting his head on Rock's arm. "I watched you for months, but couldn't approach you. I think I fell for you when you stood up to my mother when I couldn't, and—" He cut himself off, not wanting to go into his stupidity once again. Justin rolled his head and lightly kissed Rock's skin. Slowly, he pressed Rock onto his back and pushed away the covers. "You know you're mine too," Justin said, and Rock hummed his agreement as Justin kissed down Rock's chest and belly before sucking Rock into his mouth.

Justin wasn't as experienced as Rock, but he threw himself into what he was doing. Rock slowly rocked his hips on the mattress, and Justin met each movement. He loved Rock's cock sliding along his tongue and reveled in the flavor of his lover. Justin stroked Rock's hips and belly, sucking for all he was worth, with Rock's little whimpers egging him on. He loved that he could reduce a man as huge as Rock to whimpering and small pleading cries.

"Jus, please, I need…." Rock groaned, and Justin sucked him as far and fast as he could. "That's it, just like that," Rock moaned. "Jesus God!"

Justin smiled around Rock's dick and continued sucking, Rock's flavor intensifying. He felt Rock rest his big hands on his head, smoothing his fingers over Justin's scalp. Tingles went through Justin's body as Rock moved in time with him. Justin pulled his mouth away, licking up and down the thick shaft, teasing the skin just below the head. Rock arched his back and cried out as Justin stroked his spit-lubed cock. "That's what I want. Just like in the hospital. Give it to me, all of it." Justin sucked as much of Rock as he could, giving as much sensation as he could. Rock continued moaning and whimpering.

"God, you're fucking amazing," Rock growled, and Justin sucked harder. "I can't wait until this cast comes off. I want to fuck you, burying myself deep inside you until we're one. So I can feel your heart beat through my cock." Justin paused. "I'm gonna fuck you until you scream," Rock yelled as he began to quiver on the bed. "I'm going to make you mine forever!" Rock pulsed and throbbed in Justin's mouth. Justin swallowed hard, again and again, taking everything Rock could give him. Then, slowly, Justin felt the tension slip out of his lover, and he let Rock slide from between his lips.

Justin settled on the sheets next to Rock, holding him and listening as he breathed heavily in his ear. "Yes," Rock said softly, and Justin draped an arm over Rock's chest. "You're perfect."

"I doubt that," Justin said, holding Rock as he closed his eyes, ready to fall back to sleep for a while, but obviously Rock wasn't, and Justin didn't want to miss anything with his new lover. "There's something I don't understand, and I've been wondering about it for the past few days." Justin yawned as he resettled on the bed. "The doctor said the effect of his treatments when I was a kid should have faded over time, but they didn't. It wasn't until he told me about them that they truly seemed to go away."

Rock shrugged, and he inched closer. "The most powerful organ in the body is the brain, and I think that at first, you reacted to people you liked because of the hypnotic suggestion. It probably did fade, but you were already expecting the reaction, so it happened. Remember, you could talk to me when you were angry or excited—your system overrode what it was afraid of." Rock kissed him lightly on the cheek, and Justin turned his head so they could share a proper kiss. "Once he told you what he'd done, the illusion was broken and the reaction went away."

"You really think so?" Justin asked.

"Sure. You don't have any problem talking to me now."

"Nope, and I don't intend to from now on," Justin said. He closed his eyes and took a deep breath, then released it slowly. "Is it too early to say what I'm feeling?" Justin shifted slightly so he could clearly see into Rock's eyes, and he instantly knew the answer to that question.

"I already know," Rock told him. "I feel the same way." Justin lowered his head, resting it on Rock's chest, and within seconds he felt Rock lightly stroking his hair. He'd never thought something so simple and gentle could feel so wonderful and... necessary. Like he needed Rock's small touches just as desperately as he needed to breathe.

"I know you know, but I need to tell you." Justin moved so he could look at Rock eye to eye, their lips so close he could feel Rock's breath. "I love you." Rock brought their lips together in a hard kiss that damned near had Justin passing out from the sheer intensity. "What is it?" Justin asked.

"You have no idea how long it's been since someone, anyone, said those words to me," Rock whispered, and Justin saw tears forming in his eyes. "I love you too," Rock said, and then he kissed him again. Justin wanted to ask what Rock meant, why it had been so long since he'd been told he was loved, but they continued kissing for a long time, and then both of them napped briefly, storing up energy, before expressing their newly declared love all over again.

Keep reading for an excerpt from
*Through the Flames*
Carlisle Fire Book 1
by Andrew Grey

# Chapter 1

IT HAD been said that the difference between love and hate could be measured as the width of a hair. Hayden Walters wasn't so sure.

"Going to bury yourself in a book, bookworm?" Jason Wilson asked. The man was a mountain of pain in the ass, and not in an "oh my God" good kind of way. But he wasn't as bad as his brother, Kyle, who had to be the biggest asshole on the planet. Maybe it was something in the water where they grew up.

Hayden gritted his teeth. "Do you actually think you're clever?" He had no idea what caused it, but those two had to be some of the worst human beings to have ever lived.

Okay, that was an exaggeration. Kyle was awful, sure, but part of Hayden's problem with Jason was hatred transference. Jason *could* be an ass, but no one at the station really paid that any attention.

Hayden could take their cue. He picked up his coffee mug to find more amenable company somewhere else. He refused to let the oaf's comments get to him. After all, Hayden had endured Kyle's bullying—including shoving him into lockers—his entire time in high school, so shit like that shouldn't get to him. Jason was nothing. Hell, Hayden didn't even know if Jason actually disliked him. He made up nicknames and teased everyone in the station.

"Knock it off, Wilson," Greg Luther said as he passed, clapping Hayden on the shoulder. Greg was the other gay firefighter in their fire company in Carlisle, Pennsylvania. He'd been part of the company for eight years, while Hayden had been hired on just a year and a half ago, fresh out of fire academy, but they only started working similar shifts a few months ago. "I know you think you're funny, but no one else does. What the hell happened to you? Your mama drop you on your head one too many times?"

"Look who thinks he's funny," Jason said.

"*You* certainly aren't." Hayden clenched his hands and left the room. Jason was an ass, but Hayden had found he was harmless—unlike his fucking brother, who could be lethal in his meanness. Maybe that was why he had such a hard time with Jason. The two men looked so alike it was uncanny, though Jason was older. Granted, so far Hayden hadn't found much to like about Jason either, but it wasn't like the guy was the antichrist… that would be Kyle. No, Hayden just needed to find a way to get along with the guy, and he had to remember that Jason wasn't his brother.

He figured he could find something to do to make himself useful out of the presence of the department clown. Hayden liked to be busy, and he wanted to make himself as productive as possible. As one of the newest members of the fire company, he still had plenty to prove, and he strove to do that every chance he got. After all, if the other guys accepted him, maybe he could figure out a way to leave behind the small, skinny, never-fit-in-anywhere kid he'd once been. He was no longer skinny, with impressively broad shoulders and a muscled chest, but that misfit kid was still inside him.

Before he could find something to do, the fire alarm blared, and everyone sprang to life. Hayden suited up as the details of the call came in. House fire on Pomfret. Union was responding and requested backup.

There were two fire companies in Carlisle. Union Fire Company was right downtown. They were also the oldest and the one with the local fire equipment museum in the old part of their facility. Carlisle Fire and Rescue was on the north side of town in a new facility. If Union was requesting backup this fast, it had to be a bad one.

Hayden climbed on the truck and took his place in the back of the cab. He held on as they screamed out of the drive and made the left turn onto Spring Road, racing toward the fire.

Lights changed color ahead of them, bringing traffic through the historic district of downtown to a halt. Hayden barely noticed the old courthouse with its clock tower and Civil War scars as they zoomed past and then made the right turn onto Pomfret, heading down the block and a half to where the other company was already setting up.

"Wet down roofs, make sure the fire doesn't spread to the other row houses," Union's chief called almost as soon as they came to a stop. "It's a bad one and growing hotter in the old house."

Breaking glass pulled Hayden's attention, and movement from behind the now fully open upstairs window caught his attention.

"There's someone in there," Hayden said.

"We were told it was empty," the Union chief said as Hayden hefted on his breathing gear.

"Go, but don't take long, for God's sake. The back of the building is where the fire started, probably in the kitchen. Stay to the front," Greg, the fire captain for their unit, told him. He had the ability to read a fire like few others, and Hayden expected him to be chief someday.

"Got it." His mind was already inside.

"The staircase is going to be right in front of you when you enter. Get up, find whoever is in there, and get the hell out fast. Don't linger," Greg told him.

Hayden pulled on his mask and started the flow of air as he raced for the door. He immediately stepped into a thick gray fog of swirling smoke, the stairs looming out of it. Glass broke behind him, but he paid little attention. It was probably the guys knocking out the windows so they could get water on the blaze.

As he reached the top of the stairs, flames shot skyward through the back of the house. What had once been a bedroom was now an inferno, and a portion of the floor had collapsed. The guys were going to have a hard time getting resources to that part of the building, but judging by the hissing that accompanied the roar of flame, they were trying their best. Picking up the pace, Hayden hurried forward. He checked the old bathroom and then the first bedroom he came to, which was empty. He closed the door and went forward to where he thought he'd seen movement.

A man lay on the floor. Hayden wasn't sure if he was still alive. Hayden pulled him up and hefted him over his shoulders, then started back toward the stairs. The fire was now running along the ceiling over his head, consuming the old horsehair plaster at a rapid pace, embers and ash falling all around him. Hayden's heart raced, but he kept his head even when he was no longer able to see.

Using his hands, he found the top of the banister, and then his foot found the first step. He didn't dare turn around, knowing the wall of fire behind him was consuming the house like a ravenous wolf. He had to get out before everything collapsed around both of them.

One step at a time, he descended, growing closer to the door. Flames jumped up to the side on the first floor, and the entire staircase shuddered as he got lower. Hayden could almost feel the building giving up under the onslaught. Three more steps and large pieces of ceiling collapsed around him, sending up more ash, feeding the flames that flared even higher. Two more steps and the staircase shook like hell. Hayden realized he only had a matter of seconds. He reached the last few steps and jumped to the floor, making for the front door with a last burst of energy as everything behind him collapsed in a conflagration, propelling Hayden and his charge out through the doorway. He would have crashed to the ground if two other firefighters hadn't caught them both.

Together, they got the man away from the building and onto a gurney, where an EMT immediately took over. Hayden continued away from the collapsing row home, pulled off his breathing gear, and sucked in beloved fresh air. Once he made it to the truck, he took off his fire coat and let the spring air get to his shirt, now plastered to his skin by sweat.

"You did good," Greg told him. "Fucking damn good."

"Is he alive?" Hayden asked. Right now, it was the only thing important to him.

"They're still working on him." Greg turned away to give more orders. "Keep spraying the home next door. I don't want to lose it now… good." Greg hurried away, and Hayden grabbed a bottle of water and sucked it down. Then he pulled his coat back on, donned his hat, and joined the rest of the men helping to get this beast of a fire out.

He manned a hose, trying to get to the heart of the fire. Their current jobs were to prevent the fire from spreading to the neighboring homes and keep the side walls from collapsing under all the strain from the heat. They were going to be weakened, that was certain, but if they gave way, the buildings on either side would be unlivable and additional families would find themselves without a home. Hayden aimed his stream of water through one of the front windows, sending it cascading through the building. They were finally making headway. A large part of the back roof was gone, but the flames had died considerably, and within an hour the chief declared the fire out.

The police had shown up, and they took over securing the exterior of the building and directing traffic around where they were working.

"Hey, Red," Greg said as he shook Red's hand.

"You guys had a big one," Red commented.

"Yeah. We're going to check out the buildings on either side. I suspect they'll need new roofs, and there's likely to be water damage." Greg directed some of the men to begin winding up the hoses.

Hayden turned off the water, and once Jason signaled that the pressure was off, he turned the hose on to bleed the water out—but the unexpected force nearly knocked him onto his butt.

"Very funny," Hayden called as the pressure bled away.

"Knock it off, Jason," Greg admonished and stalked right up to him. "This is work, not a circus. If you can't act like a professional and stop playing your games, I'm going to ask the chief to reevaluate your position here. Am I making myself clear?"

Jason scoffed. "What? I thought it was off." He clearly knew different. "Can't guys like you take a joke?"

Greg didn't back down. "Get your ass on the truck now. That's harassment, and you know it won't be tolerated. At the very least, you're going to have to do the sensitivity training… again. Maybe this time you won't sleep through it." Greg was angry, and Hayden didn't blame him. He wanted to take Jason's head off himself.

"I heard what he said," Red said as he stood behind Greg, arms folded over his chest.

For the first time since Hayden joined the company, Jason seemed to grow smaller. "It was just a joke, nothing more." He took a step back, lowering his gaze slightly. "You did good getting the man out of the building." That was Jason-speak for an apology, because he wasn't likely to compliment anyone for another reason.

"Thanks." Hayden drained his hose and started rolling it up.

"Hayden, let Jason do that. You go check on the man you rescued. They're about to transport him." Greg smiled as he gave Jason the crap job, and Hayden didn't argue, heading over to where the EMTs were loading the only person injured in the fire. That alone was some sort of miracle.

"How is he?" Hayden asked.

"He's breathing on his own now, and he's awake," Karen answered. She and Hayden had crossed paths a number of times before. She was something else. Even as far back as high school, Karen had always been an amazing person. They were in the same graduating class, but while she had been popular and outgoing, Hayden had done his best to try to blend in with the paint. "Come on, you can talk to him a minute before we take him in to be checked out. I'd say you got to him just in time." She led the way around the back of the ambulance, and Hayden followed and peered into the vehicle.

"I understand you saved me," the man said as Hayden stepped up. Hayden's breath hitched, and he blinked more than once. No way—this couldn't be right. "Thanks, man. You're a real hero." He smiled and Hayden nodded, forcing a smile as he stared into the dirty face of Kyle Wilson, Jason's brother and probably the one person on earth Hayden wished he could have simply left in the burning building. Not that he would have, but still.

"Glad I could help," Hayden mumbled and then stepped out and immediately turned away. "His brother, Jason, is one of the firefighters in my company. Does he know about Kyle?"

"Yeah. They had a gorilla-type chest-pounding argument a little while ago that the EMTs broke up." She rolled her eyes. "They're both real pieces of work as far as I can tell, though that may be just how they are." She closed the back door of the ambulance, and Hayden backed away and returned to where they guys were cleaning up and getting ready to leave.

"Did you talk to him?" Greg asked.

"Yeah. I think the guy is going to be okay." Hayden didn't really want to talk. Greg was many things: a great captain, a super mentor… and a pain in the ass when he realized there was something he didn't know. "Did you know that was Jason's brother?"

Greg nodded. "It seems they don't get along anymore. They had a falling out. Jason used to talk about Kyle all the time. Apparently, Kyle was like Superman… and then something changed, and now they don't speak."

Hayden nodded but didn't say anything. When Greg didn't continue, Hayden returned to gathering up the last of their equipment. He stowed it and then climbed onto the truck for the ride back to the station. He'd done his job and saved one of the people he hated most in the world. Maybe that bit of karmic goodness would come back to him in a good way… or maybe it would bite him in the ass. Either way, at least he wasn't likely to see Kyle ever again—and he could live with that.

# Chapter 2

"YOU DIDN'T burn down my house, did you?" Ellen asked earnestly but without heat, which was surprising. Lying in the hospital bed, breathing in oxygen, Kyle had wondered the same thing, but as far as he could recall, he had done nothing that could have started the fire.

Kyle rolled his head slowly. "No, I didn't." At least he didn't think so. His memory was a little fuzzy. Every time he tried to concentrate, his head spun and he ended up closing his eyes. The doctors said that would pass and told him to rest for a while. "You had me working in the front rooms, remember? I was repairing the plaster in the first two bedrooms. I had my ear buds in and didn't realize anything until smoke filled the room I was working in. The door to the room had been removed and was in the basement because you wanted it stripped." His throat was rough and still sore, but at least he was alive.

"So you weren't where the fire started?" Ellen had purchased the property maybe two months ago and had hired him to help her make the house livable for her and her two daughters. "I'm not sure what caused it, but they think it started in the kitchen."

"That's my guess, but I don't know. I tried to get out and broke the window to try to get breathable air, but it didn't work too well. The smoke just billowed out and the air rushed into the room from the rest of the house." The last thing he remembered was crouching on the floor, because that was where he was hoping for better air. His plan was to try to make it to the stairs, but he didn't get far. The smoke was too much. The next thing he knew, he'd come back to consciousness outside with EMTs all around him. "Apparently a firefighter went inside the house to get me and hauled me out."

"He did, yeah. And word around town is that he saved your life."

Kyle sat up but ended up coughing, and Ellen helped him back down onto the bed. "Sorry, and I'm sorry about your house too. It was going to be beautiful, I know that." He had already been working on the place for two weeks, and it had been starting to come together. Once the bedrooms were done, he had expected the new cabinets to arrive so he could put the kitchen together. After that, his next task would have been to tackle the bathrooms. He had expected another two months of solid work on the place, but now that was up in smoke right along with Ellen's house. "But I didn't start the fire." He coughed again and watched Ellen deflate.

"Thank God," she whispered. A questionable fire would delay an insurance payment.

"Was everything insured?" Kyle asked. He'd hate for her to lose everything she had. "I know you just bought the house and...." You needed insurance to get a mortgage, right?

"Yes, it was. That isn't an issue. The house was completely destroyed, and we'll need to figure out things with the insurance company, but I'm hoping we can start looking for a new home soon. But it will probably be weeks." She had troubles of her own, but so did Kyle. "I'm glad you're going to be okay and that the fire was accidental."

"Me too." It would be hard to live with himself if he knew he was at fault. "I really appreciate you stopping by to see me."

Ellen took his hand. "Has anyone else been up?"

Kyle had known Ellen for three years now. When she got the house she was in now, he had helped do the work she needed. Ellen had been one of his first clients when he'd decided to try contracting on his own.

"Jason was one of the firefighters at the house. He saw me and knows that I got out alive. I guess he'll tell anyone else who wants to know." He sighed and forced himself to relax. "When you find a house, you know I'll be there to help you with it."

Ellen smiled and patted his hand. "I know you will. I need you to put together your bill for all your work so I can get the insurance company to pay for it." He supposed if he had to in order to keep Ellen from getting screwed, they could say that it had all been in the house. "I'm hoping we can use what's on order in the new house."

"I'll do that just as soon as I get home." Breathing kept getting easier, and he closed his eyes. "When are you supposed to be out of your house?" She had already sold it, and they were waiting for closing.

"Another month. After that I'm not sure what I'll do. I could back out, but that would only complicate things even further."

Kyle nodded. "I could talk to my family." Even saying the words hurt. Yeah, he could try to contact them, but it didn't mean they'd take his call. "My parents have a house they rent out on the south side."

"No. You don't worry about us. We have friends who have offered us places to stay until we can figure things out. But we can rent if we have to." She took his hand. "Just get better and call me when you're on your feet again." Ellen stood up, leaned over the bed, and lightly kissed his cheek. Then she left the room, and Kyle relaxed, trying not to think about his breathing, because every time he did, he inhaled either too quickly or too deeply and started coughing once more. What he really needed was a job. He had turned down other work because he was going to be busy at Ellen's getting the house rehabbed, and now that was gone... along with his ability to breathe. Who knew how long that was going to keep him home.

Financially, he had a little bit of a cushion, and once he was on his feet, he could hopefully find some work to fill the time until his next bigger job, which was scheduled to a start in a few months. Kyle put all of that aside. There was nothing he could do about it in a hospital bed while they gave him oxygen and told him to rest so his lungs could heal. Maybe once he was home, he could figure all that out.


THERE WERE only two fire stations in town, and Kyle had tried Union first because they were the first unit to respond to the fire and because his brother worked at Carlisle Fire and Rescue, and he wanted to avoid him if possible.

"I don't know who it was. I wasn't on duty," the brick wall of a firefighter said before turning. "Lee, do you know who rescued the man from the home on Pomfret the other day?"

Another firefighter approached, this one equally as stunning as the first one. Together they oozed enough testosterone to nearly make Kyle drunk. "I think it was one of the guys from CFR. They arrived later, but one of their men saw the guy break a window and he charged right in." Lee's smile brightened a little as soon as he turned to the other man, and damned if the guy, as big as a house, didn't melt a little right there. Damn, Kyle wanted that so bad he could taste it. No one had to tell him that these guys were a couple. All they had to do was look at each other and Kyle knew it. Just a single look and that was it. Kyle pulled himself out of his moment of longing.

"Thanks."

"Why do you want to find him?" Lee asked.

Kyle coughed. "I'm the guy he rescued, and I wanted to thank him. I got out of the hospital a few days ago, and I really need to thank the guy. I kind of remember that he looked in on me when I was in the ambulance. I know he saved my life." He shook hands with both men. "I appreciate your help."

"You're welcome," the first man said. Kyle hadn't caught his name. Then he left the station and got into his car and headed out to the far north side of town.

Kyle pulled into the sizable parking lot and turned off the engine, but he stayed in the truck for a moment. He hoped his brother wasn't working today. He didn't need the stress of running into him. Maybe this wasn't such a good idea after all. He could just go home and write a note and send it to the station.

"Yeah, that's the chickenshit way out," he told himself and got out of the truck. He still coughed if he breathed too quickly, but it was getting better every day. Hopefully in another week he could go back to work.

In the reception area, a man sat behind a plastic window, typing on a computer. "Can I help you?" he asked as he continued typing.

"Yeah, I…. That fire the other day on Pomfret."

The man nodded. "Yeah, I'm told that was a bad one."

Kyle nodded. "It was, I guess. I was the guy that was rescued, and I wanted to thank the man who went in and got me. He saved my life, and I wanted to thank him. I don't know his name, and I only saw him briefly before they took me to the hospital. I'm told it was one of the guys from here who got me."

"Sure. Let me look," he said, typing away. "Yeah. It was Hayden, and I think…." He grabbed a sheet of paper. "Yeah, he's on shift today. Let me check and see if I can find him." He stood and left the small office area and hurried out.

Kyle sat in one of the chairs nearby and did his best to relax. The doctors said he needed to stay calm, and he didn't know why he was nerved up.

Kyle remembered the face of the guy in the ambulance. He seemed nice enough.

"He'll be right out," the man said from inside the window. Then the typing began again, and Kyle settled into his seat.

A few minutes later, the door from the back opened and a man with broad shoulders stepped out like he was ready to go into battle. His eyes were hard and his body straight and rigid.

"I'm Kyle Wilson. You probably work with my brother, Jason—" He began to cough and covered his mouth with his hand. "Sorry." He cleared his throat. "I understand you pulled me out of the fire on Pomfret."

Hayden narrowed his gaze and crossed his arms over his chest defensively. Kyle didn't get that. "I did. Yeah." Damn, his eyes were hard a flint. Kyle started wondering what the hell he had done to make the guy so angry at him.

"Well, I just wanted to thank you. You saved my life, and I really appreciate it." He had this whole little speech planned. "I know it's what you do, but I wanted to try to find you and thank you personally." God, the "go away" vibes rolled off this guy in waves.

"Well, I'm glad you're okay." He turned back toward the door and reached for it. Either this was the most modest man on earth and he just wanted to get away, or…. Kyle didn't understand.

"Thanks," Kyle said, figuring he'd done what he'd come here to do and that was it. He stepped toward the door to leave.

"You don't remember me, do you?" Hayden asked.

Kyle looked at him again, tilting his head to the side as he tried to recall where he might have seen him before. He racked his brain trying to place the guy and couldn't. And it wasn't like this man was someone he'd easily forget. He was strong, but not in a bulky way. More like firm and well built with intense eyes and short jet-black hair. But it was the short, sexy hair that caught Kyle's attention most of all. It was perfect and sexy as all hell. No, Kyle wasn't likely to forget walking-sex-on-a-stick Hayden… not in this lifetime, anyway.

"I'm sorry. Should I? Have we met before?" He hated when he was supposed to remember someone and didn't. It made him feel stupid. Although if Kyle made a list of things that made him feel that way, he'd be at it all day. He wasn't the smartest guy in the world, but he hated feeling stupid more than just about anything.

Hayden stepped forward. "Maybe it would jog your memory if you tried to push me into a locker or sent my books sliding down the wet high school hallway." The snarl was menacing, but Kyle barely heard it. He looked into Hayden's steely gaze and felt his own widen.

"My God. I remember you now." He gasped and then groaned before coughing. He pulled a tissue out of his pocket to cover his mouth, concentrated on breathing evenly, and eventually the spasm passed.

It looked like Hayden was about to leave, and Kyle knew he had to say something. Memories of how he had acted back then flooded through him, and Kyle wanted to disappear. There were times when he looked back and wondered what the hell he had been thinking. Somehow, he had thought that tearing down guys smaller than him would make him look bigger and stronger. "God, I was such a dick back then." It was all he could think of to say. It was the truth, but massively understated.

"Huh?" Hayden asked, his arms uncrossing.

"I was such a jerk to you... and to other people." There had been a lot of water under the bridge since then, and a hell of a lot had changed. "And here you're the person who saved my life." He was more than a little blown away by that. "Why would you do that after... well... everything?"

Hayden seemed shocked. "I'm a professional, and that's what I do. I don't get to decide who lives or dies, and I don't let people burn up in a fiery building because I don't like them." The set of his jaw told Kyle that he'd insulted Hayden. Maybe it was best if he simply kept his mouth shut and went on his way.

"I'm sorry for taking up your time." Kyle might as well get out of here with some piece of his dignity intact. He'd come here to thank the person who'd saved him, and he'd done that. "And once again, thank you for what you did—for whatever reason you did it." He pulled open the door and stepped out into the fresh air, breathing deeply just to try to clear his head. Of course he took in too much air and ended up coughing, only this time it didn't seem to want to stop. His eyes watered and his chest ached, and he bent over, willing the fit to end. He tried all of the things they showed him in the hospital, but nothing worked.

"Just relax." The voice was rich, and Kyle knew immediately it was Hayden. "Breathe slowly, in and out. Don't fight it. That's it." The coughing subsided, but Kyle remained bent over, breathing shallowly. "How much smoke did you get?"

"The doctor said I was lucky I was alive. Apparently there was a lot of bad stuff in that fire, and it really hurt my lungs." Kyle straightened up. "Thanks for your help... again." He moved away. "I'll be going now.

I won't darken your doorstep again." He headed to his work truck and got inside, then pulled the door closed. He breathed evenly before getting ready to leave.

He couldn't blame Hayden for not wanting anything to do with him. Back in high school, Kyle had been vicious with anyone who was different. It didn't take a shrink for him to understand why he had acted that way. If he was mean and singled out anyone who might not fit the mold, then no one would think *he* was different. Looking back on it, he knew he'd been a coward, afraid of who he was and what he wanted. Hayden had been an easy target. It had been pretty obvious back then by the way he acted and the things he liked that Hayden had fit into the easiest category of kid to pick on. The gay one, the sissy, the kid who would always be on the outside looking in. In other words, the one just like Kyle. But Hayden had been braver and stronger than anyone had given him credit for, and in the end, he'd saved Kyle's life, and now Kyle was the one on the outside, wishing he could figure out where the hell he fit in… anywhere.

ANDREW GREY is the author of more than two hundred works of Contemporary Gay Romantic fiction. After twenty-seven years in corporate America, he has now settled down in Central Pennsylvania with his husband of more than twenty-five years, Dominic, and his laptop. An interesting ménage. Andrew grew up in western Michigan with a father who loved to tell stories and a mother who loved to read them. Since then he has lived throughout the country and traveled throughout the world. He is a recipient of the RWA Centennial Award, has a master's degree from the University of Wisconsin–Milwaukee, and now writes full-time. Andrew's hobbies include collecting antiques, gardening, and leaving his dirty dishes anywhere but in the sink (particularly when writing). He considers himself blessed with an accepting family, fantastic friends, and the world's most supportive and loving partner. Andrew currently lives in beautiful, historic Carlisle, Pennsylvania.

Email: andrewgrey@comcast.net

Website:www.andrewgreybooks.com

Follow me on BookBub

# THROUGH the FLAMES
# ANDREW GREY

Carlisle
Fire

1

Carlisle Fire Book 1

Kyle Wilson hasn't had it easy. His insecurities and nasty home life made him lash out as a kid, and when he finally came out as gay, his family disowned him. Then, just when he's pulled his life together and gotten his construction company running, he's caught in a fire and forced to take costly time off.

When firefighter Hayden Walters rescues a man from a burning building, he's just doing his job. He doesn't expect it to turn his life upside-down, but the man is none other than Hayden's high school bully.

He definitely doesn't expect Kyle to come to the station to thank him in person.

With awkward apologies out of the way, Kyle and Hayden realize they have a lot in common. And when it turns out someone set the fire at Kyle's construction site to target him, they find they can solve each other's problems too: Hayden needs a place to stay while his apartment is renovated, and Kyle doesn't want to be alone in case the firebug strikes again. Things between the two of them quickly heat up—but so does the arsonist's agenda. Can they track down the would-be killer before it's too late?

# www.dreamspinnerpress.com

# FIRE AND SAND
# ANDREW GREY

Carlisle Troopers Book One

Can a single dad with a criminal past find love with the cop who pulled him over?

When single dad Quinton Jackson gets stopped for speeding, he thinks he's lost both his freedom and his infant son, who's in the car he's been chasing down the highway. Amazingly, State Trooper Wyatt Nelson not only believes him, he radios for help and reunites Quinton with baby Callum.

Wyatt should ticket Quinton, but something makes him look past Quinton's record. Watching him with his child proves he made the right decision. Quinton is a loving, devoted father—and he's handsome. Wyatt can't help but take a personal interest.

For Quinton, getting temporary custody is a dream come true… or it would be, if working full-time and caring for an infant left time to sleep. As if that weren't enough, Callum's mother will do anything to get him back, including ruining Quinton's life. Fortunately, Quinton has Wyatt for help, support, and as much romance as a single parent can schedule.

But when Wyatt's duties as a cop conflict with Quinton's quest for permanent custody, their situation becomes precarious. Can they trust each other, and the courts, to deliver justice and a happy ever after?

# www.dreamspinnerpress.com

# FIRE AND FLINT

# ANDREW GREY

CARLISLE
DEPUTIES
1

Carlisle Deputies Book 1

Jordan Erichsohn suspects something is rotten about his boss, Judge Crawford. Unfortunately he has nowhere to turn and doubts anyone will believe his claims—least of all the handsome deputy, Pierre Ravelle, who has been assigned to protect the judge after he received threatening letters. The judge has a long reach, and if he finds out Jordan's turned on him, he might impede Jordan adopting his son, Jeremiah.

When Jordan can no longer stay silent, he gathers his courage and tells Pierre what he knows. To his surprise and relief, Pierre believes him, and Jordan finds an ally… and maybe more. Pierre vows to do what it takes to protect Jordan and Jeremiah and see justice done. He's willing to fight for the man he's growing to love and the family he's starting to think of as his own. But Crawford is a powerful and dangerous enemy, and he's not above ripping apart everything Jordan and Pierre are trying to build in order to save himself….

# www.dreamspinnerpress.com

# FIRE AND WATER

# ANDREW GREY

CARLISLE
COPS

1

Carlisle Cops Book 1

Officer Red Markham knows about the ugly side of life after a car accident left him scarred and his parents dead. His job policing the streets of Carlisle, PA, only adds to the ugliness, and lately, drug overdoses have been on the rise. One afternoon, Red is dispatched to the local Y for a drowning accident involving a child. Arriving on site, he finds the boy rescued by lifeguard Terry Baumgartner. Of course, Red isn't surprised when gorgeous Terry won't give him and his ugly mug the time of day.

Overhearing one of the officer's comments about him being shallow opens Terry's eyes. Maybe he isn't as kindhearted as he always thought. His friend Julie suggests he help those less fortunate by delivering food to the elderly. On his route he meets outspoken Margie, a woman who says what's on her mind. Turns out, she's Officer Red's aunt.

Red and Terry's worlds collide as Red tries to track the source of the drugs and protect Terry from an ex-boyfriend who won't take no for an answer. Together they might discover a chance for more than they expected—if they can see beyond what's on the surface.

# www.dreamspinnerpress.com

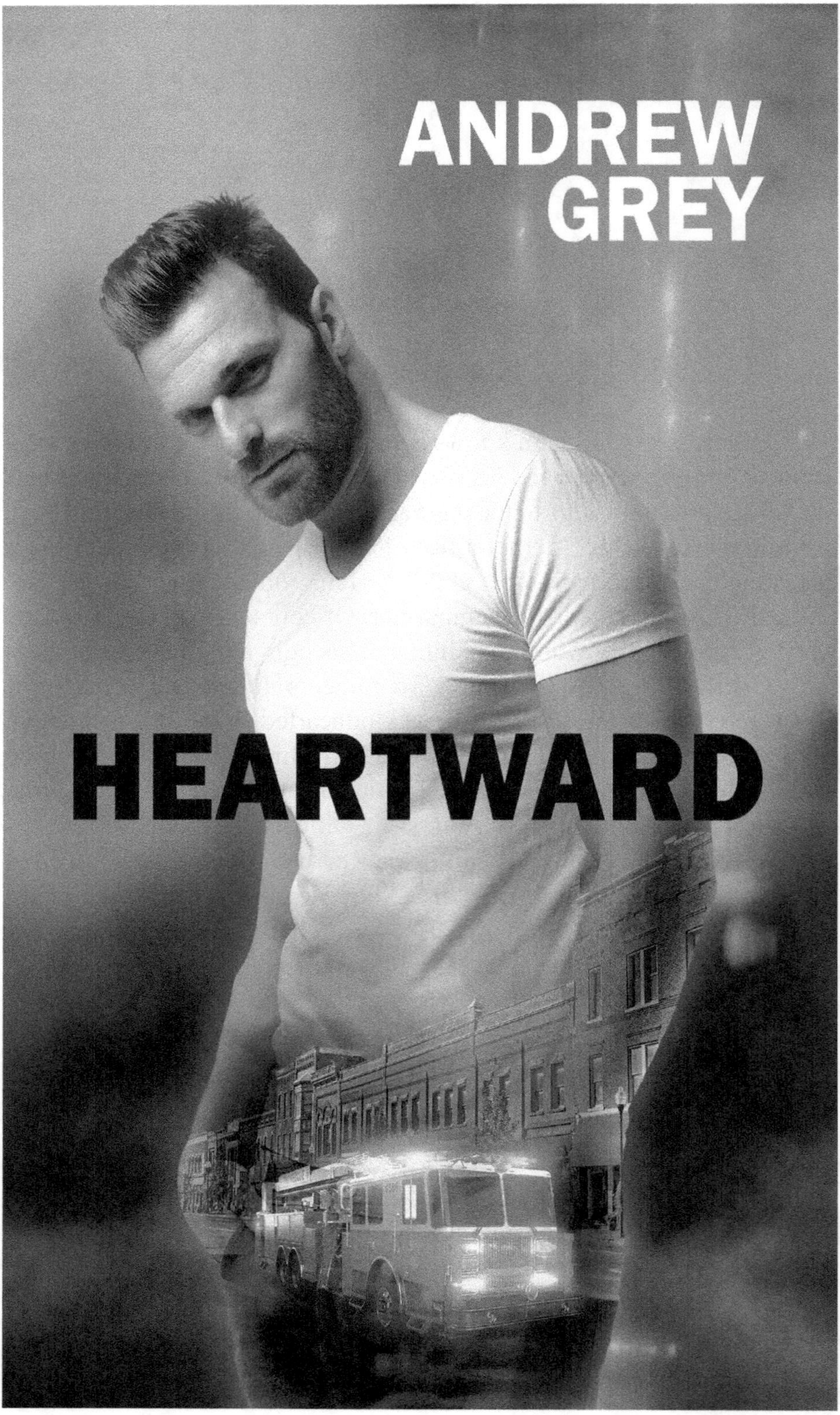
ANDREW
GREY
HEARTWARD

He doesn't know that home is where his heart will be….

Firefighter Tyler Banik has seen his share of adventure while working disaster relief with the Red Cross. But now that he's adopted Abey, he's ready to leave the danger behind and put down roots. That means returning to his hometown—where the last thing he anticipates is falling for his high school nemesis.

Alan Pettaprin isn't the boy he used to be. As a business owner and council member, he's working hard to improve life in Scottville for everyone. Nobody is more surprised than Alan when Tyler returns, but he's glad. For him, it's a chance to set things right. Little does he guess he and Tyler will find the missing pieces of themselves in each other. Old rivalries are left in the ashes, passion burns bright, and the possibility for a future together stretches in front of them….

But not everyone in town is glad to see Tyler return….

# www.dreamspinnerpress.com